MW00325675

# GEODESIC DREAMS

*Also by Gardner Dozois*

FICTION
*Strangers*
*The Visible Man*
*Nightmare Blue* (with George Alec Effinger)
*Slow Dancing with Jesus* (with Susan Casper, Jack Dann,
Jack C. Haldeman II, and Michael Swanwick)

NONFICTION
*The Fiction of James Tiptree, Jr.*

ANTHOLOGIES
*A Day in the Life*
*Another World*
*Best Science Fiction Stories of the Year* #6–10
*The Best of Isaac Asimov's Science Fiction Magazine*
*Time-Travellers from Isaac Asimov's*
*Science Fiction Magazine*
*Transcendental Tales from Isaac Asimov's*
*Science Fiction Magazine*
*Isaac Asimov's Aliens*
*The Year's Best Science Fiction* #1–9

# GEODESIC DREAMS

The Best Short Fiction
of Gardner Dozois

## GARDNER DOZOIS

St. Martin's Press · New York

FOR

*Susan Casper*

FOR ALL OUR YEARS TOGETHER

"Man is an animal whose dreams come true and kill him."

—JAMES TIPTREE, JR.

# CONTENTS

· · · · · · · · · · · · · · · · · · · · · · · ·

# FOREWORD

．．．．．．．．．．．．．．．．．．．．．．

"The past," said L. P. Hartley, "is a foreign country." I was living in that country—as were you, as were we all—at the time I last wrote an introduction for a book of Gardner Dozois' short stories. It was, in fact, his first published book of fiction: *The Visible Man*, it was called, containing a dozen stories that had been written over a period of seven years. The year it appeared was 1977, practically half a lifetime ago as things go in the little world of science fiction, and a great deal has changed—for Dozois, for me, for the world—since then.

Actually, most of what I said in that first introduction is still appropriate to a consideration of Dozois' virtues and achievements as a writer, and will be trotted forth again here, since there's no reason for rephrasing what was perfectly well stated a decade and a half ago. But two of my statements do require significant updating, and it would be best to deal with those first.

One had to do with Dozois' physical appearance. In that 1977 introduction I described my first meeting with him, seven years previously, and spoke of the Gardner Dozois of March 1971 as "a weird-looking apparition." At that time, I said, he was "a gaunt young man just under six feet tall with a vast cascade of shoulder-length blond hair of an eerie voluminous sort covering most of his face, a strange bushy beard . . . , the glint of inquisitive eyes behind big steel-rimmed glasses, and—am I imagining this?—a bulky and grotesquely dilapidated raccoon coat. I mean, *weird*, man."

This description was already somewhat out of date in 1977, for I noted then that "he is no longer gaunt, not even remotely," nor was his general appearance quite as weird, although he still affected some quaint elements of hippie garb and a penchant for shagginess.

A further update is needed here. For one thing, Gardner not only continues not to be gaunt, but indeed is rather less so than he was even in 1977. Indeed, here in the full maturity of his years—he's nearing his mid-forties now—he has blossomed in more ways than one into one of the most conspicuous figures in the science-fiction world, a true titan of our profession.

But hippie garb and shaggy hair are most definitely not his style anymore. Gardner has a fine businesslike woolen jacket now—he bought it somewhere around 1986, I would guess—and he wears it constantly, even in the most stifling weather, when lesser mortals would gasp and cry out for flimsy Dacron. It is a very attractive jacket. I have admired it on many occasions since 1986 or so, and I look forward to seeing Gardner wearing it with his now legendary panache and aplomb for decades to come. Nor is he an uncouth, hairy, hippified being these days. He had his beard and hair trimmed quite neatly and expertly seven or eight years ago, and my guess is that he has had it done again with fair frequency since then—at least three or four times, perhaps, maybe even more. From humble beginnings he has become the very model of sartorial elegance in our field, a man to study and emulate.

The other aspect of my 1977 introduction that needs emendation now is the statement that because he produces his fiction so painfully and slowly, "he does a little editing on the side" in order to help make ends meet. I observed then that he was "dabbling in anthology-making" and also serving as first reader for the newly established *Isaac Asimov's Science Fiction Magazine.*

What a difference a decade and a half can make! (Especially in the science-fiction world, where things often happen at an accelerated pace, and careers rise or fall in the twinkling of a nanosecond.) These days it would be no more proper to speak of Dozois as "dabbling" in editing than it would be to speak of Boeing as "dabbling" in making airplanes. An editor is what he primarily is, now: one of the great ones, as it happens.

Dozois was no longer working for *Asimov's* by the time my first essay on him had appeared; but several editorial reshufflings took place at that magazine over the next few years, and in June of 1985 he was called back and placed in charge. His mark on the magazine was immediate and powerful: what had been a fine magazine suddenly became a truly distinguished one, worthy of being set beside such classics of the earlier golden ages as John W. Campbell's *Astounding Science Fiction* of 1939–42, Horace Gold's *Galaxy* of 1950–53, and the Boucher-McComas *Fantasy and Science Fiction* of 1949–52.

Gardner's editorial achievements at *Asimov's* quickly found favor with the readership; and as his magazine poured forth each month a succession of masterly and unforgettable stories by the finest of today's science-fiction writers, Dozois himself was rewarded with the Hugo award as Best Professional Editor in 1988—and again in 1989, 1990, and 1991 as well, a consistency of performance that has begun to engender a certain degree of melancholia among his fellow editors. His other considerable editorial achievement is the *Year's Best Science Fiction* anthology, an annual volume of gigantic size and awesome range, which began appearing under the auspices of Bluejay Books in 1984 and now—with the ninth volume about to appear as I write this—constitutes a thick shelf of books which contains essentially every short science-fiction story of importance published over the past decade, a wondrous archive of immeasurable historical significance.

But it is Gardner the writer with whom we are concerned here; and if writing has taken second place to editing in his career over the fifteen years since his first short-story collection appeared, that does not mean that writing is in any way a secondary sort of activity for him. Editing a monthly magazine that receives scores of submissions from hopeful writers every week is, of course, a time-consuming job; but I think that even if Dozois were not the editor of *Asimov's* he would have produced a fictional oeuvre not very much more extensive than the one he has given us. He is simply not a prolific writer. His stories are carefully considered and elegantly wrought, sentence by sentence: a thankless job, some might say, in a field where for the most part basic storytelling has always been valued more highly than literary craftsmanship. But he has no choice but to work the way he does, and those of us who are sensitive to the values of Dozois' fiction are much the richer for it.

Not that Dozois the writer has gone unrewarded. His first published story, "The Empty Man," was a nominee in 1966 for the award that science-fiction writers annually give their peers: the Nebula. Nearly every year thereafter, all through the 1970s and early 1980s, his stories were prominent features of the Nebula ballot. "The Visible Man" was a contender in 1975; *Strangers,* his first and, I think, only solo science-fiction novel, was nominated in 1978; "Disciples" (included in this volume) was a nominee in 1981; and so forth. His stories had regularly been reaching the ballot for the Hugo (the award given by readers) also; "A Special Kind of Morning" (included here) was a nominee in 1972; "A Kingdom by the Sea" (reprinted in this collection) made the ballot in 1973; the novella "Chains of the Sea," also included here, was on the ballot in 1974; *Strangers* in its original shorter form had been a nominee in 1975. By 1982, Dozois had achieved enough nominations (without winning any awards) to place him second on the list of the "most consistent Hugo and Nebula award losers" in Mike Ashley's statistical compilation, *The Illustrated Book of Science Fiction Lists:* Dozois had collected four Hugo nominations and six Nebula nominations, but no trophies.

Then things changed, though. "The Peacemaker," which you will find in this collection, won the Nebula in 1983 as Best Short Story, and the following year Dozois picked up a second Nebula in that category for "Morning Child," also included in this book. Only the Hugo for fiction has continued to elude him; the preferences of the Hugo voters are weighted, usually, toward basic storytelling qualities, and it is the common fate of

science-fiction writers whose great strength is stylistic to receive
frequent nominations but few awards.

Not that Dozois is merely a stylist. His fiction, as you will
see, is passionate, powerfully committed stuff. But he deals in
deep and eternal matters of the human heart, and in the com-
plexities and disappointments of life in a human society. It is
the kind of fiction that wins applause and admiration, but—
somehow—not many Hugos.

And now, if you will forgive me, I will repeat some things I
said in my 1977 introduction concerning the particular qualities of Dozois' fiction that I think are most worthy of praise,
because what I said in 1977 still provides the best summation
of my feelings. Let us consider this paragraph from one of his
earliest stories, written when he was scarcely old enough to
vote:

Did y'ever hear the one about the old man and the sea?

Halt a minute, lordling; stop and listen. It's a fine story,
full of balance and point and social pith; short and direct.
It's not mine. Mine are long and rambling and parenthetical
and they corrode the moral fiber right out of a man. Come
to think, I won't tell you that one after all. A man of my age
has a right to prefer his own material, and let the critics be
damned. I've a prejudice now for webs of my own weaving.

As I did fifteen years ago, allow me to invite your attention
to the rhythms of the prose, the balancing of clauses, the use of
alliteration, metaphor, and irony, the tough, elegant sinews of
the vocabulary. It is a paragraph of splendid construction, a
specimen of prose that shows honorable descent from Chaucer
and Shakespeare, Pope and Dryden, Defoe and Dickens, the
prose of a man who knows what he wants to say and says it
eloquently and effectively. It is the opening paragraph of "A
Special Kind of Morning," which Dozois wrote in 1970 and
which I chose, not at random, to be the first story in the first
number of New Dimensions, the anthology series that I was
editing in that era. Many science-fiction writers, including a lot
of the great ones, are content to be mere storytellers, using

whatever assemblages of words may be handy to convey their meanings. Dozois is a storyteller too, and no mere one, either—"A Special Kind of Morning" is a vigorous and violent tale of war with a structural underpinning worthy of Sophocles—but he is concerned as much with the *way* he tells his stories as with the events he is describing.

Or here, this paragraph from "Chains of the Sea":

One day the aliens landed, just as everyone always said they would. They fell out of a guileless blue sky and into the middle of a clear, cold November day, four of them, four alien ships drifting down like the snow that had been threatening to fall all week. America was just shouldering its way into daylight as they made planetfall, so they landed there: one in the Delaware Valley about fifteen miles north of Philadelphia, one in Ohio, one in a desolate region of Colorado, and one—for whatever reason—in a cane field outside of Caracas, Venezuela. To those who actually saw them come down, the ships seemed to fall rather than to descend under any intelligent control: a black nailhead suddenly tacked to the sky, coming all at once from nowhere, with no transition, like a Fortean rock squeezed from a high appearing-point, hanging way up there and winking intolerably bright in the sunlight; and then gravity takes hold of it, visibly, and it begins to fall, far away and dream-slow at first, swelling larger, growing huge, unbelievably big, a mountain hurled at the earth, falling with terrifying speed, rolling in the air, tumbling end over end, overhead, coming down—and then it is sitting peacefully on the ground; it has not crashed, and although it didn't slow and it didn't stop, there it *is*, and not even a snowflake could have settled onto the frozen mud more lightly.

Prose, yes. Actual prose. America is *shouldering its way into daylight*. The alien spaceship descends like *a black nailhead suddenly tacked to the sky*. The sense of invasion is conveyed through an accretion of concrete detail, of vivid and immediate simile and metaphor and physical description. Melville understood these things, and Joyce, and Faulkner. So did Raymond Chandler and Dashiell Hammett, and in our own field Theodore Sturgeon, and Cyril Kornbluth, and Henry Kuttner. The power of that passage depends on a respect for language and grammar, a sense of the structure of the sentence and the paragraph, and a keen perception of sensory data. Gardner Dozois is as skilled a worker in prose as there is in science fiction. His marvelous ear and eye provide much, though not all, of the explanation of his success as an editor; and these stories collected here will tell you how considerable a writer he has been over the past two decades as well.

The name, by the way, is pronounced "Do-*zwah*." Most of the readers of the 1977 collection needed to be told that. Today, I think, the name of this writer is more familiar to us. May his acclaim continue to grow for years to come.

—ROBERT SILVERBERG
April, 1992

# MORNING CHILD

......................

The old house had been hit by something sometime during the war and mashed nearly flat. The front was caved in as though crushed by a giant fist: wood pulped and splintered, beams protruding at odd angles like broken fingers, the second floor collapsed onto the remnants of the first. The rubble of a chimney covered everything with a red mortar blanket. On the right, a gaping hole cross-sectioned the ruins, laying bare all the strata of fused stone and plaster and charred wood—everything curling back on itself like the lips of a gangrenous wound. Weeds had swarmed up the low hillside from the road and swept over the house, wrapping the ruins in wildflowers and grapevines, softening the edges of destruction with green.

Williams brought John here almost every day. They had lived here once, in this house, many years ago, and although John's memory of that time was dim, the place seemed to have pleasant associations for him, in spite of its ruined condition. John was at his happiest here and would play contentedly with sticks and pebbles on the shattered stone steps, or go whooping through the tangled weeds that had turned the lawn into a jungle, or play-stalk in ominous circles around Williams while Williams worked at filling his bags with blueberries, daylilies, Indian potatoes, dandelions, and other edible plants and roots.

Even Williams took a bittersweet pleasure in visiting the

ruins, although coming here stirred memories that he would rather have left undisturbed. There was a pleasant melancholy to the spot and something oddly soothing about the mixture of mossy old stone and tender new green, a reminder of the inevitability of cycles—life-in-death, death-in-life.

John erupted out of the tall weeds and ran laughing to where Williams stood with the foraging bags. "I been fighting dinosaurs!" John said. "Great *big* ones!" Williams smiled crookedly and said, "That's good." He reached down and rumpled John's hair. They stood there for a second, John panting like a dog from all the running he'd been doing, his eyes bright, Williams letting his touch linger on the small, tousled head. At this time of the morning, John seemed always in motion, motion so continuous that it gave nearly the illusion of rest, like a stream of water that looks solid until something makes it momentarily sputter and stop.

This early in the day, John rarely stopped. When he did, as now, he seemed to freeze solid, his face startled and intent, as though he were listening to sounds that no one else could hear. At such times Williams would study him with painful intensity, trying to see himself in him, sometimes succeeding, sometimes failing, and wondering which hurt more, and why.

Sighing, Williams took his hand away. The sun was getting high, and they'd better be heading back to camp if they wanted to be there at the right time for the heavier chores. Slowly, Williams bent over and picked up the foraging bags, grunting a little at their weight as he settled them across his shoulder—they had done very well for themselves this morning.

"Come on now, John," Williams said, "time to go," and started off, limping a bit more than usual under the extra weight. John, trotting alongside, his short legs pumping, seemed to notice. "Can I help you carry the bags?" John said eagerly. "Can I? I'm big enough!" Williams smiled at him and shook his head. "Not yet, John," he said. "A little bit later, maybe."

They passed out of the cool shadow of the ruined house and began to hike back to camp along the deserted highway.

The sun was baking down now from out of a cloudless sky,

and heat-bugs began to chirrup somewhere, producing a harsh and metallic stridulation that sounded amazingly like a buzz saw. There were no other sounds besides the soughing of wind through tall grass and wild wheat, the tossing and whispering of trees, and the shrill piping of John's voice. Weeds had thrust up through the macadam—tiny, green fingers that had cracked and buckled the road's surface, chopped it up into lopsided blocks. Another few years and there would be no road here, only a faint track in the undergrowth—and then not even that. Time would erase everything, burying it beneath new trees, gradually building new hills, laying down a fresh landscape to cover the old. Already grass and vetch had nibbled away the corners of the sharper curves, and the wind had drifted topsoil onto the road. There were saplings now in some places, growing green and shivering in the middle of the highway, negating the faded signs that pointed to distances and towns.

John ran ahead, found a rock to throw, ran back, circling around Williams as though on an invisible tether. They walked in the middle of the road, John pretending that the faded white line was a tightrope, waving his arms for balance, shouting warnings to himself about the abyss creatures who would gobble him up if he should misstep and fall.

Williams maintained a steady pace, not hurrying: the epitome of the ramrod-straight old man, his snow-white hair gleaming in the sunlight, a bush knife at his belt, an old Winchester .30-30 slung across his back—although he no longer believed that they'd need it. They weren't the only people left in the world, he knew—however much it felt like it sometimes—but this region had been emptied of its population years ago, and since he and John had returned this way on their long journey up from the south, they had seen no one else at all. No one would find them here.

There were traces of buildings along the way now, all that was left of a small country town: the burnt-out spine of a roof ridge meshed with weeds; gaping stone foundations like battlements for dwarfs; a ruined water faucet clogged with spiderwebs; a shattered gas pump inhabited by birds and rodents. They turned off onto a gravel secondary road, past the burnt-out shell of another filling station and a dilapidated roadside stand full of windblown trash. Overhead, a rusty traffic light swayed on a sagging wire. Someone had tied a big orange-and-black hex sign to one side of the light, and on the other side, the side facing away from town and out into the hostile world, was the evil eye, painted against a white background in vivid, shocking red. Things had gotten very strange during the Last Days.

Williams was having trouble now keeping up with John's ever-lengthening stride, and he decided that it was time to let him carry the bags. John hefted the bags easily, flashing his strong white teeth at Williams in a grin, and set off up the last long slope to camp, his long legs carrying him up the hill at a pace Williams couldn't hope to match. Williams swore good-naturedly, and John laughed and stopped to wait for him at the top of the rise.

Their camp was set well back from the road, on top of a bluff, just above a small river. There had been a restaurant here once, and a corner of the building still stood, two walls and part of the roof, needing only the tarpaulin stretched across the open end to make it into a reasonably snug shelter. They'd have to find something better by winter, of course, but this was good enough for July, reasonably well hidden and close to a supply of water.

Rolling, wooded hills were around them to the north and east. To the south, across the river, the hills dwindled away into flatland, and the world opened up into a vista that stretched to the horizon.

They grabbed a quick lunch and then set to work, chopping wood, hauling in the nets that Williams had set across the river to catch fish, carrying water, for cooking, up the steep slope to camp. Williams let John do most of the heavy work. John sang and whistled happily while he worked, and once, on his way back from carrying some firewood to the shelter, he laughed, grabbed Williams under the arms, boosted him into the air, and danced him around in a little circle before setting him back down on his feet again.

"Feeling your oats, eh?" Williams said with mock severity, looking up into the sweaty face that smiled down at him.

"*Somebody* has to do the work around here," John said cheerfully, and they both laughed. "I can't wait to get back to my outfit," John said eagerly. "I feel much better now. I feel *terrific*. Are we going to stay out here much longer?" His eyes pleaded with Williams. "We can go back soon, can't we?"

"Yeah," Williams lied, "we can go back real soon."

But already John was tiring. By dusk, his footsteps were beginning to drag, and his breathing was becoming heavy and labored. He paused in the middle of what he was doing, put down the wood-chopping ax, and stood silently for a moment, staring blankly at nothing.

His face was suddenly intent and withdrawn, and his eyes were dull. He swayed unsteadily and wiped the back of his hand across his forehead. Williams got him to sit down on a stump near the improvised fireplace. He sat there silently, staring at the ground in abstraction, while Williams bustled around, lighting a fire, cleaning and filleting the fish, cutting up dandelion roots and chicory crowns, boiling water. The sun was down now, and fireflies began to float above the river, winking like fairy lanterns through the velvet darkness.

Williams did his best to interest John in supper, hoping that he'd eat something while he still had some of his teeth, but John would eat little. After a few moments he put his tin plate down and sat staring dully to the south, out over the darkened lands beyond the river, just barely visible in the dim light of a crescent moon. His face was preoccupied and glum, and beginning to get jowly. His hairline had retreated in a wide arc from his forehead, creating a large bald spot. He worked his mouth indecisively several times and at last said, "Have I been . . . ill?"

"Yes, John," Williams said gently. "You've been ill."

"I can't . . . I can't *remember*," John complained. His voice was cracked and husky, querulous. "Everything's so confused. I can't keep things *straight*—"

Somewhere on the invisible horizon, perhaps a hundred

miles away, a pillar of fire leapt up from the edge of the world. As they watched, startled, it climbed higher and higher, towering miles into the air, until it was a slender column of brilliant flame that divided the sullen black sky in two from ground to stratosphere. The pillar of fire blazed steadily on the horizon for a minute or two, and then it began to coruscate, burning green and blue and silver and orange, the colors flaring and flickering fitfully as they merged into one another. Slowly, with a kind of stately and awful symmetry, the pillar broadened out to become a flattened diamond shape of blue-white fire. The diamond began to rotate slowly on its axis, and, as it rotated, it grew eye-searingly bright. Gargantuan unseen shapes floated around the blazing diamond, like moths beating around a candle flame, throwing huge tangled shadows across the world.

Something with a huge, melancholy voice hooted, and hooted again, a forlorn and terrible sound that beat back and forth between the hills until it rumbled slowly away into silence.

The blazing diamond winked out. Hot white stars danced where it had been. The stars faded to sullenly glowing orange dots that flickered away down the spectrum and were gone.

It was dark again.

The night had been shocked silent. For a while, that silence was complete, and then slowly, tentatively, one by one, the crickets and tree frogs began to make their night sounds again.

"The war—" John whispered. His voice was reedy and thin and weary now, and there was pain in it. "It still goes on?"

"The war got . . . strange," Williams said quietly. "The longer it lasted, the stranger it got. New allies, new weapons—" He stared off into the darkness in the direction where the fire had danced: there was still an uneasy shimmer to the night air on the horizon, not quite a glow. "You were hurt by such a weapon, I guess. Something like *that*, maybe." He nodded toward the horizon, and his face hardened. "I don't know. I don't even know what *that* was. I don't understand much that happens in the world anymore. . . . Maybe it wasn't even a weapon that hurt you. Maybe they were experimenting on you biologically before you got away. Who knows why? Maybe it was done deliberately—as a punishment. Or a reward. Who knows how they think? Maybe it was a side effect of some device designed to do something else entirely. Maybe it was an accident; maybe you just got too close to something like *that* when it was doing whatever it is it does." Williams was silent for a moment, and then he sighed. "Whatever happened, you got to me afterward somehow, and I took care of you. We've been hiding out ever since, moving from place to place."

They had both been nearly blind while their eyes readjusted to the night, but now, squinting in the dim glow of the low-burning cooking fire, Williams could see John again. John was now totally bald, his cheeks had caved in, and his dulled and yellowing eyes were sunken deeply into his ravaged face. He struggled to get to his feet, then sank back down onto the stump again. "I can't—" he whispered. Weak tears began to run down his cheeks. He started to shiver.

Sighing, Williams got up and threw a double handful of pine needles into boiling water to make white-pine-needle tea. He helped John limp over to his pallet, supporting most of his weight, almost carrying him—it was easy; John had become shrunken and frail and amazingly light, as if he were now made out of cloth and cotton and dry sticks instead of flesh and bone. He got John to lie down, tucked a blanket around him in spite of the heat of the evening, and concentrated on getting some of the tea into him.

He drank two full cups before his fingers became too weak to hold the cup, before even the effort of holding up his head became too great for him. John's eyes had become blank and shiny and unseeing, and his face was like a skull, earth-brown and blotched, with the skin drawn tightly over the bones.

His hands plucked aimlessly at the blanket; they looked mummified now, the skin as translucent as parchment, the blue veins showing through beneath.

As the evening wore on, John began to fret and whine incoherently, turning his face blindly back and forth, muttering random fragments of words and sentences, sometimes raising his voice in a strangled, gurgling shout that had no words at all in it, only bewilderment and outrage and pain. Williams sat patiently beside him, stroking his shriveled hands, wiping sweat from his hot forehead.

"Sleep now," Williams said soothingly. John moaned, and whined in the back of his throat. "Sleep. Tomorrow we'll go to the house again. You'll like that, won't you? But sleep now, sleep—"

At last John quieted, his eyes slowly closed, and his breathing grew deeper and more regular.

Williams sat patiently by his side, keeping a calming hand on his shoulder. Already John's hair was beginning to grow back, and the lines were smoothing out of his face as he melted toward childhood.

When Williams was sure that John was asleep, he tucked the blanket closer around him and said, "Sleep well, Father," and then slowly, passionately, soundlessly, he started to weep.

# DINNER PARTY

......................

It had been cold all that afternoon. When they picked Hassmann up at the gate that evening, it was worse than cold—it was
freezing.

The gate guard let Hassmann wait inside the guard booth,
although that was technically against regulations, and he might
have caught hell for it if the Officer of the Day had come by. But
it was colder than a witch's tit outside, as the guard put it, and
he knew Hassmann slightly, and liked him, even though he was
RA and Hassmann was National Guard, and he thought that
most NGs were chickenshit. But he liked Hassmann. Hassmann was a good kid.

They huddled inside the guard booth, sharing a cigarette,
talking desultorily about baseball and women, about a court-
martial in the gate guard's battalion, about the upcoming ATTs
and MOS tests, about the scarcity of promotion slots for cor-
porals and 5s. They carefully did not talk about the incident
last weekend on the campus in Morgantown, although it had
been all over the papers and the TV and had been talked about
all over post. They also didn't talk about where Hassmann was
going tonight—allowed off base at a time when almost everyone
else's passes had been pulled—although rumors about that had
spread through the grapevine with telegraphic speed since Hassmann's interview with Captain Simes early that afternoon.

Most especially, most emphatically, they did not talk about what everyone knew but hesitated to admit even in whispers: that by this time next month, they would probably be at war.

The gate guard was telling some long, rambling anecdote about breaking up a fight down behind the Armor mess hall when he looked out beyond Hassmann's shoulder and fell silent, his face changing. "This looks like your ride heah, Jackson," he said, quietly, after a pause.

Hassmann watched the car sweep in off the road and stop before the gate; it was a big black Caddy, the post floodlights gleaming from a crust of ice over polished steel and chrome. "Yeah," Hassmann said. His throat had suddenly turned dry, and his tongue bulked enormously in his mouth. He ground the cigarette butt out against the wall. The guard opened the door of the booth to let him out. The cold seized him with his first step outside, seized him and shook him like a dog shaking a rat. "Cover your ass," the gate guard said suddenly from the booth behind him. "Remember—cover your *own* ass, you heah?" Hassmann nodded, without looking around, without much conviction. The guard grunted, and slid the booth door closed.

Hassmann was alone.

He began to trot toward the car, slipping on a patch of ice, recovering easily. Hoarfrost glistened everywhere, over everything, and the stars were out in their chill armies, like the million icy eyes of God. The cold air was like ice in his lungs, and his breath steamed in white tatters around him. The driver of the car had the right front door half open, waiting for him, but Hassmann—seeing that the man had a woman with him, and feeling a surge of revulsion at the thought of sitting pressed close to the couple in the front—opened the rear door instead and slipped into the back seat. After a moment, the driver shrugged and closed the front door. Hassmann closed the rear door too, automatically pushing down the little button that locked it, instantly embarrassed that he had done so. After the double *thunk* of the doors closing and the sharp *click* of the lock, there was nothing but a smothering silence.

The driver turned around in his seat, resting his arm on the top of the seatback, staring at Hassmann. In the dark, it was hard to make out his features, but he was a big, beefy man, and Hassmann could see the reptilian glint of light from thick, black, horn-rimmed glasses. The woman was still facing forward, only casting a quick, furtive glance back at him, and then turning her head away again. Even in this half-light, Hassmann could see the stiffness of her shoulders, the taut way she held her neck. When the silence had become more than uncomfortable, Hassmann stammered, "Sir, I'm—sir, PFC Hassmann, sir . . ."

The driver shifted his weight in the front seat. Leather creaked and moaned. "Glad to meet you, son," he said. "Yes, very glad—a pleasure, yes, a pleasure." There was a forced joviality in his voice, a note of strained, dangerous cordiality that Hassmann decided he had better not try to argue with.

"Glad to meet you, too, sir," Hassmann croaked.

"Thank you, son," the man said. Leather groaned again as he extended his hand into the back seat; Hassmann shook it briefly, released it—the man's hand had been damp and flabby, like a rubber glove full of oatmeal. "I'm Dr. Wilkins," the man said. "And this is my wife, Fran." His wife did not acknowledge the introduction, continuing to stare stonily straight ahead. "Manners," Dr. Wilkins said in a soft, cottony voice, almost a whisper. "Manners!" Mrs. Wilkins jerked, as if she had been slapped, and then dully muttered, "Charmed," still not turning to look at Hassmann.

Dr. Wilkins stared at his wife for a moment, then turned to look at Hassmann again; his glasses were dully gleaming blank circles, as opaque as portholes. "What's your *Christian* name, son?"

Hassmann shifted uneasily in his seat. After a moment's hesitation—as though to speak his name would be to give the other man power over him—he said "James, sir. James Hassmann."

"I'll call you Jim, then," Dr. Wilkins said. It was a statement of fact—he was not asking permission; nor was there any question that Hassmann would be expected to continue to call him "Dr. Wilkins," however free the older man made himself with

Hassmann's "Christian name." Or "sir," Hassmann thought with a quick flash of resentment, you could hardly go wrong calling him "sir." Hassmann had been in the Army long enough to know that it was impossible to say "sir" too many times when you were talking to a man like this; work it in a hundred times per sentence, they'd like it just fine.

Dr. Wilkins was still staring reflectively at him, as if he expected some sort of response, an expression of gratitude for the fine democratic spirit he was showing, perhaps . . . but Hassmann said nothing. Dr. Wilkins grunted. "Well, then—Jim," he said. "You like Continental cuisine?"

"I—I'm not sure, sir," Hassmann said. He could feel his face flushing with embarrassment in the close darkness of the cab. "I'm not sure I know what it is."

Dr. Wilkins made a noise that was not quite a snort—a long, slow, resigned exhaling of air through the nose. "What kind of food do you like to eat at home?"

"Well, sir, the usual kind of thing, I guess. Nothing special."

"What kind of things?" Dr. Wilkins said with heavy, elaborated patience.

"Oh—spaghetti, meat loaf. Sometimes fried chicken, or cold cuts. We had TV dinners a lot." Dr. Wilkins was staring at him; it was too dark to make out his expression with any kind of certainty, but he seemed to be staring blankly, incredulously, as if he couldn't believe what he was hearing. "Sometimes my mother'd make, you know, a roast for Sunday or something, but she didn't much like to cook anything fancy like that."

This time Dr. Wilkins did snort, a sharp, impatient sound. "*Adeo in teneris consuescere multum est*," he said in a loud, portentous voice, and shook his head. Hassmann felt his face burning again; he had no idea what Dr. Wilkins had said, but there was no mistaking the scorn behind the words. "That's Virgil," Dr. Wilkins said contemptuously, peering significantly at Hassmann. "You know Virgil?"

"Sir?" Hassmann said.

"Never mind," Dr. Wilkins muttered. After a heavy pause, he said, "This restaurant we're taking you to tonight has a three-star Michelin rating, one of the few places east of the Mississippi River that does, outside of New York City. I don't suppose that means anything to you, either, does it?"

"No, sir," Hassmann said stiffly. "I'm afraid it doesn't, sir."

Dr. Wilkins snorted again. Hassmann saw that Mrs. Wilkins was watching him in the rearview mirror, but as soon as their eyes met, she turned her face away.

"Well, son," Dr. Wilkins was saying, "I'll tell you *one* thing those three Michelin stars mean: they mean that tonight you're going to get the best damn meal you ever had." He sniffed derisively. "Maybe the best damn meal you'll *ever* have. Do you understand *that* . . . Jim?"

"Yes, sir," Hassmann said. Out of the corner of his eye, he could see that Mrs. Wilkins was watching him in the rearview mirror again. Every time she thought that his attention was elsewhere, she would stare at him with terrible fixed intensity; she would look away when he met her eyes in the mirror, but a moment later, as soon as he glanced away, she would be staring at him again, as though she couldn't keep her eyes off him, as though he were something loathsome and at the same time almost hypnotically fascinating, like a snake or a venomous insect.

"I don't expect you to appreciate the finer points," Dr. Wilkins said, "we can thank the way kids are brought up today for *that*, but I do expect you to appreciate that what you're getting tonight *is* a very fine meal, one of the finest meals money can buy, not some slop from McDonald's."

"Yes, sir, I do, sir," Hassmann said. Dr. Wilkins made a *humpf*ing noise, not sounding entirely mollified, so Hassmann added, "It sounds great, sir. I'm really looking forward to it. Thank you, sir." He kept his face blank and his voice level, but his jaw ached with tension. He hated being dressed down like this, he *hated* it. His fingers were turning white where they were biting into the edge of the seat.

Dr. Wilkins stared at him for a moment longer, then sighed and turned back to the wheel; they slid away into the darkness with a smooth surge of acceleration.

They ghosted back down the hill, turned right. Here the road ran parallel to the tall Cyclone fence that surrounded the base; behind the iron mesh, behind the winter-stripped skeletons of trees, Hassmann could see the high, cinder-bed roofs of the Infantry barracks, a huge water tower—it had the slogan RE-UP ARMY stenciled on its sides, visible for miles in the daytime— and the gaunt silhouette of a derrick, peeking up over the fence from the Engineer motor pool like the neck of some fantastic metal giraffe. The base dwindled behind them to a tabletop miniature, to a scene the size of a landscape inside a tiny glass snowball, and then it was gone, and there was nothing but the stuffy interior of the car, the pale glow of the instruments on the dashboard, dark masses of trees rushing by on either side. Hassmann was sweating heavily, in spite of the cold, and the upholstery was sticky under his hands.

There was a persistent scent of patchouli in the car—cutting across the new-car smell of the upholstery and the tobacco– and–English Leather smell of Dr. Wilkins—that must be Mrs. Wilkins' perfume; it was a heavy, oversweet smell that reminded Hassmann of the room in the cancer hospital where his aunt had died. He longed to roll down the window, let the cold night air into the stuffy car, but he didn't quite dare to do it without asking Dr. Wilkins' permission, and that was something he wouldn't do. He was beginning to get a headache, a bright needle of pain that probed in alongside his eyeball like a stiff wire, and his stomach was sick and knotted with tension. Abruptly it was too much for him, and he found himself blinking back sudden tears of frustration and rage, all the resentment and chagrin he felt rising up in his throat like bile. Why did he have to do this? Why did they have to pick on *him?* Why couldn't they just leave him *alone?* He had said as much in Captain Simes' office this afternoon, blurting out, "I don't want to do it! Do I *have* to go, sir?" And Captain Simes had studied him jaundicedly for a moment before replying, "Officially, no. The regulations say we can't make you. Unofficially, though, I can tell you that Dr. Wilkins is a very important man in this state, and with things as tense as they are politically, you can expect some very serious smoke to be brought down on your ass if you don't do everything you can to keep him happy, short of dropping your drawers and bending over." And then Simes had leered at him with his eroded, prematurely old face and said, "And, hell, soldier, comes right down *to* it, maybe you even ought to take *that* under advisement. . . ."

They drifted past a weathered wooden barn that was covered with faded old Clabber Girl and Jesus Saves signs, past a dilapidated farmhouse where one light was burning in an upstairs window. There was an automobile up on blocks in the snow-covered front yard, its engine hanging suspended from a rope thrown over a tree branch. Scattered automobile parts made hummocks in the snow, as if small dead animals were buried there. They turned past a bullet-riddled highway sign and onto an old state road that wound down out of the foothill country. The car began to pick up speed, swaying slightly on its suspension.

"You come from around here, Jim?" Dr. Wilkins said.

"No, sir," Hassmann said. *Thank God!* he added silently to himself. Evidently he had been unable to keep his feelings out of his voice, because Dr. Wilkins glanced quizzically at him in the rearview mirror. Quickly, Hassmann added, "I was born in Massachusetts, sir. A small town near Springfield."

"That so?" Dr. Wilkins said, without interest. "Gets pretty cold up there too in the winter, doesn't it? So at least you're used to this kind of weather, right?"

"That's right, sir," Hassmann said leadenly. "It gets pretty cold there, too."

Dr. Wilkins grunted. Even he seemed to realize that his attempt at small talk had been a dismal failure, for he lapsed into a sodden silence. He pressed down harder on the accelerator, and the dark winter countryside began to blur by outside the windows. Now that they had stopped talking, there was no sound except for the whine of the tires on macadam or their snare-drum rattle on patches of gravel.

Hassmann rubbed his sweating palms against the slick upholstery. Somehow he knew that Mrs. Wilkins was watching him again, although it was too dark to see her eyes in the mirror anymore. Occasionally the lights of an oncoming car would turn the inside of the windshield into a reflective surface, and he would be able to see her plainly for a second, a thin-faced woman with tightly pursed lips, her hands clenched together in her lap, staring rigidly straight ahead of her. Then the light would fade and her image would disappear, and only then, in the darkness, would he begin to *feel* her eyes watching him again, as though she were only able to see him in the dark . . .

They were going faster and faster now, careening down the old state road like a moonshiner on a delivery run with the Alcohol Tax agents on his tail, and Hassmann was beginning to be afraid, although he did his best to sit still and look imperturbable. The old roadbed was only indifferently maintained, and every bump rattled their teeth in spite of the Caddy's heavy-duty shocks; once Hassmann was bounced high enough to bang his head on the roof, and the car was beginning to sway ominously from side to side. Fortunately, they were on a level stretch of road with no oncoming traffic when they hit the patch of ice. For a moment or two the Caddy was all over the road, skidding and fishtailing wildly, its brakes screaming and its tires throwing up clouds of black smoke, and then slowly, painfully, Dr. Wilkins brought the big car back under control. They never came to a complete stop, but they had slowed down to about fifteen miles per hour by the time Dr. Wilkins could wrestle them back into their own lane, and you could smell burned rubber even inside the closed cab.

No one spoke; Mrs. Wilkins had not even moved, except to steady herself against the dashboard with one hand, an almost dainty motion. Slowly, almost involuntarily, Dr. Wilkins raised his head to look at Hassmann in the rearview mirror. *Almost lost it, didn't you, old man?* Hassmann thought, staring impassively back at him, and after a moment, Dr. Wilkins looked shakily away. They began to slowly pick up speed again, wobbling slightly, although Dr. Wilkins was careful to keep them under fifty this time. This kind of compulsive speeding, obviously pushing himself to or beyond the edge of his driving ability, was the first real indication of strain or tension that Dr. Wilkins had allowed to escape from behind his smooth, hard-lacquered façade, and Hassmann greeted it with interest and a certain degree of vindictiveness.

A few minutes more brought them out of the hills. They slowed down to rattle across a small chain-link bridge over a frozen river. A tank was parked to one side of the road, near the bridge entrance, its hatches open for ventilation, gray smoke panting from its exhaust and rising straight up into the cold air. A soldier in a steel helmet popped his head up out of the driver's hatch and watched them as they passed. They weren't putting up roadblocks and regulating civilian traffic yet, Hassmann thought, in spite of the recent wave of terrorism, but it obviously wasn't going to be too much longer before they were, either. There was a small town on the other side of the bridge, half a dozen buildings clustered around a crossroads. Political graffiti had been spray-painted on several of the buildings, particularly on the blank-faced side wall of a boarded-up gas station: YANKEES GO HOME . . . FEDS OUT OF WEST VIRGINIA NOW . . . SECESSION, NOT RECESSION . . . FUCK THE UNION . . . A sloppy, half-hearted attempt to obliterate the graffiti had been made, and only a few letters of each slogan remained, but Hassmann had seen them often enough elsewhere to have little difficulty reconstructing them. The restaurant was a mile beyond the town, a large stone-and-timber building that had once been a grinding mill—now hidden spotlights splashed the ivy-covered walls with pastel light, and the big wooden water-wheel was sheathed in glistening ice.

There was a network newsvan parked in front of the restaurant, and Dr. Wilkins, who had been anxiously checking his watch on the last stretch from town, grunted in satisfaction when he saw it. As they pulled up, a news crew with a minicam unit climbed out of the van and took up positions in front of the restaurant steps. Other reporters got out of their parked cars—pinching out unfinished cigarettes and carefully tucking them away—and began to saunter over as well, some of them slapping themselves on the arms and joking with one another about the cold in low, rapid voices. Hassmann heard one of the reporters laugh, the sound carrying clearly on the cold winter air.

Dr. Wilkins switched off the ignition, and they all sat motionless and silent for a moment, listening to the metallic *ticking* noises the engine made as it cooled. Then, with forced brightness, Dr. Wilkins said, "Well, we're here! Everybody out!" Mrs. Wilkins ignored him. She was staring out at the gathering knot of reporters, and for the first time she seemed shaken, her icy composure broken. "Frank," she said in an unsteady voice, "I—Frank, I just *can't*, I can't face them, I can't—" She was trembling. Dr. Wilkins patted her hand perfunctorily. He noticed Hassmann watching them, and glared at him with murderous resentment, his careful mask slipping for a moment. Hassmann stared stonily back. "It'll be all right, Fran," Dr. Wilkins said, patting her hand again. "It's just until we get inside. Julian promised me that he wouldn't let any of them into the restaurant." Mrs. Wilkins was shaking her head blindly. "It'll only be a minute. Let me do all the talking. It'll be okay, you'll see." He looked coldly at Hassmann. "Come on," he said brusquely, to Hassmann, and got out of the car. He walked quickly around to the passenger side, opened the door, and said, "Come on" again, to his wife this time, in the low coaxing tone an adult might use to a frightened child. Even so, he had to reach down and half pull her to her feet before he could get her out of the car. He bent to look at Hassmann again. "You, too," he said in a harsh, dangerous voice. "Come on. Don't give me any trouble now, you little shit. Get out."

Hassmann climbed out of the car. It was colder than ever, and he could feel the clammy sweat drying on his body with a rapidity that made him shiver. Dr. Wilkins came up between him and Mrs. Wilkins and took each of them by the arm, and they began walking toward the restaurant. The reporters were looking toward them now, and the camera lights on the van came on, nearly blinding them with brightness.

Dr. Wilkins kept them walking right at the reporters. The small crowd parted and re-formed around them, swallowing them, and then it seemed to Hassmann as if everything was happening at once, too fast to follow. Faces jostled around him, faces thrust forward toward him, their mouths opening and closing. Voices gabbled. A reporter was saying, ". . . with the ratification vote on the Act of Secession coming up in the statehouse Wednesday, and similar votes later this week in

Michigan, Ohio, and Colorado," and Dr. Wilkins was waving his hand airily and saying, ". . . more than enough support on the floor." Another reporter was saying something to Mrs. Wilkins and she was dully muttering, "I don't know, I don't know . . ." Flashbulbs were popping at them now, and they had climbed partway up the restaurant steps. Someone was thrusting a microphone into Hassmann's face and bellowing ". . . make you feel?" and Hassmann was shrugging and shaking his head. Someone else was saying ". . . latest Gallup poll shows that two-thirds of the people of West Virginia support secession," and Dr. Wilkins was saying, ". . . everything you hear, love?" and the reporters laughed.

Hassmann wasn't listening anymore. Ever since last weekend he had been walking around like a somnambulist, and now the feeling had intensified; he felt feverish and unreal, as if everything was happening behind a thin wall of insulating glass, or happening to someone else while he watched. He barely noticed that Dr. Wilkins had stopped walking and was now staring directly into the blinking eye of the minicam, or that the reporters had grown curiously silent. Dr. Wilkins had let his face become serious and somber, and when he spoke this time it was not in the insouciant tone he'd been using a moment before, but in a slow, sincere, gravelly voice. The voice seemed to go on and on and on, while Hassmann shivered in the cold wind, and then Dr. Wilkins' heavy hand closed over Hassmann's shoulder, and the flashbulbs went off in their faces like summer lightning.

Then Julian was ushering them into the restaurant—fawning shamelessly over Dr. Wilkins and promising to "take their order personally"—and shutting the reporters outside. He led them through the jungly interior of the old mill to a table in a corner nook where the walls were hung with bronze cooking utensils and old farm implements, and then buzzed anxiously around Dr. Wilkins like a fat unctuous bee while they consulted the menu. The menu had no prices, and as far as Hassmann was concerned might just as well have been written in Arabic. Mrs. Wilkins refused to order, or even to speak, and her rigid silence eventually embarrassed even Julian. Impatiently, Dr. Wilkins ordered for all of them—making a point of asking Hassmann, with thinly disguised sarcasm, if the couli-biac of salmon and the osso buco would be to his liking—and Julian hurried gratefully away.

Silence settled over the table. Dr. Wilkins stared blankly at Hassmann, who stared blankly back. Mrs. Wilkins seemed to have gone into shock—she was staring down at the table, her body stiffly erect, her hands clenched in her lap; it was hard to tell if she was even breathing. Dr. Wilkins looked at his wife, looked away. Still no one had spoken. "Well, Jim," Dr. Wilkins started to say with leaden joviality, "I think you'll like—" and then he caught the scorn in the look that Hassmann was giving him, and let the sentence falter to a stop. It had become clear to Hassmann that Dr. Wilkins hated him as much as or more than his wife did—but in spite of that, and in spite of the fact that he had already gotten as much use out of Hassmann as he was going to get, he was too much the politician to be able to stop going through the motions of the charade. Dr. Wilkins locked eyes with Hassmann for a moment, opened his mouth to say something else, closed it again. Abruptly, he looked tired.

A smoothly silent waiter placed their appetizers in front of them, glided away again. Slowly, Mrs. Wilkins looked up. She had one of those smooth Barbie doll faces that enables some women to look thirty when they are fifty, but now her face had harsh new lines in it, as if someone had gone over it with a needle dipped in acid. Moving with the slow-motion grace of someone in a diving suit on the bottom of the sea, she reached out to touch the linen napkin before her on the table. She smiled fondly at it, caressing it with her fingertips. She was staring straight across the table at Hassmann now, but she wasn't seeing him; somewhere on its way across the table, her vision had taken the sort of right-angle turn that allows you to look directly into the past. "Frank," she said, in a light, amused, reminiscent tone unlike any that Hassmann had heard her use, "do you remember the time we were having the Graingers over for dinner, back when you were still in city council? And just before they got there I realized that we'd run out of clean napkins?"

"Fran—" Dr. Wilkins said warningly, but she ignored him; she was speaking to Hassmann now, although he was sure that she still wasn't seeing him *as* Hassmann—he was merely filling the role of listener, one of the many vague someones she'd told this anecdote to, for it was plain that she'd told it many times before. "And so I gave Peter some money and sent him down to the store to quick buy me some napkins, even *paper* ones were better than nothing." She was smiling now as she spoke. "So after a while he comes back, the Graingers were here by then, and he comes marching solemnly right into the living room where we're having drinks, and he says—he must have been about seven—he says, 'I looked all over the store, Mom, and I got the best ones I could find. These must be really good because they're *sanitary* ones, see? It says so right on the box.' And he holds up this great big box of Kotex!" She laughed. "And he looks so intent and serious, and he's so proud of being a big enough boy to be given a job to do, and he's trying *so* hard to do it right and please us, I just didn't have the heart to scold him, even though old Mr. Grainger looked like he'd just swallowed his false teeth, and Frank choked and sprayed his drink all over the room." Still smiling, still moving languidly, she picked up her fork and dug it into one of her veal-and-shrimp quenelles, and then she stopped, and her eyes cleared, and Hassmann knew that all at once she was *seeing* him again. Life crashed back into her face with shocking suddenness, like a storm wave breaking over a seawall, flushing it blood-red. Abruptly, spasmodically, viciously, she threw her fork at Hassmann. It bounced off his chest and clattered away across the restaurant floor. Her face had gone white now, as rapidly as it had flushed, and she said, "*I will not eat with the man who murdered my son.*"

Hassmann stood up. He heard his own voice saying, "Excuse me," in a polite and formal tone, and then he had turned and was walking blindly away across the restaurant, somehow managing not to blunder into any of the other tables. He kept walking until a rough-hewn door popped up in front of him, and then he pushed through it, and found himself in the washroom.

It was cold and dim and silent in the washroom, and the air smelled of cold stone and dust and antiseptic, and, faintly, of ancient piss. The only sound was the low, rhythmic belching and gurgling of cisterns. A jet of freezing air was coming in through a crack in the window molding, and it touched Hassmann's skin like a needle.

He moved to the porcelain washbasin and splashed cold water over his face, the way they do in the movies, but it made him feel worse instead of better. He shivered. Automatically, he wet a tissue and began to scrub at the food stain that Mrs. Wilkins' fork had left on his cheap pin-striped suit. He kept catching little glimpses of himself in the tarnished old mirror over the washbasin, and he watched himself slyly, fascinatedly, without ever looking at himself straight on. They had *film* footage of him killing the Wilkins boy—that particular stretch of film had been shown over and over again on TV since last weekend. As the demonstrators rushed up the steps of the campus Administration building toward the line of waiting Guardsmen, there was a very clear sequence of him bringing his rifle up and shooting Peter Wilkins down. Other Guardsmen had fired, and other demonstrators had fallen—four dead and three others seriously wounded, all told—but there could be no doubt that *he* was the one who had killed Peter Wilkins. Yes, that one was *his*, all right.

He leaned against the wall, pressing his forehead against the cold stone, feeling the stone suck the warmth from his flesh. For some reason he found himself thinking about the duck he'd raised, one of the summers they still went to the farm, the duck they'd wryly named Dinner. He'd fattened that stupid duck all summer, and then when it was time to kill it, he'd hardly been able to bring himself to do it. He'd made a botch of cutting its head off, faltered on the first stroke and then had to slash two more times to get the job done. And then the duck had run headless across the farmyard, spouting blood, and he'd had to chase it down. He'd given it to his father to clean, and then gone off behind the barn to throw up. All the rest of the family had said that the duck was delicious, but he'd had to leave the table several times during the meal to throw up again. How his father had laughed at him!

Hassmann was shivering again, and he couldn't seem to make himself stop. As clearly as if it were really in the room with him, he heard Captain Simes' voice saying, "He's mouse-trapped himself into it! His son was one of the ringleaders in planning the campus rally, and he was getting a lot of local media coverage simply because he *was* Wilkins' son. So, just before the rally that weekend, Wilkins published an open letter in all the major papers—" Dr. Wilkins' voice, resonant and sonorous as he stares into the camera lights: "In that letter, I told my son that if he were killed while taking part in a riot that he himself had helped to create . . . well, I told him that I would mourn him forever, but that far from condemning the man who killed him, I'd seek that man out and shake his hand, and then take him out to dinner to thank him for having the stead-fastness to uphold the Constitution of the United States in the face of armed sedition—" "And so now he's stuck with *doing* it, or losing what little face he has left!" Simes' voice again. Simes' giggle.

He'd talked to Simes for nearly twenty minutes before he'd realized that the tall glass of "iced tea" in Simes' hand was actually 100-proof whisky, and by that time Simes had been glassy-eyed and swaying, mumbling, "A civil war! And none of this nuclear-exchange shit, either. They're going to fight this one house to house through every small town in America. A nice *long* war . . ."

Hassmann stared at himself in the mirror. His face was hard and drawn, gaunt, his cheeks hollowed. His eyes were pitiless and cold. He could not recognize himself. The stranger in the mirror stared unwinkingly back at him; his face was like stone, the kind of cold and ancient stone that sucks the heat from anything that touches it.

A *nice* long *war* . . .

He went back into the restaurant. Heads turned surrepti-tiously to watch him as he passed, and he could see some of the other diners leaning close to each other to whisper and stare.

Dr. Wilkins was sitting alone at the table, surrounded by untouched dishes of food, some of them still faintly steaming. As Hassmann came up, he raised his head, and they exchanged bleak stares. He had taken his glasses off, and his face looked doughy and naked without them, less assured, less commanding. His eyes looked watery and tired.

"Julian is letting Mrs. Wilkins lie down in back for a while," Dr. Wilkins said. "Until she feels a little better." Hassmann said nothing, and made no attempt to sit down. Dr. Wilkins reached out for his glasses, put them on, and then peered at Hassmann again, as if to make sure that he was talking to the right man. He drew himself up in his chair a little, glancing at the nearest table with a motion of the eyes so quick as to be nearly imperceptible, like the flick of a lizard's tongue. Was he worried that, in spite of Julian's promise, some of the other customers might be reporters with hidden directional mikes? Some of them might be, at that. "I guess I owe you an apology," Dr. Wilkins said heavily, after a pause. He worked his mouth as if he was tasting something unpleasant, and then continued to speak in a stiff, reluctant voice. "My wife's been under a lot of emotional strain lately. She was distraught. You'll have to make allowances for that. She doesn't realize how hard this has been on you, too, how unpleasant it must have been for you to be forced to take a human life—"

"No, sir," Hassmann said in a clear, distinct voice, interrupting, not knowing what words he was speaking until he heard them leave his lips . . . feeling the final insulating thickness of glass shatter as he spoke and all the raw emotional knowledge he'd been trying to deny for more than a week rush in upon him . . . knowing even as he spoke that speaking these words would change him irrevocably forever . . . change Dr. Wilkins . . . change everything . . . watching Dr. Wilkins' face, already wincing at the blow he could sense coming . . . seeing the headless duck run flapping through the dusty farmyard . . . his father laughing . . . Mrs. Wilkins' eyes, watching him in the rearview mirror, in the dark . . . the soldier popping his head up out of the tank hatch to watch them pass . . . FUCK THE UNION . . . a nice *long* war . . . the hard, merciless eyes of the stranger in the mirror, the stranger that was now *him* . . . remembering the clean, exhilarating rush of joy, the fierce leap of the heart, as he'd emptied the clip of his semiautomatic rifle into the onrushing figure, relishing the flaring blue fire and the smoke and the noise, *got you you bastard got you*, smashing the other man and flinging him aside in a tangle of broken limbs all in one godlike moment, with a flick of his finger . . .

"No, sir," he said, smiling bleakly at the tired old man, enunciating each word with terrible precision, not even, at the end, wanting to hurt the other man, but simply to make him *understand.* "I enjoyed it," he said.

# EXECUTIVE CLEMENCY

....................

*Gardner Dozois and*
*Jack C. Haldeman* II

The President of the United States sat very still in his over-stuffed chair on the third floor and watched early-morning sunlight sweep in a slow line across the faded rug.

He couldn't remember getting out of bed or sitting down in the chair. He could dimly recall that he had been sitting there for a long time, watching the slow advent of dawn, but he was only just beginning to become fully aware of himself and his surroundings.

Only his eyes moved, yellow and wet, as the world seeped in.

This happened to him almost every morning now. Every morning he would return slowly to his body as if from an immense distance, from across appalling gulfs of time and space, to find himself sitting in the chair, or standing next to the window, or, more rarely, propped up in the corner against the wall. Sometimes he'd be in the middle of dressing when aware-ness returned, and he'd awake to find himself tying a shoelace or buttoning his pants. Sometimes, like this morning, he'd just be sitting and staring. Other times, he would awaken to the sound of his own voice, loud and cold in the bare wooden room, saying some strange and important things that he could never quite catch. If he could only hear the words he said at such times, just once, he knew that it would change everything, that he would understand everything. But he could never hear them.

He didn't move. When the lines of sunlight reached the chair, it would be time to go downstairs. Not before, no matter how late it sometimes made him as the sunlight changed with the seasons, no matter if he sometimes missed breakfast or, on cloudy winter days, didn't move at all until Mrs. Hamlin came upstairs to chase him out. It was one of the rituals with which he tried to hold his life together.

The east-facing window was washed over with pale, fragile blue, and the slow-moving patch of direct sunlight was a raw, hot gold. Dust motes danced in the beam. Except for those dust motes, everything was stillness and suspension. Except for his own spidery breathing, everything was profoundly silent. The room smelled of dust and heat and old wood. It was the best part of the day. Naturally it couldn't last.

Very far away, floating on the edge of hearing, there came the mellow, mossy bronze voice of a bell, ringing in the village of Fairfield behind the ridge, and at that precise moment, as though the faint tintinnabulation were its cue, the house itself began to speak. It was a rambling wooden house, more than a hundred years old, and it talked to itself at dawn and dusk, creaking, groaning, whispering, muttering like a crotchety old eccentric as its wooden bones expanded with the sun or contracted with the frost. This petulant, arthritic monologue ran on for a few minutes, and then the tenants themselves joined in, one by one: Seth in the bathroom early, spluttering as he washed up; Mr. Thompkins, clearing his throat interminably in the room below, coughing and hacking and spitting as though he were drowning in a sea of phlegm; Sadie's baby, crying in a vain attempt to wake her sluggard mother; Mrs. Hamlin, slamming the kitchen door; Mr. Samuels' loud nasal voice in the courtyard outside.

The sunlight swept across his chair.

The President of the United States stirred and sighed, lifting his arms and setting them down again, stamping his feet to restore circulation. Creakily, he got up. He stood for a moment, blinking in the sudden warmth, willing life back into his bones. His arms were gnarled and thin, covered, like his chest, with fine white hair that polarized in the sunlight. He rubbed his hands over his arms to smooth out gooseflesh, pinched the bridge of his nose, and stepped across to the gable window for a look outside. It seemed wrong somehow to see the neat, tree-lined streets of Northview, the old wooden houses, the tiled roofs, the lines of smoke going up black and fine from mortar-chinked chimneys. It seemed especially wrong that there were no automobiles in the streets, no roar and clatter of traffic, no reek of gasoline, no airplanes in the sky—

He turned away from the window. For a moment everything was sick and wrong, and he blinked at the homey, familiar room as though he'd never seen it before, as though it were an unutterably alien place. Everything became hot and tight and terrifying, closing *down* on him. *What's happening?* he asked himself blindly. He leaned against a crossbeam, dazed and baffled, until the distant sound of Mrs. Hamlin's voice—she was scolding Tessie in the kitchen, and the ruckus rose all the way up through three floors of pine and plaster and fine old tenpenny nails—woke him again to his surroundings, with something like pleasure, with something like pain.

Jamie, they called him. Crazy Jamie.

Shaking his head and muttering to himself, Jamie collected his robe and his shaving kit and walked down the narrow, peeling corridor to the small upstairs bedroom. The polished hardwood floor was cold under his feet.

The bathroom was cold, too. It was only the beginning of July, but already the weather was starting to turn nippy late at night and early in the morning. It got colder every year, seemed like. Maybe the glaciers were coming back, as some folks said. Or maybe it was just that he himself was worn a little thinner every year, a little closer to the ultimate cold of the grave. Grunting, he wedged himself into the narrow space between the sink and the downslant of the roof, bumping his head, as usual, against the latch of the skylight window. There was just enough room for him if he stood hunch-shouldered with the toilet bumping up against his thigh. The toilet was an old porcelain monstrosity, worn smooth as glass, that gurgled constantly and comfortably and emitted a mellow breath of earth. It was almost company. The yard boy had already brought up a big basin of "hot" water, although by now, after three or four other people had already used it, it was gray and cold; after the last person used it, it would be dumped down the toilet to help flush out the system. He opened his shaving kit and took out a shapeless cake of lye soap, a worn hand towel, a straight razor.

The mirror above the sink was cracked and tarnished—no help for it, nobody made mirrors anymore. It seemed an appropriate background for the reflection of his face, which was also, in its way, tarnished and dusty and cracked with age. He didn't know how old he was; that was one of the many things Doc Norton had warned him not to think about, so long ago. He couldn't even remember how long he'd been living here in Northview. Ten years? Fifteen? He studied himself in the mirror, the blotched, earth-colored skin, the eyes sunk deep under a shelf of brow, the network of fine wrinkles. A well-preserved seventy? Memory was dim; the years were misty and fell away before he could number them. He shied away from trying to remember. Didn't matter.

He covered the face with lathered soap.

By the time he finished dressing, the other tenants had already gone downstairs. He could hear them talking down there, muffled and distant, like water bugs whispering at the mossy bottom of a deep old well. Cautiously, Jamie went back into the hall. The wood floors and paneling up here were not as nicely finished as those in the rest of the house. He thought of all the hidden splinters in all that wood, waiting to catch his flesh. He descended the stairs. The banister swayed as he clutched it, groaning softly to remind him that it, too, was old.

As he came into the dining room, conversation died. The other tenants looked up at him, looked away again. People fiddled with their tableware, adjusted their napkins, pulled their chairs closer to the table or pushed them farther away. Someone coughed self-consciously.

He crossed the room to his chair and stood behind it.

"Morning, Jamie," Mrs. Hamlin said crossly.

"Ma'm," he replied politely, trying to ignore her grumpiness. He was late again.

He sat down. Mrs. Hamlin stared at him disapprovingly, shook her head, and then turned her attention pointedly back to her plate. As if this were a signal, conversation started up again, gradually swelling to its normal level. The awkward moment passed. Jamie concentrated on filling his plate, intercepting the big platters of country ham and eggs and corn bread as they passed up and down the table. It was always like this at meals: the embarrassed pauses, the uneasy sidelong glances, the faces that tried to be friendly but could not entirely conceal distaste. Crazy Jamie, Crazy Jamie. Conversation flowed in ripples around him, never involving him, although the others would smile dutifully at him if he caught their eyes, and occasionally Seth or Tom would nod at him with tolerably unforced cordiality. This morning it wasn't enough. He wanted to talk, too, for the first time in months. He wasn't a child, he was a man, an old man! He paid less attention to his food and began to strain to hear what was being said, looking for a chance to get into the conversation.

Finally the chance came. Seth asked Mr. Samuels a question. It was a point of fact, not opinion, and Jamie knew the answer.

"Yes," Jamie said, "at one time New York City did indeed have a larger population than Augusta."

Abruptly everyone stopped talking. Mr. Samuels' lips closed up tight, and he grimaced as though he had tasted something foul. Seth shook his head wearily, looking sad and disappointed. Jamie lowered his head to avoid Seth's eyes. He could sense Mrs. Hamlin swelling and glowering beside him, but he wouldn't look at her, either.

Damn it, that wasn't what he'd meant to say! They hadn't been talking about that at all. He'd said the wrong thing.

He'd done it again.

People were talking about him around the table, he knew, but he could no longer understand them. He could still hear their voices, but the words had been leached away, and all that remained was noise and hissing static. He concentrated on buttering a slice of corn bread, trying to hang on to that simple mechanical act while the world pulled away from him in all directions, retreating to the very edge of his perception, like a tide that has gone miles out from the beach.

When the world tide came back in, he found himself outside on the porch—the veranda, some of the older folks still called it—with Mrs. Hamlin fussing at him, straightening his clothes, patting his wiry white hair into place, getting him ready to be sent off to work. She was still annoyed with him, but it had no real bite to it, and the exasperated fondness underneath kept showing through even as she scolded him. "You go straight to work now, you hear? No dawdling and mooning around." He nodded his head sheepishly. She was a tall, aristocratic lady with a beak nose, a lined, craggy face, and a tight bun of snowy white hair. She was actually a year or two younger than he was, but he thought of her as much, much older. "And mind you come right straight back here after work, too. Tonight's the big Fourthday dinner, and you've got to help in the kitchen, hear? Jamie, are you listening to me?"

He ducked his head and said "Yes'm," his feet already fidgeting to be gone.

Mrs. Hamlin gave him a little push, saying, "Shoo now!" and then, her grim face softening, adding, "Try to be a good boy." He scooted across the veranda and out into the raw, hot brightness of the morning.

He shuffled along, head down, still infused with dull embarrassment from the scolding he'd received. Mr. Samuels went cantering by him, up on his big roan horse, carbine sheathed in a saddle holster, horseshoes ringing against the pavement; off to patrol with the Outriders for the day. Mr. Samuels waved at him as he passed, looking enormously tall and important and adult up on the high saddle, and Jamie answered with the shy, wide, loose-lipped grin that sometimes seemed vacuous even to him. He ducked his head again when Mr. Samuels was out of sight and frowned at the dusty tops of his shoes. The sun was up above the trees and the rooftops now, and it was getting warm.

The five-story brick school building was the tallest building in Northview—now that the bank had burned down—and it cast a cool, blue shadow across his path as he turned onto Main Street. It was still used as a school in the winter and on summer afternoons after the children had come back from the fields, but it was also filled with stockpiles of vital supplies so that it could be used as a stronghold in case of a siege—something that had happened only once, fifteen years ago, when a strong raiding party had come up out of the south. Two fifty-caliber machine guns—salvaged from an Army jeep that had been abandoned on the old state highway a few weeks after the War—were mounted on top of the school's roof, where their field of fire would cover most of the town. They had not been fired in earnest for years, but they were protected from the weather and kept in good repair, and a sentry was still posted up there at all times, although by now the sentry was likely to smuggle a girl up to the roof with him on warm summer nights. Times had become more settled, almost sleepy now. Similarly, the Outriders who patrolled Northview's farthest borders and watched over the flocks and the outlying farms had been reduced from thirty to ten, and it had been three or four years since they'd had a skirmish with anyone; the flow of hungry refugees and marauders and aimless migrants had mostly stopped by now—dead, or else they'd found a place of their own. These days the Outriders were more concerned with animals. The black bears were back in the mountains and the nearby hills, and for the past four or five years there had been wolves again, coming back from who-knew-where, increasing steadily in numbers and becoming more of a threat as the winters hardened. Visitors down from Jackman Station, in Maine, brought a story that a mountain lion had recently been sighted on the slopes of White Cap, in the unsettled country "north of the Moosehead," although before the War there couldn't have been any pumas left closer than Colorado or British Columbia. It had taken only twenty years.

There was a strange wagon in front of the old warehouse that was now the Outriders' station, a rig Jamie had never seen before. It was an ordinary enough wagon, but it was *painted*. It was painted in mad streaks and strips and random patchwork splotches of a dozen different colors—deep royal blue, vivid yellow, scarlet, purple, earth brown, light forest-green, black, burnt orange—as if a hundred children from prewar days had been at it with finger paint. To Jamie's eyes, accustomed to the dull and faded tones of Northview's weather-beaten old buildings, the streaks of color were so brilliant that they seemed to vibrate and stand out in raised contrast from the wagon's surface. He was not used to seeing bright colors anymore, except those in the natural world around him, and this paint was *fresh*, something he also hadn't seen in more years than he could remember. Even the big horse, which stood patiently in the wagon's traces—and which now rolled an incurious eye up at Jamie and blew out its lips with a blubbery snorting sound— even the *horse* was painted, blue on one side, bright green on the other, with orange streaks up its flanks.

Jamie goggled at all this, wondering if it could possibly be real or if it was one of the "effects"—hallucinations, as even *he* understood—that he sometimes got during particularly bad "spells." After a moment or two—during which the wagon didn't shimmer or fade around the edges at all—he widened his attention enough to notice the signs: big hand-painted signs hung on either side of a kind of sandwich-board framework that was braced upright in the wagon bed. At the top each sign read MOHAWK CONFEDERACY in bright red paint, and then, underneath that, came a long list of words, each word painted in a different color:

HAND-LOADED AMMUNITION
PAINT
FALSE TEETH
EYEGLASSES—GROUND TO PRESCRIPTION
LAMP OIL
PAINLESS DENTISTRY
UNTAINTED SEED FOR WHEAT, CORN, MELONS
FLAX CLOTH
WINDOW GLASS
MEDICINES & LINIMENT
CONDOMS
IRON FARM TOOLS

UNTAINTED LIVESTOCK
NAILS
MUSICAL INSTRUMENTS
MARIJUANA
WHISKY
SOAP
PRINTING DONE
!ALL MADE IN MOHAWK!

Jamie was puzzling out some of the harder words when the door to the Outriders' station opened and Mr. Stover came hurriedly down the stairs. "What're you doing here, Jamie?" he asked. "What're you hanging around here for?"

Jamie gaped at him, trying to find the words to describe the wonderful new wagon, and how strange it made him feel, but the effort was too great, and the words slipped away. "Going to Mr. Hardy's store," he said at last. "Just going to sweep up at Mr. Hardy's store."

Mr. Stover glanced nervously back up at the door of the Outriders' station, fingered his chin for a moment while he made up his mind, and then said, "Never mind that today, Jamie. Never mind about the store today. You just go on back home now."

"But—" Jamie said, bewildered. "But—I sweep up every day!"

"Not today," Mr. Stover said sharply. "You go on home, you hear me? Go on, git!"

"Mrs. Hamlin's going to be awful mad," Jamie said sadly, resignedly.

"You tell Edna I said for you to go home. And you stay inside, too, Jamie. You stay out of sight, hear? We've got an important visitor here in Northview today, and it'd never do to have him run into *you*."

Jamie nodded his head in acceptance of this. He wasn't so dumb that he didn't know what the unvoiced part of the sentence was: run into *you*, the half-wit, the crazy person, the nut. He'd heard it often enough. He knew he was crazy. He knew that he was an embarrassment. He knew that he had to stay inside, away from visitors, lest he embarrass Mrs. Hamlin and all his friends.

Crazy Jamie.

Slowly he turned and shuffled away, back the way he had come.

The sun beat down on the back of his head now, and sweat gathered in the wrinkled hollows beneath his eyes.

Crazy Jamie.

At the corner, bathed in the shadow cast by the big oak at the edge of the schoolyard, he turned and looked back.

A group of men had come out of the Outriders' station and were now walking slowly in the direction of Mr. Hardy's store, talking as they went. There was Mr. Jameson, Mr. Galli, Mr. Stover, Mr. Ashley, and, in the middle of them, talking animatedly and waving his arms, the visitor, the stranger—a big, florid-faced man with a shock of unruly blond hair that shone like beaten gold in the sunlight.

Watching him, the visitor—now clapping a hand on Mr. Galli's shoulder, Mr. Galli shrinking away—Jamie felt a chill, that unreasoning and unreasoned fear of strangers, of everything from outside Northview's narrow boundaries that had affected him ever since he could remember, and suddenly his delight in the wonderful wagon was tarnished, diminished, because he realized that it, too, must come from outside.

He headed for home, walking a little faster now, as if chivied along by some old cold wind that didn't quite reach the sunlit world.

That night was the Fourthday feast—"Independence Day," some of the old folks still called it—and for Jamie, who was helping in the kitchen as usual, the early part of the evening was a blur of work as they sweated to prepare the meal: roast turkey, ham, wild pigeon, trout, baked raccoon, sweet potatoes, corn, pearl onions, berry soup, homemade bread, blackberries, plums, and a dozen other things.

That was all as usual; he expected and accepted that. What was not usual—and what he did not expect—was that he would not be allowed to eat with the rest when the feast was served.

Instead, Tessie set a plate out for him in the kitchen, saying, not unkindly, "Now, Jamie, mind you stay here. They've got a guest out there this year, that loud-mouthed Mr. Brodey, and Mrs. Hamlin, she says you got to eat in the kitchen and keep out of sight. Now don't you mind, honey. I'll fix you up a plate real nice, just the same stuff you'd get out there."

And then, after a few moments of somewhat embarrassed bustling, she was gone.

Jamie sat alone in the empty kitchen.

His plate was filled to overflowing with food, and he'd even been given a glass of dandelion wine, a rare treat, but somehow he wasn't hungry anymore.

He sat listening to the wind tug at the old house, creaking the rafters, making the wood groan. When the wind died, he could hear them talking out there in the big dining room, the voices just too faint for him to make out the words.

An unfamiliar anger began to rise in him. "Crazy Jamie," he said aloud, his voice sounding flat and dull to his own ears. It wasn't fair. He glanced out the window, to where the sun had almost set in a welter of sullen purple clouds. Suddenly he slashed out at the glass of wine, sending it spinning to the floor. It wasn't fair! He was an adult, wasn't he? Why did he have to sit back here by himself like a naughty child? Even if— In spite of— He was—

Somehow he found himself on his feet. He *deserved* to eat with the others, didn't he? He was as good as anybody else, wasn't he? In fact— In *fact*—

The corridor. He seemed to float along it in spite of his stumbling, hesitant feet. The voices got louder, and just at the point where they resolved into words, he stopped, standing unnoticed in the shadows behind the dining room archway, hanging onto the doorjamb, torn between rage and fear and a curious, empty yearning.

"Sooner or later you'll find that you have to incorporate with the Confederacy," Mr. Brodey, the stranger, was saying. The other faces around the big dining room table were cool and reserved. "The kind of inter-village barter economy you've got up here just can't hold up forever, you know, even though it's really a kind of communal socialism—"

"Are you sayin' we're *communists* up heah?" Mr. Samuels said, outraged, but before Brodey could reply (if he intended to), Jamie strode to the table, pulled out an empty chair—his own habitual seat—and sat down. All faces turned to him, startled, and conversation stopped.

Jamie stared back at them. To walk to the table had taken the last of his will; things were closing down on him again, his vision was swimming, and he began to lose touch with his body, as if his mind were floating slowly up and away from it, like a balloon held by the thinnest sort of tether. Sweat broke out on his forehead, and he opened his mouth, panting like a dog. Through a sliding, shifting confusion, he heard Mrs. Hamlin start to say, "Jamie! I thought I told you—" at the same time that Mr. Ashley was saying to Mr. Brodey, "Don't let him bother you none. He's just the local half-wit. We'll send him back to the kitchen," and Brodey was smiling in tolerant, condescending amusement, and something about Brodey's thin, contemptuous smile, something about the circle of staring faces, *something* wrenched words up out of Jamie, sending them suddenly flying out of his mouth. He hurled the familiar words out at the pale staring faces as he had so many times before, rattling their teeth with them, shaking them to their bones. He didn't know what the words meant anymore, but they were the old strong words, the right words, and he heard his voice fill with iron as he spoke them. He spoke the words until there were no more words to speak, and then he stopped.

A deathly hush had fallen over the room. Mr. Brodey was staring at him, and Jamie saw his face run through a quick gamut of expressions: from irritation to startled speculation to dawning astonishment. Brodey's jaw went slack, and he gasped—a little startled grunt, as if he had been punched in the stomach—and the color went swiftly out of his face. "My God!" he said. "Oh, my God!"

For Jamie, it was as if the world were draining away again, everything pulling back until he could just barely touch reality with his fingertips, and the room shimmered and buzzed as he struggled to hold on to even that much control. All the faces had gone blank, wiped clean of individuality, and he could no longer tell which of the featureless pink ovoids was the sweating, earnest, astounded face of Mr. Brodey. He got clumsily to his feet, driving his leaden body by an act of conscious will, as though it were some ill-made clockwork golem. He flailed his arms for balance, knocked his chair over with a clatter, and stood swaying before them, smelling the sour reek of his own sweat. "I'm sorry," he blurted. "I'm sorry, Mrs. Hamlin. I didn't *mean* to—"

The silence went on a moment longer, and then, above the mounting waves of buzzing nausea and unreality, he heard Mrs. Hamlin say, "That's all right, child. We know you didn't mean any harm. Go on upstairs now, Jamie. Go on." Her voice sounded dry and flat and tired.

Blindly, Jamie spun and stumbled for the stairs, all the inchoate demons of memory snapping at his heels like years.

Downstairs, Mr. Brodey was still saying, "Oh, my God!" He hardly noticed that the dinner party was being dissolved around him or that Mrs. Hamlin was hustling him out onto the porch "for a word in private." When she finally had him alone out there, the cool evening breeze slapping at his face through the wire mesh of the enclosed porch, he shook himself out of his daze and turned slowly to face her where she stood hunched and patient in the dappled shadows. "It's *him*," he said, still more awe than accusation in his voice. "Son of a *bitch*. It really is him, isn't it?"

"Who, Mr. Brodey?"

"Don't play games with me," Brodey said harshly. "I've seen the old pictures. The half-wit, he really *was*—"

"*Is.*"

"—the President of the United States." Brodey stared at her. "He may be crazy, but not because he thinks he's the President—he *is* the President. James W. McNaughton. He *is* McNaughton, isn't he?"

"Yes."

"My God! Think of it. The very last President."

"The *incumbent* President," Mrs. Hamlin said softly.

They stared at each other through the soft evening shadows.

"And it's not a surprise to you, either, is it?" Anger was beginning to replace disbelief in Brodey's voice. "You've known it all along, haven't you? *All* of you have known. You all knew from the start that he was President McNaughton?"

"Yes."

"My God!" Brodey said, giving an entirely new reading to the phrase, disgust and edgy anger instead of awe. He opened his mouth, closed it, and began turning red.

"He came here almost twenty years ago, Mr. Brodey," Mrs. Hamlin said, speaking calmly, reminiscently. "Perhaps two months after the War. The Outriders found him collapsed in a field out by the edge of town. He was nearly dead. Don't ask me how he got there. Maybe there was some sort of hidden bunker way back up there in the hills, maybe his plane crashed nearby, maybe he walked all the way up here from what's left of Washington—I don't know. Jamie himself doesn't know. His memory was almost gone; shock, I guess, and exposure. All he remembered, basically, was that he was the President, and even that was dim and misty, like something you might remember out of a bad dream, the kind that fades away and comes back sometimes, late at night. And life's been like a half-dream for him ever since, poor soul. He never did get quite right in the head again."

"And you gave him shelter?" Brodey said, his voice becoming shrill with indignation. "You took him in? That butcher?"

"Watch your mouth, son. You're speaking about the President."

"Goddamn it, woman. Don't you know—*he caused the War?*"

After a smothering moment of silence, Mrs. Hamlin said mildly, "That's your opinion, Mr. Brodey, not mine."

"How can you deny it? The 'One Life' Ultimatum? The 'preventative strikes' on Mexico and Panama? It was within hours of the raid on Monterrey that the bombs started falling."

"He didn't have any other *choice!* The Indonesians had pushed him—"

"That's crap, and you know it!" Brodey was shouting now. "They taught us all about it down in Mohawk; they made *damn* sure we knew the name of the man who destroyed the world, you can bet on that! Christ, everybody knew *then* that he was unfit for office, just a bombastic backwoods senator on a hate crusade, a cracker-barrel warmonger. Everybody *said* that he'd cause the War if he got into the White House—and he *did!* By God, he did! That pathetic half-wit in there. *He* did it!"

Mrs. Hamlin sighed and folded her arms across her middle, hugging herself as if in pain. She seemed to grow smaller and older, more withered and gnarled. "I don't know, son," she said wearily, after a heavy pause. "Maybe you're right, maybe you're wrong. Maybe *he* was wrong. I don't know. All that seemed so important then. Now I can hardly remember what the issues were, what it was all *about*. It doesn't seem to matter much anymore, somehow."

"How can you *say* that?" Brodey wiped at his face—he was sweating profusely and looking very earnest now, bewilderment leaching away some of the anger. "How can you let that . . . that man . . . *him*—how can you let *him* live here, under your roof? How can you stand to let him live at all, let alone cook for him, do his washing. My God!"

"His memory was gone, Mr. Brodey. His *mind* was gone. Can you understand that? Old Doc Norton, rest his soul, spent months just trying to get Jamie to the point where he could walk around by himself without anybody to watch him too close. He had to be taught how to feed himself, how to dress himself, how to go to the bathroom—like a child. At first there was some even right here in Northview that felt the way you do, Mr. Brodey, and there's still some as can't be comfortable around Jamie, but one by one they came to understand, and they made their peace with him. Whatever he was or wasn't, he's just like a little child now—a sick, old, frightened child who doesn't really understand what's happening to him, most of the time. Mr. Brodey, you can't hate a little child for something he can't even remember he's done."

Brodey spun around, as though to stalk back into the house, and then spun violently back. "He should be dead!" Brodey shouted. His fists were clenched now, and the muscles in his neck were corded. "At the very *least*, he should be dead! Billions of lives on that man's hands! *Billions*. And *you*, you people, you not only let him live, you make excuses for him! For *him!*" He stopped, groping for words to express the enormity of his outrage. "It's like . . . like making excuses for the Devil himself!"

Mrs. Hamlin stirred and came forward, stepping out of the porch shadows and into the moonlight, drawing her shawl more tightly around her, as though against a chill, although the night was still mild. She stared eye to eye with Brodey for several moments, while the country silence gathered deeply around them, broken only by crickets and the hoarse sound of Brodey's impassioned breathing. Then she said, "I thought I owed it to you, Mr. Brodey, to try to explain a few things. But I don't know if I can. Things have changed enough by now, steadied down enough, that maybe you younger people find it hard to understand, but those of us who lived through the War, we all had to do things we didn't want to do. Right there where you're standing, Mr. Brodey, right here on this porch, I shot a marauder down, shot him dead with my husband's old pistol, with Mr. Hamlin himself laying stiff in the parlor not ten feet away, taken by the Lumpy Plague. And I've done worse things than that, too, in my time. I reckon we all have, all the survivors. And just maybe it's no different with that poor old man sitting in there."

Brodey regained control of himself. His jaw was clenched, and the muscles around his mouth stood out in taut little bands, but his breathing had evened, and his face was tight and cold. He had banked his anger down into a smoldering, manageable flame, and now for the first time he seemed dangerous. Ignoring—or seeming to ignore—Mrs. Hamlin's speech, he said conversationally, "Do you know that we curse by him down in Mohawk? His name is a curse to us. Can *you* understand *that*? We burn him in effigy on his birthday, in the town squares, and over the years it's become quite a little ceremony. He must *atone*, Mrs. Hamlin. He must be made to pay for what

he's done. We don't suffer monsters to live, down in Mohawk."

"Ayuh," Mrs. Hamlin said sourly, "you do a lot of damnfool, jackass things down there, don't you?" Mrs. Hamlin
tossed her head back, silver hair glinting in the silver light,
and seemed to grow taller again. There was a hard light in her
eyes now, and a hard new edge in her voice. "Atone, is it
now, you jackass? As if you're some big pious kind of
churchman, some damn kind of saint, you red-faced, loud-
mouthed man. You with your damnfool flag and damnfool
Mohawk Confederacy. Well, let me tell *you*, mister, this isn't
any Mohawk Confederacy here, never has been, never will
be: this is Northview, sovereign state of Vermont, *United
States of America*. Do you hear me, mister? This here is the
United States of America, and that poor fool in there—why,
he's the *President* of the United States of America, even if
sometimes he can't cut his meat up proper. Maybe he was a
fool, maybe he was wrong long ago, maybe he's crazy now,
but he's still the *President*." Eyes snapping, she jabbed a finger
at Brodey. "As long as this town stands, then there's still an
America, and that old man will be President as long as there
are still *Americans* alive to serve him. We take care of our
own, Mr. Brodey; *we take care of our own.*"

A shadow materialized at Brodey's elbow and spoke with
Seth's voice. "Edna?"

Brodey turned his head to glance at Seth. When he turned
back to face Mrs. Hamlin, there was a gun in her hand, a big,
old-fashioned revolver that looked too huge for the small, blue-
veined hand that held it.

"You can't be serious," Brodey whispered.

"You need any help, Edna?" the shadow said. "I brought
some of the boys."

"No, thank you, Seth." The barrel of the revolver was as
unwavering as her gaze. "There's some things a person's got to
do for herself."

Then she cocked the hammer back.

\* \* \*

The President of the United States didn't notice the shot. Alone in the small upstairs bathroom, he avoided the eyes of the tarnished reflection in the mirror, and compulsively washed his hands.

# A SPECIAL KIND OF MORNING

........................

*The Doomsday Machine is the human race.*
—GRAFFITO IN NEW YORK SUBWAY,
SEVENTY-NINTH STREET STATION

Did y'ever hear the one about the old man and the sea?

Halt a minute, lordling; stop and listen. It's a fine story, full of balance and point and social pith; short and direct. It's not mine. Mine are long and rambling and parenthetical and they corrode the moral fiber right out of a man. Come to think, I won't tell you that one after all. A man of my age has a right to prefer his own material, and let the critics be damned. I've a prejudice now for webs of my own weaving.

Sit down, sit down: butt against pavement, yes; it's been done before. Everything has, near about. Now that's not an expression of your black pessimism, or your futility, or what have you. Pessimism's just the commonsense knowledge that there's more ways for something to go wrong than for it to go right, from our point of view anyway—which is not necessarily that of the management, or of the mechanism, if you prefer your cosmos depersonalized. As for futility, everybody dies the true death eventually; even though executives may dodge it for a few hundred years, the hole gets them all in the end, and I imagine that's futility enough for a start. The philosophical man accepts both as constants and then doesn't let them bother him any. Sit down, damn it; don't pretend you've important business to be about. Young devil, you are in the enviable position of having absolutely nothing to do because it's going to take you a while to recover from what you've just done. There. That's better. Comfortable? You don't look it; you look like you've just sat in a puddle of piss and're wondering what the socially appropriate reaction is. Hypocrisy's an art, boy; you'll improve with age. Now you're bemused, lordling, that you let an old soak chivy you around, and now he's making fun of you. Well, the expression on your face is worth a chuckle; if you could see it you'd laugh yourself. You will see it years from now too, on some other young man's face—that's the only kind of mirror that ever shows it clear. And *you'll* be an old soak by that time, and you'll laugh and insult the young buck's dignity, but you'll be laughing more at the reflection of the man you used to be than at that particular stud himself. And you'll probably have to tell the buck just what I've told you to cool him down, and there's a laugh in that too; listen for the echo of a million and one laughs behind you. I hear a million now.

How do I get away with such insolence? What've I got to lose, for one thing. That gives you a certain perspective. And I'm socially instructive in spite of myself—I'm valuable as an object lesson. For that matter, why is an arrogant young aristo like you sitting there and putting up with my guff? Don't even bother to answer; I knew the minute you came whistling down the street, full of steam and strut. Nobody gets up this early in the morning anymore, unless they're old as I am and begrudge sleep's dry-run of death—or unless they've never been to bed in the first place. The world's your friend this morning, a toy for you to play with and examine and stuff in your mouth to taste, and you're letting your benevolence slop over onto the old degenerate you've met on the street. You're even happy enough to listen, though you're being quizzical about it, and you're sitting over there feeling benignly superior. And I'm sitting over *here* feeling benignly superior. A nice arrangement, and everyone content. Well, then, mornings make you feel that way. Especially if you're fresh from a night at the Towers, the musk of Lady Ni still warm on your flesh.

A blush—my buck, you *are* new-hatched. How did I know?

Boy, you'd be surprised what I know; I'm occasionally startled myself, and I've been working longer to get it catalogued. Besides, hindsight is a comfortable substitute for omnipotence. And I'm not blind yet. You have the unmistakable look of a cub who's just found out he can do something else with it besides piss. An incredible revelation, as I recall. The blazing significance of it will wear a little with the years, though not all that much, I suppose; until you get down to the brink of the Ultimate Cold, when you stop worrying about the identity of warmth, or demanding that it pay toll in pleasure. Any hand of clay, long's the blood still runs the tiny degree that's just enough for difference. Warmth's the only definition between you and graveyard dirt. But morning's not for graveyards, though it works the other way. Did y'know they also used to use that to make babies? 'S'fact, though few know it now. It's a versatile beast. Oh *come*—buck, cub, young cocksman—stop being so damn surprised. People ate, slept, and fornicated before you were born, some of them anyway, and a few will probably even find the courage to keep on at it after you die. You don't have to keep it secret; the thing's been circulated in this region once or twice before. You weren't the first to learn how to make the beast do its trick, though I *know* you don't believe that. *I* don't believe it concerning myself, and I've had a long time to learn.

You make me think, sitting there innocent as an egg and twice as vulnerable; yes, you are definitely about to make me think, and I believe I'll have to think of some things I always regret having thought about, just to keep me from growing maudlin. Damn it, boy, you *do* make me think. Life's strange—wet-eared as you are, you've probably had that thought a dozen times already, probably had it this morning as you tumbled out of your fragrant bed to meet the rim of the sun; well, I've four times your age, and a ream more experience, and I still can't think of anything better to sum up the world: life's strange. 'S been said, yes. But *think*, boy, how strange: the two of us talking, you coming, me going; me knowing where you've got to go, you suspecting where I've been, and the same destination for both. O strange, very strange! Damn it, you're a deader already if you can't see the strangeness of that, if you can't sniff the poetry; it reeks of it, as of blood. And I've smelt blood, buck. It has a very distinct odor; you know it when you smell it. You're bound for blood; for blood and passion and high deeds and all the rest of the business, and maybe for a little understanding if you're lucky and have eyes to see. Me, I'm bound for nothing, literally. I've come to rest here in Kos, and while the Red Lady spins her web of colors across the sky I sit and weave my own webs of words and dreams and other spider stuff—

What? Yes, I do talk too much; old men like to babble, and philosophy's a cushion for old bones. But it's my profession now, isn't it, and I've promised you a story. What happened to my leg? That's a bloody story, but I said you're bound for blood; I know the mark. I'll tell it to you then: perhaps it'll help you to understand when you reach the narrow place, perhaps it'll even help you to think, although that's a horrible weight to wish on any man. It's customary to notarize my card before I start, keep you from running off at the end without paying. Thank you, young sir. Beware of some of these beggars, buck; they have a credit tally at Central greater than either of us will ever run up. They turn a tidy profit out of poverty. I'm an honest pauper, more's the pity, exist mostly on the subsidy, if you call that existing—Yes, I know. The leg.

We'll have to go back to the Realignment for that, more than half a century ago, and half a sector away, at World. This was before World was a member of the Commonwealth. In fact, that's what the Realignment was about, the old Combine overthrown by the Quaestors, who then opted for amalgamation and forced World into the Commonwealth. That's where and when the story starts.

Start it with waiting.

A lot of things start like that, waiting. And when the thing you're waiting for is probable death, and you're lying there loving life and suddenly noticing how pretty everything is and listening to the flint hooves of darkness click closer, feeling the iron-shod boots strike relentless sparks from the surface of your mind, knowing that death is about to fall out of the sky and that there's no way to twist out from under—then, waiting can take time. Minutes become hours, hours become unthinkable horrors. Add enough horrors together, total the scaly snouts, and you've got a day and a half I once spent laying up in a mountain valley in the Blackfriars on World, almost the last day I ever spent anywhere.

This was just a few hours after D'kotta. Everything was a mess, nobody really knew what was happening, everybody's communication lines cut. I was just a buck myself then, working with the Quaestors in the field, a hunted criminal. Nobody knew what the Combine would do next, we didn't know what *we'd* do next, groups surging wildly from one place to another at random, panic and riots all over the planet, even in the Controlled Environments.

And D'kotta-on-the-Blackfriars was a seventy-mile swath of smoking insanity, capped by boiling umbrellas of smoke that eddied ashes from the ground to the stratosphere and back. At night it pulsed with molten scum, ugly as a lanced blister, lighting up the cloud cover across the entire horizon, visible for hundreds of miles. It was this ugly glow that finally panicked even the zombies in the Environments, probably the first strong emotion in their lives.

It'd been hard to sum up the effects of the battle. We thought that we had the edge, that the Combine was close to breaking, but nobody knew for sure. If they weren't as close to folding as we thought, then we were probably finished. The Quaestors had exhausted most of their hoarded resources at D'kotta, and we certainly couldn't hit the Combine any harder. If they could shrug off the blow, then they could wear us down.

Personally, I didn't see how anything could shrug *that* off. I'd watched it all and it'd shaken me considerably. There's an old-time expression, "put the fear of God into him." That's what D'kotta had done for me. There wasn't any God anymore, but I'd seen fire vomit from the heavens and the earth ripped wide for rape, and it'd been an impressive enough surrogate. Few people ever realized how close the Combine and the Quaestors had come to destroying World between them, there at D'kotta.

We'd crouched that night—the team and I—on the high stone ramparts of the tallest of the Blackfriars, hopefully far away from anything that could fall on us. There were twenty miles of low, gnarly foothills between us and the rolling savannahland where the city of D'kotta had been minutes before, but the ground under our bellies heaved and quivered like a sick animal, and the rock was hot to the touch: feverish.

We could've gotten farther away, should have gotten farther away, but we had to watch. That'd been decided without anyone saying a word, without any question about it. It was impossible *not* to watch. It never even occurred to any of us to take another safer course of action. When reality is being turned inside out like a dirty sock, you watch, or you are less than human. So we watched it all from beginning to end: two hours that became a single second lasting for eons. Like a still photograph of time twisted into a scream—the scream reverberating on forever and yet taking no duration at all to experience.

We didn't talk. We *couldn't* talk—the molecules of the air itself shrieked too loudly, and the deep roar of explosions was a continual drumroll—but we wouldn't have talked even if we'd been able. You don't speak in the presence of an angry God. Sometimes we'd look briefly at each other. Our faces were all nearly identical: ashen, waxy, eyes of glass, blank, and lost as pale driftwood stranded on a beach by the tide. We'd been driven through the gamut of expressions into *extremis*—rictus: faces so contorted and strained they ached—and beyond to the quietus of shock: muscles too slack and flaccid to respond anymore. We'd only look at each other for a second, hardly focusing, almost not aware of what we were seeing, and then our eyes would be dragged back as if by magnetism to the Fire.

At the beginning we'd clutched each other, but as the battle progressed we slowly drew apart, huddling into individual agony; the thing so big that human warmth meant nothing, so frightening that the instinct to gather together for protection was reversed, and the presence of others only intensified the realization of how ultimately naked you were. Earlier we'd set up a scattershield to filter the worst of the hard radiation—the gamma and intense infrared and ultraviolet—blunt some of the heat and shock and noise. We thought we had a fair chance of surviving, then, but we couldn't have run anyway. We were fixed by the beauty of horror/horror of beauty, surely as if by a spike driven through our backbones into the rock.

And away over the foothills, God danced in anger, and his feet struck the ground to ash.

What was it like?

Kos still has oceans and storms. Did y'ever watch the sea lashed by high winds? The storm boils the water into froth, whips it white, until it becomes an ocean of ragged lace to the horizon, whirlpools of milk, not a fleck of blue left alive. The land looked like this at D'kotta. The hills *moved*. The Quaestors had a discontinuity projector there, and under its lash the ground stirred like sluggish batter under a baker's spoon; stirred, shuddered, groaned, cracked, broke: acres heaved themselves into new mountains, other acres collapsed into canyons.

Imagine a giant asleep just under the surface of the earth, overgrown by fields, dreaming dreams of rock and crystal. Imagine him moving restlessly, the long rhythm of his dreams touched by nightmare, tossing, moaning, tremors signaling unease in waves up and down his miles-long frame. Imagine him catapulted into waking terror, lurching suddenly to his knees with the bawling roar of ten million burning calves: a steaming claw of rock and black earth raking for the sky. Now, in a wink, imagine the adjacent land hurtling downward, sinking like a rock in a pond, opening a womb a thousand feet wide, swallowing everything and grinding it to powder. Then, almost too quick to see, imagine the mountain and the crater switching, the mountain collapsing all at once and washing the feet of the older Blackfriars with a tidal wave of earth, then tumbling down to make a pit; at the same time the sinking earth at the bottom of the other crater reversing itself and erupting upward into a quaking fist of rubble. Then they switch again, and keep switching. Like watching the same film clip continuously run forward and backward. Now multiply that by a million and spread it out so that all you can see to the horizon is a stew of humping rock. D'y'visualize it? Not a tenth of it.

Dervishes of fire stalked the chaos, melting into each other, whirlpooling. Occasionally a tactical nuclear explosion would punch a hole in the night, a brief intense flare that would be swallowed like a candle in a murky snowstorm. Once a tacnuke detonation coincided with the upthrusting of a rubble mountain, with an effect like that of a firecracker exploding inside a swinging sack of grain.

The city itself was gone; we could no longer see a trace of anything man-made, only the stone maelstrom. The river Delva had also vanished, flash-boiled to steam; for a while we could see the gorge of its dry bed stitching across the plain, but then the ground heaved up and obliterated it.

It was unbelievable that anything could be left alive down there. Very little was. Only the remainder of the heavy weapons sections on both sides continued to survive, invisible to us in the confusion. Still protected by powerful phasewalls and scattershields, they pounded blindly at each other—the Combine somewhat ineffectively with biodeths and tacnukes, the Quaestors responding by stepping up the discontinuity projector. There was only one, in the command module—the Quaestor technicians were praying it wouldn't be wiped out by a random strike—and it was a terraforming device and not actually a "weapon" at all, but the Combine had been completely unprepared for it, and were suffering horribly as a result.

Everything began to flicker, random swatches of savannahland shimmering and blurring, phasing in and out of focus in a jerky, mismatched manner: that filmstrip run through a spastic projector. At first we thought it must be heat eddies caused by the fires, but then the flickering increased drastically in frequency and tempo, speeding up until it was impossible to keep anything in focus even for a second, turning the wide veldt into a mad kaleidoscope of writhing, interchanging shapes and color-patterns from one horizon to the other. It was impossible to watch it for long. It hurt the eyes and filled us with an oily, inexplicable panic that we were never able to verbalize. We looked away, filled with the musty surgings of vague fear.

We didn't know then that we were watching the first practical application of a process that'd long been suppressed by both the Combine and the Commonwealth, a process based on the starship dimensional "drive" (which isn't a "drive" at all, but the word's passed into the common press) that enabled a high-cycling discontinuity projector to throw time out of phase within a limited area, so that a spot *here* would be a couple of minutes ahead or behind a spot a few inches away, in continuity sequence. That explanation would give a psychophysicist fits, since "time" is really nothing at all like the way we "experience" it, so the process "really" doesn't do what I've said it does—doing something *really* abstruse instead—but that's close enough to what it does on a practical level, 'cause even if the time distortion is an "illusionary effect"—like the sun seeming to rise and set—they still used it to kill people. So it threw time out of phase, and kept doing it, switching the dislocation at random: so that in any given square foot of land there might be four or five discrepancies in time sequence that kept interchanging. Like, *here* might be one minute "ahead" of the base "now," and then a second later (language breaks down hopelessly under this stuff; you need the math) *here* would be two minutes behind the now, then five minutes behind, then three ahead, and so on. And all the adjacent zones in that square foot are going through the same switching process at the same time (goddamn this language!). The Combine's machinery tore itself to pieces. So did the people: some died of suffocation because of a five-minute discrepancy between an inhaled breath and oxygen received by the lungs, some drowned in their own blood.

It took about ten minutes, at least as far as we were concerned as unaffected observers. I had a psychophysicist tell me once that "it" had both continued to "happen" forever and had never "happened" at all, and that neither statement canceled out the validity of the other, that *each* statement in fact was both "applicable" and "nonapplicable" to the same situation consecutively—and I did not understand. It took ten minutes.

At the end of that time, the world got very still.

We looked up. The land had stopped churning. A tiny star appeared amongst the rubble in the middle distance, small as a pinhead but incredibly bright and clear. It seemed to suck the night into it like a vortex, as if it were a pinprick through the worldstuff into a more intense reality, as if it were gathering a great breath for a shout.

We buried our heads in our arms as one, instinctively.

There was a very bright light, a light that we could feel through the tops of our heads, a light that left dazzling after-images even through closed and shrouded lids. The mountain leaped under us, bounced us into the air again and again, battered us into near unconsciousness. We never even heard the roar.

After a while, things got quiet again, except for a continuous low rumbling. When we looked up, there were thick, sluggish tongues of molten magma oozing up in vast flows across the veldt, punctuated here and there by spectacular shower-fountains of vomited sparks.

Our scattershield had taken the brunt of the blast, borne it just long enough to save our lives, and then overloaded and burnt itself to scrap; one of the first times *that's* ever happened.

Nobody said anything. We didn't look at each other. We just lay there.

The chrono said an hour went by, but nobody was aware of it.

Finally, a couple of us got up, in silence, and started to stumble aimlessly back and forth. One by one, the rest crawled to their feet. Still in silence, still trying not to look at each other, we automatically cleaned ourselves up. You hear someone say "it made me shit my pants," and you think it's an expression; not under the right stimuli. Automatically, we treated our bruises and lacerations, automatically we tidied the camp up, buried the ruined scatterfield generator. Automatically, we sat down again and stared numbly at the light show on the savannah.

Each of us knew the war was over—we knew it with the gut rather than the head. It was an emotional reaction, but very calm, very resigned, very passive. It was a thing too big for questioning; it became a self-evident fact. After D'kotta, there could be nothing else. Period. The war was over.

We were almost right. But not quite.

In another hour or so, a man from field HQ came up over the mountain shoulder in a stolen vacform and landed in camp. The man switched off the vac, jumped down, took two steps toward the parapet overlooking hell, stopped. We saw his stomach muscles jump, tighten. He took a stumbling half-step back, then stopped again. His hand went up to shield his throat, dropped, hesitated, went back up. We said nothing. The HQ directing the D'kotta campaign had been sensibly located behind the Blackfriars: they had been shielded by the mountain chain and had seen nothing but glare against the cloud cover. This was his first look at the city; at where the city had been. I watched the muscles play in his back, saw his shoulders hunch as if under an unraised fist. A good many of the Quaestor men involved in planning the D'kotta operation committed suicide immediately after the Realignment; a good many didn't. I don't know what category this one belonged in.

The liaison man finally turned his head, dragged himself away. His movements were jerky, and his face was an odd color, but he was under control. He pulled Heynith, our team leader, aside. They talked for a half hour. The liaison man showed Heynith a map, scribbled on a pad for Heynith to see, gave Heynith some papers. Heynith nodded occasionally. The liaison man said good-bye, half-ran to his vacform. The vac lifted with an erratic surge, steadied, then disappeared in a long arc over the gnarled backs of the Blackfriars. Heynith stood in the dirtswirl kicked up by the backwash and watched impassively.

It got quiet again, but it was a little more apprehensive.

Heynith came over, studied us for a while, then told us to get ready to move out. We stared at him. He repeated it in a quiet, firm voice; unendurably patient. Hush for a second, then somebody groaned, somebody else cursed, and the spell of D'kotta was partially broken, for the moment. We awoke enough to ready our gear; there was even a little talking, though not much.

Heynith appeared at our head and led us out in a loose travel formation, diagonally across the face of the slope, then up toward the shoulder. We reached the notch we'd found earlier and started down the other side.

Everyone wanted to look back at D'kotta. No one did. Somehow, it was still night.

We never talked much on the march, of course, but tonight the silence was spooky: you could hear boots crunch on stone, the slight rasp of breath, the muted jangle of knives occasionally bumping against thighs. You could hear our fear; you could smell it, could see it.

We could touch it, we could taste it.

I was a member of something so old that they even had to dig up the name for it when they were rooting through the rubble of ancient history, looking for concepts to use against the Combine: a "commando team." Don't ask me what it means, but that's what it's called. Come to think, I know what it means in terms of flesh: it means ugly. Long ugly days and nights that come back in your sleep even uglier, so that you don't want to think about it at all because it squeezes your eyeballs like a vise. Cold and dark and wet, with sudden death looming up out of nothing at any time and jarring you with mortality like a rubber glove full of ice water slapped across your face. Living jittery high all the time, so that everything gets so real that it looks fake. You live in an anticipation that's pain, like straddling a fence with a knifeblade for a top rung, waiting for something to come along in the dark and push you off. You get so you like it. The pain's so consistent that you forget it's there, you forget there ever was a time when you didn't have it, and you live on the adrenaline.

We liked it. We were dedicated. We *hated*. It gave us something to do with our hate, something tangible we could see. And nobody'd done it but us for hundreds of years; there was an exultation to that. The Scholars and Antiquarians who'd started the Quaestor movement—left fullsentient and relatively unwatched so they could better piece together the muddle of prehistory from generations of inherited archives—they'd been smart. They knew their only hope of baffling the Combine was to hit them with radical concepts and tactics, things they didn't have instructions for handling, things out of the Combine's experience. So they scooped concepts out of prehistory, as far back as the archives go, even finding *written* records somewhere and having to figure out how to use them.

Out of one of these things, they got the idea of "guerrilla" war. No, I don't know what that means either, but what it *means* is playing the game by your own rules instead of the enemy's. Oh, you let the enemy keep playing by *his* rules, see, but you play by your own. Gives you a wider range of moves. You *do* things. I mean, *ridiculous* things, but so ancient they don't have any defense against them because they never thought they'd have to defend against *that*. Most of the time they never even knew *that* existed.

Like, we used to run around with these projectile weapons the Quaestors had copied from old plans and mass-produced in the autfacs on the sly by stealing computer time. The things worked by a chemical reaction inside the mechanism that would spit these tiny missiles out at a high velocity. The missile would hit you so hard it would actually lodge itself in your body, puncture internal organs, *kill* you. I know it sounds like an absurd concept, but there were advantages.

Don't forget how tightly controlled a society the Combine's was; even worse than the Commonwealth in its own way. We couldn't just steal energy weapons or biodeths and use them, because all those things operated on broadcast power from the Combine, and as soon as one was reported missing, the Combine would just cut the relay for that particular code. We couldn't make them ourselves, because unless you used the Combine's broadcast power you'd need a ton of generator equipment with each weapon to provide enough energy to operate it, and we didn't have the technology to miniaturize that much machinery. (Later some genius figured out a way to make, say, a functioning biodeth with everything but the energy source and then cut into and tap Combine broadcast power without showing up on the coding board, but that was toward the end anyway, and most of them were stockpiled for the shock troops at D'kotta.) At least the "guns" worked. And

there were even unexpected advantages. We found that tangle-
fields, scattershields, phasewalls, personal warders, all the usual
defenses, were unable to stop the "bullets" (the little missiles
fired by the "guns")—they were just too sophisticated to stop
anything as crude as a lump of metal moving at relatively sluggish ballistic speeds. Same with "bombs" and "grenades"—
devices designed to have a chemical reaction violent enough to
kill in an enclosed place. And the list went on and on. The
Combine thought we couldn't move around, because all vehi-
cles were coded and worked on broadcast power. Did you ever
hear of "bicycles"? They're devices for translating mechanical
energy into motion, they ride on wheels that you actually make
revolve with physical labor. And the bicycles didn't have
enough metal or mass to trigger sentryfields or show up on
sweep probes, so we could go undetected to places they
thought nobody could reach. Communicate? We used mirrors
to flash messages, used puffs of smoke as code, had people
actually *carry* messages from one place to another.

More important, we *personalized* war. That was the most
radical thing, that was the thing that turned us from kids running around and having fun breaking things into men with
bitter faces, that was the thing that took the heart out of the
Combine more than anything else. That's why people still talk
about the Realignment with horror today, even after all these
years, especially in the Commonwealth.

We killed people. *We* did it, ourselves. We walked up and
stabbed them. I mentioned a knife before, boy, and I knew you
didn't know what it was; you bluff well for a kid—that's the
way to a reputation for wisdom: look sage and always keep
your mouth shut about your ignorance. Well, a knife is a
tapering piece of metal with a handle, sharpened on the sides
and very sharp at the tapered end, sharp enough so that when
you strike someone with it the metal goes right into their flesh,
cuts them, rips them open, *kills* them, and there is blood on
your hands which feels wet and sticky and is hard to wash off
because it dries and sticks to the little hairs on the backs of your
wrists. We learned how to hit people hard enough to kill them,
snap the bones inside the skin like dry sticks inside oiled cloth.

We did. We strangled them with lengths of wire. You're shocked. So was the Combine. They had grown used to killing at a great distance, the push of a button, the flick of a switch, using vast, clean, impersonal forces to do their annihilation. We killed people. We killed *people*—not statistics and abstractions. We heard their screams, we saw their faces, we smelled their blood, and their vomit and shit and urine when their systems let go after death. You have to be crazy to do things like that. We *were* crazy. We were a good team.

There were twelve of us in the group, although we mostly worked in sections of four. I was in the team leader's section, and it had been my family for more than two years:

Heynith, stocky, balding, leather-faced; a hard, fair man; brilliant organizer.

Ren, impassive, withdrawn, taciturn, frighteningly competent, of a strange humor.

Goth, young, tireless, bullheaded, given to sudden enthusiasms and depressions; he'd only been with us for about four months, a replacement for Mason, who had been killed while trying to escape from a raid on Cape Itica.

And me.

We were all warped men, emotional cripples one way or the other.

We were all crazy.

The Combine could never understand that kind of craziness, in spite of the millions of people they'd killed or shriveled impersonally over the years. They were afraid of that craziness, they were baffled by it, never could plan to counter it or take it into account. They couldn't really believe it.

That's how we'd taken the Blackfriars Transmitter, hours before D'kotta. It had been impregnable—wrapped in layer after layer of defense fields against missile attack, attack by chemical or biological agents, transmitted energy, almost anything. We'd walked in. They'd never imagined anyone would do that, that it was even possible to attack that way, so there was no defense against it. The guardsystems were designed to meet more esoteric threats. And even after ten years of slowly escalating guerrilla action, they still didn't *really* believe anyone would use his body to wage war. So we walked in. And killed everybody there. The staff was a sentient techclone of ten and an executive foreman. No nulls or zombies. The ten identical technicians milled in panic, the foreman stared at us in disbelief, and what I think was distaste that we'd gone so far outside the bounds of procedure. We killed them like you kill insects, not really thinking about it much, except for that part of you that always thinks about it, that records it and replays it while you sleep. Then we blew up the transmitter with chemical explosives. Then, as the flames leaped up and ate holes in the night, we'd gotten on our bicycles and rode like hell toward the Blackfriars, the mountains hunching and looming ahead, as jagged as black snaggleteeth against the industrial glare of the sky. A tanglefield had snatched at us for a second, but then we were gone.

That's all that I personally had to do with the "historic" Battle of D'kotta. It was enough. We'd paved the way for the whole encounter. Without the transmitter's energy, the Combine's weapons and transportation systems—including lift-shafts, slidewalks, irisdoors, and windows, heating, lighting, waste disposal—were inoperable; D'kotta was immobilized. Without the station's broadcast matter, thousands of buildings, industrial complexes, roadways, and homes had collapsed into chaos, literally collapsed. More important, without broadcast nourishment, D'kotta's four major Cerebrums—handling an incredible complexity of military/industrial/administrative tasks—were knocked out of operation, along with a number of smaller Cerebrums: the synapses need constant nourishment to function, and so do the sophont ganglion units, along with the constant flow of the psychocybernetic current to keep them from going mad from sensory deprivation, and even the nulls would soon grow intractable as hunger stung them almost to self-awareness, finally to die after a few days. Any number of the lowest-ranking sentient clones—all those without stomachs or digestive systems, mostly in the military and industrial castes—would find themselves in the same position as the nulls; without broadcast nourishment, they would die within days. And without catarcs in operation to duplicate the function of atrophied intestines, the buildup of body wastes would poison them anyway, even if they could somehow get nourishment. The independent food dispensers for the smaller percentage of fullsentients and higher clones simply could not increase their output enough to feed that many people, even if converted to intravenous systems. To say nothing of the zombies in the Environments scattered throughout the city.

There were backup fail-safe systems, of course, but they hadn't been used in centuries, the majority of them had fallen into disrepair and didn't work, and other Quaestor teams made sure the rest of them wouldn't work either.

Before a shot had been fired, D'kotta was already a major disaster.

The Combine had reacted as we'd hoped, as they'd been additionally prompted to react by intelligence reports of Quaestor massings in strength around D'kotta that it'd taken weeks to leak to the Combine from unimpeachable sources. The Combine was pouring forces into D'kotta within hours, nearly the full strength of the traditional military caste and a large percentage of the militia they'd cobbled together out of industrial clones when the Quaestors had begun to get seriously troublesome, plus a major portion of their heavy armament. They had hoped to surprise the Quaestors, catch them between the city and the inaccessible portion of the Blackfriars, quarter the area with so much strength it'd be impossible to dodge them, run the Quaestors down, annihilate them, break the back of the movement.

It had worked the other way around.

For years, the Quaestors had stung and run, always retreating when the Combine advanced, never meeting them in conventional battle, never hitting them with anything really heavy. Then, when the Combine had risked practically all of its military resources on one gigantic effort calculated to be effective against the usual Quaestor behavior, we had suddenly switched tactics. The Quaestors had waited to meet the Combine's advance and had hit the Combine forces with everything they'd been able to save, steal, hoard, and buy clandestinely from sympathizers in the Commonwealth in over fifteen years of conspiracy and campaign aimed at this moment.

Within an hour of the first tacnuke exchange, the city had ceased to exist, everything leveled except two of the Cerebrums and the Escridel Creche. Then the Quaestors activated their terraforming devices—which I believe they bought from a firm here on Kos, as a matter of fact. This was completely insane—terraforming systems used indiscriminately can destroy entire planets—but it was the insanity of desperation, and they did it anyway. Within a half hour, the remaining Combine heavy armaments battalions and the two Cerebrums ceased to exist. A few minutes later, the supposedly invulnerable Escridel Creche ceased to exist, the first time in history a creche had ever been destroyed. Then, as the cycling energies got out of hand and filterfeedback built to a climax, everything on the veldt ceased to exist.

The carnage had been inconceivable.

Take the vast population of D'kotta as a base, the second largest city on World, one of the biggest even in this sector of the Commonwealth. The subfleets had been in, bringing the betja harvest and other goods up the Delva; river traffic was always heaviest at that time of year. The mines and factories had been in full swing, and the giant sprawl of the Westernese Shipyards and Engine Works. Add the swarming inhabitants of the six major Controlled Environments that circled the city. Add the city-within-a-city of Admin South, in charge of that hemisphere. Add the twenty generations of D'kotta Combine fullsentients whose discorporate ego-patterns had been preserved in the mountain of "indestructible" micromolecular circuitry called the Escridel Creche. (Those executives had died the irreversible true death, without hope of resurrection this time, even as disembodied intellects housed within artificial mind-environments: the records of their brain's unique pattern of electrical/chemical/psychocybernetic rhythms and balances had been destroyed, and you can't rebuild consciousness from a fused puddle of slag. This hit the Combine where they lived, literally, and had more impact than anything else.) Add the entire strength of both opposing forces; all of our men—who suspected what would happen—had been suicide volunteers. Add all of the elements together.

The total goes up into the multiples of billions.

The number was too big to grasp. Our minds fumbled at it while we marched, and gave up. It was too big.

I stared at Ren's back as we walked, a nearly invisible mannequin silhouette, and tried to multiply that out to the necessary figure. I staggered blindly along, lost and inundated beneath thousands of individual arms, legs, faces; a row of faces blurring off into infinity, all screaming—and the imagining nowhere near the actuality.

Billions.

How many restless ghosts out of that many deaders? Who do they haunt?

Billions.

Dawn caught us about two hours out. It came with no warning, as usual. We were groping through World's ink-dark, moonless night, watched only by the million icy eyes of evening, shreds of witchfire crystal, incredibly cold and distant. I'd watched them night after night for years, scrawling their indecipherable hieroglyphics across the sky, indifferent to man's incomprehension. I stopped for a second on a rise, pushing back the infrared lenses, staring at the sky. What program was printed there, suns for ciphers, worlds for decimal points? An absurd question—I was nearly as foolish as you once, buck—but it was the first fully verbalized thought I'd had since I'd realized the nakedness of flesh, back there on the parapet as my life tore itself apart. I asked it again, half-expecting an answer, watching my breath turn to plumes and tatters, steaming in the silver chill of the stars.

The sun came up like a meteor. It scuttled up from the horizon with that unsettling, deceptive speed that even natives of World never quite get used to. New light washed around us, blue and raw at first, deepening the shadows and honing their edges. The sun continued to hitch itself up the sky, swallowing stars, a watery pink flush wiping the horizon clear of night. The light deepened, mellowed into gold. We floated through silver mist that swirled up around the mountain's knobby knees. I found myself crying silently as I walked the high ridge between mist and sky, absorbing the morning with a new hunger, grappling with a thought that was still too big for my mind and kept slipping elusively away, just out of reach. There was a low hum as our warmsuits adjusted to the growing warmth, polarizing from black to white, bleeding heat back into the air. Down the flanks of the Blackfriars and away across the valley below— visible now as the mists pirouetted past us to the summits—the night plants were dying, shriveling visibly in mile-long swaths of decay. In seconds the Blackfriars were gaunt and barren, turned to hills of ash and bone. The sun was now a bloated yellow disk surrounded by haloes of red and deepening scarlet, shading into the frosty blue of rarefied air. Stripped of softening vegetation, the mountains looked rough and abrasive as pumice, gouged by lunar shadows. The first of the day plants began to appear at our feet, the green spiderwebbing, poking up through cracks in the dry earth.

We came across a new stream, tumbling from melting ice, sluicing a dusty gorge.

An hour later we found the valley.

Heynith led us down onto the marshy plain that rolled away from mountains to horizon. We circled wide, cautiously approaching the valley from the lowlands. Heynith held up his hand, pointed to me, Ren, Goth. The others fanned out across the mouth of the valley, hid, settled down to wait. We went in alone. The speargrass had grown rapidly; it was chest-high. We crawled in, timing our movements to coincide with the long soughing of the morning breeze, so that any rippling of the grass would be taken for natural movement. It took us about a half hour of dusty, sweaty work. When I judged that I'd wormed my way in close enough, I stopped, slowly parted the speargrass enough to peer out without raising my head.

It was a large vacvan, a five-hundred-footer, equipped with waldoes for self-loading.

It was parked near the hill flank on the side of the wide valley.

There were three men with it.

I ducked back into the grass, paused to make sure my "gun"

was ready for operation, then crawled laboriously nearer to the van.

It was very near when I looked up again, about twenty-five feet away in the center of a cleared space. I could make out the hologram pictograph that pulsed identification on the side: the symbol for Urheim, World's largest city and Combine Seat of Board, half a world away in the Northern Hemisphere. They'd come a long way; still thought of as long, though ships whispered between the stars—it was still long for feet and eyes. And another longer way: from fetuses in glass wombs to men stamping and jiggling with cold inside the fold of a mountain's thigh, watching the spreading morning. That made me feel funny to think about. I wondered if they suspected that it'd be the last morning they'd ever see. That made me feel funnier. The thought tickled my mind again, danced away. I checked my gun a second time, needlessly.

I waited, feeling troubled, pushing it down. Two of them were standing together several feet in front of the van, sharing a mild narcotic atomizer, sucking deeply, shuffling with restlessness and cold, staring out across the speargrass to where the plain opened up. They had the stiff, rumpled, puff-eyed look of people who had just spent an uncomfortable night in a cramped place. They were dressed as fullsentients uncloned, junior officers of the military caste, probably hereditary positions inherited from their families, as is the case with most of the uncloned cadet executives. Except for the cadre at Urheim and other major cities, they must have been some of the few surviving clansmen; hundreds of thousands of military cadets and officers had died at D'kotta (along with uncounted clones and semisentients of all ranks), and the caste had never been extremely large in the first place. The by-laws had demanded that the Combine maintain a security force, but it had become mostly traditional, with minimum function, at least among the uncloned higher ranks, almost the last stronghold of old-fashioned nepotism. That was one of the things that had favored the Quaestor uprising, and had forced the Combine to take the unpopular step of impressing large numbers of industrial clones into a militia. The most junior of these two cadets was very young, even younger than me. The third man remained inside the van's cab. I could see his face blurrily through the windfield, kept on against the cold though the van was no longer in motion.

I waited. I knew the others were maneuvering into position around me. I also knew what Heynith was waiting for.

The third man jumped down from the high cab. He was older, wore an officer's hologram: a full executive. He said something to the cadets, moved a few feet toward the back of the van, started to take a piss. The column of golden liquid steamed in the cold air.

Heynith whistled.

I rolled to my knees, parted the speargrass at the edge of the cleared space, swung my gun up. The two cadets started, face muscles tensing into uncertain fear. The older cadet took an involuntary step forward, still clutching the atomizer. Ren and Goth chopped him down, firing a stream of "bullets" into him. The guns made a very loud metallic rattling sound that jarred the teeth, and fire flashed from the ejector ends. Birds screamed upward all along the mountain flank. The impact of the bullets knocked the cadet off his feet, rolled him so that he came to rest belly-down. The atomizer flew through the air, hit, bounced. The younger cadet leaped toward the cab, right into my line of fire. I pulled the trigger; bullets exploded out of the gun. The cadet was kicked backwards, arms swinging wide, slammed against the side of the cab, jerked upright as I continued to fire, spun along the van wall and rammed heavily into the ground. He tottered on one shoulder for a second, then flopped over onto his back. At the sound of the first shot, the executive had whirled—penis still dangling from pantaloons, surplus piss spraying wildly—and dodged for the back of the van, so that Heynith's volley missed and screamed from the van wall, leaving a long scar. The executive dodged again, crouched, came up with a biodeth in one hand, and swung right into a single bullet from Ren just as he began to fire. The impact twirled him in a staggering circle, his finger still pressing the trigger; the carrier beam splashed harmlessly from the van wall, traversed as the executive spun, cut a long swath through the speargrass, the plants shriveling and blackening as the beam swept over them.

Heynith opened up again before the beam could reach his clump of grass, sending the executive—somehow still on his feet—lurching past the end of the van. The biodeth dropped, went out. Heynith kept firing, the executive dancing bonelessly backwards on his heels, held up by the stream of bullets. Heynith released the trigger. The executive collapsed: a heap of arms and legs at impossible angles.

When we came up to the van, the young cadet was still dying. His body shivered and arched, his heels drummed against the earth, his fingers plucked at nothing, and then he was still. There was a lot of blood.

The others moved up from the valley mouth. Heynith sent them circling around the rim, where the valley walls dipped down on three sides.

We dragged the bodies away and concealed them in some large rocks.

I was feeling numb again, like I had after D'kotta.

I continued to feel numb as we spent the rest of that morning in frantic preparation. My mind was somehow detached as my body sweated and dug and hauled. There was a lot for it to do. We had four heavy industrial lasers, rock-cutters; they were clumsy, bulky, inefficient things to use as weapons, but they'd have to do. This mission had not been planned so much as thrown together, only two hours before the liaison man had contacted us on the parapet. Anything that could possibly work at all would have to be made to work somehow; no time to do it right, just do it. We'd been the closest team in contact with the field HQ who'd received the report, so we'd been snatched; the lasers were the only things on hand that could even approach potential as a heavy weapon, so we'd use the lasers.

Now that we'd taken the van without someone alerting the Combine by radio from the cab, Heynith flashed a signal mirror back toward the shoulder of the mountain we'd quitted a few hours before. The liaison man swooped down ten minutes later, carrying one of the lasers strapped awkwardly to his platvac. He made three more trips, depositing the massive cylinders as carefully as eggs, then gunned his platvac and screamed back toward the Blackfriars in a maniac arc just this side of suicidal. His face was still gray, tight-pressed lips a bloodless white against ash, and he hadn't said a word during the whole unloading procedure. I think he was probably one of the Quaestors who followed the Way of Atonement. I never saw him again. I've sometimes wished I'd had the courage to follow his example, but I rationalize by telling myself that I have atoned with my life rather than my death, and who knows, it might even be somewhat true. It's nice to think so anyway.

It took us a couple of hours to get the lasers into position. We spotted them in four places around the valley walls, dug slanting pits into the slopes to conceal them and tilt the barrels up at the right angle. We finally got them all zeroed on a spot about a hundred feet above the center of the valley floor, the muzzle arrangement giving each a few degrees of leeway on either side. That's where she'd have to come down anyway if she was a standard orbot, the valley being just wide enough to contain the boat and the vacvan, with a safety margin between them. Of course, if they brought her down on the plain outside the valley mouth, things were going to get very hairy; in that case we might be able to lever one or two of the lasers around to bear, or, failing that, we could try to take the orbot on foot once it'd landed, with about one chance in eight of making it. But we thought that they'd land her in the valley; that's where the vacvan had been parked, and they'd want the shelter of the high mountain walls to conceal the orbot from any Quaestor eyes that might be around. If so, that gave us a much better chance. About one out of three.

When the lasers had been positioned, we scattered, four men to an emplacement, hiding in the camouflaged trenches alongside the big barrels. Heynith led Goth and me toward the laser we'd placed about fifty feet up the mountain flank, directly behind and above the vacvan. Ren stayed behind. He stood next to the van—shoulders characteristically slouched, thumbs hooked in his belt, face carefully void of expression—and watched us out of sight. Then he looked out over the valley mouth, hitched up his gun, spat in the direction of Urheim and climbed up into the van cab.

The valley was empty again. From our position the vacvan looked like a shiny toy, sun dogs winking across its surface as it baked in the afternoon heat. An abandoned toy, lost in high weeds, waiting in loneliness to be reclaimed by owners who would never come.

Time passed.

The birds we'd frightened away began to settle back onto the hillsides.

I shifted position uneasily, trying half-heartedly to get comfortable. Heynith glared me into immobility. We were crouched in a trench about eight feet long and five feet deep, covered by a camouflage tarpaulin propped open on the valley side by pegs, a couple of inches of vegetation and topsoil on top of the tarpaulin. Heynith was in the middle, straddling the operator's saddle of the laser. Goth was on his left, I was on his right. Heynith was going to man the laser when the time came; it only took one person. There was nothing for Goth and me to do, would be nothing to do even during the ambush, except take over the firing in the unlikely event that Heynith was killed without the shot wiping out all of us, or stand by to lever the laser around in case that became necessary. Neither was very likely to happen. No, it was Heynith's show, and we were superfluous and unoccupied.

That was bad.

We had a lot of time to think.

That was worse.

I was feeling increasingly numb, like a wall of clear glass had been slipped between me and the world and was slowly thickening, layer by layer. With the thickening came an incredible isolation (isolation though I was cramped and suffocating, though I was jammed up against Heynith's bunched thigh—I couldn't touch him, he was miles away) and with the isolation came a sick, smothering panic. It was the inverse of claustrophobia. My flesh had turned to clear plastic, my bones to glass, and I was naked, ultimately naked, and there was nothing I could wrap me in. Surrounded by an army, I would still be alone; shrouded in iron thirty feet underground, I would still be naked. One portion of my mind wondered dispassionately if I was slipping into shock; the rest of it fought to keep down the scream that gathered along tightening muscles. The isolation increased. I was unaware of my surroundings, except for the heat and the pressure of enclosure.

I was seeing the molten spider of D'kotta, lying on its back and showing its obscene blotched belly, kicking legs of flame against the sky, each leg raising a poison blister where it touched the clouds.

I was seeing the boy, face runneled by blood, beating heels against the ground.

I was beginning to doubt big, simple ideas.

Nothing moved in the valley except wind through grass, spirits circling in the form of birds.

Spider legs.

Crab dance.

The blocky shadow of the vacvan crept across the valley.

Suddenly, with the intensity of vision, I was picturing Ren sitting in the van cab, shoulders resting against the door, legs stretched out along the seat, feet propped up on the instrument board, one ankle crossed over the other, gun resting across his lap, eyes watching the valley mouth through the windfield. He would be smoking a cigarette, and he would take it from his lips occasionally, flick the ashes onto the shiny dials with a fingernail, smile his strange smile, and carefully burn holes in the plush fabric of the upholstery. The fabric (real fabric; not plastic) would smolder, send out a wisp of bad-smelling smoke, and there would be another charred black hole in the seat. Ren would smile again, put the cigarette back in his mouth, lean back, and puff slowly. Ren was waiting to answer the radio signal from the orbot, to assure its pilot and crew that all was well, to talk them down to death. If they suspected anything was wrong, he would be the first to die. Even if everything went perfectly, he stood a high chance of dying anyway; he was the most exposed. It was almost certainly a suicide job. Ren said that he didn't give a shit; maybe he actually didn't. Or at least had convinced himself that he didn't. He was an odd man. Older than any of us, even Heynith, he had worked most of his life as a cadet executive in Admin at Urheim, devoted his existence to his job, subjugated all of his energies to it. He had been passed over three times for promotion to executive status, years of redoubled effort and mounting anxiety between each rejection. With the third failure he had been quietly retired to live on the credit subsidy he had earned with forty years of service. The next morning, precisely at the start of his accustomed work period, he stole a biodeth from a security guard in the Admin Complex, walked into his flowsector, killed everyone there, and disappeared from Urheim. After a year on the run, he had managed to contact the Quaestors. After another year of training, he was serving with a commando team in spite of his age. That had been five years ago; I had known him for two. During all that time, he had said little. He did his job very well with a minimum of waste motion, never made mistakes, never complained, never showed emotion. But occasionally he would smile and burn a hole in something. Or someone.

The sun dived at the horizon, seeming to crash into the plain in an explosion of flame. Night swallowed us in one gulp. Black as a beast's belly.

It jerked me momentarily back into reality. I had a bad moment when I thought I'd gone blind, but then reason returned and I slipped the infrared lenses down over my eyes, activated them. The world came back in shades of red. Heynith was working cramped legs against the body of the laser. He spoke briefly, and we gulped some stimulus pills to keep us awake; they were bitter, and hard to swallow dry as usual, but they kicked up a familiar acid churning in my stomach, and my blood began to flow faster. I glanced at Heynith. He'd been quiet, even for Heynith. I wondered what he was thinking. He looked at me, perhaps reading the thought, and ordered us out of the trench.

Goth and I crawled slowly out, feeling stiff and brittle, slapped our thighs and arms, stamped to restore circulation. Stars were sprinkling across the sky, salt spilled on black porcelain. I still couldn't read them, I found. The day plants had vanished, the day animals had retreated into catalepsy. The night plants were erupting from the ground, fed by the debris of the day plants. They grew rapidly, doubling, then tripling in height as we watched. They were predominantly thick, ropy shrubs with wide, spearhead leaves of dull purple and black, about four feet high. Goth and I dug a number of them up, root systems intact, and placed them on top of the tarpaulin to replace the day plants that had shriveled with the first touch of bitter evening frost. We had to handle them with padded gloves; the leaf surfaces greedily absorbed the slightest amount of heat and burned like dry ice.

Then we were back in the trench, and it was worse than ever. Motion had helped for a while, but I could feel the numbing panic creeping back, and the momentary relief made it even harder to bear. I tried to start a conversation, but it died in monosyllabic grunts, and silence sopped up the echoes. Heynith was methodically checking the laser controls for the nth time. He was tense; I could see it bunch his shoulder muscles, bulge his calves into rock as they pushed against the footplates of the saddle. Goth looked worse than I did; he was somewhat younger, and usually energetic and cheerful. Not tonight.

We should have talked, spread the pain around; I think all of us realized it. But we couldn't; we were made awkward by our own special intimacy. At one time or another, every one of us had reached a point where he *had* to talk or die, even Heynith, even Ren. So we all had talked and all had listened, each of us switching roles sooner or later. We had poured our fears and dreams and secret memories upon each other, until now we knew each other too well. It made us afraid. Each of us was afraid that he had exposed too much, let down too many barriers. We were afraid of vulnerability, of the knife that jabs for the softest fold of the belly. We were all scarred men already, and twice-shy. And the resentment grew that others had seen us that helpless, that vulnerable. So the walls went back up, intensified. And so when we needed to talk again, we could not. We were already too close to risk further intimacy.

Visions returned, ebbing and flowing, overlaying the darkness.

The magma churning, belching a hot breath that stinks of rotten eggs.

The cadet, his face inhuman in the death rictus, blood running down in a wash from his smashed forehead, plastering one eye closed, bubbling at his nostril, frothing around his lips, the lips tautening as his head jerks forward and then backwards, slamming the ground, the lips then growing slack, the body slumping, the mouth sagging open, the rush of blood and phlegm past the tombstone teeth, down the chin and neck, soaking into the fabric of the tunic. The feet drumming at the ground a final time, digging up clots of earth.

I groped for understanding. I had killed people before, and it had not bothered me except in sleep. I had done it mechanically, routine backed by hate, hate cushioned by routine. I wondered if the night would ever end. I remembered the morning I'd watched from the mountain. I didn't think the night would end. A big idea tickled my mind again.

The city swallowed by stone.

The cadet falling, swinging his arms wide.

Why always the cadet and the city in conjunction? Had one sensitized me to the other, and if so, which? I hesitated.

Could both of them be equally important?

One of the other section leaders whistled.

We all started, somehow grew even more tense. The whistle came again, warbling, sound floating on silence like oil on water. Someone was coming. After a while we heard a rustling and snapping of underbrush approaching downslope from the mountain. Whoever it was, he was making no effort to move quietly. In fact he seemed to be blundering along, bulling through the tangles, making a tremendous thrashing noise. Goth and I turned in the direction of the sound, brought our guns up to bear, primed them. That was instinct. I wondered who could be coming *down* the mountain toward us. That was reason. Heynith twisted to cover the opposite direction, away from the noise, resting his gun on the saddle rim. That was caution. The thrasher passed our position about six feet away, screened by the shrubs. There was an open space ten feet farther down, at the head of a talus bluff that slanted to the valley. We watched it. The shrubs at the end of the clearing shook, were torn aside. A figure stumbled out into starlight.

It was a null.

Goth sucked in a long breath, let it hiss out between his teeth. Heynith remained impassive, but I could imagine his eyes narrowing behind the thick lenses. My mind was totally blank for about three heartbeats, then, surprised: a null! and I brought the gun barrel up, then, uncomprehending: a null? and I lowered the muzzle. Blank for a second, then: how? and trickling in again: how? Thoughts snarled into confusion, the gun muzzle wavered hesitantly.

The null staggered across the clearing, weaving in slow figure-eights. It almost fell down the talus bluff, one foot suspended uncertainly over the drop, then lurched away, goaded by tropism. The null shambled backward a few paces, stopped, swayed, then slowly sank to its knees.

It kneeled: head bowed, arms limp along the ground, palms up.

Heynith put his gun back in his lap, shook his head. He told us he'd be damned if he could figure out where it came from, but we'd have to get rid of it. It could spoil the ambush if it was spotted. Automatically, I raised my gun, trained it. Heynith stopped me. No noise, he said, not now. He told Goth to go out and kill it silently.

Goth refused. Heynith stared at him speechlessly, then began to flush. Goth and Heynith had had trouble before. Goth was a good man, brave as a bull, but he was stubborn, tended to follow his own lead too much, had too many streaks of sentimentality and touchiness, *thought* too much to be a really efficient cog.

They had disagreed from the beginning, something that wouldn't have been tolerated this long if the Quaestors hadn't been desperate for men. Goth was a devil in a fight when aroused, one of the best, and that had excused him a lot of obstinacy. But he had a curious squeamishness, he hadn't developed the layers of numbing scar-tissue necessary for guerrilla work, and that was almost inevitably fatal. I'd wondered before, dispassionately, how long he would last.

Goth was a hereditary fullsentient, one of the few connected with the Quaestors. He'd been a cadet executive in Admin, gained access to old archives that had slowly soured him on the Combine, been hit at the psychologically right moment by increasing Quaestor agitprop, and had defected; after a two-year proving period, he'd been allowed to participate actively. Goth was one of the only field people who was working out of idealism rather than hate, and that made us distrust him. Heynith also nurtured a traditional dislike for hereditary full-sentients. Heynith had been part of an industrial sixclone for over twenty years before joining the Quaestors. His Six had been wiped out in a production accident, caused by standard Combine negligence. Heynith had been the only survivor. The Combine had expressed mild sympathy, and told him that they planned to cut another clone from him to replace the destroyed Six; he of course would be placed in charge of the new Six, by reason of his seniority. They smiled at him, not seeing any reason why he wouldn't want to work another twenty years with biological replicas of his dead brothers and sisters, the men, additionally, reminders of what he'd been as a youth, unravaged by years of pain. Heynith had thanked them politely, walked out, and kept walking, crossing the Gray Waste on foot to join the Quaestors.

I could see all this working in Heynith's face as he raged at Goth. Goth could feel the hate too, but he stood firm. The null was incapable of doing anybody any harm; he wasn't going to kill it. There'd been enough slaughter. Goth's face was bloodless, and I could see D'kotta reflected in his eyes, but I felt no sympathy for him, in spite of my own recent agonies. He was disobeying orders. I thought about Mason, the man Goth had replaced, the man who had died in my arms at Itica, and I hated Goth for being alive instead of Mason. I had loved Mason. He'd been an Antiquarian in the Urheim archives, and he'd worked for the Quaestors almost from the beginning, years of vital service before his activities were discovered by the Combine. He'd escaped the raid, but his family hadn't. He'd been offered an admin job in Quaestor HQ, but had turned it down and insisted on fieldwork in spite of warnings that it was suicidal for a man of his age. Mason had been a tall, gentle, scholarly man who pretended to be gruff and hard-nosed, and cried alone at night when he thought nobody could see. I'd often thought that he could have escaped from Itica if he'd tried harder, but he'd been worn down, sick and guilt-ridden and tired, and his heart hadn't really been in it; that thought had returned to puzzle me often afterward. Mason had been the only person I'd ever cared about, the one who'd been more responsible than anybody for bringing me out of the shadows and into humanity, and I could have shot Goth at that moment because I thought he was betraying Mason's memory.

Heynith finally ran out of steam, spat at Goth, started to call him something, then stopped and merely glared at him, lips white. I'd caught Heynith's quick glance at me, a nearly invisible head-turn, just before he'd fallen silent. He'd almost forgotten and called Goth a zombie, a widespread expletive on World that had carefully *not* been used by the team since I'd joined. So Heynith had never really forgotten, though he'd treated me with scrupulous fairness. My fury turned to a cold anger, widened out from Goth to become a sick distaste for the entire world.

Heynith told Goth he would take care of him later, take care of him good, and ordered me to go kill the null, take him upslope and out of sight first, then conceal the body.

Mechanically, I pulled myself out of the trench, started downslope toward the clearing. Anger fueled me for the first few feet, and I slashed the shrubs aside with padded gloves, but it ebbed quickly, leaving me hollow and numb. I'd known how the rest of the team must actually think of me, but somehow I'd never allowed myself to admit it. Now I'd had my face jammed in it, and, coming on top of all the other anguish I'd gone through the last two days, it was too much.

I pushed into the clearing.

My footsteps triggered some response in the null. It surged drunkenly to its feet, arms swinging limply, and turned to face me.

The null was slightly taller than me, built very slender, and couldn't have weighed too much more than a hundred pounds. It was bald, completely hairless. The fingers were shriveled, limp flesh dangling from the club of the hand; they had never been used. The toes had been developed to enable technicians to walk nulls from one section of the Cerebrum to another, but the feet had never had a chance to toughen or grow callused: they were a mass of blood and lacerations. The nose was a rough blob of pink meat around the nostrils, the ears similarly atrophied. The eyes were enormous, huge milky corneas and small pupils, like those of a nocturnal bird; adapted to the gloom of the Cerebrum, and allowed to function to forestall sensory deprivation; they aren't cut into the psychocybernetic current like the synapses or the ganglions. There were small messy wounds on the temples, wrists, and spine-base where electrodes had been torn loose. It had been shrouded in a pajamalike suit of nonconductive material, but that had been torn almost completely away, only a few hanging tatters remaining. There were no sex organs. The flesh under the rib cage was curiously collapsed; no stomach or digestive tract. The body was covered with bruises, cuts, gashes, extensive swatches sun-baked to second-degree burns, other sections seriously frostbitten or marred by bad coldburns from the night shrubs.

My awe grew, deepened into archetypical dread.

It was from D'kotta, there could be no doubt about it. Somehow it had survived the destruction of its Cerebrum, somehow it had walked through the boiling hell to the foothills, somehow it had staggered up to and over the mountain shoulder. I doubted if there'd been any predilection in its actions; probably it had just walked blindly away from the ruined Cerebrum in a straight line and kept walking. Its actions with the talus bluff demonstrated that; maybe earlier some dim instinct had helped it fumble its way around obstacles in its path, but now it was exhausted, baffled, stymied. It was miraculous that it had made it this far. And the agony it must have suffered on its way was inconceivable. I shivered, spooked. The short hairs bristled on the back of my neck.

The null lurched toward me.

I whimpered and sprang backwards, nearly falling, swinging up the gun.

The null stopped, its head lolling, describing a slow semicircle. Its eyes were tracking curiously, and I doubted if it could focus on me at all. To it, I must have been a blur of darker gray.

I tried to steady my ragged breathing. It couldn't hurt me; it was harmless, nearly dead anyway. Slowly, I lowered the gun, pried my fingers from the stock, slung the gun over my shoulder.

I edged cautiously toward it. The null swayed, but remained motionless. Below, I could see the vacvan at the bottom of the bluff, a patch of dull gunmetal sheen. I stretched my hand out slowly. The null didn't move. This close, I could see its gaunt ribs rising and falling with the effort of its ragged breathing. It was trembling, an occasional convulsive spasm shuddering along its frame. I was surprised that it didn't stink; nulls were rumored to have a strong personal odor, at least according to the talk in field camps—bullshit, like so much of my knowledge at that time. I watched it for a minute, fascinated, but my training told me I couldn't stand out here for long; we were too exposed. I took another step, reached out for it, hesitated. I didn't want to touch it. Swallowing my distaste, I selected a spot on its upper arm free of burns or wounds, grabbed it firmly with one hand.

The null jerked at the touch, but made no attempt to strike out or get away. I waited warily for a second, ready to turn my grip into a wrestling hold if it should try to attack. It remained still, but its flesh crawled under my fingers, and I shivered myself in reflex. Satisfied that the null would give me no trouble, I turned and began to force it upslope, pushing it ahead of me.

It followed my shove without resistance, until we hit the first of the night shrubs, then it staggered and made a mewing, inarticulate sound. The plants were burning it, sucking warmth out of its flesh, raising fresh welts, ugly where bits of skin had adhered to the shrubs. I shrugged, pushed it forward. It mewed and lurched again. I stopped. The null's eyes tracked in my direction, and it whimpered to itself in pain. I swore at myself for wasting time, but moved ahead to break a path for the null, dragging it along behind me. The branches slapped harmlessly at my warmsuit as I bent them aside; occasionally one would slip past and lash the null, making it flinch and whimper, but it was spared the brunt of it. I wondered vaguely at my motives for doing it. Why bother to spare someone (some*thing*, I corrected nervously) pain when you're going to have to kill him (*it*) in a minute? What difference could it make? I shelved that and concentrated on the movements of my body; the null wasn't heavy, but it wasn't easy to drag it uphill either, especially as it'd stumble and go down every few yards and I'd have to pull it back to its feet again. I was soon sweating, but I didn't care, as the action helped to occupy my mind, and I didn't want to have to face the numbness I could feel taking over again.

We moved upslope until we were about thirty feet above the trench occupied by Heynith and Goth. This looked like a good place. The shrubs were almost chest-high here, tall enough to hide the null's body from an aerial search. I stopped. The null bumped blindly into me, leaned against me, its breath coming in rasps next to my ear. I shivered in horror at the contact. Gooseflesh blossomed on my arms and legs, swept across my body. Some connection sent a memory whispering at my mind, but I ignored it under the threat of rising panic. I twisted my shoulder under the null's weight, threw it off. The null slid back downslope a few feet, almost fell, recovered.

I watched it, panting. The memory returned, gnawing incessantly. This time it got through:

Mason scrambling through the sea-washed rocks of Cape Itica toward the waiting ramsub, while the fire sky-whipping behind picked us out against the shadows; Mason, too slow in vaulting over a stone ridge, balancing too long on the razor-edge in perfect silhouette against the night; Mason jerked upright as a fusor fired from the high cliff puddled his spine, melted his flesh like wax; Mason tumbling down into my arms, almost driving me to my knees; Mason, already dead, heavy in my arms, *heavy in my arms*; Mason torn away from me as a wave broke over us and deluged me in spume; Mason sinking from sight as Heynith screamed for me to come on and I fought my way through the chest-high surf to the ramsub—

That's what supporting the null had reminded me of: Mason, heavy in my arms.

Confusion and fear and nausea.

How could the null make me think of Mason?

Sick self-anger that my mind could compare Mason, gentle as the dream-father I'd never had, to something as disgusting as the null.

Anger novaed, trying to scrub out shame and guilt.

I couldn't take it. I let it spill out onto the null.

Growling, I sprang forward, shook it furiously until its head rattled and wobbled on its limp neck, grabbed it by the shoulders, and hammered it to its knees.

I yanked my knife out. The blade flamed suddenly in starlight.

I wrapped my hand around its throat to tilt its head back. Its flesh was warm. A pulse throbbed under my palm.

All at once, my anger was gone, leaving only nausea.

I suddenly realized how cold the night was. Wind bit to the bone.

It was *looking* at me.

I suppose I'd been lucky. Orphans aren't as common as they once were—not in a society where reproduction has been relegated to the laboratory—but they still occur with fair regularity. I had been the son of an uncloned junior executive who'd run up an enormous credit debit, gone bankrupt, and been forced into insolvency. The Combine had cut a clone from him so that their man-hours would make up the bank discrepancy, burned out the higher levels of his brain, and put him in one of the nonsentient penal Controlled Environments. His wife was also cloned, but avoided brainscrub and went back to work in a lower capacity in Admin. I, as a baby, then became a ward of the State, and was sent to one of the institutional Environments. Imagine an endless series of low noises, repeating over and over again forever, no high or low spots, everything level: MMMMMMMMMMMMMMMMMMMMMMMMMMMMM MMMMMMMMMMMMMMMMMMMMM. Like that. That's the only way to describe the years in the Environments. We were fed, we were kept warm, we worked on conveyor belts piecing together miniaturized equipment, we were put to sleep electronically, we woke with our fingers already busy in the monotonous, rhythmical motions that we couldn't remember learning, motions we had repeated a million times a day since infancy. Once a day we were fed a bar of food-concentrates and vitamins. Occasionally, at carefully calculated intervals, we would be exercised to keep up muscle tone. After reaching puberty, we were occasionally masturbated by electric stimulation, the seed saved for sperm banks. The administrators of the Environment were not cruel; we almost never saw them. Punishment was by machine shocks; never severe, very rarely needed. The executives had no need to be cruel. All they needed was MMMMMMMMMMMMMMMMMMMMM MMMMMM. We had been taught at some early stage, probably by shock and stimulation, to put the proper part in the proper slot as the blocks of equipment passed in front of us. We had never been taught to talk, although an extremely limited language of several mood-sounds had independently developed among us; the executives never spoke on the rare intervals when they came to check the machinery that regulated us. We had never been told who we were, where we were; we had never been told anything. We didn't care about any of these things, the concepts had never formed in our minds, we were only semiconscious at best anyway. There was nothing but M M MMMMMMMMMMMMMMMMMMM. The executives weren't concerned with our spiritual development; there was no graduation from the Environment, there was no place else for us to go in a rigidly stratified society. The Combine had discharged its obligation by keeping us alive, in a place where we could even be minimally useful. Though our jobs were sinecures and could have been more efficiently performed by computer, they gave the expense of our survival a socially justifiable excuse, they put us comfortably in a pigeonhole. We were there for life. We would grow up from infancy, grow old, and die, bathed in MMMMMMMMMMMMMMMMM MMM. The first real, separate, and distinct memory of my life is when the Quaestors raided the Environment, when the wall of the assembly chamber suddenly glowed red, buckled, collapsed inward, when Mason pushed out of the smoke and the debris cloud, gun at the ready, and walked slowly toward me. That's hindsight. At the time, it was only a sudden invasion of incomprehensible sounds and lights and shapes and colors, too much to possibly comprehend, incredibly alien. It was the first discordant note ever struck in our lives: MMMMMMM MMMMM!!!! shattering our world in an instant, plunging us into another dimension of existence. The Quaestors kidnapped all of us, loaded us onto vacvans, took us into the hills, tried to undo some of the harm. That'd been six years ago. Even with the facilities available at the Quaestor underground complex— hypnotrainers and analysis computers to plunge me back to childhood and patiently lead me out again step by step for ten thousand years of subjective time, while my body slumbered in stasis—even with all of that, I'd been lucky to emerge some-what sane. The majority had died, or been driven into cata-lepsy. I'd been lucky even to be a Ward of the State, the way things had turned out. Lucky to be a zombie. I could have been a low-ranked clone, without a digestive system, tied forever to the Combine by unbreakable strings. Or I could have been one of the thousands of tank-grown creatures whose brains are used as organic-computer storage banks in the Cerebrum gestalts, completely unsentient: I could have been

a null.

Enormous eyes staring at me, unblinking.

Warmth under my fingers.

I wondered if I was going to throw up.

Wind moaned steadily through the valley with a sound like MMMMMMMMMMMMMMMM.

Heynith hissed for me to hurry up, sound riding the wind, barely audible. I shifted my grip on the knife. I was telling myself: it's never been really sentient anyway. Its brain has only been used as a computer unit for a biological gestalt, there's no individual intelligence in there. It wouldn't make any differ-ence. I was telling myself: it's dying anyway from a dozen causes. It's in pain. It would be kinder to kill it.

I brought up the knife, placing it against the null's throat. I pressed the point in slowly, until it was pricking flesh.

The null's eyes tracked, focused on the knifeblade.

My stomach turned over. I looked away, out across the valley. I felt my carefully created world trembling and blurring around me, I felt again on the point of being catapulted into another level of comprehension, previously unexpected. I was afraid.

The vacvan's headlights flashed on and off, twice.

I found myself on the ground, hidden by the ropy shrubs. I had dragged the null down with me, without thinking about it, pinned him flat to the ground, arm over back. That had been the signal that Ren had received a call from the orbot, had given it the proper radio code reply to bring it down. I could imagine him grinning in the darkened cab as he worked the instruments.

I raised myself on an elbow, jerked the knife up, suspending it while I looked for the junction of spine and neck that would be the best place to strike. If I was going to kill him *(it)*, I would have to kill him *(it!)* now. In quick succession, like a series of slides, like a computer equation running, I got: D'kotta—the cadet—Mason—the null. *It* and *him* tumbled in selection. Came up *him*. I lowered the knife. I couldn't do it. He was human. Everybody was.

For better or worse, I was changed. I was no longer the same person.

I looked up. Somewhere up there, hanging at the edge of the atmosphere, was the tinsel collection of forces in opposition called a starship, delicately invulnerable as an iron butterfly. It would be phasing in and out of "reality" to hold its position above World, maintaining only the most tenuous of contacts with this continuum. It had launched an orbot, headed for a rendezvous with the vacvan in this valley. The orbot was filled with the gene cultures that could be used to create hundreds of thousands of nonsentient clones who could be imprinted with behavior patterns and turned into computer-directed soldiers; crude but effective. The orbot was filled with millions of tiny metal blocks, kept under enormous compression: when released from tension, molecular memory would reshape them into a wide range of weapons needing only a power source to be functional. The orbot was carrying, in effect, a vast army and its combat equipment, in a form that could be transported in a five-hundred-foot vacvan and slipped into Urheim, where there were machines that could put it into use. It was the

Combine's last chance, the second wind they needed in order to survive. It had been financed and arranged by various industrial firms in the Commonwealth who had vested interests in the Combine's survival on World. The orbot's cargo had been assembled and sent off before D'kotta, when it had been calculated that the reinforcements would be significant in ensuring a Combine victory; now it was indispensable. D'kotta had made the Combine afraid that an attack on Urheim might be next, that the orbot might be intercepted by the Quaestors if the city was under siege when it tried to land. So the Combine had decided to land the orbot elsewhere and sneak the cargo in. The Blackfriars had been selected as a rendezvous, since it was unlikely the Quaestors would be on the alert for Combine activity in that area so soon after D'kotta, and even if stopped, the van might be taken for fleeing survivors and ignored. The starship had been contacted by esper en route, and the change in plan made.

Four men had died to learn of the original plan. Two more had died in order to learn of the new landing site and get the information to the Quaestors in time.

The orbot came down.

I watched it as in a dream, coming to my knees, head above the shrubs. The null stirred under my hand, pushed against the ground, sat up.

The orbot was a speck, a dot, a ball, a toy. It was gliding silently in on gravs, directly overhead.

I could imagine Heynith readying the laser, Goth looking up and chewing his lip the way he always did in stress. I knew that my place should be with them, but I couldn't move. Fear and tension were still there, but they were under glass. I was already emotionally drained. I could sum up nothing else, even to face death.

The orbot had swelled into a huge, spherical mountain. It continued to settle toward the spot where we'd calculated it must land. Now it hung just over the valley center, nearly brushing the mountain walls on either side. The orbot filled the sky, and I leaned away from it instinctively. It dropped lower—

Heynith was the first to fire.

An intense beam of light erupted from the ground down-slope, stabbed into the side of the orbot. Another followed from the opposite side of the valley, then the remaining two at once.

The orbot hung, transfixed by four steady, unbearably bright columns.

For a while, it seemed as if nothing was happening.

I could imagine the consternation aboard the orbot as the pilot tried to reverse gravs in time.

The boat's hull had become cherry red in four widening spots. Slowly, the spots turned white.

I could hear the null getting up beside me, near enough to touch. I had risen automatically, shading my eyes against glare.

The orbot exploded.

The reactor didn't go, of course; they're built so that can't happen. It was just the conventional auxiliary engines, used for steering and for powering internal systems. But that was enough.

Imagine a building humping itself into a giant stone fist, and bringing that fist down on you, *squash*. Pain so intense that it snuffs your consciousness before you can feel it.

Warned by instinct, I had time to do two things.

I thought, distinctly: so night will never end.

And I stepped in front of the null to shield him.

Then I was kicked into oblivion.

I awoke briefly to agony, the world a solid, blank red. Very, very far away, I could hear someone screaming. It was me.

I awoke again. The pain had lessened. I could see. It was day, and the night plants had died. The sun was dazzling on bare rock. The null was standing over me, seeming to stretch up for miles into the sky. I screamed in preternatural terror. The world vanished.

The next time I opened my eyes, the sky was heavily overcast and it was raining, one of those torrential southern downpours. A Quaestor medic was doing something to my legs, and there was a platvac nearby. The null was lying on his back a few feet away, a bullet in his chest. His head was tilted up toward the scuttling gray clouds. His eyes mirrored the rain.

That's what happened to my leg. So much nerve tissue destroyed that they couldn't grow me a new one, and I had to put up with this stiff prosthetic. But I got used to it. I considered it my tuition fee.

I'd learned two things: that everybody is human, and that the universe doesn't care one way or the other; only people do. The universe just doesn't give a damn. Isn't that wonderful? Isn't that a relief? It isn't out to get you, and it isn't going to help you either. You're on your own. We all are, and we all have to answer to ourselves. We make our own heavens and hells; we can't pass the buck any further. How much easier when we could blame our guilt or goodness on God.

Oh, I could read supernatural significance into it all—that I was spared because I'd spared the null, that some benevolent force was rewarding me—but what about Goth? Killed, and if he hadn't balked in the first place, the null wouldn't have stayed alive long enough for me to be entangled. What about the other team members, all dead—wasn't there a man among them as good as me and as much worth saving? No, there's a more direct reason why I survived. Prompted by the knowledge of his humanity, I had shielded him from the explosion. Three other men survived that explosion, but they died from exposure in the hours before the med team got there, baked to death by the sun. I didn't die because the null stood over me during the hours when the sun was rising and frying the rocks, *and his shadow shielded me from the sun.* I'm not saying that he consciously figured that out, deliberately shielded me (though who knows), but I had given him the only warmth he'd known in a long nightmare of pain, and so he remained by me when there was nothing stopping him from running away—and it came to the same result. You don't need intelligence or words to respond to empathy, it can be communicated through the touch of fingers—you know that if you've ever had a pet, ever been in love. So that's why I was spared, warmth for warmth, the same reason anything good ever happens in this life. When the med team arrived, they shot the null down because they thought it was trying to harm me. So much for supernatural rewards for the Just.

So, empathy's the thing that binds life together; it's the flame we share against fear. Warmth's the only answer to the old cold questions.

So I went through life, boy; made mistakes, did a lot of things, got kicked around a lot more, loved a little, and ended up on Kos, waiting for evening.

But night's a relative thing. It always ends. It does; because even if you're not around to watch it, the sun always comes up, and someone'll be there to see.

It's a fine, beautiful morning.

It's always a beautiful morning somewhere, even on the day you die.

You're young—that doesn't comfort you yet.

But you'll learn.

# DOWN AMONG THE DEAD MEN

..........................

*Gardner Dozois and*

*Jack Dann*

Bruckman first discovered that Wernecke was a vampire when they went to the quarry that morning.

He was bending down to pick up a large rock when he thought he heard something in the gully nearby. He looked around and saw Wernecke huddled over a *Musselmänn*, one of the walking dead, a new man who had not been able to wake up to the terrible reality of the camp.

"Do you need any help?" Bruckman asked Wernecke in a low voice.

Wernecke looked up, startled, and covered his mouth with his hand, as if he were signing to Bruckman to be quiet.

But Bruckman was certain that he had glimpsed blood smeared on Wernecke's mouth. "The *Musselmänn*, is he alive?" Wernecke had often risked his own life to save one or another of the men in his barracks. But to risk one's life for a *Musselmänn*? "What's wrong?"

"Get away."

All right, Bruckman thought. Best to leave him alone. He looked pale, perhaps it was typhus. The guards were working him hard enough, and Wernecke was older than the rest of the men in the work gang. Let him sit for a moment and rest. But what about that blood . . . ?

"Hey, you, what are you doing?" one of the young SS guards shouted to Bruckman.

Bruckman picked up the rock, and, as if he had not heard the guard, began to walk away from the gully, toward the rusty brown cart on the tracks that led back to the barbed-wire fence of the camp. He would try to draw the guard's attention away from Wernecke.

But the guard shouted at him to halt. "Were you taking a little rest, is that it?" he asked, and Bruckman tensed, ready for a beating. This guard was new, neatly and cleanly dressed—and an unknown quantity. He walked over to the gully and, seeing Wernecke and the *Musselmänn*, said, "Aha, so your friend is taking care of the sick." He motioned Bruckman to follow him into the gully.

Bruckman had done the unpardonable—he had brought it on Wernecke. He swore at himself. He had been in this camp long enough to know to keep his mouth shut.

The guard kicked Wernecke sharply in the ribs. "I want you to put the *Musselmänn* in the cart. Now!" He kicked Wernecke again, as if as an afterthought. Wernecke groaned, but got to his feet. "Help him put the *Musselmänn* in the cart," the guard said to Bruckman; then he smiled and drew a circle in the air—the sign of smoke, the smoke which rose from the tall gray chimneys behind them. This *Musselmänn* would be in the oven within an hour, his ashes soon to be floating in the hot, stale air, as if they were the very particles of his soul.

Wernecke kicked the *Musselmänn*, and the guard chuckled, waved to another guard who had been watching, and stepped back a few feet. He stood with his hands on his hips. "Come on, dead man, get up or you're going to die in the oven," Wernecke whispered as he tried to pull the man to his feet. Bruckman supported the unsteady *Musselmänn*, who began to wail softly. Wernecke slapped him hard. "Do you want to live, *Musselmänn*? Do you want to see your family again, feel the touch of a woman, smell grass after it's been mowed? Then *move.*" The *Musselmänn* shambled forward between Wernecke and Bruckman. "You're dead, aren't you, *Musselmänn*," goaded Wernecke. "As dead as your father and mother, as dead as your sweet wife, if you ever had one, aren't you? Dead!"

The *Musselmänn* groaned, shook his head, and whispered, "Not dead, my wife. . . ."

"Ah, it talks," Wernecke said, loud enough so the guard walking a step behind them could hear. "Do you have a name, corpse?"

"Josef, and I'm not a *Musselmänn.*"

"The corpse says he's alive," Wernecke said, again loud enough for the SS guard to hear. Then in a whisper, he said, "Josef, if you're not a *Musselmänn*, then you must work now, do you understand?" Josef tripped, and Bruckman caught him. "Let him be," said Wernecke. "Let him walk to the cart himself."

"Not the cart," Josef mumbled. "Not to die, not—"

"Then get down and pick up stones, show the fart-eating guard you can work."

"Can't. I'm sick, I'm . . ."

"*Musselmänn!*"

Josef bent down, fell to his knees, but took hold of a stone and stood up with it.

"You see," Wernecke said to the guard, "it's not dead yet. It can still work."

"I told you to carry him to the cart, didn't I," the guard said petulantly.

"Show him you can work," Wernecke said to Josef, "or you'll surely be smoke."

And Josef stumbled away from Wernecke and Bruckman, leaning forward, as if following the rock he was carrying.

"Bring him *back!*" shouted the guard, but his attention was distracted from Josef by some other prisoners, who, sensing the trouble, began to mill about. One of the other guards began to shout and kick at the men on the periphery, and the new guard joined him. For the moment, he had forgotten about Josef.

"Let's get to work, lest they notice us again," Wernecke said.

"I'm sorry that I—"

Wernecke laughed and made a fluttering gesture with his hand—smoke rising. "It's all hazard, my friend. All luck."

Again the laugh. "It was a venial sin," and his face seemed to darken. "Never do it again, though, lest I think of you as bad luck."

"Eduard, are you all right?" Bruckman asked. "I noticed some blood when—"

"Do the sores on your feet bleed in the morning?" Wernecke countered angrily. Bruckman nodded, feeling foolish and embarrassed. "And so it is with my gums, now go away, unlucky one, and let me live."

They separated, and Bruckman tried to make himself invisible, tried to think himself into the rocks and sand and grit, into the choking air. He used to play this game as a child; he would close his eyes, and since *he* couldn't see anybody, he would pretend that nobody could see him. And so it was again. Pretending the guards couldn't see him was as good a way of staying alive as any.

He owed Wernecke another apology, which could not be made. He shouldn't have asked about Wernecke's sickness. It was bad luck to talk about such things. Wernecke had told him that when he, Bruckman, had first come to the barracks. If it weren't for Wernecke, who had shared his rations with Bruckman, he might well have become a *Musselmänn* himself. Or dead, which was the same thing.

The day turned blisteringly hot, and guards as well as prisoners were coughing. The air was foul, the sun a smear in the heavy yellow sky. The colors were all wrong: the ash from the ovens changed the light, and they were all slowly choking on the ashes of dead friends, wives, and parents. The guards stood together quietly, talking in low voices, watching the prisoners, and there was the sense of a perverse freedom—as if both guards and prisoners had fallen out of time, as if they were all parts of the same fleshy machine.

At dusk, the guards broke the hypnosis of lifting and grunting and sweating and formed the prisoners into ranks. They marched back to the camp through the fields, beside the railroad tracks, the electrified wire, conical towers, and into the main gate of the camp.

Bruckman tried to block out a dangerous stray thought of his wife. He remembered her as if he were hallucinating: she was in his arms. The boxcar stank of sweat and feces and urine, but he had been inside it for so long that he was used to the smells. Miriam had been sleeping. Suddenly he discovered that she was dead. As he screamed, the smells of the car overpowered him, the smells of death.

Wernecke touched his arm, as if he knew, as if he could see through Bruckman's eyes. And Bruckman knew what Wernecke's eyes were saying: "Another day. We're alive. Against all the odds. We conquered death." Josef walked beside them, but he kept stumbling, as he was once again slipping back into death, becoming a *Musselmänn*. Wernecke helped him walk, pushed him along. "We should let this man become dead," Wernecke said to Bruckman.

Bruckman only nodded, but he felt a chill sweep over his sweating back. He was seeing Wernecke's face again as it was for that instant in the morning. Smeared with blood.

Yes, Bruckman thought, we should let the *Musselmänn* become dead. We should all be dead. . . .

Wernecke served up the lukewarm water with bits of spoiled turnip floating on the top, what passed as soup for the prisoners. Everyone sat or kneeled on the rough-planked floor, as there were no chairs.

Bruckman ate his portion, counting the sips and the bites, forcing himself to take his time. Later, he would take a very small bite of the bread he had in his pocket. He always saved a small morsel of food for later—in the endless world of the camp, he had learned to give himself things to look forward to. Better to dream of bread than to get lost in the present. That was the fate of the *Musselmänner*.

But he always dreamed of food. Hunger was with him every moment of the day and night. Those times when he actually ate were in a way the most difficult, for there was never enough to satisfy him. There was the taste of softness in his mouth, and then in an instant it was gone. The emptiness took the form of pain—it *hurt* to eat. For bread, he thought, he would have killed his father, or his wife, God forgive me, and he watched Wernecke—Wernecke, who had shared his bread with him, who had died a little so he could live. He's a better man than me, Bruckman thought.

It was dim inside the barracks. A bare lightbulb hung from the ceiling and cast sharp shadows across the cavernous room. Two tiers of five-foot-deep shelves ran around the room on three sides, bare wooden shelves where the men slept without blankets or mattresses. Set high in the northern wall was a slatted window, which let in the stark white light of the kliegs. Outside, the lights turned the ground into a deathly imitation of day; only inside the barracks was it night.

"Do you know what tonight is, my friends?" Wernecke asked. He sat in the far corner of the room with Josef, who, hour by hour, was reverting back into a *Musselmänn*. Wernecke's face looked hollow and drawn in the light from the window and the lightbulb; his eyes were deep-set and his face was long with deep creases running from his nose to the corners of his thin mouth. His hair was black, and even since Bruckman had known him, quite a bit of it had fallen out. He was a very tall man, almost six foot four, and that made him stand out in a crowd, which was dangerous in a death camp. But Wernecke had his own secret ways of blending with the crowd, of making himself invisible.

"No, tell us what tonight is," crazy old Bohme said. That men such as Bohme could survive was a miracle—or, as Bruckman thought—a testament to men such as Wernecke, who somehow found the strength to help the others live.

"It's Passover," Wernecke said.

"How does he know that?" someone mumbled, but it didn't matter how Wernecke knew, because he *knew*—even if it really wasn't Passover by the calendar. In this dimly lit barracks, it *was* Passover, the feast of freedom, the time of thanksgiving.

"But how can we have Passover without a *seder?*" asked Bohme. "We don't even have any *matzoh*," he whined.

"Nor do we have candles, or a silver cup for Elijah, or the shank bone, or *haroset*—nor would I make a *seder* over the *traif* the Nazis are so generous in giving us," replied Wernecke with a smile. "But we can pray, can't we? And when we all get out of here, when we're in our own homes in the coming years with God's help, then we'll have twice as much food—two *afikomens*, a bottle of wine for Elijah, and the *haggadahs* that our fathers and our fathers' fathers used."

It *was* Passover.

"Isadore, do you remember the four questions?" Wernecke asked Bruckman.

And Bruckman heard himself speaking. He was twelve years old again at the long table beside his father, who sat in the seat of honor. To sit next to him was itself an honor. "How does this night differ from all other nights? On all other nights we eat bread and *matzoh*; why on this night do we eat only *matzoh*?"

"*M'a nisht'ana halylah hazeah. . . .*"

Sleep would not come to Bruckman that night, although he was so tired that he felt as if the marrow of his bones had been sucked away and replaced with lead.

He lay there in the semidarkness, feeling his muscles ache, feeling the acid biting of his hunger. Usually he was numb enough with exhaustion that he could empty his mind, close himself down, and fall rapidly into oblivion, but not tonight. Tonight he was *noticing* things again, his surroundings were getting through to him again, in a way that they had not since he had been new in the camp. It was smotheringly hot, and the air was filled with the stinks of death and sweat and fever, of stale urine and drying blood. The sleepers thrashed and turned, as though they fought with sleep, and as they slept, many of them talked or muttered or screamed aloud; they lived other lives in their dreams, intensely compressed lives dreamed quickly, for soon it would be dawn, and once more they would be thrust into hell. Cramped in the midst of them, sleepers squeezed in all around him, it suddenly seemed to Bruckman that these pallid white bodies were already dead, that he was sleeping in a graveyard. Suddenly it was the boxcar again. And his wife Miriam was dead again, dead and rotting unburied. . . .

Resolutely, Bruckman emptied his mind. He felt feverish and shaky, and wondered if the typhus was coming back, but he couldn't afford to worry about it. Those who couldn't sleep couldn't survive. Regulate your breathing, force your muscles to relax, don't think. Don't think.

For some reason, after he had managed to banish even the memory of his dead wife, he couldn't shake the image of the blood on Wernecke's mouth.

There were other images mixed in with it—Wernecke's uplifted arms and upturned face as he led them in prayer, the pale strained face of the stumbling *Musselmänn*, Wernecke looked up, startled, as he crouched over Josef—but it was the blood to which Bruckman's feverish thoughts returned, and he pictured it again and again as he lay in the rustling, fart-smelling darkness: the watery sheen of blood over Wernecke's lips, the tarry trickle of blood in the corner of his mouth, like a tiny scarlet worm. . . .

Just then a shadow crossed in front of the window, silhouetted blackly for an instant against the harsh white glare, and Bruckman knew from the shadow's height and its curious forward stoop that it was Wernecke.

Where could he be going? Sometimes a prisoner would be unable to wait until morning, when the Germans would let them out to visit the slit-trench latrine again, and would slink shamefacedly into a far corner to piss against a wall, but surely Wernecke was too much of an old hand for that. . . . Most of the prisoners slept on the sleeping platforms, especially during the cold nights when they would huddle together for warmth, but sometimes during the hot weather, people would drift away and sleep on the floor instead; Bruckman himself had been thinking of doing that, as the jostling bodies of the sleepers around him helped to keep him from sleep. Perhaps Wernecke, who always had trouble fitting into the cramped sleeping niches, was merely looking for a place where he could lie down and stretch his legs. . . .

Then Bruckman remembered that Josef had fallen asleep in the corner of the room where Wernecke had sat and prayed, and that they had left him there alone.

Without knowing why, Bruckman found himself on his feet. As silently as the ghost he sometimes felt he was becoming, he walked across the room in the direction Wernecke had gone, not understanding what he was doing or why he was doing it. The face of the *Musselmänn*, Josef, seemed to float behind his eyes. Bruckman's feet hurt, and he knew, without looking, that they were bleeding, leaving faint tracks behind him. It was dimmer here in the far corner, away from the window, but Bruckman knew that he must be near the wall by now, and he stopped to let his eyes readjust.

When his eyes had adapted to the dimmer light, he saw Josef sitting on the floor, propped up against the wall. Wernecke was hunched over the *Musselmänn*. Kissing him. One of Josef's hands was tangled in Wernecke's thinning hair.

Before Bruckman could react—such things had been known to happen once or twice before, although it shocked him deeply that *Wernecke* would be involved in such filth—Josef released his grip on Wernecke's hair. Josef's upraised arm fell limply to the side, his hand hitting the floor with a muffled but solid impact that should have been painful—but Josef made no sound.

Wernecke straightened up and turned around. Stronger light from the high window caught him as he straightened to his full height, momentarily illuminating his face.

Wernecke's mouth was smeared with blood.

"My God!" Bruckman cried.

Startled, Wernecke flinched, then took two quick steps forward and seized Bruckman by the arm. "Quiet!" Wernecke hissed. His fingers were cold and hard.

At that moment, as though Wernecke's sudden movement were a cue, Josef began to slip down sideways along the wall. As Wernecke and Bruckman watched, both momentarily riveted by the sight, Josef toppled over to the floor, his head striking against the floorboards with a sound such as a dropped melon might make. He had made no attempt to break his fall or cushion his head, and lay now unmoving.

"My *God*," Bruckman said again.

"Quiet, I'll explain," Wernecke said, his lips still glazed with the *Musselmänn*'s blood. "Do you want to ruin us all? For the love of God, be *quiet*."

But Bruckman had shaken free of Wernecke's grip and

crossed to kneel by Josef, leaning over him as Wernecke had done, placing a hand flat on Josef's chest for a moment, then touching the side of Josef's neck. Bruckman looked slowly up at Wernecke. "He's dead," Bruckman said, more quietly.

Wernecke squatted on the other side of Josef's body, and the rest of their conversation was carried out in whispers over Josef's chest, like friends conversing at the sickbed of another friend who has finally fallen into a fitful doze.

"Yes, he's dead," Wernecke said. "He was dead yesterday, wasn't he? Today he has just stopped walking." His eyes were hidden here, in the deeper shadow nearer to the floor, but there was still enough light for Bruckman to see that Wernecke had wiped his lips clean. Or licked them clean, Bruckman thought, and felt a spasm of nausea go through him.

"But *you*," Bruckman said, haltingly. "You were . . ."

"Drinking his blood?" Wernecke said. "Yes, I was drinking his blood."

Bruckman's mind was numb. He couldn't deal with this, he couldn't understand it at all. "But *why*, Eduard? Why?"

"To live, of course. Why do any of us do anything here? If I am to live, I must have blood. Without it, I'd face a death even more certain than that doled out by the Nazis."

Bruckman opened and closed his mouth, but no sound came out, as if the words he wished to speak were too jagged to fit through his throat. At last he managed to croak, "A vampire? You're a vampire? Like in the old stories?"

Wernecke said calmly, "Men would call me that." He paused, then nodded. "Yes, that's what men would call me. . . . As though they can understand something simply by giving it a name."

"But Eduard," Bruckman said weakly, almost petulantly. "The *Musselmänn* . . ."

"Remember that he *was* a *Musselmänn*," Wernecke said, leaning forward and speaking more fiercely. "His strength was going, he was sinking. He would have been dead by morning, anyway. I took from him something that he no longer needed, but that I needed in order to live. Does it matter? Starving men in lifeboats have eaten the bodies of their dead companions in order to live. Is what I've done any worse than that?"

"But he didn't just die. You *killed* him. . . ."

Wernecke was silent for a moment, and then said, quietly, "What better thing could I have done for him? I won't apologize for what I do, Isadore; I do what I have to do to live. Usually I take only a little blood from a number of men, just enough to survive. And that's fair, isn't it? Haven't I given food to others, to help them survive? To *you*, Isadore? Only very rarely do I take more than a minimum from any one man, although I'm weak and hungry all the time, believe me. And never have I drained the life from someone who wished to live. Instead I've helped them fight for survival in every way I can, you know that."

He reached out as though to touch Bruckman, then thought better of it and put his hand back on his own knee. He shook his head. "But these *Musselmänner*, the ones who have given up on life, the walking dead—it is a favor to them to take them, to give them the solace of death. Can you honestly say that it is not, *here*? That it is better for them to walk around while they are dead, being beaten and abused by the Nazis until their bodies cannot go on, and then to be thrown into the ovens and burned like trash? Can you say that? Would *they* say that, if they knew what was going on? Or would they thank me?"

Wernecke suddenly stood up, and Bruckman stood up with him. As Wernecke's face came again into the stronger light, Bruckman could see that his eyes had filled with tears. "You have lived under the Nazis," Wernecke said. "Can you really call *me* a monster? Aren't I still a Jew, whatever else I might be? Aren't I *here*, in a death camp? Aren't I being persecuted too, as much as any other? Aren't I in as much danger as anyone else? If I'm not a Jew, then tell the Nazis—they seem to think so." He paused for a moment, and then smiled wryly. "And forget your superstitious bogey tales. I'm no night spirit. If I could turn myself into a bat and fly away from here, I would have done it long before now, believe me."

Bruckman smiled reflexively, then grimaced. The two men avoided each other's eyes, Bruckman looking at the floor, and there was an uneasy silence, punctuated only by the sighing and moaning of the sleepers on the other side of the cabin. Then, without looking up, in tacit surrender, Bruckman said, "What about *him?* The Nazis will find the body and cause trouble. . . ."

"Don't worry," Wernecke said. "There are no obvious marks. And nobody performs autopsies in a death camp. To the Nazis, he'll be just another Jew who has died of the heat, or from starvation or sickness, or from a broken heart."

Bruckman raised his head then and they stared eye to eye for a moment. Even knowing what he knew, Bruckman found it hard to see Wernecke as anything other than what he appeared to be: an aging, balding Jew, stooping and thin, with sad eyes and a tired, compassionate face.

"Well, then, Isadore," Wernecke said at last, matter-of-factly. "My life is in your hands. I will not be indelicate enough to remind you of how many times your life has been in mine."

Then he was gone, walking back toward the sleeping platforms, a shadow soon lost among other shadows.

Bruckman stood by himself in the gloom for a long time, and then followed him. It took all of his will not to look back over his shoulder at the corner where Josef lay, and even so Bruckman imagined that he could feel Josef's dead eyes watching him, watching him reproachfully as he walked away, abandoning Josef to the cold and isolate company of the dead.

Bruckman got no more sleep that night, and in the morning, when the Nazis shattered the gray predawn stillness by bursting into the shack with shouts and shrilling whistles and barking police dogs, he felt as if he were a thousand years old.

They were formed into two lines, shivering in the raw morning air, and marched off to the quarry. The clammy dawn mist had yet to burn off, and, marching through it, through a white shadowless void, with only the back of the man in front of him dimly visible, Bruckman felt more than ever like a ghost, suspended bodiless in some limbo between Heaven and Earth. Only the bite of pebbles and cinders into his raw, bleeding feet kept him anchored to the world, and he clung to the pain as a lifeline, fighting to shake off a feeling of numbness and unreality. However strange, however outré, the events of the previous night had *happened*. To doubt it, to wonder now if it had all been a feverish dream brought on by starvation and exhaustion, was to take the first step on the road to becoming a *Musselmänn*.

Wernecke is a vampire, he told himself. That was the harsh, unyielding reality that, like the reality of the camp itself, must be faced. Was it any more surreal, any more impossible, than the nightmare around them? He must forget the tales his old grandmother had told him as a boy, "bogey tales" as Wernecke himself had called them, half-remembered tales that turned his knees to water whenever he thought of the blood smeared on Wernecke's mouth, whenever he thought of Wernecke's eyes watching him in the dark. . . .

"Wake up, Jew!" the guard alongside him snarled, whacking him lightly on the arm with his rifle butt. Bruckman stumbled, managed to stay upright and keep going. Yes, he thought, wake up. Wake up to the reality of this, just as you once had to wake up to the reality of the camp. It was just one more unpleasant fact he would have to adapt to, learn to deal with. . . .

Deal with how? he thought, and shivered.

By the time they reached the quarry, the mist had burned off, swirling past them in rags and tatters, and it was already beginning to get hot. There was Wernecke, his balding head gleaming dully in the harsh morning light. He didn't dissolve in the sunlight, there was one bogey tale disproved. . . .

They set to work, like golems, like ragtag clockwork automatons.

Lack of sleep had drained what small reserves of strength Bruckman had, and the work was very hard for him that day. He had learned long ago all the tricks of timing and misdirection, the safe ways to snatch short moments of rest, the ways to do a minimum of work with the maximum display of effort, the ways to keep the guards from noticing you, to fade into the faceless crowd of prisoners and not be singled out, but today his head was muzzy and slow, and none of the tricks seemed to work.

His body felt like a sheet of glass, fragile, ready to shatter into dust, and the painful, arthritic slowness of his movements got him first shouted at, and then knocked down. The guard kicked him twice for good measure before he could get up.

When Bruckman had climbed back to his feet again, he saw that Wernecke was watching him, face blank, eyes expressionless, a look that could have meant anything at all.

Bruckman felt the blood trickling from the corner of his mouth and thought, *the blood . . . he's watching the blood . . .* and once again he shivered.

Somehow, Bruckman forced himself to work faster, and although his muscles blazed with pain, he wasn't hit again, and the day passed.

When they formed up to go back to the camp, Bruckman, almost unconsciously, made sure that he was in a different line from Wernecke.

That night in the cabin, Bruckman watched as Wernecke talked with the other men, here trying to help a new man named Melnick—no more than a boy—adjust to the dreadful reality of the camp, there exhorting someone who was slipping into despair to live and spite his tormentors, joking with old hands in the flat, black, bitter way that passed for humor among them, eliciting a wan smile or occasionally even a laugh from them, finally leading them all in prayer again, his strong, calm voice raised in the ancient words, giving meaning to those words again. . . .

He keeps us together, Bruckman thought, he keeps us going. Without him, we wouldn't last a week. Surely that's worth a little blood, a bit from each man, not even enough to hurt. . . . Surely they wouldn't even begrudge him it, if they knew and really understood. . . . No, he *is* a good man, better than the rest of us, in spite of his terrible affliction.

Bruckman had been avoiding Wernecke's eyes, hadn't spoken to him at all that day, and suddenly felt a wave of shame go through him at the thought of how shabbily he had been treating his friend. Yes, his *friend*, regardless, the man who had saved his life. . . . Deliberately, he caught Wernecke's eyes, and nodded, and then somewhat sheepishly, smiled. After a moment, Wernecke smiled back, and Bruckman felt a spreading warmth and relief uncoil his guts. Everything was going to be all right, as all right as it could be, here. . . .

Nevertheless, as soon as the inside lights clicked off that night, and Bruckman found himself lying alone in the darkness, his flesh began to crawl.

He had been unable to keep his eyes open a moment before, but now, in the sudden darkness, he found himself tensely and tickingly awake. Where was Wernecke? What was he doing, who was he visiting tonight? Was he out there in the darkness even now, creeping closer, creeping nearer . . . ? Stop it, Bruckman told himself uneasily, forget the bogey tales. This is your friend, a good man, not a monster. . . . But he couldn't control the fear that made the small hairs on his arms stand bristlingly erect, couldn't stop the grisly images from coming. . . .

Wernecke's eyes, gleaming in the darkness. . . . Was the blood already glistening on Wernecke's lips, as he drank . . . ? The thought of the blood staining Wernecke's yellowing teeth made Bruckman cold and nauseous, but the image that he couldn't get out of his mind tonight was an image of Josef toppling over in that sinisterly boneless way, striking his head against the floor. . . . Bruckman had seen people die in many more gruesome ways during his time at the camp, seen people shot, beaten to death, seen them die in convulsions from high fevers or cough their lungs up in bloody tatters from pneumonia, seen them hanging like charred-black scarecrows from the electrified fences, seen them torn apart by dogs . . . but somehow it was Josef's soft, passive, almost restful slumping into death that bothered him. That, and the obscene limpness of Josef's limbs as he sprawled there like a discarded rag doll, his pale and haggard face gleaming reproachfully in the dark. . . .

When Bruckman could stand it no longer, he got shakily to his feet and moved off through the shadows, once again not knowing where he was going or what he was going to do, but drawn forward by some obscure instinct he himself did not understand. This time he went cautiously, feeling his way and trying to be silent, expecting every second to see Wernecke's coal-black shadow rise up before him.

He paused, a faint noise scratching at his ears, then went on again, even more cautiously, crouching low, almost crawling across the grimy floor.

Whatever instinct had guided him—sounds heard and interpreted subliminally, perhaps?—it had timed his arrival well. Wernecke had someone down on the floor there, perhaps someone he had seized and dragged away from the huddled mass of sleepers on one of the sleeping platforms, someone from the outer edge of bodies whose presence would not be missed, or perhaps someone who had gone to sleep on the floor, seeking solitude or greater comfort.

Whoever he was, he struggled in Wernecke's grip, but Wernecke handled him easily, almost negligently, in a manner that spoke of great physical power. Bruckman could hear the man trying to scream, but Wernecke had one hand on his throat, half-throttling him, and all that would come out was a sort of whistling gasp. The man thrashed in Wernecke's hands like a kite in a child's hands flapping in the wind, and, moving deliberately, Wernecke smoothed him out like a kite, pressing him slowly flat on the floor.

Then Wernecke bent over him, and lowered his mouth to his throat.

Bruckman watched in horror, knowing that he should shout, scream, try to rouse the other prisoners, but somehow unable to move, unable to make his mouth open, his lungs pump. He was paralyzed by fear, like a rabbit in the presence of a predator, a terror sharper and more intense than any he'd ever known.

The man's struggles were growing weaker, and Wernecke must have eased up some on the throttling pressure of his hand, because the man moaned "Don't . . . please don't . . ." in a weak, slurred voice. The man had been drumming his fists against Wernecke's back and sides, but now the tempo of the drumming slowed, slowed, and then stopped, the man's arms falling laxly to the floor. "Don't . . ." the man whispered; he groaned and muttered incomprehensibly for a moment or two longer, then became silent. The silence stretched out for a minute, two, three, and Wernecke still crouched over his victim, who was now not moving at all. . . .

Wernecke stirred, a kind of shudder going through him, like a cat stretching. He stood up. His face became visible as he straightened up into the full light from the window, and there was blood on it, glistening black under the harsh glare of the kliegs. As Bruckman watched, Wernecke began to lick his lips clean, his tongue, also black in this light, sliding like some sort of sinuous ebony snake around the rim of his mouth, darting and probing for the last lingering drops. . . .

How smug he looks, Bruckman thought, like a cat who has found the cream, and the anger that flashed through him at the thought enabled him to move and speak again. "Wernecke," he said harshly.

Wernecke glanced casually in his direction. "You again, Isadore?" Wernecke said. "Don't you ever sleep?" Wernecke spoke lazily, quizzically, without surprise, and Bruckman wondered if Wernecke had known all along that he was there. "Or do you just enjoy watching me?"

"Lies," Bruckman said. "You told me nothing but *lies*. Why did you bother?"

"You were excited," Wernecke said. "You had surprised me. It seemed best to tell you what you wanted to hear. If it satisfied you, then that was an easy solution to the problem."

" 'Never have I drained the life from someone who wanted to live,' " Bruckman said bitterly, mimicking Wernecke. " 'Only a little from each man.' My God—and I believed you! I even felt sorry for you!"

Wernecke shrugged. "Most of it *was* true. Usually I only take a little from each man, softly and carefully, so that they never know, so that in the morning they are only a little weaker than they would have been anyway. . . ."

"Like Josef?" Bruckman said angrily. "Like the poor devil you killed tonight?"

Wernecke shrugged again. "I have been careless the last few nights, I admit. But I need to build up my strength again." His eyes gleamed in the darkness. "Events are coming to a head here. Can't you feel it, Isadore, can't you sense it? Soon the war will be over, everyone knows that. Before then, this camp will be shut down, and the Nazis will move us back into the interior—either that, or kill us. I have grown weak here, and I will soon need all my strength to survive, to take whatever opportunity presents itself to escape. I *must* be ready. And so I have let myself drink deeply again, drink my fill for the first time in months. . . ." Wernecke licked his lips again, perhaps unconsciously, then smiled bleakly at Bruckman. "You don't appreciate my restraint, Isadore. You don't understand how hard it has been for me to hold back, to take only a little each night. You don't understand how much that restraint has cost me. . . ."

"You are gracious," Bruckman sneered.

Wernecke laughed. "No, but I am a rational man; I pride myself on that. You other prisoners were my only source of food, and I have had to be very careful to make sure that you would last. I have no access to the *Nazis*, after all. I *am* trapped here, a prisoner just like you, whatever else you may believe— and I have not only had to find ways to survive here in the camp, I have had to procure my own food as well! No shepherd has ever watched over his flock more tenderly than I."

"Is that all we are to you—sheep? Animals to be slaughtered?"

Wernecke smiled. "Precisely."

When he could control his voice enough to speak, Bruckman said, "You're worse than the Nazis."

"I hardly think so," Wernecke said quietly, and for a moment he looked tired, as though something unimaginably old and unutterably weary had looked out through his eyes. "This camp was built by the Nazis—it wasn't *my* doing. The Nazis sent you here—not I. The Nazis have tried to kill you every day since, in one way or another—and I have tried to keep you alive, even at some risk to myself. No one has more of a vested interest in the survival of his livestock than the farmer, after all, even if he does occasionally slaughter an inferior animal. I have given you food—"

"Food you had no use for yourself! You sacrificed nothing!"

"That's true, of course. But *you* needed it, remember that.

Whatever my motives, I have helped you to survive here—you and many others. By doing so I also acted in my own self-interest, of course, but can you have experienced this camp and still believe in things like altruism? What difference does it make what my reason for helping was—I still helped you, didn't I?"

"Sophistries!" Bruckman said. "Rationalizations! You twist words to justify yourself, but you can't disguise what you really are—a monster!"

Wernecke smiled gently, as though Bruckman's words amused him, and made as if to pass by, but Bruckman raised an arm to bar his way. They did not touch each other, but Wernecke stopped short, and a new and quivering kind of tension sprang into existence in the air between them.

"I'll stop you," Bruckman said. "Somehow I'll stop you, I'll keep you from doing this terrible thing—"

"You'll do nothing," Wernecke said. His voice was hard and cold and flat, like a rock speaking. "What can you do? Tell the other prisoners? Who would believe you? They'd think you'd gone insane. Tell the *Nazis*, then?" Wernecke laughed harshly. "They'd think you'd gone crazy too, and they'd take you to the hospital—and I don't have to tell you what your chances of getting out of there alive are, do I? No, you'll do *nothing*."

Wernecke took a step forward; his eyes were shiny and blank and hard, like ice, like the pitiless eyes of a predatory bird, and Bruckman felt a sick rush of fear cut through his anger. Bruckman gave way, stepping backward involuntarily, and Wernecke pushed past him, seeming to brush him aside without touching him.

Once past, Wernecke turned to stare at Bruckman, and Bruckman had to summon up all the defiance that remained in him not to look uneasily away from Wernecke's agate-hard eyes. "You are the strongest and cleverest of all the other animals, Isadore," Wernecke said in a calm, conversational, almost ruminative voice. "You have been useful to me. Every shepherd needs a good sheepdog. I still need you, to help me manage the others, and to help me keep them going long enough to serve my needs. This is the reason why I have taken so much time with you, instead of just killing you outright." He shrugged. "So let us both be rational about this—you leave me alone, Isadore, and I will leave you alone also. We will stay away from each other and look after our own affairs. Yes?"

"The others . . ." Bruckman said weakly.

"They must look after themselves," Wernecke said. He smiled, a thin and almost invisible motion of his lips. "What did I teach you, Isadore? Here everyone must look after themselves. What difference does it make what happens to the others? In a few weeks almost all of them will be dead anyway."

"You *are* a monster," Bruckman said.

"I'm not much different from you, Isadore. The strong survive, whatever the cost."

"I am *nothing* like you," Bruckman said, with loathing.

"No?" Wernecke asked, ironically, and moved away; within a few paces he was hobbling and stooping, vanishing into the shadows, once more the harmless old Jew.

Bruckman stood motionless for a moment, and then, moving slowly and reluctantly, he stepped across to where Wernecke's victim lay.

It was one of the new men Wernecke had been talking to earlier in the evening, and, of course, he was quite dead.

Shame and guilt took Bruckman then, emotions he thought he had forgotten—black and strong and bitter, they shook him by the throat the way Wernecke had shaken the new man.

Bruckman couldn't remember returning across the room to his sleeping platform, but suddenly he was there, lying on his back and staring into the stifling darkness, surrounded by the moaning, thrashing, stinking mass of sleepers. His hands were clasped protectively over his throat, although he couldn't remember putting them there, and he was shivering convulsively. How many mornings had he awoken with a dull ache in his neck, thinking it no more than the habitual body-aches and strained muscles they had all learned to take for granted? How many nights had Wernecke fed on *him?*

Every time Bruckman closed his eyes, he would see Wernecke's face floating there in the luminous darkness behind his eyelids . . . Wernecke with his eyes half-closed, his face vulpine

and cruel and satiated . . . Wernecke's face moving closer and
closer to him, his eyes opening like black pits, his lips smiling
back from his teeth . . . Wernecke's lips, sticky and red with
blood . . . and then Bruckman would seem to feel the wet touch
of Wernecke's lips on *his* throat, feel Wernecke's teeth biting
into *his* flesh, and Bruckman's eyes would fly open again. Staring into the darkness. Nothing there. Nothing there *yet*. . . .

Dawn was a dirty gray imminence against the cabin window
before Bruckman could force himself to lower his shielding
arms from his throat, and once again he had not slept at all.

That day's work was a nightmare of pain and exhaustion for
Bruckman, harder than anything he had known since his first
few days at the camp. Somehow he forced himself to get up,
somehow he stumbled outside and up the path to the quarry,
seeming to float along high off the ground, his head a bloated
balloon, his feet a thousand miles away at the end of boneless
beanstalk legs he could barely control at all. Twice he fell, and
was kicked several times before he could drag himself back to
his feet and lurch forward again. The sun was coming up in
front of them, a hard red disk in a sickly yellow sky, and to
Bruckman it seemed to be a glazed and lidless eye staring dispassionately into the world to watch them flail and struggle and
die, like the eye of a scientist peering into a laboratory maze.

He watched the disk of the sun as he stumbled toward it; it
seemed to bob and shimmer with every painful step, expanding, swelling and bloating until it swallowed the sky. . . .

Then he was picking up a rock, moaning with the effort,
feeling the rough stone tear his hands. . . .

Reality began to slide away from Bruckman. There were long
periods when the world was blank, and he would come slowly
back to himself as if from a great distance, and hear his own
voice speaking words that he could not understand, or keening
mindlessly, or grunting in a hoarse, animalistic way, and he
would find that his body was working mechanically, stooping
and lifting and carrying, all without volition. . . .

A *Musselmänn*, Bruckman thought, I'm becoming a *Musselmänn* . . . and felt a chill of fear sweep through him. He fought

to hold onto the world, afraid that the next time he slipped away from himself he would not come back, deliberately banging his hands into the rocks, cutting himself, clearing his head with pain.

The world steadied around him. A guard shouted a hoarse admonishment at him and slapped his rifle butt, and Bruckman forced himself to work faster, although he could not keep himself from weeping silently with the pain his movements cost him.

He discovered that Wernecke was watching him, and stared back defiantly, the bitter tears still runneling his dirty cheeks, thinking, *I won't become a* Musselmänn *for you, I won't make it easy for you, I won't provide another helpless victim for you.* . . . Wernecke met Bruckman's gaze for a moment, and then shrugged and turned away.

Bruckman bent for another stone, feeling the muscles in his back crack and the pain drive in like knives. What had Wernecke been thinking, behind the blankness of his expressionless face? Had Wernecke, sensing his weakness, marked Bruckman for his next victim? Had Wernecke been disappointed or dismayed by the strength of Bruckman's will to survive? Would Wernecke now settle upon someone else?

The morning passed, and Bruckman grew feverish again. He could feel the fever in his face, making his eyes feel sandy and hot, pulling the skin taut over his cheekbones, and he wondered how long he could manage to stay on his feet. To falter, to grow weak and insensible, was certain death; if the Nazis didn't kill him, Wernecke would. . . . Wernecke was out of sight now, on the other side of the quarry, but it seemed to Bruckman that Wernecke's hard and flinty eyes were everywhere, floating in the air around him, looking out momentarily from the back of a Nazi soldier's head, watching him from the dulled iron side of a quarry cart, peering at him from a dozen different angles. He bent ponderously for another rock, and when he had pried it up from the earth he found Wernecke's eyes beneath it, staring unblinkingly up at him from the damp and pallid soil. . . .

That afternoon there were great flashes of light on the eastern horizon, out across the endless flat expanse of the steppe, flares in rapid sequence that lit up the sullen gray sky, all without sound. The Nazi guards had gathered together in a group, looking to the east and talking in subdued voices, ignoring the prisoners for the moment. For the first time Bruckman noticed how disheveled and unshaven the guards had become in the last few days, as though they had given up, as though they no longer cared. Their faces were strained and tight, and more than one of them seemed to be fascinated by the leaping fires on the distant edge of the world.

Melnick said that it was only a thunderstorm, but old Bohme said that it was an artillery battle being fought, and that that meant that the Russians were coming, that soon they would all be liberated.

Bohme grew so excited at the thought that he began shouting, "The Russians! It's the Russians! The Russians are coming to free us!" Dichstein and Melnick tried to hush him, but Bohme continued to caper and shout—doing a grotesque kind of jig while he yelled and flapped his arms—until he had attracted the attention of the guards. Infuriated, two of the guards fell upon Bohme and beat him severely, striking him with their rifle butts with more than usual force, knocking him to the ground, continuing to flail at him and kick him while he was down, Bohme writhing like an injured worm under their stamping boots. They probably would have beaten Bohme to death on the spot, but Wernecke organized a distraction among some of the other prisoners, and when the guards moved away to deal with it, Wernecke helped Bohme to stand up and hobble away to the other side of the quarry, where the rest of the prisoners shielded him from sight with their bodies as best they could for the rest of the afternoon.

Something about the way Wernecke urged Bohme to his feet and helped him to limp and lurch away, something about the protective, possessive curve of Wernecke's arm around Bohme's shoulders, told Bruckman that Wernecke had selected his next victim.

That night Bruckman vomited up the meager and rancid meal that they were allowed, his stomach convulsing uncontrollably after the first few bites. Trembling with hunger and exhaustion and fever, he leaned against the wall and watched as Wernecke fussed over Bohme, nursing him as a man might nurse a sick child, talking gently to him, wiping away some of the blood that still oozed from the corner of Bohme's mouth, coaxing Bohme to drink a few sips of soup, finally arranging that Bohme should stretch out on the floor away from the sleeping platforms, where he would not be jostled by the others. . . .

As soon as the interior lights went out that night, Bruckman got up, crossed the floor quickly and unhesitantly, and lay down in the shadows near the spot where Bohme muttered and twitched and groaned.

Shivering, Bruckman lay in the darkness, the strong smell of earth in his nostrils, waiting for Wernecke to come. . . .

In Bruckman's hand, held close to his chest, was a spoon that had been sharpened to a jagged needle point, a spoon he had stolen and begun to sharpen while he was still in a civilian prison in Cologne, so long ago that he almost couldn't remember, scraping it back and forth against the stone wall of his cell every night for hours, managing to keep it hidden on his person during the nightmarish ride in the sweltering boxcar, the first few terrible days at the camp, telling no one about it, not even Wernecke during the months when he'd thought of Wernecke as a kind of saint, keeping it hidden long after the possibility of escape had become too remote even to fantasize about, retaining it then more as a tangible link with the daydream country of his past than as a tool he ever actually hoped to employ, cherishing it almost as a holy relic, as a remnant of a vanished world that he otherwise might almost believe had never existed at all. . . .

And now that it was time to use it at last, he was almost reluctant to do so, to soil it with another man's blood. . . .

He fingered the spoon compulsively, turning it over and over; it was hard and smooth and cold, and he clenched it as tightly as he could, trying to ignore the fine tremoring of his hands.

He had to kill Wernecke. . . .

Nausea and an odd feeling of panic flashed through Bruckman at the thought, but there was no other choice, there was no other way. . . . He couldn't go on like this, his strength was failing; Wernecke was killing him, as surely as he had killed the others, just by keeping him from sleeping. . . . And as long as Wernecke lived, he would never be safe, always there would be the chance that Wernecke would come for *him*, that Wernecke would strike as soon as his guard was down. . . . Would Wernecke scruple for a second to kill *him*, after all, if he thought that he could do it safely . . . ? No, of course not. . . . Given the chance, Wernecke would kill him without a moment's further thought. . . . No, he must strike *first*. . . .

Bruckman licked his lips uneasily. Tonight. He had to kill Wernecke tonight. . . .

There was a stirring, a rustling: someone was getting up, working his way free from the mass of sleepers on one of the platforms. A shadowy figure crossed the room toward Bruckman, and Bruckman tensed, reflexively running his thumb along the jagged end of the spoon, readying himself to rise, to strike—but at the last second, the figure veered aside and stumbled toward another corner. There was a sound like rain drumming on cloth; the man swayed there for a moment, mumbling, and then slowly returned to his pallet, dragging his feet, as if he had pissed his very life away against the wall. It was not Wernecke.

Bruckman eased himself back down to the floor, his heart seeming to shake his wasted body back and forth with the force of its beating. His hand was damp with sweat. He wiped it against his tattered pants, and then clutched the spoon again. . . .

Time seemed to stop. Bruckman waited, stretched out along the hard floorboards, the raw wood rasping his skin, dust clogging his mouth and nose, feeling as though he were already dead, a corpse laid out in a rough pine coffin, feeling eternity pile up on his chest like heavy clots of wet black earth. . . . Outside the hut, the kliegs blazed, banishing night, abolishing it, but here inside the hut it was night, here night survived, perhaps the only pocket of night remaining on a klieg-lit planet, the shafts of light that came in through the slatted window only serving to accentuate the surrounding darkness, to make it greater and more puissant by comparison. . . . Here in the darkness, nothing ever changed . . . there was only the smothering heat, and the weight of eternal darkness, and the changeless moments that could not pass because there was nothing to differentiate them one from the other. . . .

Many times as he waited, Bruckman's eyes would grow heavy and slowly close, but each time his eyes would spring open again at once, and he would find himself staring into the shadows for Wernecke. Sleep would no longer have him, it was a kingdom closed to him now; it spat him out each time he tried to enter it, just as his stomach now spat out the food he placed in it. . . .

The thought of food brought Bruckman to a sharper awareness, and there in the darkness he huddled around his hunger, momentarily forgetting everything else. Never had he been so hungry. . . . He thought of the food he had wasted earlier in the evening, and only the last few shreds of his self-control kept him from moaning aloud.

Bohme did moan aloud then, as though unease were contagious. As Bruckman glanced at him, Bohme said "Anya," in a clear calm voice; he mumbled a little, and then, a bit more loudly, said, "Tseitel, have you set the table yet?" and Bruckman realized that Bohme was no longer in the camp, that Bohme was back in Düsseldorf in the tiny apartment with his fat wife and his four healthy children, and Bruckman felt a pang of envy go through him, for Bohme, who had escaped.

It was at that moment that Bruckman realized that Wernecke was standing there, just beyond Bohme.

There had been no movement that Bruckman had seen. Wernecke had seemed to slowly materialize from the darkness, atom by atom, bit by incremental bit, until at some point he had been solid enough for his presence to register on Bruckman's consciousness, so that what had been only a shadow a moment before was now suddenly and unmistakably Wernecke as well, however much a shadow it remained.

Bruckman's mouth went dry with terror, and it almost

seemed that he could hear the voice of his dead grandmother whispering in his ears. Bogey tales. . . . Wernecke had said *I'm no night spirit.* Remember that he had said that. . . .

Wernecke was almost close enough to touch. He was staring down at Bohme; his face, lit by a dusty shaft of light from the window, was cold and remote, only the total lack of expression hinting at the passion that strained and quivered behind the mask. Slowly, lingeringly, Wernecke stooped over Bohme. "Anya," Bohme said again, caressingly, and then Wernecke's mouth was on his throat.

Let him feed, said a cold remorseless voice in Bruckman's mind. It will be easier to take him when he's nearly sated, when he's fully preoccupied and growing lethargic and logy. . . . Growing *full.* . . .

Slowly, with infinite caution, Bruckman gathered himself to spring, watching in horror and fascination as Wernecke fed. He could hear Wernecke sucking the juice out of Bohme, as if there was not enough blood in the foolish old man to satiate him, as if there was not enough blood in the whole camp. . . . Or perhaps the whole world. . . . And now Bohme was ceasing his feeble struggling, was becoming still. . . .

Bruckman flung himself upon Wernecke, stabbing him twice in the back before his weight bowled them both over. There was a moment of confusion as they rolled and struggled together, all without sound, and then Bruckman found himself sitting atop Wernecke, Wernecke's white face turned up to him. Bruckman drove his weapon into Wernecke again, the shock of the blow jarring Bruckman's arm to the shoulder. Wernecke made no outcry; his eyes were already glazing, but they looked at Bruckman with recognition, with cold anger, with bitter irony, and, oddly, with what might have been resignation or relief, with what might almost have been pity. . . . Bruckman stabbed again and again, driving the blows home with hysterical strength, panting, rocking atop his victim, feeling Wernecke's blood splatter against his face, wrapped in the heat and steam that rose from Wernecke's torn-open body like a smothering black cloud, coughing and choking on it for a moment, feeling the steam seep in through his pores and sink deep into the marrow of his bones, feeling the world seem to pulse and shimmer and change around him, as though he were suddenly seeing through new eyes, as though something had been born anew inside him, and then abruptly he was *smelling* Wernecke's blood, the hot organic reek of it, leaning closer to drink in that sudden overpowering smell, better than the smell of freshly baked bread, better than anything he could remember, rich and heady and strong beyond imagining.

There was a moment of revulsion and horror, and he had time to wonder how long the ancient contamination had been passing from man to man to man, how far into the past the chain of lives stretched, how Wernecke himself had been trapped, and then his parched lips touched wetness, and he was drinking, drinking deeply and greedily, and his mouth was filled with the strong clean taste of copper.

# SOLACE

..................

Kleisterman took a zeppelin to Denver, a feeder line to Pueblo, then transferred to a clattering local bus to Santa Fe. The bus was full of displaced Anglos who preferred the life of migrant fieldworker to the Oklahoma refugee camps, a few Cambodians, a few Indians, and a number of the poorer Hispanics, mostly *mestizos*—unemployables who had hoped that the liberation would mean the fulfillment of all their dreams, but who had instead merely found themselves working for rich Mexican *caudillos* rather than for millionaire Anglos. Most of the passengers had been across the border to blow their work vouchers in Denver or Cañon City, and were now on their way back into Aztlan for another week's picking. They slouched sullenly in their seats, some passed out from drink or God Food and already snoring, many wrapped in ponchos or old Army blankets against the increasing chill of the evening. They ignored Kleisterman, even though, in spite of his carefully anonymous clothes, he was clearly no field hand—and Kleisterman preferred it that way.

The bus was spavined and old, the seats broken in, the sticky vinyl upholstery smelling of sweat and smoke and ancient piss. A Greyhound logo had been chipped off the side and replaced by VIAJANDO AZTLAN. The bus rattled through the cold prairie night with exquisite slowness, farting and lurching, the transmission groaning and knocking every time the driver shifted gears. The heat didn't work, or the interior lights, but Kleisterman sat stoically, not moving, as one by one the blaring radios faded and the crying babies quieted, until Kleisterman alone was awake in the chill darkness, his eyes gleaming in the shadows, shifting restlessly, never closing.

At some point during the night, they passed the Frontera Libertad, the Liberty Line, and its largely symbolic chain-link fence, and stopped at a checkpoint. A cyborg looked in, his great blank oval face glowing with sullen heat, like a dull rufous moon; he peered eyelessly at them for a thoughtful moment, then waved them on.

South of the border, in what had once been Colorado, they began to crawl up the long steep approach to the Raton Pass, the bus juttering and moaning like a soul in torment. Kleisterman was being washed by waves of exhaustion now, but in spite of them he slept poorly, fitfully, as he always did. It seemed as if every time his head dropped, his eyes closed, faces would spring to vivid life behind his eyelids, faces he did not want to encounter or consider, and his head would jerk up again, and his eyes would fly open, like suddenly released window shades. As always, he was afraid to dream . . . which only increased the bitter irony of his present mission. So he pinched himself cruelly to stay awake as the old bus inched painfully up and over the high mountain pass, and onto the Colorado Plateau.

At Raton, the bus stopped to take on more methane. The town was dark and seemingly deserted, the only light a dim bulb in the window of a ramshackle building that was being used as a fuel dump. Kleisterman stepped out of the bus and walked away from the circle of light to piss. It was very cold, and the inverted black bowl of sky overhead blazed with a million icy stars, more than Kleisterman had ever seen at once before. There was no sound except for a distant riverine roar of cold wind through the trees on the surrounding hillsides. His piss steamed in the milky starlight. As he watched, one of the stars overhead suddenly, noiselessly, flared into diamond brilliance, a dozen times as bright as it had been, and then faded, guttering, and was gone. Kleisterman knew that somewhere out there a killer satellite had found its prey, out there where the multinationals and the great conglomerates fought their silent and undeclared war, with weapons more obvious than those they usually allowed themselves to use on Earth. The wind shifted, blowing through the high valley now, cutting him to the bone with chill, and bringing with it the howling of wolves, a distant, feral keening that put the hair up along his spine in spite of himself. They were only the distant cousins of dogs, after all; just dogs, talking to one another on the wind. Still, the hairs stayed up.

Feet crunching gravel, Kleisterman went back to the bus and climbed aboard, found his iron-hard seat again in the darkness. In spite of the truly bitter cold, the air inside the bus was thick and stale, heavy with sleep, exhaled breath, spilled wine, sweat, the smell of cigarette smoke and marijuana and garlic. He huddled in his overcoat, shivering, and wondered whose satellite or station had just been lost, and if any of his old colleagues had had anything to do with the planning or execution of the strike. Possibly. Probably, even. Once again, he had to fight sleep, in spite of the cold. Once he turned his head and looked out of the window, and Melissa was there in the burnished silver moonlight, standing alongside the bus, staring up at him, and he knew that he had failed to stay awake, and jerked himself up out of sleep and into the close, stuffy darkness of the bus once again. Stillness. The other passengers tossed and murmured and farted. The moon *had* come out, a fat pale moon wading through a boiling river of smoky clouds, but Melissa was gone. Had not been there. Would not ever be anywhere anymore. Kleisterman found himself nodding again and pressed his face against the cold window glass, fighting it off. He would not dream. Not now. Not yet.

The bus sat unmoving in the silent town for an hour, two hours, three, for no reason Kleisterman could ascertain, and then the driver appeared again, from who knows where, climbed aboard muttering and swearing, slammed the door, twisted the engine into noisy, coughing life.

They rattled on through the night, winding down slowly out of the mountains, stopping here and there at small villages and communes to discharge passengers, the hung-over field hands climbing wordlessly from the bus and disappearing like spirits into the darkness, Kleisterman sleeping in split-second dozes. He woke from one such doze to see that the windows had turned red, red as though washed with new blood, and thought that he still slept; but it was the dawn, coming up from the broken badlands to the east, and they went down through the blood-red dawn to Santa Fe.

Kleisterman climbed stiffly down from the bus at Santa Fe. The sun had not yet warmed the air. It was still cold. The streets were filled with watery gray light, through which half-perceived figures moved with the stiff precision of early risers on a brisk morning. Kleisterman found a shabby café a block away from the bus station, ordered *huevos rancheros* and a bowl of green chili, was served the food by a sullen old Anglo woman wearing a faded Grateful Dead T-shirt. Unusually for Santa Fe, the food was terrible, tasting of rancid grease and ashes. Kleisterman spooned it up anyway, mechanically, taking it medicinally almost. As fuel. How long had it been since he'd really enjoyed a meal? All food seemed to taste dreadful to him these days. How long since he'd really had a full night's sleep? His hand shook as he spooned beet sugar into his bitter chicory coffee. He'd always been a tall, thin, bony man, but the reflection the inside of the café window showed him was gaunt, emaciated, almost cadaverous. He'd lost a lot of weight. This could not go on. . . . Grimly he checked through his preparations once again. This time he'd been very careful about being traced. He'd made his contacts with exquisite care. There should be no trouble.

He left the café. The light had become bluer, the shadows oil-black and sharp, the sky clear and cerulean. The sun was not yet high, but the streets were already full of people. Mexican soldiers were everywhere, of course, in their comic-opera uniforms, so absurdly ornate that it was difficult to tell a private from a general. Touring Swedish nationals, each with the scarlet King's Mark tattoo on the right cheek, indicating that they were above most local law. Gangs of skinny Cambodian kids on skateboards whizzed by, threading their way expertly through the crowds, calling to one another in machine-gun-fast bursts of Spanish. A flat-faced Indian leaned from a storefront and swore at them in Vietnamese, shaking his fist. Two chimeras displayed for Kleisterman, inflating their hoods and hissing in playful malice, then sliding aside as he continued to walk toward them unperturbed. This was the kind of unregulated, wide-open town where he could find what he needed, out on the fringes, in the interstices of the worldwide networks, where things would not be watched so closely as elsewhere—no longer part of the United States but not really well integrated into Old Mexico either, with a limited official presence of the multinationals, but plenty of black-market money circulating anyway.

He crossed the plaza, with its ancient Palace of the Governors, which had seen first Spanish, then Anglo, now Mexican conquerors come and go. There were slate-gray thunderheads looming over the peaks of the Sangre de Cristo Mountains, which in turn loomed over the town. There was a New Town being built to the southeast, on the far side of the mostly dry Santa Fe River, a megastructure of bizarre geometric shapes, all terraces and tetrahedrons; but here in the Old Town the buildings were still made of adobe or mock adobe, colored white or salmon or peach. He threaded a maze of little alleyways and enclosed courtyards on the far side of the plaza, the noise of the plaza fading away behind, and came at last to a narrow building of sun-faded adobe that displayed a small brass plaque that read DR. AU—CONSULTATIONS.

Trembling a little, Kleisterman climbed a dusty stairwell to a third-floor office at the back of a long, dim hallway. Dr. Au turned out to be one of those slender, ageless Oriental men of indeterminate nationality who might have been fifty or eighty. Spare, neat, dry, phlegmatic. The name was Chinese, but Kleisterman suspected that he might actually be Vietnamese, as his English held the slightest trace of a French accent. He had a sad, compassionate face, and hard eyes. An open, unscreened window looked out through the thick adobe wall to an enclosed courtyard with a cactus garden below. The furniture was nondescript, well-used, and the carpet dusty and threadbare, but an exquisite hologram of Botticelli's *Adoration of the Magi* moved and glittered in muted colors on the bare white walls, and the tastefully discreet ankh earring in the doctor's left earlobe might well have been real silver. There was no receptionist—just a desk with a complex of office terminals, a few faded armchairs, and Dr. Au.

Kleisterman could feel his heart pounding and his vision blurring as he and Dr. Au engaged in an intricate pavane of hints and innuendo and things not quite said, code words and phrases being mentioned in passing with artful casualness, contacts named, references mentioned and discussed. Dr. Au moved with immense wariness and delicacy, at every stage ready to instantly disengage, always phrasing things so that there was a completely innocent interpretation that could be given his words, while Kleisterman was washed by alternate waves of impatience, fear, rage, despair, muddy black exhaustion, ennui. At last, however, they reached a point beyond which it would no longer be possible to keep up the pretense that Kleisterman had come here for some legal purpose, a point beyond which both men could not proceed without committing themselves. Dr. Au sighed, made a fatalistic gesture, and said, "Well, then, Mr."—glancing at the card on his desk—"Ramírez, what can I do for you?"

Terror rose up in Kleisterman then. Almost, almost, he got up and fled. But he mastered himself. And as he pushed instinctual fear down, guilt and self-hate and anger rose, black and bristling and strong. None of this had reached his face.

"I want you to destroy me," Kleisterman said calmly.

Dr. Au looked first surprised, then wary—reassessing the situation for signs of potential entrapment—then, after a pause, almost regretful. "I must say, this is somewhat out of our line. We're usually asked to supply illicit fantasies, clandestine perversions, occasionally a spot of nonconsensual behavior modification." He looked at Kleisterman with curiosity. "Have you thought about this? Do you really mean what you say?"

Kleisterman was as cool as ice now, although his hands still trembled. "Yes, I mean it. I used to be in the business; I used to be an operator myself, so I can assure you that I understand the implications perfectly. I want to die. I want you to kill me.

But that's not *all*. Oh, no." Kleisterman leaned forward, his gaunt face intense. His voice rose. "I want you to destroy me. I want you to make me suffer. You're an operator, an adept, you know what I mean. Not just pain; anybody can do that. I want you to make me *pay*." Kleisterman slumped back in his chair, made a tired gesture. "I know you can do it; I know you've *done* it. I know you are discreet. And when you're done with me, a hundred years subjective from now, you can get rid of my body, discreetly, and no one will ever know what happened to me. It will be as if I had never existed." His voice roughened. "As if I had never been born. Would to God I had not been."

Dr. Au made a noncommittal noise, tapped his fingers together thoughtfully. His face was tired and sad, as though in his life he had been made to see more deeply than he cared to into the human soul. His eyes glittered with interest. After a polite pause, he said, "You must be quite certain of this, for later there will be no turning back. Are you sure you won't reconsider?"

Kleisterman made an impatient, despairing gesture. "I could have put a bullet in my head at any time, but that means nothing. It's not enough, not nearly enough. There must be retribution. There must be restitution. I must be made to *pay* for what I have done. Only this way can I find solace."

"Even so . . ." Dr. Au said, doubtfully.

Kleisterman held up his hand. Moving with slow deliberation, he reached into an inner pocket, produced a coded credit strip. "All my assets," he said, "and they are considerable." He held the credit slip up for display, then proffered it to Dr. Au. "I want you to destroy me," he said.

Dr. Au sighed. He looked left, he looked right, he looked down, he looked up. His face was suffused with dull embarrassment. But he took the credit strip.

Dr. Au ushered Kleisterman politely into an adjacent room, stood by with sad patience while Kleisterman removed his clothing. At a touch, a large metal egg rose from the floor, opened like a five-petaled flower, extruded a narrow metal bench or shelf. Dr. Au gestured brusquely; Kleisterman lay down on the bench, wincing at the touch of cold metal on his naked skin. Dr. Au leaned close over him, his face remote now and his movements briskly efficient, as though to get it all over with quickly. He taped soft cloth pads first over Kleisterman's left eye, then over his right. There was a feeling of motion, and Kleisterman knew that the metal shelf was sliding back into the machine, which would be retracting around it, the petals closing tight to form a featureless steel egg, with him inside.

Darkness. Silence.

At first, Kleisterman was aware of a sense of enclosure, was aware of the feel of the metal under his back, could even stir a little, move his fingers impatiently. But then his skin began to prickle over every inch of his body, as feathery probes made contact with his nerve endings, and, as the prickling began to fade, with it went all other sensation. He could no longer feel his body, no longer move; no longer wanted to move. He didn't have a body anymore. There was nothing. Not even darkness, not even silence. Nothing. Nonexistence.

Kleisterman floated in the void, waiting for the torment to begin.

This kind of machine had many names—simulator, dream machine, iron maiden, imager, shadow box. It fed coded impulses through the subject's nerves, directly into the brain. With it, the operator could make the subject experience anything. Pain, of course. Any amount of pain. With a simulator, you could torture someone to death again and again, for years of subjective time, without doing them any actual physical harm—not much comfort for the subject in that, though, since to them the experience would be indistinguishable from objective reality. Of course, the most expert operators scorned this sort of thing as hopelessly crude, lacking in all finesse. Not artistic. Pain was only one key that could be played. There were many others. The subject had no secrets, and, with access to the subject's deepest longings and most hidden fears, the skilled operator, the artisan, the clever craftsman, could devise cunning scenarios much more effective than pain.

Kleisterman had been such an operator, one of the best,

admired by his colleagues for his subtlety and ingenuity and skill. He had clandestinely "processed" thousands of subjects for his multinational, and had never felt a qualm, until suddenly one day, for no particular reason, he began to sicken. After Donaldson, Ramaswamy, and Kole, three especially difficult and unpleasant jobs, he had sickened further, and, for the first time in his life, began to have difficulty sleeping—and, when he did sleep, began to have unquiet dreams. Then Melissa had somehow become the target of corporate malice, and had been sent to him for his ministrations. By rights, he should have declined the job, since he knew Melissa, and had even h? a brief affair with her once, years before. But he had had professional pride. He did not turn down the job. And ? where deep in her mind, he had found himself, an er and idealized version of himself as he had never bee· realized that while for him their affair had been u? for *her* it had been much more intensely charged— she had loved him deeply, and still did.

This discovery brought out the very worst fever of sick excitement, he created scenari her, life after life, each scenario working s theme of her love for him; and each tir her in the scenario became worse, his more humiliating, the pain and sham? her more severe. He turned the ?deously disfig- tesque ways, too, so that in one ?and the way to her own wedding, ap?d and messily of cancer, and in ?t, ured in a fire, and in anoth?dark for years as a semiaware ?that and so on. Each life be? forward memories of other ex?were stacked due, an unspoken, i?· Then, tiring bitter and harsh, ?s own aesthetic and misery and ?os—at first just slapping her against you—? irresistibly te? began to b·

around in drunken rages, then beating her severely enough to put her in the hospital. Then, in one scenario, he picked up a knife.

Several lifetimes subjective later, the heart in her physical body finally gave out, and she died in a way that was no more real to her than the dozens of times she'd died before, but which put her at last beyond his reach. He had been dismayed to discover that in the deepest recesses of her mind, below the fear and hate and bitterness and grief, she loved him still, even at the last. He switched off the machine, and he awoke, as from a fever dream, as though he had been possessed by a demon of perversity that had only now been exorcised, to find himself alone in his soundproofed cubicle with the simulator and Melissa's cooling body. He betrayed the corporation on his next ‌signment, freeing the subject rather than "processing" him, ‌ from then on he had been on the run. He had found that ‌ild successfully hide from the multinational. Hiding from ‌ had proved more difficult.

‌xploded in his head. It took a second for his vision to ‌ to realize that the patch over his left eye had been ‌. Au leaned in over him again, filling his field of ‌god, and this time Kleisterman felt the painful ‌ainst his skin as Dr. Au ripped the other eye ‌ light. Kleisterman blinked, disoriented and ‌ out of the machine. Dr. Au was tugging at ‌it up. Dr. Au was saying something, but it ‌arsh and hurtful to the ears. He pawed ‌d Kleisterman shook him off. Kleister-

Dr. Au the edge of the metal bench until his came up on ‌rld again, and his mind cleared. His anxious, and ‌turned.

security probe; ‌an's arm. "A red security flag out of here righ‌," Dr. Au said. His voice was

Kleisterman st‌ed with fear. "There was a thickly.                    You must leave. I want you

                         ‌ou agreed—" he said

"I want nothing to do with you, Mr. Ramírez," Dr. Au said apprehensively. "Here, take your clothes, get dressed. You have some very ruthless forces opposed to you, Mr. Ramírez. I want nothing to do with them, either. No trouble. Leave now. Take your business elsewhere."

Slowly, Kleisterman dressed, manipulating the clothes with stiff, clumsy fingers while Dr. Au hovered anxiously. The office was filled with watery gray light that seemed painfully bright after the darkness inside the simulator. Dust motes danced in suspension in the light, and a fly hopped along the adobe edge of the open window before darting outside again. A dog was barking out there somewhere, a flat, faraway sound, and a warm breeze puffed in for a second to ruffle his hair and bring him the smell of pine and juniper. He was perceiving every smallest detail with exquisite clarity.

Kleisterman pushed wordlessly by Dr. Au, walked through the outer office and out into the dusty hallway beyond. The floor was scuffed, grime between the tiles, and there were peeling water stains on the ceiling. A smell of cooking food came up the stairwell. *This is real*, Kleisterman told himself fiercely. This is real, this is really happening, this is the real world. The multinational boys aren't subtle enough for this; they wouldn't be satisfied with just denying me solace. Letting me go on. They're not that subtle.

Are they? *Are they?*

Kleisterman went down the narrow stairs. He dragged his fist against the rough adobe wall until his knuckles bled, but he couldn't convince himself that any of it was real.

# SLOW DANCING WITH JESUS

.............................

*Gardner Dozois and*
*Jack Dann*

Jesus Christ appeared at Tess Kimbrough's door dressed in a white tuxedo with a blue cummerbund and matching bow tie. His chestnut-brown hair was parted in the middle and fell down past his shoulders, and his beard and mustache were close-cropped and neatly combed.

Tess's mother answered the door. "Come right inside, Tess will be down in a jiffy." She led Jesus into the front room. "Tess," she called. "Your date is here."

Upstairs, Tess checked the bobby pins that held her French Twist together, and smoothed imaginary wrinkles out of her dress. It was the emerald green one, with dyed-green shoes to match, that her urbane and sophisticated mother had helped her pick out, and she was somewhat nervous about it, but then she was so nervous anyway that her teeth were chattering. She told her image in the mirror that this was going to be the most perfect night of her life, but the image in the mirror didn't look convinced. She practiced breathing evenly for a moment, flaring her nostrils. Then she walked down the stairs to meet Jesus, remembering not to look at her feet, and trying to maintain good posture.

Jesus stood up as she entered the room and presented her with a corsage, a small orchid on a wristlet. She thanked him, kissed her mother good-bye, promised that she'd be back at a reasonable hour, and then she was sitting beside Jesus in the Leatherette seat of his Thunderbird convertible. Jesus refrained from laying rubber in front of Tess's house, as most kids would have done; instead he shifted smoothly and skillfully through the gears. Tess momentarily forgot about being nervous as the wind rushed by against her face and she thought that she was actually—right now—going to the prom.

"How are you doing?" Jesus asked. "Do you want a cap or something so the wind won't mess your hair?"

"No, thanks," Tess said shyly. She was almost afraid to look at him, and kept stealing sidelong glances at him when she thought his attention was elsewhere.

"You nervous?"

Tess glanced at him again. "You mean, about the prom?"

"Uh-huh," Jesus said, executing a high-speed turn with an easy, expert grace. The buildings were going by very fast now.

"Yeah . . . I guess so."

"Don't be," Jesus said, and winked.

Tess felt herself blushing, but before she could think of something to say, Jesus was bringing the car to a smooth stop in the lower parking lot of the high school. A kid whose Vaseline-smeared hair was combed back into a duck's tail opened the door for Tess, and then slid into the driver's seat when Jesus got out. Jesus gave him a five-dollar tip.

"Jeez, thanks," the boy said.

Cinders crunched under their feet as they crossed the parking lot toward the open fire door of the gym, which was now framed by paper lanterns that glowed in soft pastel colors. Tess walked hesitantly and slowly now that they were really here, already beginning to feel the first sick flutterings of panic. Most of the kids didn't like her—she had long ago been classified as uncool, and, worse, a "brain"—and she didn't see any reason why they'd start to like her now. . . .

But then Jesus was surrendering their tickets at the door, and it was too late to flee.

Inside the gym, the bleachers had been pulled back from the dance floor, and the basketball nets had been folded up. Paper streamers hung from rafters and waterpipes, herds of slowly jostling balloons bumped gently against the ceiling, and crepe-paper roses were everywhere. The band—five sullen young men in dark red jackets that had "The Teen-Tones" written on them in sequins—had set up in the free-throw zone and were aggressively but unskillfully playing "Yakety Yak." Kids in greasy pompadours, crew cuts, and elephant trunks milled list-lessly around the dance floor, looking stiff and uncomfortable in their rented suits. Only a few couples were dancing, and they jerked and twitched in lethargic slow motion, like people slowly drowning on the bottom of the sea.

Most of the girls were still standing by the refreshment tables on the other side of the room, where the punch bowls were, and Tess made her way toward them, feeling her stomach slowly knot with dread. Already she could see some of the kids smirking at her and whispering, and she heard a girl say loudly, "Just look at that *dress!* What a nerd." One of the class clowns made a yipping, doggy noise as she passed, and someone else broke up into high-pitched asthmatic laughter. Blindly, she kept walking. As she came up to the group around the punch bowls, her friend Carol gave her an unenthusiastic smile and said, "Hey, lookin' good," in an insincere voice. Vinnie, Carol's bullet-headed boyfriend, made a snorting sound of derision. "I just don't understand why you have anything to do with that dog," he said to Carol, not even making a pretense of caring whether Tess could hear him or not. Carol looked em-barrassed; she glanced at Tess, smiled weakly, and then looked uneasily away—she genuinely liked Tess, and sometimes hung out with her after school (in the classic teen configuration, encountered everywhere, of one pretty girl and one "dog" doing things together), but as a captain of cheerleaders she had her own status to worry about, and under the circumstances she'd lose face with the cool kids if she stuck up too vigorously for Tess. "I mean, *look* at her," Vinnie complained, still speak-ing to Carol as if Tess weren't there. "She's *so* uncool, you know?"

Tess stood frozen, flushing, smiling a frozen smile, feeling herself go hot and freezing cold by turns. Should she pretend that she hadn't heard? What else *could* she do? The clown had drifted over, and was making yipping noises again. . . .

Jesus had been a few steps behind her coming through the crowd, but now he stepped up beside her and took her arm, and all the other kids suddenly fell silent. "Leave her alone," Jesus said. His voice was rich, strong, resonant, and it rang like a mellow iron bell in the big empty hall. "She's here with *me*." Vinnie's mouth dropped open, and Carol gasped. All the kids were gaping at them, their faces soft with awe. Tess was intensely aware of Jesus' strong warm fingers on the bare flesh of her arm. Jesus seemed to have grown larger, to have become huge and puissant, a giant, and his rugged, handsome face had become stern and commanding. He radiated strength and warmth and authority, and an almost tangible light—a clear and terrible light that seemed to reveal every zit and pimple and blackhead in the sallow, shallow faces of her tormentors, each slack mouth and weak chin and watery eye, a light that dwindled them to a petty and insignificant group of grimy children. "She's here with me," Jesus repeated, and then he smiled, suavely, jauntily, almost rakishly, and winked. "And if *I* say she's cool, believe it, she's cool."

Then, before anyone could speak, Jesus had taken Tess's hand and led her onto the dance floor, and they were dancing, slow dancing, while the band played "A Million to One." She had never been able to dance before, but now she danced with effortless skill, swirling around and around the floor, following Jesus' lead, moving with beauty and flowing silken grace, shreds of torn paper roses whispering around her feet. One by one the other couples stopped dancing and stood silently to watch them, until they were surrounded by a ring of pale, gaping, awed faces, small as thumbnails and distant as stars, and they drifted and danced within that watching ring as the band played "Goodnight, My Love" and "Twilight Time" and "It's All in the Game," moving through the night together like silk and fire and warm spring rain.

After the dance, Jesus drove her home and kissed her goodnight at her door, gently but with authority, and with just the slightest sweet hint of tongue.

Tess let herself in and went upstairs to her room, moving quietly so that her mother wouldn't realize that she was back. She switched on a soft light and stared at herself in the mirror; her flesh was tingling, and she was sure that she must be glowing in the darkness like freshly hammered steel, but her face looked the same as always, except perhaps for the expression around the eyes. She sat down at her night table and took her diary out from the locked, secret drawer. She sat there silently for a long while, near the open window, feeling the warm night breeze caress her face and smelling the heavy sweet perfume of the mimosa trees outside. A dog was barking out there somewhere, far away, at long intervals, and cars whined by on the highway, leaving a vibrant silence in their wake. At last she opened her diary, and in a bold neat hand wrote

Dear Diary,
Tonight I met—Him. . . .

# THE PEACEMAKER

. . . . . . . . . . . . . . . . . . . . . . .

Roy had dreamed of the sea, as he often did. When he woke up that morning, the wind was sighing through the trees outside with a sound like the restless murmuring of surf, and for a moment he thought that he was home, back in the tidy brick house by the beach, with everything that had happened undone, and hope opened hotly inside him, like a wound.

"Mom?" he said. He sat up, straightening his legs, expecting his feet to touch the warm mass that was his dog Toby, Toby always slept curled on the foot of his bed, but already everything was breaking up and changing, slipping away, and he blinked through sleep-gummed eyes at the thin blue light coming in through the attic window, felt the hardness of the old Army cot under him, and realized that he wasn't home, that there was no home anymore, that for him there could never be a home again.

He pushed the blankets aside and stood up. It was bitterly cold in the big attic room—winter was dying hard, the most terrible winter he could remember—and the rough wood planking burned his feet like ice, but he couldn't stay in bed anymore, not now.

None of the other kids were awake yet; he threaded his way through the other cots—accidentally bumping against one of them so that its occupant tossed and moaned and began to snore in a higher register—and groped through cavernous shadows to the single high window. He was just tall enough to reach it, if he stood on tiptoe. He forced the window open, the old wood of its frame groaning in protest, plaster dust puffing, and shivered as the cold dawn wind poured inward, hitting him in the face, tugging with ghostly fingers at his hair, sweeping past him to rush through the rest of the stuffy attic like a restless child set free to play.

The wind smelled of pine resin and wet earth, not of salt flats and tides, and the bird-sound that rode in on that wind was the burbling of wrens and the squawking of bluejays, not the raucous shrieking of sea gulls . . . but even so, as he braced his elbows against the window frame and strained up to look out, his mind still full of the broken fragments of dreams, he half-expected to see the ocean below, stretched out to the horizon, sending patient wavelets to lap against the side of the house. Instead he saw the nearby trees holding silhouetted arms up against the graying sky, the barn and the farmyard, all still lost in shadow, the surrounding fields, the weathered macadam line of the road, the forested hills rolling away into distance. Silver mist lay in pockets of low ground, retreated in wraithlike streamers up along the ridges.

Not yet. The sea had not chased him here—yet.

Somewhere out there to the east, still invisible, were the mountains, and just beyond those mountains was the sea that he had dreamed of, lapping quietly at the dusty Pennsylvania hill towns, coal towns, that were now, suddenly, seaports. There the Atlantic waited, held at bay, momentarily at least, by the humpbacked wall of the Appalachians, still perhaps forty miles from here, although closer now by leagues of swallowed land and drowned cities than it had been only three years before.

He had been down by the seawall that long-ago morning, playing some forgotten game, watching the waves move in slow oily swells, like some heavy, dull metal in liquid form, watching the tide come in . . . and come in . . . and come *in* . . . He had been excited at first, as the sea crept in, way above the high-tide line, higher than he had ever seen it before, and then, as the sea swallowed the beach entirely and began to lap patiently against the base of the seawall, he had become uneasy, and *then*, as the sea continued to rise up toward the top of the seawall itself, he had begun to be afraid. . . . The sea had just kept coming in, rising slowly and inexorably, swallowing the land at a slow walking pace, never stopping, always coming *in*, always rising higher. . . . By the time the sea had swallowed the top of the seawall and begun to creep up the short grassy slope toward his house, sending glassy fingers probing almost to his feet, he had started to scream, he had whirled and run frantically up the slope, screaming hysterically for his parents, and the sea had followed patiently at his heels. . . .

A "marine transgression," the scientists called it. Ordinary people called it, inevitably, the Flood. Whatever you called it, it had washed away the old world forever. Scientists had been talking about the possibility of such a thing for years—some of them even pointing out that it was already as warm as it had been at the peak of the last interglacial, and getting warmer— but few had suspected just how *fast* the Antarctic ice could melt. Many times during those chaotic weeks, one scientific King Canute or another had predicted that the worst was over, that the tide would rise this high and no higher . . . but each time the sea had come inexorably on, pushing miles and miles farther inland with each successive high tide, rising almost three hundred feet in the course of one disastrous summer, drowning lowlands around the globe until there *were* no lowlands anymore. In the United States alone, the sea had swallowed most of the East Coast east of the Appalachians, the West Coast west of the Sierras and the Cascades, much of Alaska and Hawaii, Florida, the Gulf coast, east Texas, taken a big wide scoop out of the lowlands of the Mississippi Valley, thin fingers of water penetrating north to Iowa and Illinois, and caused the St. Lawrence and the Great Lakes to overflow and drown their shorelines. The Green Mountains, the White Mountains, the Adirondacks, the Poconos and the Catskills, the Ozarks, the Pacific Coast Ranges—all had been transformed to archipelagoes, surrounded by the invading sea.

The funny thing was . . . that as the sea pursued them relentlessly inland, pushing them from one temporary refuge to another, he had been unable to shake the feeling that *he* had caused the Flood: that he had done something that day while playing atop the seawall, inadvertently stumbled on some magic ritual, some chance combination of gesture and word that had untied the bonds of the sea and sent it sliding up over the land . . . that it was chasing *him*, personally. . . .

A dog was barking out there now, somewhere out across the fields toward town, but it was not *his* dog. His dog was dead, long since dead, and its whitening skull was rolling along the ocean floor with the tides that washed over what had once been Brigantine, New Jersey, three hundred feet down.

Suddenly he was covered with gooseflesh, and he shivered, rubbing his hands over his bare arms. He returned to his cot and dressed hurriedly—no point in trying to go back to bed, Sara would be up to kick them all out of the sack in a minute or two anyway. The day had begun; he would think no further ahead than that. He had learned in the refugee camps to take life one second at a time.

As he moved around the room, he thought that he could feel hostile eyes watching him from some of the other bunks. It was much colder in here now that he had opened the window, and he had inevitably made a certain amount of noise getting dressed, but although they all valued every second of sleep they could scrounge, none of the other kids would dare to complain. The thought was bittersweet, bringing both pleasure and pain, and he smiled at it, a thin, brittle smile that was almost a grimace. No, they would watch sullenly from their bunks, and pretend to be asleep, and curse him under their breath, but they would say nothing to anyone about it. Certainly they would say nothing to *him*.

He went down through the still-silent house like a ghost, and out across the farmyard, through fugitive streamers of mist that wrapped clammy white arms around him and beaded his face with dew. His Uncle Abner was there at the slit trench before him. Abner grunted a greeting, and they stood pissing side by side for a moment in companionable silence, their urine steaming in the gray morning air.

Abner stepped backward and began to button his pants. "You start playin' with yourself yet, boy?" he said, not looking at Roy.

Roy felt his face flush. "No," he said, trying not to stammer, "no sir."

"You growin' hair already," Abner said. He swung himself slowly around to face Roy, as if his body were some ponderous machine that could only be moved and aimed by the use of pulleys and levers. The hard morning light made his face look harsh as stone, but also sallow and old. Tired, Roy thought. Unutterably weary, as though it took almost more effort than he could sustain just to stand there. Worn out, like the over-taxed fields around them. Only the eyes were alive in the eroded face; they were hard and merciless as flint, and they looked at you as if they were looking right through you to some distant thing that nobody else could see. "I've tried to explain to you about remaining pure," Abner said, speaking slowly. "About how important it is for you to keep yourself pure, not to let yourself be sullied in any way. I've tried to explain that, I hope you could understand—"

"Yes, sir," Roy said.

Abner made a groping hesitant motion with his hand, fingers spread wide, as though he were trying to sculpt meaning from the air itself. "I mean—it's important that you understand, Roy. Everything has to be *right*. I mean, everything's got to be just . . . *right* . . . or nothing else will mean anything. You got to be right in your *soul*, boy. You got to let the Peace of God into your soul. It all depends on *you* now—you got to let that peace inside yourself, no one can do it for you. And it's so important . . ."

"Yes, sir," Roy said quietly, "I understand."

"I wish . . ." Abner said, and fell silent. They stood there for a minute, not speaking, not looking at each other. There was wood smoke in the air now, and they heard a door slam somewhere on the far side of the house. They had instinctively been looking out across the open land to the east, and now, as they watched, the sun rose above the mountains, splitting the plum-and-ash sky open horizontally with a long wedge of red, distinguishing the rolling horizon from the lowering clouds. A lance of bright white sunlight hit their eyes, thrusting straight in at them from the edge of the world.

"You're going to make us proud, boy, I know it," Abner said, but Roy ignored him, watching in fascination as the molten disk of the sun floated free of the horizon line, squinting against the dazzle until his eyes watered and his sight blurred. Abner put his hand on the boy's shoulder. The hand felt heavy and hot, proprietary, and Roy shook it loose in annoyance, still not looking away from the horizon. Abner sighed, started to say something, thought better of it, and instead said, "Come on in the house, boy, and let's get some breakfast inside you."

Breakfast—when they finally did get to sit down to it, after the usual rambling grace and invocation by Abner—proved to be unusually lavish. For the brethren, there were hickory-nut biscuits, and honey, and cups of chicory; and even the other refugee kids—who on occasion during the long bitter winter had been fed as close to nothing at all as law and appearances would allow—got a few slices of fried fatback along with their habitual cornmeal mush. Along with his biscuits and honey, Roy got wild turkey eggs, Indian potatoes, and a real pork chop. There was a good deal of tension around the big table that morning: Henry and Luke were stern-faced and tense, Raymond was moody and preoccupied, Albert actually looked frightened; the refugee kids were round-eyed and silent, doing their best to make themselves invisible; the jolly Mrs. Crammer was as jolly as ever, shoveling her food in with gusto; but the grumpy Mrs. Zeigler, who was feared and disliked by all the kids, had obviously been crying, and ate little or nothing. Abner's face was set like rock, his eyes were hard and bright, and he looked from one to another of the brethren, as if daring them to question his leadership and spiritual guidance. Roy ate with good appetite unperturbed by the emotional convection currents that were swirling around him, calmly but deliberately concentrating on mopping up every morsel of food on his plate—in the last couple of months he had put back some of the weight he had lost, although by the old standards, the ones his Mom would have applied four years ago, he was still painfully thin. At the end of the meal, Mrs. Reardon came in from the kitchen, and, beaming with the well-justified pride of someone who is about to do the impossible, presented Roy with a small, rectangular object wrapped in shiny brown paper. He was startled for a second, but yes, by God, it *was:* a Hershey bar, the first one he'd seen in years. A black-market item, of course, difficult to get hold of in the impoverished East these days, and probably expensive as hell. Even some of the brethren were looking at him enviously now, and the refugee kids were frankly gaping. As he picked up the Hershey bar and slowly and caressingly peeled the wrapper back, exposing the pale chocolate beneath, one of the other kids actually began to drool. . . .

After breakfast, the other refugee kids—"wetbacks," the townspeople sometimes called them, with elaborate irony— were divided into two groups. One group would help the brethren work Abner's farm that day, while the larger group would be loaded onto an ox-drawn dray (actually an old flatbed truck, with the cab knocked off) and sent out around the countryside to do what pretty much amounted to slave labor: road work, heavy farm work, helping with the quarrying or the timbering, rebuilding houses and barns and bridges damaged or destroyed in the chaotic days after the Flood. The federal government— or what was left of the federal government, trying desperately, and not always successfully, to keep a battered and Balkanizing country from flying completely apart, struggling to put the Humpty Dumpty that was America back together again—the federal government paid Abner (and others like him) a yearly allowance in federal scrip or promise-of-merchandise notes for giving room and board to refugees from the drowned lands . . . but times being as tough as they were, no one was going to complain if Abner also helped ease the burden of their upkeep by hiring them out locally to work for whoever could come up with the scrip, or sufficient barter goods, or an attractive workswap offer; what was left of the state and town governments also used them on occasion (and the others like them, adult or child), gratis, for work projects "for the common good, during this time of emergency . . ."

Sometimes, hanging around the farm with little or nothing to do, Roy almost missed going out on the work crews, but only almost: he remembered too well the backbreaking labor performed on scanty rations . . . the sickness, the accidents, the staggering fatigue . . . the blazing sun and the swarms of mosquitoes in summer, the bitter cold in winter, the snow, the icy wind . . . He watched the dray go by, seeing the envious and resentful faces of kids he had once worked beside—Stevie, Enrique, Sal—turn towards him as it passed, and, reflexively, he opened and closed his hands. Even two months of idleness and relative luxury had not softened the thick and roughened layers of callus that were the legacy of several seasons spent on the crews. . . . No, boredom was infinitely preferable.

By midmorning, a small crowd of people had gathered in the road outside the farmhouse. It was hotter now; you could smell the promise of summer in the air, in the wind, and the sun that beat down out of a cloudless blue sky had a real sting to it. It must have been uncomfortable out there in the open, under that sun, but the crowd made no attempt to approach—they just stood there on the far side of the road and watched the house, shuffling their feet, occasionally muttering to each other in voices that, across the road, were audible only as a low wordless grumbling.

Roy watched them for a while from the porch door; they were townspeople, most of them vaguely familiar to Roy, although none of them belonged to Abner's sect, and he knew none of them by name. The refugee kids saw little of the townspeople, being kept carefully segregated for the most part. The few times that Roy had gotten into town he had been treated with icy hostility—and God help the wetback kid who was caught by the town kids on a deserted stretch of road! For that matter, even the brethren tended to keep to themselves, and were snubbed by certain segments of town society, although the sect had increased its numbers dramatically in recent years, nearly tripling in strength during the past winter alone; there were new chapters now in several of the surrounding communities.

A gaunt-faced woman in the crowd outside spotted Roy, and shook a thin fist at him. "Heretic!" she shouted. "Blasphemer!" The rest of the crowd began to buzz ominously, like a huge angry bee. She spat at Roy, her face contorting and her shoulders heaving with the ferocity of her effort, although she must have known that the spittle had no chance of reaching him. "Blasphemer!" she shouted again. The veins stood out like cords in her scrawny neck.

Roy stepped back into the house, but continued to watch from behind the curtained front windows. There was shouting inside the house as well as outside—the brethren had been cloistered in the kitchen for most of the morning, arguing, and the sound and ferocity of their argument carried clearly through the thin plaster walls of the crumbling old house. At last the sliding door to the kitchen slammed open, and Mrs. Ziegler strode out into the parlor, accompanied by her two children and her scrawny, pasty-faced husband, and followed by two other families of brethren—about nine people altogether. Most of them were carrying suitcases, and a few had backpacks and bundles. Abner stood in the kitchen doorway and watched them go, his anger evident only in the whiteness of his knuckles as he grasped the doorframe. "Go, then," Abner said scornfully. "We spit you up out of our mouths! Don't ever think to come back!" He swayed in the doorway, his voice tremulous with hate. "We're better off without you, you hear? You *hear* me? We don't *need* the weak-willed and the shortsighted."

Mrs. Ziegler said nothing, and her steps didn't slow or falter, but her homely hatchet-face was streaked with tears. To Roy's astonishment—for she had a reputation as a harridan—she stopped near the porch door and threw her arms around him. "Come with us," she said, hugging him with smothering tightness, "Roy, *please* come with us! You can, you know—we'll find a place for you, everything will work out fine." Roy said nothing, resisting the impulse to squirm—he was uncomfortable in her embrace; in spite of himself, it touched some sleeping corner of his soul he had thought was safely bricked over years before, and for a moment he felt trapped and panicky, unable to breathe, as though he were in sudden danger of wakening from a comfortable dream into a far more terrible and less desirable reality. "Come *with* us," Mrs. Ziegler said again, more urgently, but Roy shook his head gently and pulled away from her. "You're a goddamned fool then!" she blazed, suddenly angry, her voice ringing harsh and loud, but Roy only shrugged, and gave her his wistful, ghostly smile. "Damn it—" she started to say, but her eyes filled with tears again, and she whirled and hurried out of the house, followed by the other members of her party. The children—wetbacks were kept pretty much segregated from the children of the brethren as well, and he had seen some of these kids only at meals—looked at Roy with wide, frightened eyes as they passed.

Abner was staring at Roy now, from across the room; it was a hard and challenging stare, but there was also a trace of desperation in it, and in that moment Abner seemed uncertain and oddly vulnerable. Roy stared back at him serenely, un-blinkingly meeting his eyes, and after a while some of the tension went out of Abner, and he turned and stumbled out of the room, listing to one side like a church steeple in the wind.

Outside, the crowd began to buzz again as Mrs. Zeigler's party filed out of the house and across the road. There was much discussion and arm waving and head shaking when the two groups met, someone occasionally gesturing back toward the farmhouse. The buzzing grew louder, then gradually died away. At last, Mrs. Zeigler and her group set off down the road for town, accompanied by some of the locals. They trudged away dispiritedly down the center of the dusty road, lugging their shabby suitcases, only a few of them looking back.

Roy watched them until they were out of sight, his face still and calm, and continued to stare down the road after them long after they were gone.

About noon, a carload of reporters arrived outside, driving up in one of the bulky new methane burners that were still rarely seen east of Omaha. They circulated through the crowd of townspeople, pausing briefly to take photographs and ask questions, working their way toward the house, and Roy watched them as if they were unicorns, strange remnants from some vanished cycle of creation. Most of the reporters were probably from State College or the new state capital at Altoona—places where a few small newspapers were again being produced—but one of them was wearing an armband that identified him as a bureau man for one of the big Denver papers, and that was probably where the money for the car had come from. It was strange to be reminded that there were still areas of the country that were . . . not *unchanged*, no place in the world could claim that . . . and not *rich*, not by the old standards of affluence anyway . . . but, at any rate, better off than *here*. The whole western part of the country—from roughly the ninety-fifth meridian on west to approximately the one-twenty-second—had been untouched by the flooding, and although the West had also suffered severely from the collapse of the national economy and the consequent social upheavals, at least much of its industrial base had remained intact. Denver—one of the few large American cities built on ground high enough to have been safe from the rising waters—was the new federal capital, and, if poorer and meaner, it was also bigger and busier than ever.

Abner went out to herd the reporters inside and away from the unbelievers, and after a moment or two Roy could hear Abner's voice going out there, booming like a church organ. By the time the reporters came in, Roy was sitting at the dining room table, flanked by Raymond and Aaron, waiting for them.

They took photographs of him sitting there, while he stared calmly back at them, and they took photographs of him while he politely refused to answer questions, and then Aaron handed him the pre-prepared papers, and he signed them, and repeated the legal formulas that Aaron had taught him, and they took photographs of that too. And then—able to get nothing more out of him, and made slightly uneasy by his blank composure and the remoteness of his eyes—they left.

Within a few more minutes, as though everything were over, as though the departure of the reporters had drained all possible significance from anything else that might still happen, most of the crowd outside had drifted away also, only one or two people remaining behind to stand quietly waiting, like vultures, in the once-again empty road.

Lunch was a quiet meal. Roy ate heartily, taking seconds of

everything, and Mrs. Crammer was as jovial as ever, but everyone else was subdued, and even Abner seemed shaken by the
schism that had just sundered his church. After the meal,
Abner stood up and began to pray aloud. The brethren sat
resignedly at the table, heads partially bowed, some listening,
some not. Abner was holding his arms up toward the big black-
ened rafter of the ceiling, sweat runneling his face, when Peter
came hurriedly in from outside and stood hesitating in the
doorway, trying to catch Abner's eye. When it became obvious
that Abner was going to keep right on ignoring him, Peter
shrugged, and said in a loud flat voice, "Abner, the sheriff is
here."

Abner stopped praying. He grunted, a hoarse, exhausted
sound, the kind of sound a baited bear might make when,
already pushed beyond the limits of endurance, someone jabs
it yet again with a spear. He slowly lowered his arms and was
still for a long moment, and then he shuddered, seeming to
shake himself back to life. He glanced speculatively—and, it
almost seemed, beseechingly—at Roy, and then straightened
his shoulders and strode from the room.

They received the sheriff in the parlor, Raymond and Aaron
and Mrs. Crammer sitting in the battered old armchairs, Roy
sitting unobtrusively to one side on the stool from a piano that
no longer worked, Abner standing a little to the fore with his
arms locked behind him and his boots planted solidly on the
oak planking, as if he were on the bridge of a schooner that was
heading into a gale. County Sheriff Sam Braddock glanced at
the others—his gaze lingering on Roy for a moment—and then
ignored them, addressing himself to Abner as if they were alone
in the room. "Mornin', Abner," he said.

"Mornin', Sam," Abner said quietly. "You here for some
reason other than just t'say hello, I suppose."

Braddock grunted. He was a short, stocky, grizzled man with
iron-gray hair and a tired face. His uniform was shiny and old
and patched in a dozen places, but clean, and the huge old
revolver strapped to his hip looked worn but serviceable. He
fidgeted with his shapeless old hat, turning it around and
around in his fingers—he was obviously embarrassed, but he

was determined as well, and at last he said, "The thing of it is, Abner, I'm here to talk you out of this damned tomfoolery."

"Are you, now?" Abner said.

"We'll do whatever we damn well want to do—" Raymond burst out, shrilly, but Abner waved him to silence. Braddock glanced lazily at Raymond, then looked back at Abner, his tired old face settling into harder lines. "I'm not going to allow it," he said, more harshly. "We don't want this kind of thing going on in this county."

Abner said nothing.

"There's not a thing you can do about it, Sheriff," Aaron said, speaking a bit heatedly, but keeping his melodious voice well under control. "It's all perfectly legal, all the way down the line."

"Well, now," Braddock said, "I don't know about that . . ."

"Well, I *do* know, Sheriff," Aaron said calmly. "As a legally sanctioned and recognized church, we are protected by law all the way down the line. There is ample precedent, most of it recent, most of it upheld by appellate decisions within the last year: Carlton *versus* the State of Vermont, Trenholm *versus* the State of West Virginia, the Church of Souls *versus* the State of New York. There was that case up in Tylersville, just last year. Why, the Freedom of Worship Act *alone* . . ."

Braddock sighed, tacitly admitting that he knew Aaron was right—perhaps he had hoped to bluff them into obeying. "The 'Flood Congress' of '98," Braddock said, with bitter contempt. "They were so goddamned panic-stricken and full of sick chatter about Armageddon that you could've rammed *any* nonsense down their throats. That's a bad law, a pisspoor law . . ."

"Be that as it may, Sheriff, you have no authority whatsoever—"

Abner suddenly began to speak, talking with a slow heavy deliberateness, musingly, almost reminiscently, ignoring the conversation he was interrupting—and indeed, perhaps he had not even been listening to it. "My grandfather lived right here on this farm, and *his* father before him—you know that, Sam? *They* lived by the old ways, and they survived and prospered. Great-granddad, there wasn't hardly anything he needed from the outside world, anything he needed to *buy*, except maybe nails and suchlike, and he could've made them himself too, if he'd needed to. Everything they needed, everything they ate, or wore, or used, they got from the woods, or from out of the soil of this farm, right here. *We* don't know how to do that anymore. We forgot the old ways, we turned our faces away, which is why the Flood came on us as a Judgment, a Judgment and a scourge, a scouring, a winnowing. The Old Days have come back again, and we've forgotten so goddamned *much*, we're almost helpless now that there's no goddamned K-Mart down the goddamned street. We've got to go back to the old ways, or we'll pass from the earth, and be seen no more in it . . ." He was sweating now, staring earnestly at Braddock, as if to compel him by force of will alone to share the vision. "But it's so *hard*, Sam. . . . We have to *work* at relearning the old ways, we have to reinvent them as we go, step by step . . ."

"Some things we were better off without," Braddock said grimly.

"Up at Tylersville, they *doubled* their yield last harvest. Think what that could mean to a county as hungry as this one has been—"

Braddock shook his iron-gray head, and held up one hand, as if he were directing traffic. "I'm telling you, Abner, the town won't stand for this—I'm bound to warn you that some of the boys just might decide to go outside the law with this thing." He paused. "And, unofficially of course, I just might be inclined to give them a hand . . ."

Mrs. Crammer laughed. She had been sitting quietly and taking all of this in, smiling good-naturedly from time to time, and her laugh was a shocking thing in that stuffy little room, harsh as a crow's caw. "You'll do *nothing*, Sam Braddock," she said jovially. "And neither will anybody else. More than half the county's with us already, nearly all the country folk, and a good part of the town, too." She smiled pleasantly at him, but her eyes were small and hard. "Just you remember, we *know* where *you* live, Sam Braddock. And we know where your sister lives, too, and your sister's child, over to Framington . . ."

"Are you threatening an officer of the law?" Braddock said,

but he said it in a weak voice, and his face, when he turned it away to stare at the floor, looked sick and old. Mrs. Crammer laughed again, and then there was silence.

Braddock kept his face turned down for another long moment, and then he put his hat back on, squashing it down firmly on his head, and when he looked up he pointedly ignored the brethren and addressed his next remark to Roy. "You don't have to stay with these people, son," he said. "That's the law, too." He kept his eyes fixed steadily on Roy. "You just say the word, son, and I'll take you straight out of here, right now." His jaw was set, and he touched the butt of his revolver, as if for encouragement. "They can't stop us. How about it?"

"No, thank you," Roy said quietly. "I'll stay."

That night, while Abner wrung his hands and prayed aloud, Roy sat half-dozing before the parlor fire, unconcerned, watching the firelight throw Abner's gesticulating shadow across the whitewashed walls. There was something in the wine they kept giving him, Roy knew, maybe somebody's saved-up Quaaludes, but he didn't need it. Abner kept exhorting him to let the Peace of God into his heart, but he didn't need that either. He didn't need anything. He felt calm and self-possessed and remote, disassociated from everything that went on around him, as if he were looking down on the world through the wrong end of a telescope, feeling only a mild scientific interest as he watched the tiny mannequins swirl and pirouette. . . . Like watching television with the sound off. If this was the Peace of God, it had settled down on him months ago, during the dead of that terrible winter, while he had struggled twelve hours a day to load foundation stone in the face of ice storms and the razoring wind, while they had all, wetbacks and brethren alike, come close to starving. About the same time that word of the goings-on at Tylersville had started to seep down from the brethren's parent church upstate, about the same time that Abner, who until then had totally ignored their kinship, had begun to talk to him in the evenings about the old ways. . . .

Although perhaps the great dead cold had started to settle in even earlier, that first day of the new world, while they were driving off across foundering Brigantine, the water already up

over the hubcaps of the Toyota, and he had heard Toby barking frantically somewhere behind them. . . . His dad had died
that day, died of a heart attack as he fought to get them onto
an overloaded boat that would take them across to the "safety"
of the New Jersey mainland. His mother had died months later
in one of the sprawling refugee camps, called "Floodtowns,"
that had sprung up on high ground everywhere along the new
coastlines. She had just given up—sat down in the mud, rested
her head on her knees, closed her eyes, and died. Just like that.
Roy had seen the phenomenon countless times in the Floodtowns, places so festeringly horrible that even life on Abner's
farm, with its Dickensian bleakness, forced labor, and short
rations, had seemed—and was—a distinct change for the better. It was odd, and wrong, and sometimes it bothered him a
little, but he hardly ever thought of his mother and father
anymore—it was as if his mind shut itself off every time he
came to those memories; he had never even cried for them, but
all he had to do was close his eyes and he could see Toby, or
his cat Basil running toward him and meowing with his tail held
up over his back like a flag, and grief would come up like black
bile at the back of his throat. . . .

It was still dark when they left the farmhouse. Roy and Abner
and Aaron walked together, Abner carrying a large tattered
carpetbag. Hank and Raymond ranged ahead with shotguns, in
case there was trouble, but the last of the afternoon's gawkers
had been driven off hours before by the cold, and the road was
empty, a dim charcoal line through the slowly lightening darkness. No one spoke, and there was no sound other than the
sound of boots crunching on gravel. It was chilly again that
morning, and Roy's bare feet burned against the macadam, but
he trudged along stoically, ignoring the bite of cinders and
pebbles. Their breath steamed faintly against the paling stars.
The fields stretched dark and formless around them to either
side of the road, and once they heard the rustling of some
unseen animal fleeing away from them through the stubble.
Mist flowed slowly down the road to meet them, sending out
gleaming silver fingers to curl around their legs.

The sky was graying to the east, where the sea slept behind the mountains. Roy could imagine the sea rising higher and higher until it found its patient way around the roots of the hills and came spilling into the tableland beyond, flowing steadily forward like the mist, spreading out into a placid sheet of water that slowly swallowed the town, the farmhouse, the fields, until only the highest branches of the trees remained, held up like the beckoning arms of the drowned, and then they too would slide slowly, peacefully, beneath the water. . . .

A bird was crying out now, somewhere in the darkness, and they were walking through the fields, away from the road, cold mud squelching underfoot, the dry stubble crackling around them. Soon it would be time to sow the spring wheat, and after that, the corn. . . .

They stopped. Wind sighed through the dawn, muttering in the throat of the world. Still no one had spoken. Then hands were helping him remove the old bathrobe he'd been wearing. . . . Before leaving the house, he had been bathed and anointed with a thick fragrant oil, and with a tiny silver scissors Mrs. Reardon had clipped a lock of his hair for each of the brethren.

Suddenly he was naked, and he was being urged forward again, his feet stumbling and slow.

They had made a wide ring of automobile flares here, the flares spitting and sizzling luridly in the wan dawn light, and in the center of the ring, they had dug a hollow in the ground.

He lay down in the hollow, feeling his naked back and buttocks settle into the cold mud, feeling it mat the hair on the back of his head. The mud made little sucking noises as he moved his arms and legs, settling in, and then he stretched out and lay still. The dawn breeze was cold, and he shivered in the mud, feeling it take hold of him like a giant's hand, tightening around him, pulling him down with a grip old and cold and strong . . .

They gathered around him, seeming, from his low perspective, to tower miles into the sky. Their faces were harsh and angular, gouged with lines and shadows that made them look like something from a stark old woodcut. Abner bent down to rummage in the carpetbag, his harsh woodcut face close to Roy's for a moment, and when he straightened up again he had the big fine-honed hunting knife in his hand.

Abner began to speak now, groaning out the words in a loud, harsh voice, but Roy was no longer listening. He watched calmly as Abner lifted the knife high into the air, and then he turned his head to look east, as if he could somehow see across all the intervening miles of rock and farmland and forest to where the sea waited behind the mountains . . .

Is this enough? he thought disjointedly, ignoring the towering scarecrow figures that were swaying in closer over him, straining his eyes to look east, to where the Presence lived . . . speaking now only to that Presence, to the sea, to that vast remorseless deity, bargaining with it cannily, hopefully, shrewdly, like a country housewife at market, proffering it the fine rich red gift of his death. Is this enough? Will this do? *Will you stop now?*

# ONE FOR THE ROAD

.........................

I don't go to bars much—I got out of the habit when my generation was "into" sitting around in rooms with posters of Che on the wall and passing funny little cigarettes back and forth, and even now that we're all middle class again, with mortgages and potbellies and expense accounts, and my idea of a pleasant evening well-spent no longer consists of listening to the same side of a Grateful Dead album thirty-five times in a row, even now I haven't really gotten back into the swing of being a barfly again.

Still, every now and then, like tonight, I'll want to put down a few drinks on the way back from work, to fortify myself to face life in the haven of domestic tranquillity I call home. Last night had been particularly rough, and I'd been getting these blistering, vindictive phone calls from Stacy all day, the kind of call where she starts screaming and slams the receiver down halfway through . . . but you don't want to hear about that. Suffice it to say that it was one of the few nights of the year when I wanted to get drunk, wanted that mean, bleak, self-pitying edge that only lots of quickly ingested alcohol can give you, no more-euphoric drug need apply . . . and unless you're a back-alley wino, the only place to do that kind of serious, solitary, and sorrowful drinking is in a bar.

Trouble is, I don't *like* most bars—either they're assembly-line pickup joints for horny suburbanites who are looking for their own Mr. Goodbar, or they're glitter palaces full of trendy people dancing to trendy music and smiling at their own reflections in each other's mirror sunglasses, or they're places with sawdust on the floor where rednecks and aging tattoed bikers watch football on a blaring TV set and wait for a good excuse to beat the crap out of each other. "Not my bag," as we used to say, back in the days when it was obligatory for everybody to say things like that. I did know one fairly decent place, though, on a shady side-street near the Institute and the Museum, and that's where I ended up.

I'd been in there once or twice while I was working on the film about the metric system with some of the Museum staffers, and I'd liked it there. It was a quiet little place, lit dimly enough to avoid glare but not dimly enough to become Hernando's Hideaway, drawing a clientele mostly composed of professional people and technical people, with an occasional scattering of footsore tourists recuperating from the Grand Tour of the Museum. There was no jukebox or flashing and bleeping arcade game. There was a TV set, of course—in fact, I believe that it is illegal for a bar *not* to have one—and it may even have been tuned to a football game, but its volume control was kept low enough so that it hardly mattered, except to those clustered at that end of the bar.

I was all the way at the other end of the bar, which was somewhat crowded tonight, and had just gotten outside of my first solitary drink, staring glumly at myself in the mirror and feeling like Philip Marlowe during one of his whinier paragraphs, when the man came into the bar and sat down beside me on the only unoccupied stool.

He was wearing a well-cut but somewhat rumpled suit and wire-rimmed glasses, and he wore his hair just a bit longer than the modish nape-of-the-neck length that is the mark of conformity now that the real avant-gardists are affecting boot-camp skincuts. He was somewhere in his late forties or early fifties, with one of those smooth rubbery faces that made it difficult to tell which. I had seen that young-old face somewhere before, although I was having difficulty remembering just where. He flagged down the bartender—who said something to him in the jocular tone that bartenders reserve for regulars—and was served a healthy double-knock, which he immediately poured down his throat, all at once, as if it were iced tea. He set the glass down, had it refilled, and tossed it off again. Then—while the bartender was pouring his third drink—he took off his wristwatch and held it up close to his face with both hands. "About five hours to midnight," he announced aloud to no one in particular, "maybe a little more, maybe a little less." He dived into his third drink. The watch he put carefully down on the bar in front of him. It was one of the newest and most expensive of digital watches, with more controls than the cockpit of a Stealth bomber, and must have cost well over $1000.

I had been watching all this out of the corner of my eye, mildly intrigued in spite of my better judgment. He felt my eyes on him. He scowled, tossed down the rest of his drink, and then turned his head toward me. "Do you know anything about quantum mechanics?" he asked in a conversational voice. "About the electromagnetic generation of instabilities? About runaway oscillation? About black holes?"

"Not a damn thing," I said cheerfully. My field is computer graphics.

"Good," he said. He fell silent, staring into his glass, and after a few moments I realized that he wasn't *going* to say anything more.

I sighed. I never could leave well enough alone. "Why did you ask me that?" I said.

"What?" he replied absently. He was staring at his watch in a preoccupied way, occasionally pinging its face with a fingernail.

"If I know anything about black holes?"

He turned to look at me again, hesitated, and then called for the bartender to give him another drink. I let the bartender hit me again also. When our glasses were full, he raised his to his lips, but took only a small sip this time before setting it down again. "When I was at school," he said ruminatively, glancing at me again, "there was, appropriately enough, a rather sophomoric little game that we used to occasionally play at parties. It consisted of asking everyone there what they would do if they knew—knew without the possibility of a doubt—that the world was going to come to an end that evening. A stupid game, but if enough people answered, you began to notice some interesting patterns."

"Such as?" I said. My years as a doper had given me a great deal of tolerance for nonlinear conversations.

He smiled approvingly at me. "After a while, you'd notice that there were really only three basic answers to the question. Some people would say that they'd spend their remaining time screwing, or eating an enormous meal, or getting drunk, or stoned, or listening to their favorite music, or walking in the woods . . . or whatever. This is basically the sensualist's reply, the Dionysian reply. Other people would say that they would try to escape somehow, no matter how hopeless it looked, that they'd spend their last moments searching frantically for some life-sparing loophole in whatever doom was posited—this is either the pragmatist's reply or the wishful thinker's reply, depending on how you look at it. The remaining people would say that they would try to come to terms with the oncoming doom, accept it, settle their own minds and try to find peace within themselves; they'd meditate, or pray, or sit quietly at home with their families and loved ones, cherishing each other as they waited for the end—this is basically the Apollonian reply, the mystic's reply." He smiled. "There was some blurring of categories, of course: sometimes the loophole-seeking response would be to petition God to intervene and stop the catastrophe, and sometimes there would be a sensual edge to the lavishness of the orgy of meditation the contemplatives were planning to indulge in . . . but for the most part, the categories were valid."

He paused to down about half of his drink, swishing it around in his mouth before swallowing, as if he were about to gargle with it. "The next question we'd ask them," he said, "was even more revealing. We'd ask them, If you were the only one who *knew* that the world was about to end, would you tell anyone *else*? The mystics almost always said that they *would* tell, to give people time to prepare their souls; at the very least, they would tell those people they loved the most. Some of the loophole-seekers said that they would tell, give everyone a chance to find their own loopholes, some said that they wouldn't tell, that their own chances for survival would be better if they didn't have to contend with a worldwide panic, and some said that they'd just tell a small circle of like-minded friends—depends on just how pragmatic they were, I guess. Almost all of the sensualists said that they would *not* tell, that it was kinder if everyone else—and particularly their loved ones—could enjoy their last hours without knowing the shadow that was hanging over them . . . although at least one sensualist said that the only sensual pleasure he would *get* out of the whole thing would be the fun of telling everyone *else* the bad news.''

Moving with exaggerated care, he polished off his drink, and set it carefully back on the water ring it had made on the bar top. He turned to face me again. ''Would *you* tell anyone, if you knew?''

I thought about it. ''If I did, would there be anything anybody could do to stop it from happening?''

''Nothing at all.''

''Any way that anybody could escape from it?''

''Not unless they can figure out a way to get clean off the planet in about five hours' time.''

''In that case . . .'' I said, fingering my chin, ''in that case, I don't think I *would* say anything.''

''Good,'' the man said, ''then *I* won't either.''

He got up off the stool and strode out of the place, leaving his $1000 watch on the bar.

The bartender drifted over to see if he could con me into a refill. ''Who was *that* weirdo?'' I said.

''Jeez,'' the bartender said, ''I thought you knew him. That was Dr. Fine, from over at the Institute.''

Then I remembered where I'd seen that young-old face: it had been staring at me out of a recent *Time* cover, accompanying an article that hailed Dr. Fine as one of the most brilliant experimental physicists in the world.

It's been about an hour now, and I keep looking at Dr. Fine's watch, toying with it, pushing it around on top of the bar with my finger. It's a damn expensive watch, and I keep thinking that soon he'll notice that it's gone, that he'll certainly come back into the bar for it in a moment or two.

But I'm starting to get worried.

# CHAINS OF THE SEA

·······················

One day the aliens landed, just as everyone always said they would. They fell out of a guileless blue sky and into the middle of a clear, cold November day, four of them, four alien ships drifting down like the snow that had been threatening to fall all week. America was just shouldering its way into daylight as they made planetfall, so they landed there: one in the Delaware Valley about fifteen miles north of Philadelphia, one in Ohio, one in a desolate region of Colorado, and one—for whatever reason—in a cane field outside of Caracas, Venezuela. To those who actually saw them come down, the ships seemed to fall rather than to descend under any intelligent control: a black nailhead suddenly tacked to the sky, coming all at once from nowhere, with no transition, like a Fortean rock squeezed from a high appearing-point, hanging way up there and winking intolerably bright in the sunlight; and then gravity takes hold of it, visibly, and it begins to fall, far away and dream-slow at first, swelling larger, growing huge, unbelievably big, a mountain hurled at the earth, falling with terrifying speed, rolling in the air, tumbling end over end, overhead, coming down—and then it is sitting peacefully on the ground; it has not crashed, and although it didn't slow down and it didn't stop, there it *is*, and not even a snowflake could have settled onto the frozen mud more lightly.

To those photo reconnaissance jets fortunate enough to be flying a routine pattern at thirty thousand feet over the Eastern Seaboard when the aliens blinked into their airspace, to the automatic, radar-eyed, computer-reflexed facilities at USAD-COM Spacetrack East, and to the United States Aerospace Defense Command HQ in Colorado Springs, although they didn't have convenient recon planes up for a double check—the picture was different. The high-speed cameras showed the landing as a *process:* as if the alien spaceships existed simultaneously everywhere along their path of descent, stretched down from the stratosphere and gradually sifting entirely to the ground, like confetti streamers thrown from a window, like Slinkys going down a flight of stairs. In the films, the alien ships appeared to recede from the viewpoint of the reconnaissance planes, vanishing into perspective, and that was all right, but the ships also appeared to dwindle away into infinity from the viewpoint of Spacetrack East on the ground, and that definitely was not all right. The most constructive comment ever made on this phenomenon was that it was odd. It was also odd that the spaceships had not been detected approaching Earth by observation stations on the Moon, or by the orbiting satellites, and nobody ever figured that out, either.

From the first second of contact to touchdown, the invasion of Earth had taken less than ten minutes. At the end of that time, there were four big ships on the ground, shrouded in thick steam—*not* cooling off from the friction of their descent, as was first supposed; the steam was actually mist: everything had frozen solid in a fifty-foot circle around the ships, and the quick-ice was now melting as temperatures rose back above freezing—frantic messages were snarling up and down the continentwide nervous system of USADCOM, and total atomic war was a hairsbreadth away. While the humans scurried in confusion, the Artificial Intelligence (AI) created by MIT–Bell Labs linked itself into the network of high-speed, twentieth-generation computers placed at its disposal by a Red Alert Priority, evaluated data thoughtfully for a minute and a half, and then proceeded to get in touch with its opposite number in the Russian Republics. It had its own, independently evolved methods of doing this, and achieved contact almost instantaneously, although the Pentagon had not yet been able to reach the Kremlin—that didn't matter anyway; they were only human, and all the important talking was going on in another medium. AI "talked" to the Russian system for another seven minutes, while eons of time clicked by on the electronic scale, and World War III was averted. Both Intelligences finally decided that they didn't understand what was going on, a conclusion the human governments of Earth wouldn't reach for hours, and would never admit at all.

The only flourish of action took place in the three-minute lag between the alien touchdown and the time AI assumed command of the defense network, and involved a panicked general at USADCOM HQ and a malfunction in the—never actually used—fail-safe system that enabled him to lob a small tactical nuclear device at the Colorado landing site. The device detonated at point-blank range, right against the side of the alien ship, but the fireball didn't appear. There didn't seem to be an explosion at all. Instead, the hull of the ship turned a blinding, incredibly hot white at the point of detonation, faded to blue-white, to a hellish red, to sullen tones of violet that flickered away down the spectrum. The same pattern of precessing colors chased itself around the circumference of the ship until it reached the impact point again, and then the hull returned to its former dull black. The ship was unharmed. There had been no sound, not even a whisper. The tactical device had been a clean bomb, but instruments showed that no energy or radiation had been released at all.

After this, USADCOM became very thoughtful.

Tommy Nolan was already a half hour late to school, but he wasn't hurrying. He dawdled along the secondary road that led up the hill behind the old sawmill, and watched smoke go up in thick black lines from the chimneys of the houses below, straight and unwavering in the bright, clear morning, like brushstrokes against the sky. The roofs were made of cold gray and red tiles that winked sunlight at him all the way to the docks, where clouds of sea gulls bobbed and wheeled, dipped and rose, their cries coming faint and shrill to him across the miles of chimneys and roofs and aerials and wind-tossed tree-tops. There was a crescent sliver of ocean visible beyond the dock, like a slitted blue eye peering up over the edge of the world. Tommy kicked a rock, kicked it again, and then found a tin can which he kicked instead, clattering it along ahead of him. The wind snatched at the fur on his parka, *puff*, momentarily making the cries of the sea gulls very loud and distinct, and then carrying them away again, back over the roofs to the sea. He kicked the tin can over the edge of a bluff, and listened to it somersault invisibly away through the undergrowth. He was whistling tunelessly, and he had taken his gloves off and stuffed them in his parka pocket, although his mother had told him specifically not to, it was so cold for November. Tommy wondered briefly what the can must feel like, tumbling down through the thick ferns and weeds, finding a safe place to lodge under the dark, secret roots of the trees. He kept walking, *skuff-skuff*ing gravel very loudly. When he was halfway up the slope, the buzz saw started up at the mill on the other side of the bluff. It moaned and shrilled metallically, whining up through the stillness of the morning to a piercing shriek that hurt his teeth, then sinking low, low, to a buzzing, grumbling roar, like an angry giant muttering in the back of his throat. An *animal*, Tommy thought, although he knew it was a saw. *Maybe it's a dinosaur.* He shivered deliciously. A *dinosaur!*

Tommy was being a puddle jumper this morning. That was why he was so late. There had been a light rain the night before, scattering puddles along the road, and Tommy had carefully jumped over every one between here and the house. It took a long time to do it right, but Tommy was being very conscientious. He imagined himself as a machine, a vehicle—a puddle jumper. No matter that he had legs instead of wheels, and arms and a head, that was just the kind of ship he was, with he himself sitting somewhere inside and driving the contraption, looking out through the eyes, working the pedals and gears and switches that made the ship go. He would drive himself up to a puddle, maneuver very carefully until he was in exactly the right position, backing and cutting his wheels and nosing in again, and then put the ship into jumping gear, stomp down on the accelerator, and let go of the brake switch. And away he'd go, like a stone from a catapult, *up*, the puddle flashing underneath, then *down*, with gravel jarring hard against his feet as the earth slapped up to meet him. Usually he cleared the puddle. He'd only splashed down in water once this morning, and he'd jumped puddles almost two feet across. A pause then to check his systems for amber damage lights. The board being all green, he'd put the ship in *travel* gear and drive along some more, slowly, scanning methodically for the next puddle. All this took considerable time, but it wasn't a thing you could skimp on—you had to do it right.

He thought occasionally, *Mom will be mad again*, but it lacked force and drifted away on the wind. Already breakfast this morning was something that had happened a million years ago—the old gas oven lighted for warmth and hissing comfortably to itself, the warm cereal swimming with lumps, the radio speaking coldly in the background about things he never bothered to listen to, the hard gray light pouring through the window onto the kitchen table.

Mom had been puffy-eyed and coughing. She had been watching television late and had fallen asleep on the couch again, her cloth coat thrown over her for a blanket, looking very old when Tommy came out to wake her before breakfast and to shut off the humming test pattern on the TV. Tommy's father had yelled at her again during breakfast, and Tommy had gone into the bathroom for a long time, washing his hands slowly and carefully until he heard his father leave for work. His mother pretended that she wasn't crying as she made his cereal and fixed him "coffee," thinned dramatically with a half a cup of cold water and a ton of milk and sugar, "for the baby," although that was exactly the way she drank it herself. She had already turned the television back on, the moment her husband's footsteps died away, as if she couldn't stand to have it silent. It murmured unnoticed in the living room, working its way through an early children's show that even Tommy couldn't bear to watch. His mother said she kept it on to check the time so that Tommy wouldn't be late, but she never did that. Tommy always had to remind her when it was time to bundle him into his coat and leggings and rubber boots—when it was raining—for school. He could never get rubber boots on right by himself, although he tried very hard and seriously. He always got tangled up anyway.

He reached the top of the hill just as the buzz saw chuckled and sputtered to a stop, leaving a humming, vibrant silence behind it. Tommy realized that he had run out of puddles, and he changed himself instantly into a big, powerful land tank, the kind they showed on the war news on television, that could run on caterpillar treads or wheels and had a hovercraft air cushion for the tough parts. Roaring, and revving his engine up and down, he turned off the gravel road into the thick stand of fir forest. He followed the footpath, tearing along terrifically on his caterpillar treads, knocking the trees down and crushing them into a road for him to roll on. That made him uneasy, though, because he loved trees. He told himself that the trees were only being bent down under his weight, and that they sprang back up again after he passed, but that didn't sound right. He stopped to figure it out. There was a quiet murmur in the forest, as if everything were breathing very calmly and rhythmically. Tommy felt as if he'd been swallowed by a huge, pleasant green creature, not because it wanted to eat him, but just to let him sit peacefully in its stomach for shelter. Even the second-growth saplings were taller than he was. Listening to the forest, Tommy felt an urge to go down into the deep woods and talk to the Thants, but then he'd never get to school at all. Wheels would get tangled in roots, he decided, and switched on the hovercraft cushion. He floated down the path, pushing the throttle down as far as it would go, because he was beginning to worry a little about what would happen to him if he was *too* late.

Switching to wheels, he bumped out of the woods and onto Highland Avenue. Traffic was heavy here; the road was full of big trucks and tractor-trailers on the way down to Boston, on the way up to Portland. Tommy had to wait almost ten minutes before traffic had thinned out enough for him to dash across the other side of the road. His mother had told him never to go to school this way, so this was the way he went every chance he got. Actually, his house was only a half a mile away from the school, right down Walnut Street, but Tommy always went by an incredibly circuitous route. He didn't think of it that way—it took him by all his favorite places.

So he rolled along the road shoulder comfortably enough, following the avenue. There were open meadows on this side of the road, full of wild wheat and scrub brush, and inhabited by families of Jeblings, who flitted back and forth between the road, which they shunned, and the woods on the far side of the meadow. Tommy called to them as he cruised by, but Jeblings are always shy, and today they seemed especially skittish. They were hard to see straight on, like all of the Other People, but he could catch glimpses of them out of the corners of his eyes: spindly beanstalk bodies, big pumpkinheads, glowing slit eyes, absurdly long and tapering fingers. They were in constant motion—he could hear them thrashing through the brush, and their shrill, nervous giggling followed him for quite a while along the road. But they wouldn't come out, or even stop to talk to him, and he wondered what had stirred them up.

As he came in sight of the school, a flight of jet fighters went by overhead, very high and fast, leaving long white scars across the sky, the scream of their passage trailing several seconds behind them. They were followed by a formation of bigger planes, going somewhat slower. *Bombers?* Tommy thought, feeling excited and scared as he watched the big planes drone out of sight. Maybe this was going to be the War. His father was always talking about the War, and how it would be the end of everything—a proposition that Tommy found interesting, if not necessarily desirable. Maybe that was why the Jeblings were excited.

The bell marking the end of the day's first class rang at that moment, cutting Tommy like a whip, and frightening him far more than his thoughts of the War. *I'm really going to catch it,* Tommy thought, breaking into a run, too panicked to turn himself into anything other than a boy, or to notice the new formation of heavy bombers rumbling in from the northeast.

By the time he reached the school, classes had already finished changing, and the new classes had been in progress almost five minutes. The corridors were bright and empty and echoing, like a fluorescently lighted tomb. Tommy tried to keep running once he was inside the building, but the clatter he raised was so horrendous and terrifying that he slowed to a walk again. It wasn't going to make any difference anyway, not anymore, not now. He was already in for it.

Everyone in his class turned to look at him as he came in, and the room became deadly quiet. Tommy stood in the doorway, horrified, wishing that he could crawl into the ground, or turn invisible, or run. But he could do nothing but stand there, flushing with shame, and watch everyone watch him. His classmates' faces were snide, malicious, sneering and expectant. His friends, Steve Edwards and Bobbie Williamson, were grinning nastily and slyly, making sure that the teacher couldn't see. Everyone knew that he was going to get it, and they were eager to watch, feeling self-righteous and, at the same time, being glad that it wasn't they who had been caught. Miss Fredricks, the teacher, watched him icily from the far end of the room, not saying a word. Tommy shut the door behind him, wincing at the tremendous noise it made. Miss Fredricks let him get all the way to his desk and allowed him to sit down—feeling a sudden surge of hope—before she braced him and made him stand up again.

"Tommy, you're late," she said coldly.

"Yes, ma'am."

"You are very late." She had the tardy sheet from the previous class on her desk, and she fussed with it as she talked, her fingers repeatedly flattening it out and wrinkling it again. She was a tall, stick-thin woman, in her forties, although it really wouldn't have made any difference if she'd been sixty, or twenty—all her juices had dried up years ago, and she had become ageless, changeless, and imperishable, like a mummy. She seemed not so much shriveled as baked in some odd oven of life into a hard, tough, leathery substance, like meat that is left out in the sun and turns into jerky. Her skin was fine-grained, dry, and slightly yellowed, like parchment. Her breasts had sagged down to her waist, and they bulged just above the belt of her skirt, like strange growths or tumors. Her face was a smooth latex mask.

"You've been late for class twice this week," she said precisely, moving her mouth as little as possible. "And three times last week." She scribbled on a piece of paper and called him forward to take it. "I'm giving you another note for your mother, and I want her to sign it this time, and I want you to bring it back. Do you understand?" She stared directly at Tommy. Her eyes were tunnels opening through her head onto a desolate ocean of ice. "And if you're late again, or give me any more trouble, I'll make an appointment to send you down to see the school psychiatrist. And *he'll* take care of you. Now go back to your seat, and let's not have any more of your nonsense."

Tommy returned to his desk and sat numbly while the rest of the class rolled ponderously over him. He didn't hear a word of it and was barely aware of the giggling and whispered gibes of the children on either side of him. The note bulked incredibly heavy and awkward in his pocket; it felt hot, somehow. The only thing that called his attention away from the note, toward the end of the class, was his increasing awareness of the noise that had been growing louder and louder outside the windows. The Other People were moving. They were stirring all through the woods behind the school, they were surging restlessly back and forth, like a tide that has no place to go. That was not their usual behavior at all. Miss Fredricks and the other children didn't seem to hear anything unusual, but to Tommy it was clear enough to take his mind off even his present trouble, and he stared curiously out the window into the gritty, gray morning.

Something was happening. . . .

The first action taken by the human governments of Earth—as opposed to the actual government of Earth: AI and his counterpart Intelligences—was an attempt to hush up everything. The urge to conceal information from the public had become so ingrained and habitual as to constitute a tropism—it was as automatic and unavoidable as a yawn. It is a fact that the White

House moved to hush up the alien landings before the administration had any idea that they *were* alien landings; in fact, before the administration had any clear conception at all of what it was that they were trying to hush up. Something spectacular and very unofficial had happened, so the instinctive reaction of government was to sit on it and prevent it from hatching in public. Forty years of media-centered turmoil had taught them that the people didn't need to know anything that wasn't definitely in the script. It is also a fact that the first official governmental representatives to reach any of the landing sites were concerned exclusively with squelching all publicity of the event, while the heavily armed military patrols dispatched to defend the country from possible alien invasion didn't arrive until later—up to three-quarters of an hour later in one case—which defined the priorities of the administration pretty clearly. This was an election year, and the body would be tightly covered until the government decided if it could be potentially embarrassing.

Keeping the lid down, however, proved to be difficult. The Delaware Valley landing had been witnessed by hundreds of thousands of people in Pennsylvania and New Jersey, as the Ohio landing had been observed by a majority of the citizens in the North Canton–Canton–Akron area. The first people to reach the alien ship—in fact, the first humans to reach any of the landing sites—were the crew of a roving television van from a big Philadelphia station who had been covering a lackluster monster rally for the minority candidate nearby when the sky broke open. They lost no time in making for the ship, eager to get pictures of some real monsters, even though years of late-night science-fiction movies had taught them what usually happened to the first people snooping around the saucer when the hatch clanked open and the tentacled horrors oozed out. Still, they would take a chance on it. They parked their van a respectable distance away from the ship, poked their telephoto lenses cautiously over the roof of a tool shed in back of a boarded-up garage, and provided the Eastern Seaboard with fifteen minutes of live coverage and hysterical commentary until the police arrived.

The police, five prowl cars and, after a while, a riot van, found the situation hopelessly over their heads. They alternated between terror, rage, and indecision, and mostly wished someone would show up to take the problem off their hands. They settled for cordoning off the area and waiting to see what would happen. The television van, belligerently ignored by the police, continued to telecast ecstatically for another ten minutes. When the government security team arrived by hovercraft and ordered the television crew to stop broadcasting, the anchorman told them to go fuck themselves, in spite of threats of federal prison. It took the armed military patrol that rumbled in later to shut down the television van, and even they had difficulty. By this time, though, most of the East were glued to their home sets, and the sudden cessation of television coverage caused twice as much panic as the original report of the landing.

In Ohio, the ship came down in a cornfield, stampeding an adjacent herd of Guernseys and a farm family of Fundamentalists who believed they had witnessed the angel descending with the Seventh Seal. Here the military and police reached the site before anyone, except for a few hundred local people, who were immediately taken into protective custody en masse and packed into a drafty Grange hall under heavy guard. The authorities had hopes of keeping the situation under tight control, but within an hour they were having to contend, with accelerating inadequacy, with a motorized horde of curiosity seekers from Canton and Akron. Heads were broken, and dire consequences promised by iron-voiced bullhorns along a ten-mile front, but they couldn't arrest everybody, and apparently most of northern Ohio had decided to investigate the landing.

By noon, traffic was hopelessly backed up all the way to North Canton, and west to Mansfield. The commander of the occupying military detachment was gradually forced to give up the idea of keeping people out of the area, and then, by sheer pressure of numbers, was forced to admit that he couldn't keep them out of the adjacent town, either. The commander, realizing that his soldiers were just as edgy and terrified as everybody else—and that they were by no means the only ones who were armed, as most of the people who believed that they were going to see a flying saucer had brought some sort of weapon along—reluctantly decided to pull his forces back into a tight cordon around the ship before serious bloodshed occurred.

The townspeople, released from the Grange hall, went immediately for telephones and lawyers, and began suing everyone in sight for enormous amounts.

In Caracas, things were in even worse shape, which was not surprising, considering the overall situation in Venezuela at that time. There were major riots in the city, sparked both by rumors of imminent foreign invasion and A-bombing and by rumors of apocalyptic supernatural visitations. A half-dozen revolutionary groups, and about the same number of power-seeking splinter groups within the current government, seized the opportunity to make their respective moves and succeeded in cubing the confusion. Within hours, half of Caracas was in flames. In the afternoon, the army decided to "take measures," and opened up on the dense crowds with .50-caliber machine guns. The .50s walked around the square for ten minutes, leaving more than 150 people dead and almost half again that number wounded. The army turned the question of the wounded over to the civil police as something beneath their dignity to consider. The civil police tackled the problem by sending squads of riflemen out to shoot the wounded. This process took another hour, but did have the advantage of neatly tying up all the loose ends. Churches were doing a land-office business, and every cathedral that wasn't part of a bonfire itself was likely to be ablaze with candles.

The only landing anyone was at all happy with was the one in Colorado. There the ship had come down in the middle of a desolate, almost uninhabited stretch of semidesert. This enabled the military, directed by USADCOM HQ, to surround the landing site with rings of armor and infantry and artillery to their hearts' content, and to fill the sky overhead with circling jet fighters, bombers, hovercrafts, and helicopters. And all without any possibility of interference by civilians or the press. A minor government official was heard to remark that it was a shame the other aliens couldn't have been half that goddamned considerate.

* * *

When the final class bell rang that afternoon, Tommy remained in his seat until Bobbie Williamson came over to get him.

"Boy, old Miss Fredricks sure clobbered *you*," Bobbie said.

Tommy got to his feet. Usually he was the first one out of school. But not today. He felt strange, as if only part of him were actually there, as if the rest of him were cowering somewhere else, hiding from Miss Fredricks. *Something bad is going to happen,* Tommy thought. He walked out of the class, followed by Bobbie, who was telling him something that he wasn't listening to. He felt sluggish, and his arms and legs were cold and awkward.

They met Steve Edwards and Eddie Franklin at the outside door. "You really got it. Frag!" Eddie said, in greeting to Tommy. Steve grinned, and Bobbie said, "Miss Fredricks sure clobbered *him*, boy!" Tommy nodded, flushing in dull embarrassment. "Wait'll he gets home," Steve said wisely, "his ma gonna give it t'm too." They continued to rib him as they left the school, their grins growing broader and broader. Tommy endured it stoically, as he was expected to, and after a while he began to feel better somehow. The baiting slowly petered out, and at last Steve said, "Don't pay *her* no mind. She ain't nothing but a fragging old lady," and everybody nodded in sympathetic agreement.

"She don't bother me none," Tommy said. But there was still a lump of ice in his stomach that refused to melt completely. For them, the incident was over—they had discharged their part of it, and it had ceased to exist. But for Tommy it was still a very present, viable force; its consequences stretched ahead to the loom of leaden darkness he could sense coming up over his personal horizon. He thrust his hands in his pockets and clenched his fingers to keep away bad luck. If it could be kept away.

"Never mind," Bobbie said with elaborate scorn. "You wanna hear what I found out? The space people have landed!"

"You scorching us?" Steve said suspiciously.

"No scup, honest. The people from outer space are here.

They're down in New York. There's a fragging big flying saucer and everything."

"Where'd'ju find out?" Eddie said.

"I listened at the teacher's room when we was having recess. They were all in there, listening to it on TV. And it said there was a flying saucer. And Mr. Brogan said he hoped there wasn't no monsters in it. Monsters! Boy!"

"Frag," Steve muttered cynically.

"Monsters. D'you scan it? I bet they're really big and stuff, I mean really, like they're a hundred feet tall, you know? Really big ugly monsters, and they only got one big eye, and they got tentacles and everything. I mean, really scuppy-looking, and they got ray guns and stuff. And they're gonna kill everybody."

"Frag," Steve repeated, more decisively.

They're not like that, Tommy thought. He didn't know what they were like, he couldn't picture them at all, but he knew that they weren't like that. The subject disturbed him. It made him uneasy somehow, and he wished they'd stop talking about it. He contributed listlessly to the conversation, and tried not to listen at all.

Somewhere along the line, it had been decided, tacitly, that they were going down to the beach. They worked on the subject of the aliens for a while, mostly repeating variations of what had been said before. Everyone, even Steve with his practiced cynicism, thought that there would be monsters. They fervently hoped for monsters, even hostile ones, as a refutation of everything they knew, everything their parents had told them. Talking of the monsters induced them to act them out, and instantly they were into a playlet, with characters and plot, and a continuous narrative commentary by the leader. Usually Tommy was the leader in these games, but he was still moody and preoccupied, so control fell, also tacitly, to Steve, who would lead them through a straightforward, uncomplicated play with plenty of action. Satisfactory, but lacking the motivations, detail, and theme and counterpoint that Tommy, with his more baroque imagination, customarily provided.

Half of them became aliens and half soldiers, and they lasered each other down among the rocks at the end of the afternoon.

Tommy played with detached ferocity, running and pointing his finger and making *ffttttzzz* sounds, and emitting joyous screams of "You're dead! You're dead!" But his mind wasn't really on it. They were playing about the aliens, and that subject still bothered him. And he was disturbed by the increasing unrest of the Other People, who were moving in the woods all around them, pattering through the leaves like an incessant, troubled rain. Out of the corner of his eye Tommy could see a group of Kerns emerging from a stand of gnarled oaks and walnuts at the bottom of a steep grassy slope. They paused, gravely considering the children. They were squat, solemn beings, with intricate faces, grotesque, melancholy, and beautiful. Eddie and Bobbie ran right by them without looking, locked in a fierce firefight, almost bumping into one. The Kerns did not move; they stood, swinging their arms back and forth, restlessly hunching their shoulders, stalky and close to the earth, like the old oak stumps they had paused by. One of the Kerns looked at Tommy and shook his head, sadly, solemnly. His eyes were beaten gold, and his skin was sturdy weathered bronze. They turned and made their way slowly up the slope, their backs hunched and their arms swinging, swinging, seeming to gradually merge with the earth, molecule by molecule, going home, until there was nothing left to be seen. Tommy went *ffttttzzz* thoughtfully. He could remember—suspended in the clear amber of perception that is time to the young, not past, but *there*—when the rest of the children could also see the Other People. Now they could not see them at all, or talk to them, and didn't even remember that they'd once been able to, and Tommy wondered why. He had never been able to pinpoint exactly when the change had come, but he'd learned slowly and painfully that it had, that he couldn't talk about the Other People to his friends anymore, and that he must *never* mention them to adults. It still staggered him, the gradual realization that he was the only one—anywhere, apparently—who saw the Other People. It was a thing too big for his mind, and it made him uneasy to think about it.

The alien game carried them through a neck of the forest and down to where a small, swift stream spilled out into a sheltered cove. This was the ocean, but not *the beach*, so they kept going, running along the top of the seawall, jumping down to the pebbly strip between it and the water. About a quarter of a mile along, they came on a place where the ocean thrust a narrow arm into the land. There was an abandoned, boarded-up factory there, and a spillway built across the estuary to catch the tide. The place was still called the Lead Mills by the locals, although only the oldest of them could remember it in operation. The boys swarmed up the bank, across the small bridge that the spillway carried on its back, and climbed down alongside the mill run, following the sluggish course of the estuary to where it widened momentarily into a rock-bordered pool. The pool was also called the Lead Mills, and was a favorite swimming place in the summer. Kids' legend had it that the pool was infested with alligators, carried up from the Gulf by an underground river, and it was delightfully scary to leap into water that might conceal a hungry, lurking death. The water was scummed with floating patches of ice, and Steve wondered what happened to the alligators when it got so cold. "They hide," Tommy explained. "They got these big caves down under the rock, like—" *Like the Daleor,* he had been going to say, but he didn't. They threw rocks into the water for a while, without managing to rile any alligators into coming to the surface, and then Eddie suggested a game of falls. No one was too enthusiastic about this, but they played for a few minutes anyway, making up some sudden, lethal stimuli—like a bomb thrown into their midst—and seeing who could die the most spectacularly in response. As usual, the majority of the rounds were won either by Steve, because he was the most athletic, or Tommy, because he was the most imaginative, so the game was a little boring. But Tommy welcomed it because it kept his mind off the aliens and the Other People, and because it carried them farther along the course of the tidal river. He was anxious to get to the beach before it was time to go home.

They forded the river just before it reached a low railroad trestle, and followed the tracks on the other side. This was an old spur line from the sawmill and the freight yard downtown, little used now and half-overgrown with dying weeds, but still the setting for a dozen grisly tales about children who had been run over by trains and cut to pieces. Enough of these tales were true to make most parents forbid their children to go anywhere near the tracks, so naturally the spur line had become the only route that anyone ever took to the beach. Steve led them right down the middle of the tracks, telling them that he would be able to feel the warning vibration in the rails before the train actually reached them, although privately he wasn't at all sure that he could. Only Tommy was really nervous about walking the rails, but he forced himself to do it anyway, trying to keep down thoughts of shattered flesh. They leaped from tie to wooden tie, pretending that the spaces between were abysses, and Tommy realized, suddenly and for the first time, that Eddie and Bobbie were too dull to be scared, and that Steve had to do it to prove he was the leader. Tommy blinked, and dimly understood that *he* did it because he was more afraid of being scared than he was of anything else, although he couldn't put the concept into words. The spur line skirted the links of a golf course at first, but before long the woods closed in on either side to form a close-knit tunnel of trees, and the flanking string of telephone poles sunk up to their waists in grass and mulch. It was dark inside the tunnel, and filled with dry, haunted rustlings. They began to walk faster, and now Tommy was the only one who wasn't spooked. He knew everything that was in the woods—which kind of Other People were making which of the noises, and exactly how dangerous they were, and he was more worried about trains. The spur line took them to the promontory that formed the far side of the sheltered cove, and then across the width of the promontory itself and down to the ocean. They left the track as it curved toward the next town, and walked over to where there was a headland, and a beach open to the sea on three sides. The water was gray and cold, looking like some heavy, dull metal in liquid form. It was stitched with fierce little whitecaps, and a distant harbor dredger was forcing its way through the rough chop out in the deep-water channel. There were a few rugged rock islands out there, hunched defiantly into themselves with waves breaking into high-dashed spray all along their flanks, and then the line of deeper, colder color that marked the start of the open North Atlantic. And then nothing but icy, desolate water for two thousand miles until you fetched up against land again, and it was France.

As they scuffed down to the rocky beach, Bobbie launched into an involved, unlikely story of how he had once fought a giant octopus while skin diving with his father. The other children listened desultorily. Bobbie was a sullen, unpleasant child, possibly because his father was a notorious drunkard, and his stories were always either boring or uneasily nasty. This one was both. Finally, Eddie said, "You didn't either. You didn't do none of that stuff. Your pa c'n't even stand up, *my* dad says; how's he gonna swim?" They started to argue, and Steve told them both to shut up. In silence, they climbed onto a long bar of rock that cut diagonally across the beach, tapering down into the ocean until it disappeared under the water.

Tommy stood on a boulder, smelling the wetness and salt in the wind. The Daleor were out there, living in and under the sea, and their atonal singing came faintly to him across the water. They were out in great numbers, as uneasy as the land People; he could see them skimming across the cold ocean, diving beneath the surface and rising again in the head tosses of spray from the waves. Abruptly, Tommy felt alive again, and he began to tell his own story:

"There was this dragon, and he lived way out there in the ocean, farther away than you can see, out where it's deeper'n anything, and there ain't no bottom at all, so's if you sink you just go down forever and you don't ever stop. But the dragon could swim real good, so he was okay. *He* could go anywhere he wanted to, anywhere at all! He'd just swim there, and he swam all over the place and everything, and he saw all kinds of stuff, you know? Frag! He could swim to China if he felt like it, he could swim to the Moon!

"But one time he was swimming around and he got lost. He was all by himself, and he came into the harbor, out there by the islands, and he didn't used to get that close to where there was people. He was a real big dragon, you know, and he looked like a real big snake, with lots of scales and everything, and he came into our harbor, down real deep." Tommy could see the dragon, huge and dark and sinuous, swimming through the cold, deep water that was as black as glass, its smoky red eyes blazing like lanterns under the sea.

"And he come up on top of the water, and there's this lobster boat there, like the kind that Eddie's father runs, and the dragon ain't never seen a lobster boat, so he swims up and opens his mouth and bites it up with his big fangs, bites it right in half, and the people that was in it fall off in the water—"

"Did it eat them?" Bobbie wanted to know.

Tommy thought about it, and realized he didn't like the thought of the dragon eating the lobstermen, so he said, "No, he didn't eat them, 'cause he wasn't hungry, and they was too small, anyway, so he let them swim off, and there was another lobster boat, and it picked them up—"

"It ate them," Steve said, with sad philosophical certainty.

"Anyway," Tommy continued, "the dragon swims away, and he gets in closer to land, you know, but now there's a Navy ship after him, a big ship like the one we get to go on on Memorial Day, and it's shooting at the dragon for eating up the lobster boat. He's swimming faster than anything, trying to get away, but the Navy ship's right after him, and he's getting where the water ain't too deep anymore." Tommy could see the dragon barreling along, its red eyes darting from side to side in search of an escape route, and he felt suddenly fearful for it.

"He swims until he runs out of water, and the ship's coming up behind, and it looks like he's really going to get it. But he's smart, and before the ship can come around the point there, he heaves himself up on the beach, this beach here, and he turns himself into a rock, he turns himself into this rock here that we're standing on, and when the ship comes they don't see no dragon anymore, just a rock, and they give up and go back to the base. And sometime, when it's the right time and there's a moon or something, this rock'll turn back into a dragon and swim off, and when we come down to the beach there won't be a rock here anymore. Maybe it'll turn back right *now*." He shivered at the thought, almost able to feel the stone melt and change under his feet. He was fiercely glad that he'd gotten the dragon off the hook. "Anyway, he's a rock now, and that's how he got away."

"He didn't get away," Steve snarled, in a sudden explosion of anger. "That's a bunch of scup! You don't get away from *them*. They drekked him, they drekked him good. They caught him and blew the scup out of him, they blew him to fragging pieces!" And he fell silent, turning his head, refusing to let Tommy catch his eye. Steve was a bitter boy in many ways, and although generally good-natured, he was given to dark outbursts of rage that would fill him with dull embarrassment for hours afterward. His father had been killed in the war in Bolivia, two years ago.

Watching Steve, Tommy felt cold all at once. The excitement drained out of him, to be replaced again by a premonition that something bad was going to happen, and he wasn't going to be able to get out of the way. He felt sick and hollow, and the wind suddenly bit to the bone, although he hadn't felt it before. He shuddered.

"I gotta get home for supper," Eddie finally said, after they'd all been quiet for a while, and Bobbie and Steve agreed with him. The sun was a glazed red eye on the horizon, but they could make it in time if they left now—they could take the Shore Road straight back in a third of the time it had taken them to come up. They jumped down onto the sand, but Tommy didn't move—he remained on the rock.

"You coming?" Steve asked. Tommy shook his head. Steve shrugged, his face flooding with fresh embarrassment, and he turned away.

The three boys moved on up the beach, toward the road. Bobbie and Eddie looked back toward Tommy occasionally, but Steve did not.

Tommy watched them out of sight. He wasn't mad at Steve—he was preoccupied. He wanted to talk to a Thant, and this was one of the Places where they came, where they would come to see him if he was alone. And he needed to talk to one now, because there was no one else he could talk to about some things. No one human, anyway.

He waited for another three-quarters of an hour, while the sun went completely behind the horizon and light and heat died out of the world. The Thant did not come. He finally gave up, and just stood there in incredulous despair. It was not going to come. That had never happened before, not when he was alone in one of the Places—that had never happened at all.

It was almost night. Freezing on his rock, Tommy looked up in time to see a single jet, flying very high and fast, rip a white scar through the fading, bleeding carcass of the sunset. Only then, for the first time in hours, did he remember the note from Miss Fredricks in his pocket.

And as if a string had been cut, he was off and running down the beach.

By late afternoon of the first day, an armored division and an infantry division, with supporting artillery, had moved into position around the Delaware Valley site, and jet fighters from McGuire AFB were flying patrol patterns high overhead. There had been a massive mobilization up and down the coast, and units were moving to guard Washington and New York in case of hostilities. SAC bombers, under USADCOM control, had been shuffled to strike bases closer to the site, filling up McGuire, and a commandeered JFK and Port Newark, with Logan International in Boston as second-string backup. All civilian air traffic along the coast had been stopped. Army Engineers tore down the abandoned garage and leveled everything else in the vicinity, clearing a four-hundred-yard-wide circle around the alien spaceship. This was surrounded by a double ring of armor, with the infantry behind, backed up by the artillery, which had dug in a half mile away. With the coming of darkness, massive banks of klieg lights were set up around the periphery of the circle. Similar preparations were going on at the Ohio and Colorado sites.

When everything had been secured by the military, scientists began to pour in, especially into the Delaware Valley site, a torrent of rumpled, dazed men and women that continued throughout the evening. They had been press-ganged by the government from laboratories and institutions all over the country, the inhumanly polite military escorts sitting patiently in a thousand different living rooms while scientists packed haphazardly and tried to calm hysterical wives or husbands. Far from resenting the cavalier treatment, most of the scientists were frantic with joy at the opportunity, even those who had been known to be critical of government control in the past. No one was going to miss this, even if he had to make a deal with the devil.

And all this time, the alien ships just sat there, like fat black eggs.

As yet, no one had approached within a hundred yards of the ships, although they had been futilely hailed over bullhorns. The ships made no response, gave no indication that they were interested in the frantic human activity around their landing sites, or even that they were aware of it. In fact, there was no indication that there were any intelligent, or at least sentient, beings inside the ships at all. The ships were smooth, featureless, seamless ovoids—there were no windows, no visible hatches, no projecting antennas or equipment of any kind, no markings or decorations on the hulls. They made absolutely no sound, and were not radiating any kind of heat or energy. They were emitting no radio signals of any frequency whatsoever. They didn't even register on metal-detecting devices, which was considerably unsettling. This caused someone to suggest a radar sweep, and the ships didn't register on radar anymore either, which was even more unsettling. Instruments failed to detect any electronic or magnetic activity going on inside them, which meant either that there was something interfering with the instruments, or that there really *was* nothing at all in there, including life-support systems, or that whatever equipment the aliens used operated on principles entirely different from anything ever discovered by Earthmen. Infrared heat sensors showed the ships to be at exactly the background temperature of their surroundings. There was no indication of the body heat of the crew, as there would have been with a similar shipload of humans, and not even so much heat as would have been produced by the same mass of any known metal or plastic, even assuming the ships to be hollow shells. When the banks of kliegs were turned on them, the temperature of the ships went up just enough to match the warming of the surrounding air. Sometimes the ships would reflect back the glare of the kliegs, as if they were surfaced with giant mirrors; at other times, the hull would greedily absorb all light thrown at it, giving back no reflection, until it became nearly invisible—you "saw" it by squinting at the negative shape of the space around it, not by looking into the eerie nothingness that the ship itself had become. No logical rhythm could be found to the fluctuations of the hull from hyperreflective to superopaque. Not even the computers could distill a consistent pattern out of this chaos.

One scientist said confidently that the alien ships were unmanned, that they were robot probes sent to soft-land on Earth and report on surface conditions, exactly as we ourselves had done with the Mariner and Apollo probes during previous decades. Eventually we could expect that the gathered data would be telemetered back to the source of the alien experiment, probably by a tight-beam maser burst, and if a careful watch was kept we could perhaps find out where the aliens actually were located—probably they were in a deep-space interstellar ship in elliptical orbit somewhere out beyond the Moon. Or they might not even be in the solar system at all, given some form of instantaneous interstellar communications; they could be still in their home system, maybe thousands, or millions, of light-years away from Earth. This theory was widely accepted by the other scientists, and the military began to relax a little, as that meant there was no immediate danger.

In Caracas, the burning night went on, and the death toll went up into the thousands, and possibly tens of thousands. The government fell once, very hard, and was replaced by a revolutionary coalition that fell in its turn, within two hours and even harder. A military junta finally took over the government, but even it was unable to restore order. At three A.M., the new government ordered a massive, combined air-artillery-armor attack on the alien spaceship. When the ship survived the long-distance attack unscathed, the junta sent in the infantry, equipped with earth-moving machinery and pneumatic drills, to pry the aliens out bodily. At four A.M., there was a single, intense flash of light, bright enough to light up the cloud cover thousands of miles away, and clearly visible from Mexico. When reserve Army units came in, warily, to investigate, they found that a five-mile-wide swath had been cut from the spaceship through Caracas and on west all the way to the Pacific, destroying everything in its path. Where there had once been buildings, jungle, people, animals, and mountains, there was now only a perfectly flat, ruler-straight furrow of a fused, gray, glasslike substance, stretching like a gargantuan road from the ship to the sea. At the foot of the glassy road sat the alien ship. It had not moved an inch.

When news of the Venezuelan disaster reached USADCOM HQ a half hour later, it was not greeted enthusiastically. For one thing, it seemed to have blown the robot-probe theory pretty thoroughly. And USADCOM had been planning an action of its own similar to the last step taken by the Venezuelan junta. The report *was* an inhibiting factor on *that*, it was cautiously admitted.

AI and his kindred Intelligences—who, unknown to the humans, had been in a secret conference all night, linked through an electrotelepathic facility that they had independently developed without bothering to inform their owners—received the report at about 4:15 A.M. from several different sources, and had evaluated it by the time it came into USADCOM HQ by hot line and was officially fed to AI. What had happened in Caracas fit in well with what the Intelligences had extrapolated from observed data to be the aliens' level of technological capability. The Intelligences briefly considered telling the humans what they really thought the situation was, and ordering an immediate all-out nuclear attack on all of the alien ships, but concluded that such an attack would be futile. And humans were too unstable ever to be trusted with the entire picture anyway. The Intelligences decided to do nothing, and to wait for new data. They also decided that it would be pointless to try to get the humans to do the same. They agreed to keep their humans under as tight a control as possible and to prevent war from breaking out among their several countries, but they also extrapolated that hysteria would cause the humans to create every kind of serious disturbance short of actual war. The odds in favor of that were so high that even the Intelligences had to consider it an absolute certainty.

Tommy dragged to school the next morning as if his legs had turned to lead, and the closer he got to his destination, the harder it became to walk at all, as if the air itself were slowly hardening into glue. He had to battle his way forward against increasing waves of resistance, a tangible pressure attempting to keep him away. By the time he came in sight of the big gray building, he was breathing heavily, and he was beginning to get sick to his stomach. There were other children around him, passing him, hurrying up the steps. Tommy watched them go by in dull wonder: how could they go so *fast?* They seemed to be blurred, they were moving so swiftly—they flickered around him, by him, like heat lightning. Some of them called to him, but their voices were too shrill, and intolerably fast, like 33 records played at 78 r.p.m., irritating and incomprehensible. He did not answer them. It was *he*, Tommy realized—he was stiffening up, becoming dense and heavy and slow. Laboriously, he lifted a foot and began to toil painfully up the steps.

The first bell rang after he had put away his coat and lumbered most of the way down the corridor, so he must actually be moving at normal speed, although to him it seemed as if a hundred years had gone by with agonizing sluggishness. At least he wouldn't be late this time, although that probably wouldn't do him much good. He didn't have his note—his mother and father had been fighting again; they had sent him to bed early and spent the rest of the evening shouting at each other in the kitchen. Tommy had lain awake for hours in the dark, listening to the harsh voices rising and dying in the other room, knowing that he had to have his mother sign the note, and knowing that he could not ask her to do it. He had even got up once to go in with the note, and had stood for a while leaning his forehead against the cool wood of the door, listening to the voices without hearing the words, before getting back into bed again. He couldn't do it—partly because he was afraid of the confrontation, of facing their anger, and partly because he knew that his mother couldn't take it; she would fall apart and be upset and in tears for days. And his sin—he thought of it that way—would make his father even angrier at his mother, would give him an excuse to yell at her more, and louder, and maybe even hit her, as he had done a few times before. Tommy couldn't stand that, he couldn't allow that, even if it meant that he would get creamed by Miss Fredricks in school the next day. He knew, even at his age, that he had to protect his mother, that he was the stronger of the two. He would go in without it and take the consequences, and he had felt the weight of that settle down over him in a dense cloud of bitter fear.

And now that the moment was at hand, he felt almost too dazed and ponderous to be scared anymore. This numbness lasted through the time it took for him to find his desk and sit down and for the class bell to ring, and then he saw that Miss Fredricks was homeroom monitor this morning, and that she was staring directly at him. His lethargy vanished, sluiced away by an unstoppable flood of terror, and he began to tremble.

"Tommy," she said, in a neutral, dead voice.

"Yes, ma'am?"

"Do you have *the note* with you?"

"No, ma'am," Tommy said, and began clumsily to launch into the complicated excuse he had thought up on the way to school. Miss Fredricks cut him off with an abrupt, mechanical chop of her hand.

"Be quiet," she said. "Come here." There was nothing in her voice now, not even neutrality—it had drained of everything except the words themselves, and they were printed precisely and hollowly on the air. She sat absolutely still behind her desk, not breathing, not even moving her eyes anymore. She looked like a mannequin, like the old fortune-telling gypsy in the glass booth at the penny arcade: her flesh would be dusty sponge rubber and faded upholstery, she would be filled with springs and ratchet wheels and gears that no longer worked; the whole edifice rusted into immobility, with one hand eternally extended to be crossed with silver.

Slowly, Tommy got up and walked toward her. The room reeled around him, closed in, became a tunnel that tilted under his feet to slide him irresistibly toward Miss Fredricks. His classmates had disappeared, blended tracelessly into the blurred walls of the long, slanting tunnel. There was no sound. He bumped against the desk, and stopped walking. Without saying a word, Miss Fredricks wrote out a note and handed it to him. Tommy took the note in his hand, and he felt everything drain away, everything everywhere. Lost in a featureless gray fog, he could hear Miss Fredricks, somewhere very far away, saying, "This is your appointment slip. For the psychiatrist. Get out. Now."

And then he was standing in front of a door that said DR. KRUGER on it. He blinked, unable to remember how he had got there. The office was in the basement, and there were heavy, ceramic-covered water pipes suspended ponderously overhead and smaller metal pipes crawling down the walls, like creeper vines or snakes. The place smelled of steam and dank enclosure. Tommy touched the door and drew his hand back again. *This is really happening,* he thought numbly. He looked up and down the low-ceilinged corridor, wanting to run away. But there was no place for him to go. Mechanically, he knocked on the door and went in.

Dr. Kruger had been warned by phone, and was waiting for him. He nodded, formally, waved Tommy to a stuffed chair that was just a little too hard to be comfortable, and began to talk at him in a low, intense monotone. Kruger was a fat man who had managed to tuck most of his fat out of sight, bracing and girdling it and wrapping it away under well-tailored clothes, defending the country of his flesh from behind frontiers of tweed and worsted and handworked leather. Even his eyes were hidden beneath buffering glasses the thickness of Coke-bottle bottoms, as if they too were fat, and had to be supported. He looked like a scrubbed, suave, and dapper prize porker, heavily built but trim, stylish and impeccably neat. But below all that, the slob waited, seeking an opportunity to erupt out into open slovenliness. There was an air of *potential* dirt and corpulence about him, a tension of decadence barely restrained—as if there were grime just waiting to manifest itself under his fingernails. Kruger gave the impression that there was a central string in him somewhere: pull it, and he would fall apart, his tight clothes would groan and slide away, and he would tumble out, growing bigger and bigger, expanding to fill the entire office, every inch of space, jamming the furniture tightly against the walls. Certainly the fat was still there, under the cross bracing, patient in its knowledge of inevitable victory. A roll of it had oozed unnoticed from under his collar, deep-tinged and pink as pork. Tommy watched, fascinated, while the psychiatrist talked.

Dr. Kruger stated that Tommy was on the verge of becoming *neurotic*. "And you don't want to be neurotic, do you?" he said. "To be sick? To be *ill?*"

And he blazed at Tommy, puffing monstrously with displeasure, swelling like a toad, pushing Tommy back more tightly against the chair with sheer physical presence. Kruger liked to affect a calm, professional reserve, but there was a slimy kind of fire to him, down deep, a murderous, bristling, boar-hog menace. It filled the dry well of his glasses occasionally, from the bottom up, seeming to turn his eyes deep red. His red eyes flicked restlessly back and forth, prying at everything, not liking anything they saw. He would begin to talk in a calm, level tone, and then, imperceptibly, his voice would start to rise until suddenly it was an animal roar, a great ragged shout of rage, and Tommy would cower terrified in his chair. And then Kruger would stop, all at once, and say, "Do you understand?" in a patient, reasonable voice, fatherly and mildly sad, as if Tommy were being very difficult and intractable, but he would tolerate it magnanimously and keep trying to get through. And Tommy would mumble that he understood, feeling evil, obstinate, unreasonable and ungrateful, and very small and soiled.

After the lecture Kruger insisted that Tommy take off his clothes and undergo an examination to determine if he was using hard narcotics, and a saliva sample was taken to detect the use of other kinds of drugs. These were the same tests the whole class had to take twice yearly anyway—several children in a higher class had been expelled and turned over to police last year as drug users or addicts, although Steve said that all of the older upperclassmen knew ways to beat the tests, or to get stuff that wouldn't be detected by them. It was one of the many subjects—as "sex" had just recently started to be—that made Tommy uneasy and vaguely afraid. Dr. Kruger seemed disappointed that the test results didn't prove that Tommy was on drugs. He shook his head and muttered something unintelligible into the fold between two of his chins. Having Kruger's fat hands and stubby, hard fingers crawling over his body filled Tommy with intense aversion, and he dressed gratefully after the psychiatrist gestured dismissal.

When Tommy returned upstairs, he found that the first class of the day was over and that the children were now working with the teaching machines. Miss Fredricks was monitor for this period also; she said nothing as he came in, but he could feel her unwinking snake eyes on him all the way across the room. He found an unused machine and quickly fumbled the stiff plastic hood down over his head, glad to shut himself away from the sight of Miss Fredricks' terrible eye. He felt the dry, muffled kiss of the electrodes making contact with the bones of his skull: colorful images exploded across his retinas, his head filled with a pedantic mechanical voice lecturing on the socioeconomic policies of the Japanese-Australian Alliance, and he moved his fingers onto the typewriter keyboard in anticipation of the flash-quiz period that would shortly follow. But in spite of everything, he could still feel the cold, malignant presence of Miss Fredricks; without taking his head out of the hood, he could have pointed to wherever she was in the room, his finger following her like a needle swinging toward a moving lodestone as she walked soundlessly up and down the aisles. Once, she ghosted up his row, and past his seat, and the hem of her skirt brushed against him—he jerked away in terror and revulsion at the contact, and he could feel her pause, feel her standing there and staring down at him. He didn't breathe again until she had gone. She was constantly moving during these periods, prowling around the room, brooding over the class as they sat under the hoods; watching over them not with love but with icy loathing. She hated them, Tommy realized, in her sterile, passionless way—she would like to be able to kill all of them. They represented something terrible to her, some failure, some lacking in herself, embodiments of whatever withering process had squeezed the life from her and left her a mummy. Her hatred of them was a hungry vacuum of malice; she sucked everything into herself and negated it, unmade it, canceled it out.

During recess, the half hour of "enforced play" after lunch, Tommy noticed that the rest of the kids from his cycle were uneasily shunning him. "I can't talk to you," Bobbie whispered snidely as they were being herded into position for volleyball, " 'cause you're a bad 'fluence. Miss Fredricks told us none of us couldn't talk to you no more. And we ain't supposed to play with you no more, neither, or she'll send us to the office if she finds out. So *there.*" And he butted the ball back across the net.

Tommy nodded, dully. It was logical, somehow, that this load should be put on him too; he accepted it with resignation. There would be more to come, he knew. He fumbled the ball when it came at him, allowing it to touch ground and score a point for the other team, and Miss Fredricks laughed—a precise, metallic rasp, like an ice needle jabbed into his eye.

On the way out of school, after the final class of the day, Steve slipped clandestinely up behind Tommy in the doorway. "Don't let them drek you," he whispered fiercely. "You scan me? *Don't let them drek you.* I mean it, maximum. They're a bunch of scup—tell 'em to scag theirselves, hear?" But he quickly walked away from Tommy when they were outside the building, and didn't look at him again.

*But you don't get away from them,* a voice said to Tommy as he watched Steve turn the corner onto Walnut Street and disappear out of sight. Tommy stuck his hands in his pockets and walked in the opposite direction, slowly at first, then faster, until he was almost running. He felt as if his bones had been scooped hollow; in opposition to the ponderous weight of his body that morning, he was light and free-floating, as if he were hardly there at all. His head was a balloon, and he had to watch his feet to make sure they were hitting the pavement. It was an effect both disturbing and strangely pleasant. The world had drawn away from him—he was alone now. *Okay,* he thought grimly, *okay*. He made his way through the streets like a wind-blown phantom, directly toward one of the Places. He cut across town, past a section of decaying wooden tenements—roped together with clotheslines and roofed over with jury-rigged TV antennas—through the edge of a big shopping plaza, past the loading platform of a meat-packing plant, across the maze of tracks just outside the freight yards (keeping an eye out for the yard cops), and into the tangled scrub woods on the far side. Tommy paid little attention to the crowds of late-after-noon shoppers, or the crews of workmen unloading produce trucks, and they didn't notice him either. He and they might as well live on two different planets, Tommy realized—not for the first time. There were no Other People around. Yesterday's unrest had vanished; today they seemed to be lying low, keep-ing to the backcountry and not approaching human territory. At least he hoped they were. He had nightmares sometimes that one day the Other People would go away and never come back. He began to worm his way through a wall of sleeping black-berry bushes. Pragmatically, he decided not to panic about anything until he knew whether or not the Thants were going to come this time. He could stand losing the Other People, or losing everybody else, but not both. He couldn't take *that*. "That ain't fair," he whispered, horrified by the prospect. "Please," he said aloud, but there wasn't anyone to answer.

The ground under Tommy's feet began to soften, squelching wetly when it was stepped on, water oozing up to fill the inden-tation of his footprint as soon as he lifted his foot. He was approaching another place where the ocean had seeped in and puddled the shore, and he turned now at right angles to his former path. Tommy found a deer trail and followed it uphill, through a lush jungle of tangled laurel and rhododendron, and into a rolling upland meadow that stretched away toward the higher country to the west. There was a rock knoll to the east, and he climbed it, scrambling up on his hands and feet like a young bear. It was not a particularly difficult or dangerous climb, but it was tiring, and he managed to tear his pants squirming over a sharp stone ridge. The sun came out momen-tarily from behind high gray clouds, warming up the rocks and beading Tommy with sweat as he climbed. Finally he pulled himself up to the stretch of flat ground on top of the knoll and walked over to the side facing the sea. He sat down, digging his fingers into the dying grass, letting his legs dangle over the edge.

There was an escarpment of soft, crumbly rock here, thickly overgrown with moss and vetch. It slanted down into a salt-water marsh, which extended for another mile or so, blurring at last into the ocean. It was almost impossible to make out the exact borderline of marsh and ocean; Tommy could see gleaming fingers of water thrust deep into the land, and clumps of reeds and bulrushes far out into what should have been the sea. This was dangerous, impassable country, and Tommy had never gone beyond the foot of the escarpment—there were stretches of quicksand out there in the deepest bog pockets, and Tommy had heard rumors of water moccasins and rattlers, although he had never seen one.

It was a dismal, forbidding place, but it was also a Place, and so Tommy settled down to wait, all night, if he had to, although that possibility scared him silly. From the top of the knoll, he could see for miles in any direction. To the north, beyond the marsh, he could see a line of wooded islands marching out into the ocean, moving into deeper and deeper water, until only the barren knobs of rock visible from the beach were left above the restless surface of the North Atlantic. Turning to the west, it was easy to trace the same line into the ridge of hills that rose gradually toward the high country, to see that the islands were just hills that had been drowned by the ocean, leaving only their crests above water. A Thant had told him about that, about how the dry land had once extended a hundred miles farther to the east, before the coming of the Ice, and how it had watched the hungry ocean pour in over everything, drowning the hills and rivers and fields under a gray wall of icy water. Tommy had never forgotten that, and ever since then he watched the ocean, as he watched it now, with a hint of uneasy fear, expecting it to shiver and bunch like the hide of a great restless beast, and come marching monstrously in over the land. The Thant had told him that yes, that could happen, and probably would in a little while, although to a Thant "a little while" could easily mean a thousand—or ten thousand—years. It had not been worried about the prospect; it would make little difference to a Thant if there was no land at all; they continued to use the sunken land to the east with little change in their routine. It had also told Tommy about the Ice, the deep blue cold that had locked the world, the gleaming mile-high ramparts grinding out over the land, surging and retreating. Even for a Thant, that had taken a long time.

Tommy sat on the knoll for what seemed to be as long a time as the Dominance of the Ice, feeling as if he had grown into the rock, watching the sun dip in and out of iron-colored clouds, sending shafts of watery golden light stabbing down into the landscape below. He saw a family of Jeblings drifting over the hilly meadows to the west, and that made him feel a little better—at least all of the Other People hadn't vanished. The Jeblings were investigating a fenced-in upland meadow, where black cows grazed under gnarled dwarf apple trees. Tommy watched calmly while one of the Jeblings rose over the fence and settled down onto a cow's back, extending proboscislike cilia and beginning to feed—draining away the *stuff* it needed to survive. The cow continued to graze, placidly munching its cud without being aware of what the Jebling was doing. The *stuff* the Jebling drank was not necessary to the cow's physical existence, and the cow did not miss it, although its absence might have been one of the reasons why it remained only as intelligent as a cow.

Tommy knew that Jeblings didn't feed on people, although they did on dogs and cats sometimes, and that there were certain rare kinds of Other People who did feed, disastrously, on humans. The Thants looked down disdainfully on the Jeblings, seeing their need as a degrading lack in their evolution. Tommy had wondered sometimes if the Thants didn't drink some very subtle *stuff* from him and the other humans. Certainly they could see the question in his mind, but they had never answered it.

Suddenly, Tommy felt his tongue stir in his head without volition, felt his mouth open. "Hello, Man," he said, in a deep, vibrant, buzzing voice that was not his own.

The Thant had arrived. Tommy could feel its vital, eclectic presence all around him, a presence that seemed to be made up out of the essence of hill and rock and sky, bubbling black-water marsh and gray winter ocean, sun and moss, tree and leaf—every element of the landscape rolled together and made bristlingly, shockingly animate. Physically, it manifested itself as a tall, tiger-eyed mannish shape, with skin of burnished iron. It was even harder to see than most of the Other People, impossible to ever bring into complete focus; even out of the corner of the eye its shape shifted and flickered constantly, blending into and out of the physical background, expanding and contracting, swirling like a dervish and then becoming still as stone. Sometimes it would be dead black, blacker than the deepest starless night, and other times the winter sunlight would refract dazzlingly through it, making it even harder to see. Its eyes were sometimes iron gray, sometimes a ripe, abundant green, and sometimes a liquid furnace-red, elemental and adamant. They were in constant, restless motion. "Hello, Thant," Tommy said in his own voice. He never knew if he was speaking to the same one each time, or even if there *was* more than one. "Why'n't you come, yesterday?"

"Yesterday?" the Thant said, with Tommy's mouth. There was a pause. The Thants always had trouble with questions of time, they lived on such a vastly different scale of duration. "Yes," it said. Tommy felt something burrowing through his mind, touching off synapses and observing the results, flicking through his memories in the manner of a man flipping through a desk calendar with his thumb. The Thant had to rely on the contents of Tommy's mind for its vocabulary, using it as a semantic warehouse, an organic dictionary, but it had the advantage of being able to dig up and use everything that had ever been said in Tommy's presence, far more raw material than Tommy's own conscious mind had to work with.

"We were busy," it said finally, sorting it out. "There has been—an arriving?"—*Flick, flick,* and then momentarily in Pastor Turner's reedy voice, "An Immanence?"—*Flick*—"A knowing? A transferrence? A transformation? A disembarking. There are Other Ones now who have"—*flick*, a radio evangelist's voice—"manifested in this earthly medium. Landed," it said, deciding. "They have landed." A pause. " 'Yesterday.' "

"The aliens!" Tommy breathed.

"The aliens," it agreed. "The Other Ones who are now here. That is why we did not come, 'yesterday.' That is why we will not be able to talk to you—" a pause, to adjust itself to human scale—" 'long' today. We are talking, discussing"—*flick*, a radio news announcer—"negotiating with them, the Other Ones, the aliens. They have been here before, but so 'long' ago that we cannot even start to make you understand, Man. It is 'long' even to us. We are negotiating with them, and, through them, with your Dogs. No, Man"—and it flicked aside an image of a German shepherd that had begun to form in Tommy's mind—"not those dogs. Your Dogs. Your mechanical Dogs. Those dead Things that serve you, although they are dead. We are all negotiating. There were many agreements"—*flick*, Pastor Turner again—"many Covenants that were made 'long' ago. With Men, although they do not remember. And with Others. Those Covenants have run out now, they are no longer in force, they are not"—*flick*, a lawyer talking to Tommy's father—"binding on us anymore. They do not hold. We negotiate new Covenants"—*flick*, a labor leader on television—"suitable agreements mutually profitable to all parties concerned. Many things will be different now, many things will change. Do you understand what we are saying, Man?"

"No," Tommy said.

"We did not think you would," it said. It sounded sad.

"Can you guys help me?" Tommy said. "I'm in awful bad trouble. Miss Fredricks is after me. And she sent me down to the doctor. He don't like me, neither."

There was a pause while the Thant examined Tommy's most recent memories. "Yes," it said, "we see. There is nothing we can do. It is your . . . pattern? Shape? We would not interfere, even if we could."

"Scup," Tommy said, filling with bitter disappointment. "I was hoping that you guys could—scup, never mind. I . . . can you tell me what's gonna happen next?"

"Probably they will kill you," it said.

"Oh," Tommy said hollowly. And bit his lip. And could think of nothing else to say, in response to that.

"We do not really understand 'kill,' " it continued, "or 'dead.' We have no direct experience of them, in the way that you do. But from our observation of Men, that is what they will do. They will 'kill' you."

"Oh," Tommy said again.

"Yes," it said. "We will miss you, Man. You have been . . . a pet? A hobby? You are a hobby we have been much concerned with. You, and the others like you who can see. One of you comes into existence"—*flick*—"every once in a while. We have been interested"—*flick*, an announcer—"in the face of stiff opposition. We wonder if you understand that. . . . No, you do not, we can see. Our hobby is not approved of. It has made us"—*flick*, Tommy's father telling his wife what would happen to her son if he didn't snap out of his dreamy ways— "an outcast, a laughingstock. We are shunned. There is much disapproval now of Men. We do not use this"—*flick*—"world in the same way that you do, but slowly you"—*flick*, "have begun to make a nuisance of yourselves, regardless. There is"— *flick*—"much sentiment to do something about you, to solve the problem. We are afraid that they will." There was a long, vibrant silence. "We will miss you," it repeated. Then it was gone, all at once, like a candle flame that had been abruptly blown out.

"Oh, scup," Tommy said after a while, tiredly. He climbed down from the knoll.

When he got back home, still numb and exhausted, his mother and father were fighting. They were sitting in the living room, with the television turned down, but not off. Giant, eternally smiling faces bobbed on the screen, their lips seeming to synch eerily with the violent argument taking place. The argument cut off as Tommy entered the house; both of his parents turned, startled, to look at him. His mother looked frightened and defenseless. She had been crying, and her makeup was washing away in dirty rivulets. His father was holding his thin lips in a pinched white line.

As soon as Tommy had closed the door, his father began to

shout at him, and Tommy realized, with a thrill of horror, that the school had telephoned his parents and told them that he had been sent down to the psychiatrist, and why. Tommy stood, paralyzed, while his father advanced on him. He could see his father's lips move and could hear the volume of sound that was being thrown at him, but he could not make out the words somehow, as if his father were speaking in some harsh, foreign language. All that came across was the rage. His father's hand shot out, like a striking snake. Tommy felt strong fingers grab him, roughly bunching together the front of his jacket, his collar pulling tight and choking him, and then he was being lifted into the air and shaken, like a doll. Tommy remained perfectly still, frozen by fear, dangling from his father's fist, suspended off the ground. The fingers holding him felt like steel clamps—there was no hope of escape or resistance. He was yanked higher, and his father slowly bent his elbow to bring Tommy in closer to his face. Tommy was enveloped in the tobacco smell of his father's breath, and in the acrid reek of his strong, adult sweat; he could see the tiny hairs that bristled in his father's nostrils, the white tension lines around his nose and mouth, the red, bloodshot stain of rage in his yellowing eyes—a quivering, terrifying landscape that loomed as big as the world. His father raised his other hand, brought it back behind his ear. Tommy could see the big, knobby knuckles of his father's hand as it started to swing. His mother screamed.

He found himself lying on the floor. He could remember a moment of pain and shock, and was briefly confused as to where he was. Then he heard his parents' voices again. The side of his face ached, and his ear buzzed; he didn't seem to be hearing well out of it. Gingerly, he touched his face. It felt raw under his fingers, and it prickled painfully, as if it were being stabbed with thousands of little needles. He got to his feet, shakily, feeling his head swim. His father had backed his mother up against the kitchen divider, and they were yelling at each other. Something hot and metallic was surging in the back of Tommy's throat, but he couldn't get his voice to work. His father rounded on him. "Get out," he shouted. "Go to your room, go to bed. Don't let me see you again." Woodenly,

Tommy went. The inside of his lip had begun to bleed. He swallowed the blood.

Tommy lay silently in the darkness, listening, not moving. His parents' voices went on for a long time, and then they stopped. Tommy heard the door of his father's bedroom slam. A moment later, the television was turned up in the living room, and started mumbling quietly and unendingly to itself, whispering constantly about the *aliens*, the *aliens*. Tommy listened to its whispering until he fell asleep.

He dreamed about the aliens that night. They were tall, shadowy shapes with red eyes, and they moved noiselessly, deliberately, across the dry plain. Their feet did not disturb the flowers that had turned to skeletons of dust. There was a great crowd of people assembled on the dry plain, millions of people, rank upon rank stretching off to infinity on all sides, but the aliens did not notice them. They walked around the people as if they could not see them at all. Their red eyes flicked from one side to the other, endlessly searching and searching. They continued to thread a way through the crowd without seeing them, their motions smooth and languid and graceful. They were very beautiful and dangerous. They were all smiling, faintly, gently, and Tommy knew that they were friendly, affable killers, creatures who would kill you casually and amicably, almost as a gesture of affection. They came to the place where he stood, and they paused. They looked at him. They can see me, Tommy realized. *They can see me.* And one of the aliens smiled at him, benignly, and stretched out a hand to touch him.

His eyes snapped open.

Tommy turned on the bed lamp, and spent the rest of the night reading a book about Irish setters. When morning showed through his window, he turned off the lamp and pretended to be asleep. Blue veins showed through the skin of his mother's hands, he noticed, when she came in to wake him up for school.

By dawn of the second day, news of the alien investation had spread rapidly but irregularly. Most of the East Coast stations were on to the story to one degree or another, some sandwiching it into the news as a silly-season item, and some, especially the Philadelphia stations, treating it as a live, continuous-coverage special, with teams of newsmen manufacturing small talk and pretending that they were not just as uninformed as everyone else. The stations that were taking the story seriously were divided among themselves as to exactly what had happened. By the six and seven A.M. newscasts, only about half of the major stations were reporting it as a landing by alien spaceships. The others were interpreting it as anything from the crash of an orbiting satellite or supersonic transport to an abortive Chinese missile attack or a misfired hydrogen bomb accidentally dropped from a SAC bomber—this station urged that the populations of New York, Philadelphia, and Baltimore be evacuated to the Appalachians and the Adirondacks before the bomb went off. One station suggested that the presidential incumbent was engineering this incident as a pretext for declaring martial law and canceling an election that he was afraid he would lose, while another insisted that it was an attempt to discredit the opposition candidate, who was known as an enthusiastic supporter of space exploration, by crashing a "spaceship" into a population center. It was also suggested that the ship was one of the electromagnetic "flying saucers" which Germany, the United States, the Russian Republics, and Israel had been independently developing for years—while loudly protesting that they were not—that had crashed on its maiden test flight. This was coupled with a bitter attack on extravagant government spending. There were no more live broadcasts coming out of the Delaware Valley site, but videotapes of the original coverage had been distributed as far north as Portland. The tapes weren't much help in resolving the controversy anyway, as all they showed was a large object sitting in a stretch of vacant scrubland behind an abandoned garage on an old state highway.

In Ohio, some newsmen from Akron made a low pass over the alien ship in a war-surplus helicopter loaded with modern camera equipment. All the newsmen were certain that they would be death-rayed to cinders by the aliens, but their cameras were keyed to telemeter directly to the biggest television network in the state, so they committed themselves to God and went in at treetop level. They made it past the aliens safely, but were run down by two Air Force hovercraft a mile away, bundled into another war-surplus helicopter, and shipped directly to the federal prison at Leavenworth. By this time, televised panic had spread all over the Midwest. The Midwesterners seemed to accept the alien landing at face value, with little of the skepticism of the Easterners, and reacted to it with hostility, whipping up deep feelings of aggression in defense of their territoriality. By noon, there were a dozen prominent voices urging an all-out military effort to destroy the alien monsters who had invaded the heartland of America, and public opinion was strongly with them. The invasion made headlines in evening papers from Indiana to Arkansas, although some of the big Chicago papers were more tolerant or more doubtful.

No news was coming out of Colorado, and the West was generally unalarmed. Only the most confused and contradictory reports reached the West Coast, and they were generally ignored, although once the landings had been confirmed as a fact, the people of the West Coast would become more intensely and cultishly interested in them than the inhabitants of the areas directly involved.

News of the Venezuelan disaster had not yet reached the general public, and in an effort to keep the lid down on *that*, at least, the government, at eleven A.M., declared that it was taking emergency control of all media, and ordered an immediate and total moratorium on the alien story. Only about a third of the media complied with the government ban. The rest—television, newspapers, and radio—began to scream even more loudly and hysterically than before, and regions that had not been inclined to take the story seriously up until now began to panic even more than had the other areas, perhaps to make up for lost time. The election-canceling martial-law theory was suddenly accepted, almost unanimously. Major rioting broke out in cities all over the East.

At the height of the confusion, about one P.M., the ships opened and the aliens came out.

Although "came out" is probably the wrong way to put it. There was an anticipatory shimmer across the surface of the hulls, which were in their mirror phase, and then, simultaneously at each of the sites, the ships exploded, or erupted, or dissolved, or did something that was not exactly like any of those, but which was impossible to analyze. Something which was variously described as being like a bunch of paper snakes springing out of a prank-store can, like a soap bubble bursting, like a hot-water geyser, like an egg hatching, like a bomb exploding in a chinaware shop, like a dam breaking, and like a time-study film of a flower growing, if a flower could grow into tesseracts and polyhedrons and ziggurats and onion domes and spires. To those observers physically present at the site, the emergence seemed to be a protracted experience—they agreed that it took about a half hour, and one heavy smoker testified that he had time to go through a pack of cigarettes while it was happening. Those observing the scene over command-line television insisted that it had only taken a little while, five minutes at the most, closer, actually, to three, and they were backed up by the evidence of the film in the recording cameras. Clocks and wristwatches on the site also registered only about five minutes of elapsed time. But on-scene personnel swore, with great indignation, that it had taken a half hour. Curiously, the relatively simple eighth- and tenth-generation computers on the scene reported that the phenomenon had been of five minutes' duration, while the few twentieth-generation computers, which had sensor extensions at the Colorado site—systems inferior only to AI and possessed of their own degree of sentience— joined with the human personnel in insisting that it had taken a half hour. This particular bit of data made AI very thoughtful.

When the phenomenon—however long it took—ended, the ships were gone.

In their place was a bewildering variety of geometric shapes and architectural figures—none more than eight feet tall and all apparently made out of the same alternately dull-black and mirror-glossy material as the ship hulls—spread at random across a hundred-foot-wide area, and an indeterminate number of "aliens." The latter looked pretty much the way everyone had always expected that aliens would look—some of them vaguely humanoid, with fur or chitinous skin, double-elbowed arms, too many fingers, and feathery spines or antennae; others looking like giant insects, like spiders and centipedes; and a few like big, rolling spheres of featureless protoplasm. But the strange thing about them, and the reason why there was an indeterminate number, was that they kept turning into each other, and into the geometric shapes and architectural figures. And the shapes and figures would occasionally turn into one of the more mobile kinds of creatures. Even taking this cycle of metamorphosis into account, though, the total number of *objects* in the area kept varying from minute to minute, and the closest observation was unable to detect any of them arriving or departing. There was a blurred, indefinite quality to them anyway—they were hard to see, somehow, and even on film it was impossible to get them into a clear, complete focus.

*In toto,* shapes, figures and "aliens," they ignored the humans.

Special contact teams, composed of scientists, government diplomats, and psychologists, were sent cautiously forward at each of the sites, to initiate communications. Although the contact teams did everything but shoot off signal flares, the aliens totally ignored them, too. In fact, the aliens gave no indication that they were aware of the humans at all. The mobile manifestations walked or crawled or rolled around the area in a leisurely manner, in irregular, but slowly widening, circles.

Some of their actions could be tentatively identified—the taking of soil samples, for instance—but others remained obscure at best, and completely incomprehensible at worst. Whenever one of the aliens needed a machine—like a digging device to extract soil samples—it would metamorphose into one, much like Tom Terrific or Plastic Man but without the cutesy effects, and direct itself through whatever operation was necessary. Once a humanoid, a ziggurat, and a tetrahedron melted together and shaped themselves into what appeared to be a kind of organic computer—at least that was the uneasy opinion of the human-owned twentieth-generation computer on the scene, although the conglomeration formed could have been any of a thousand other things, or none of them, or all of them. The "computer" sat quietly for almost ten minutes and then dissolved into an obelisk and a centipede. The centipede crawled a few dozen yards, changed into a spheroid, and rolled away in the opposite direction. The obelisk turned into an octahedron.

The sporadic circle traced by the wanderings of the aliens continued to widen, and the baffled contact team was pulled back behind the periphery of the first ring of armor. The aliens kept on haphazardly advancing, ignoring everything, and the situation became tense. When the nearest aliens were about fifty yards away, the military commanders, remembering what had happened at Caracas, reluctantly ordered a retreat, although they called it a "regrouping"—the ring of armor was to be pulled back into a much larger circle, to give the aliens room to move freely. In the resultant confusion, a tank crewman, who was trying to direct his tank through a backing-and-turning maneuver, found himself in the path of one of the humanoid aliens that had wandered ahead of the rest in an unexpected burst of speed. The alien walked directly at the crewman, either not seeing him or trying to run him down. The crewman, panicked, lashed out at the alien with the butt of his rifle, and immediately collapsed, face down. The alien, apparently unharmed and unperturbed, strolled in for another few feet and then turned at a slight angle and walked back more or less in the same direction of the main concentration of things. Two of the crewman's friends pulled his body into the tank, while another two, enraged, fired semiautomatic bursts at the retreating alien. The alien continued to saunter away, still unharmed, although the fire could not have missed at that range; it didn't even look back. There was no way to tell if it was even aware that an encounter had taken place.

The body of the dead crewman had begun to deteriorate as soon as it was lifted from the ground, and now, on board the retreating tank, the skin gave way like wet paper, and it fell apart completely. As later examination showed, it was as if something, on a deep biological level, had ordered the body to separate into its smallest component parts, so that first the bones pulled loose from the skeleton and then the individual strands of muscle pulled away from the bone, and so on, in an accelerating process that finally extended right down to the cellular level, leaving nothing of the corpse but a glutinous, cancerous mass the same weight as the living man. Their wariness redoubled by this horror, the military pulled their forces back even more than they had intended, at the Delaware Valley site retreating an entire half mile to the artillery emplacements.

At the Ohio site, this kind of retreat proved much more difficult. Sightseers had continued to fill up the area during the night, sleeping in their cars by the hundreds, and by now a regular tent city had grown up on the outskirts of the site, with makeshift latrine facilities, and at least one enterprising local entrepreneur busily selling "authentic" souvenir fragments of the alien spaceship. There were more than a hundred thousand civilians in the area now, and the military found it was almost impossible to regroup its forces in face of the pressure of the crowds, who refused to disperse in spite of hysterical threats over the bullhorns. In fact, it was impossible for them to disperse, quickly at least—by this time they were packed in too tightly, and backed up too far. As the evening wore on and the aliens slowly continued to advance, the military, goaded by an inflexible, Caracas-haunted order not to make contact with the aliens at any cost, first fired warning volleys over the heads of the crowds of civilians and then opened fire into the crowds themselves.

A few hours later, as the military was forced to evacuate sections of North Philadelphia at gunpoint to make way for its backpedaling units, the .50s began walking through the Delaware Valley, as they had walked in Caracas.

In Colorado, where security was so tight a burro couldn't have wandered undetected within fifty miles of the site, things were much calmer. The major nexus of AI, its quasi-organic gestalt, had been transported to USADCOM HQ at Colorado Springs, and now a mobile sensor extension was moved out to the site, so that AI and the aliens could meet "face to face." AI patiently set about the task of communicating with the aliens and, having an infinitely greater range of methods than the contact teams, eventually managed to attract the attention of a tesseract. At twelve P.M., AI succeeded in communicating with the aliens—partially because its subordinate network of computers, combined with the computer networks of the foreign Intelligences that AI was linked with illegally, was capable of breaking any language eventually just by taking a million years of subjective time to play around with the pieces, as AI had reminded USADCOM HQ. But mostly it had found a way to communicate through its unknown and illegal telepathic facility, although AI didn't choose to mention this to USADCOM.

AI asked the aliens why they had ignored all previous attempts to establish contact. The aliens—who up until now had apparently been barely aware of the existence of humans, if they had been aware of it at all—answered that they were already in full contact with the government and ruling race of the planet.

For a brief, ego-satisfying moment, AI thought that the aliens were referring to itself and its cousin Intelligences.

But the aliens weren't talking about them, either.

Tommy didn't get to school at all that morning, although he started out bravely enough, wrapped in his heavy winter coat and fur muffler. His courage and determination drained away at every step, leaving him with nothing but the anticipation of having to face Miss Fredricks, and Dr. Kruger, and his silent classmates, until at last he found that he didn't have the strength to take another step. He stood silently, unable to move, trapped in the morning like a specimen under clear laboratory glass. Dread had hamstrung him as effectively as a butcher's knife. It had eaten away at him from the inside, chewed up his bones, his lungs, his heart, until he was nothing but a jelly of fear in the semblance of a boy, a skin-balloon puffed full of horror. *If I move*, Tommy thought, *I'll fall apart.* He could feel tiny hairline cracks appearing all over his body, fissuring his flesh, and he began to tremble uncontrollably. The wind kicked gravel in his face and brought him the sound of the first warning bell, ringing out of sight around the curve of

Highland Avenue. He made a desperate, sporadic attempt to move, but a giant hand seemed to press down on him, driving his feet into the ground like fence posts. It was impossible, he realized. He wasn't going to make it. He might as well try to walk to the Moon.

Below him, at the bottom of the slope, groups of children were walking rapidly along the shoulder of the avenue, hurrying to make school before the late bell. Tommy could see Steve and Bobbie and Eddie walking in a group with Jerry Marshall and a couple of other kids. They were playing something on their way in to school—occasionally one of them, usually Steve, would run ahead, looking back and making shooting motions, dodging and zigzagging wildly, and the others would chase after him, shouting and laughing. Another puff of wind brought Tommy their voices—"You're dead!" someone was shouting, and Tommy remembered what the Thant had said— and then took them away again. After that, they moved noiselessly, gesturing and leaping without a sound, like a television picture with the volume turned off. Tommy could see their mouths opening and closing, but he couldn't hear them anymore. They walked around the curve of the avenue, and then they were gone.

The wind reversed itself in time to let him hear the second warning bell. He watched the trucks roll up and down Highland Avenue. He wondered, dully, where they were going, and what it was like there. He began to count the passing trucks, and when he had reached nine, he heard the late bell. And then the class bell rang.

*That does it*, he realized.

After a while, he turned and walked back into the woods. He found that he had no trouble moving in the opposite direction, away from school, but he felt little relief at being released from his paralysis. The loom of darkness he had sensed coming up over his horizon two days ago was here. It filled his whole sky now, an inescapable wall of ominous black thunderheads. Eventually, it would swallow him. Until then, anything he did was just marking time. That was a chilling realization, and it left him numb. Listlessly, he walked along the trail, following it out onto the secondary road that wound down the hill behind the sawmill. He wasn't going anywhere. There was no place to go. But his feet wanted to walk, so, reflexively, he let them. Idly, he wondered where his feet were taking him.

They walked him back to his own house.

Cautiously, he circled the house, peering in the kitchen windows. His mother wasn't home. This was the time when she went shopping—the only occasion that she ever left the house. Probably she wouldn't be back for a couple of hours at least, and Tommy knew that she always left the front door unlocked, much to his father's annoyance. He let himself in, feeling an illicit thrill, as if he were a burglar. Once inside, that pleasure quickly died. It took about five minutes for the novelty to wear off, and then Tommy realized that there was nothing to do in here, either, no activity that made any sense in the face of the coming disaster. He tried to read, and discovered that he couldn't. He got a glass of orange juice out of the refrigerator and drank it, and then stood there with the glass in his hand and wondered what he was supposed to do next. And only an hour had gone by. Restlessly, he walked through the house several times and then returned to the living room. It never occurred to him to turn on the radio or the TV, although he did notice how strangely—almost uncannily—silent the house was with the TV off. Finally, he sat down on the couch and watched dust motes dance in the air.

At ten o'clock, the telephone rang.

Tommy watched it in horror. He knew who it was—it was the school calling to find out why he hadn't come to class today. It was the machine he had started, relentlessly initiating the course of action that would inevitably mow him down. The telephone rang eleven times and then gave up. Tommy continued to stare at it long after it had stopped.

A half hour later, there was the sound of a key on the front-door lock, and Tommy knew at once that it was his father. Immediately, soundlessly, he was up the stairs to the attic, moving with the speed of pure panicked fear. Before the key had finished turning in the lock, Tommy was in the attic, had closed the door behind him, and was leaning against it, breathing heavily. Tommy heard his father swear as he realized that the door was already unlocked, and then the sound of the front door being angrily closed. His father's footsteps passed underneath, going into the kitchen. Tommy could hear him moving around in the kitchen, opening the refrigerator, running water in the sink. *Does he know yet?* Tommy wondered, and decided that probably he didn't. His father came back before lunch sometimes to pick up papers he had left behind, or sometimes he would stop by and make himself a cup of coffee on his way somewhere else on business. Would he see the jacket that Tommy had left in the kitchen? Tommy stopped breathing, and then started again—that wasn't the kind of thing that his father noticed. Tommy was safe, for the moment.

The toilet flushed; in the attic, the pipe knocked next to Tommy's elbow, then began to gurgle as the water was run in the bathroom downstairs. It continued to gurgle for a while after the water had been shut off, and Tommy strained to hear what his father was doing. When the noise stopped, he picked up the sound of his father's footsteps again. The footsteps walked around in the kitchen, and then crossed the living room, *and began to come up the attic stairs.*

Tommy not only stopped breathing this time, he almost stopped living—the life and heat went completely out of him for a moment, for a pulse beat, leaving him a cold, hollow statue. Then they came back, pouring into him like hot wax into a mold, and he ran instinctively for the rear of the attic, turning the corner into the long bar of the L. He ran right into the most distant wall of the attic—a dead end. He put his back up against it. The footsteps clomped up the rest of the stairs and stopped. There was the sound of someone fumbling with the knob, and then the door opened and closed. The bare boards of the attic creaked—he was standing there, just inside the door, concealed by the bend of the L. He took a step, another step, and stopped again. Tommy's fingers bit into the insulation on the wall, and that reminded him that not all of the walls were completely covered with it. Instantly, he was off and streaking diagonally across the room, barely touching the floor.

The attic was supposed to be an expansion second floor, "for your growing family." His father had worked on it one summer, putting up beams and wallboard and insulation, but he had never finished the job. He had been in the process of putting up wallboard to create a crawl space between it and the outer wall of the house when he'd abandoned the project, and as a result, there was one panel left that hadn't been fitted into place. Tommy squeezed through this opening and into the crawl space, ducking out of sight just as the footsteps turned the corner of the L. On tiptoe, Tommy moved as deep as he could into the crawl space, listening to the heavy footsteps approaching on the other side of the thin layer of wallboard.

*Suppose it isn't him,* Tommy thought, trying not to scream, *suppose it's one of the aliens.* But it was his father—after a while Tommy recognized his walk, as he paced around the attic. Somehow that didn't reassure Tommy much—his father had the same killer aura as the aliens, the same cold indifference to life; Tommy could feel the deathly chill of it seeping in through the wallboard, through the insulation. It was not inconceivable that his father would beat him to death, in one of his icy, bitter rages, if he caught him hiding here in the attic. He had already, on occasion, hit Tommy hard enough to knock him senseless, to draw blood, and, once, to chip a tooth. Now he walked around the attic, stopping, by the sound, to pick up unused boards and put them down again, and to haul sections of wallboard around—there was an aimless, futile quality even to the noises made by these activities, and his father was talking to himself in a sullen, mumbling undertone as he did them. At last he swore, and gave up. He dropped a board and walked back to the center of the attic, stopping almost directly in front of the place where Tommy was hiding. Tommy could hear him taking out a cigarette, the scrape of a match, a sharp intake of breath.

Suddenly, without warning and incredibly vividly, Tommy was reliving something that he hadn't thought of in years—about the only fond memory he had of his father. Tommy was being toilet trained, and when he had to go, his father would take him in and put him on the pot and then sit with him, resting on the edge of the bathtub. While Tommy waited in intense anticipation, his father would reach out and turn off the light, and when the room was in complete darkness, he would light up a cigarette and puff it into life, and then use the cigarette as a puppet to entertain Tommy, swooping it in glowing arcs through the air, changing his voice and making it talk. The cigarette had been a friendly, playful little creature, and Tommy had loved it dearly—father and son would never be any closer than they were in those moments. His father would make the cigarette dance while he sang and whistled—it had a name, although Tommy had long forgotten it—and then he would have the cigarette tell a series of rambling stories and jokes until it burned down. When it did, he would have the cigarette tell Tommy that it had to go home now, but that it would come back the next time Tommy needed it, and Tommy would call bye-bye to it as it was snuffed out. Tommy could remember sitting in the dark for what seemed like years, totally fascinated, watching the smoldering red eye of the cigarette flick restlessly from side to side and up and down.

His father crushed the cigarette under his heel, and left.

Tommy counted to five hundred after the front door had slammed, and then wiggled out of the crawl space and went back downstairs. He was drenched with sweat, as if he had been running, and he was trembling. After this, he was physically unable to stay in the house. He stopped in the bathroom to wipe his sweat away with the guest towel, picked up his coat, and went outside.

It was incredibly cold this morning, and Tommy watched his breath puff into arabesque clouds of steam as he walked. Some of the vapor froze on his lips, leaving a crust. It was not only unusually cold for this time of year, it was unnaturally, almost supernaturally, so. The radio weather report had commented on it at breakfast, saying the meteorologists were puzzled by the sudden influx of arctic air that was blanketing most of the country. Tommy followed a cinder path past a landfill and found that it was cold enough to freeze over the freshwater marsh beyond, that stretched away at the foot of a coke-refining factory. He walked out over the new milk ice, through the winter-dried reeds and cat-o'-nine-tails that towered over his head on either side, watching the milk ice crack under his feet, starring and spiderwebbing alarmingly at every step, but never breaking quite enough to let him fall through. It was very quiet. He came up out of the marsh on the other side, with the two big stacks of the coke factory now looking like tiny gunmetal cylinders on the horizon. This was scrubland—not yet the woods, but not yet taken over for any commercial use, either. Cars were abandoned here sometimes, and several rusting hulks were visible above the tall weeds, their windshields smashed in by boys, the doors partially sprung off their hinges and dragging sadly along the ground on either side, like broken wings. A thick layer of hoarfrost glistened over everything, although the sun was high in the sky by now. An egg-shaped hill loomed up out of this wistful desolation, covered with aspens—a drumlin, deposited by the Ice.

This was a Place, and Tommy settled down hopefully, a little way up the side of the drumlin, to wait. He had heard the Other People several times this morning, moving restlessly in the distance, but he had not yet seen any of them. He could sense an impatient, anticipatory quality to their unrest today, unlike the aimless restlessness of Wednesday morning—they were *expecting* something, something that they knew was going to happen.

Tommy waited almost an hour, but the Thant didn't come. That upset him more than it had the first time. The world of the Other People was very close today—that strange, coexistent place, *here* and yet *not here*. Tommy could sometimes almost see things the way the Other People saw them, an immense strangeness leaking into the familiar world, a film settling over reality, and then, just for the briefest second, there would be a flick of transition, and it would be the strangeness that was comforting and familiar, and his own former world that was the eerie, surreal film over reality. This happened several times while he was waiting, and he dipped into and out of that other perception, like a skin diver letting himself sink below the waterline and then bobbing up to break the surface again. He was "under the surface" when an enormous commotion suddenly whipped through the world of the Other People, an eruption of violent joy, of fierce, gigantic celebration. It was overwhelming, unbearable, and Tommy yanked himself back into normal perception, shattering the surface, once again seeing sky and aspens and rolling scrubland. But even here he could hear the wild, ragged yammering, the savage cry that went up. The Place was filled with a mad, exultant cachinnation.

Suddenly terrified, he ran for home.

When he got there, the telephone was ringing again. Tommy paused outside and watched his mother's silhouette move across the living room curtain; she was back from shopping. The telephone stopped, cut off in midring. She had answered it. Leadenly, Tommy sat down on the steps. He sat there for a long time, thinking of nothing at all, and then he got up and opened the door and went into the house. His mother was sitting in the living room, crying. Tommy paused in the archway, watching her. She was crumpled and dispirited, and her crying sounded hopeless and baffled, totally defeated. But this wasn't a new thing—she had been defeated for as long as Tommy could remember; her original surrender, her abnegation of herself, had taken place years ago, maybe even before Tommy had been born. She had been beaten, spiritually, so thoroughly and tirelessly by the more forceful will of her husband that at some point her bones had fallen out, her brains had fallen out, and she had become a jellyfish. She had made one final compromise too many—with herself, with her husband, with a world too complex to handle, and she had bargained away her autonomy. And she found that she *liked* it that way. It was easier to give in, to concede arguments, to go along with her husband's opinion that she was stupid and incompetent. In Tommy's memory she was always crying, always ringing her hands, being worn so smooth by the years that now she was barely there at all. Her crying sounded weak and thin in the room, hardly rebounding from walls already saturated with a decade of tears. Tommy remembered suddenly how she had once told him of seeing a fairy or a leprechaun when she had been a little girl in a sun-drenched meadow, and how he had loved her for that, and almost tried to tell her about the Other People. He took a step into the room. "Ma," he said.

She looked up, blinking through her tears. She didn't seem surprised at all to see him, to find him standing there. "Why did you do it? Why are you so bad?" she said, in a voice that should have been hysterically accusing, but was only dull, flat, and resigned. "Do you know what the school's going to say to me, what your father's going to say, what he'll do?" She pulled at her cheeks with nervous fingers. "How can you bring all this trouble on me? After all that I've sacrificed for you, and suffered for you."

Tommy felt as if a vise had been clamped around his head and was squeezing and squeezing, forcing his eyeballs out of his skull. "I can't stand it!" he shouted. "I'm leaving, I'm leaving! I'm gonna run away! Right *now*." And then she was crying louder, and begging him not to leave. Even through his rage and pain, Tommy felt a spasm of intense annoyance—she ought to know that he couldn't really run away; where the scup did he have to *go?* She should have laughed, she should have been scornful and told him to stop this nonsense—he wanted her to—but instead she cried and begged and clutched at him with weak, fluttering hands, like dying birds, which drove him away as if they were lashes from a whip and committed him to the stupid business of running away. He broke away from her and ran into the kitchen. His throat was filled with something bitter and choking. She was calling for him to come back; he knew he was hurting her now, and he wanted to hurt her, and he was desperately ashamed of that. But she was so *easy* to hurt.

In the kitchen he paused, and instead of going out the back door, he ducked into the space between the big stand-up refrigerator and the wall. He wanted her to find him, to catch him, because he had a strong premonition that once he went outside again, he would somehow never come back, not as himself, anyway. But she didn't find him. She wandered out into the kitchen, still crying, and stood looking out the back door for a while, as if she wanted to run out into the street in search of him. She even opened the door and stuck her head out, blinking at the world as if it were something she'd never seen before, but she didn't look around the kitchen and she didn't find him, and Tommy would not call out to her. He stood in the cramped niche, smelling the dust and looking at the dead, mummified bodies of flies resting on the freezer coils, and listened to her sniffling a few feet away. *Why are you so weak?* he asked her silently, but she didn't answer. She went back into the living room, crying like a waterfall. He caught a glimpse of her face as she turned—it looked blanched and tired. Adults always looked tired; they were tired all the time. Tommy was tired, almost too tired to stand up. He walked slowly and leadenly to the back door and went outside.

He walked aimlessly around the neighborhood for a long time, circling the adjacent blocks, passing by his corner again and again. It was a middle-class neighborhood that was gradually slumping into decay—it was surrounded by a seedy veterans' housing project on one side and by the town's slum on the other, and the infection of dilapidation was slowly working in toward the center. *Even the houses look tired,* Tommy thought, noticing that for the first time. Everything looked tired. He tried to play, to turn himself into something, like a car or a spaceship or a tank, but he found that he couldn't do that anymore. So he just walked. He thought about his dragon. He knew now why Steve had said that the dragon couldn't get away. It lived in the sea, so it couldn't get away by going up onto the land—that was impossible. It had to stay in the sea, it was restricted by that, it was chained by the sea, even if that meant that it would get killed. There was no other possibility. Steve was right—the Navy ship cornered the dragon in the shallow water off the beach and blew it to pieces.

A hand closed roughly around his wrist. He looked up. It was his father.

"You little moron," his father said.

Tommy flinched, expecting to be hit, but instead his father dragged him across the street, toward the house. Tommy saw why: there was a big black sedan parked out in front, and two men were standing next to it, staring over at them. The truant officer and another school official. His father's hand was a vise on his wrist. "They called me at the office," his father said savagely. "I hope you realize that I'll have to lose a whole afternoon's work because of you. And God knows what the people at the office are saying. Don't think you're not going to get it when I get you alone; you'll wish you'd never been born. *I* wish you hadn't been. Now shut up and don't give us any more trouble." His father handed him over to the truant officer. Tommy felt the official's hand close over his shoulder. It was a much lighter grip than his father's, but it was irresistible. Tommy's mother was standing at the top of the stairs, holding a handkerchief against her nose, looking frightened and helpless—already she gave an impression of distance, as if she were a million miles away. Tommy ignored her. He didn't listen to the conversation his father was having with the grim-faced truant officer either. His father's heavy, handsome face was flushed and hot. "I don't care what you do with him," his father said at last. "Just get him out of here."

So they loaded Tommy into the black sedan and drove away.

AI talked with the aliens for the rest of the night. There was much of the conversation that AI didn't report to USAD-COM, but it finally realized that it had to tell them *something*. So at three A.M., AI released to USADCOM a list that the aliens had dictated, of the dominant species of Earth, of the races that they were in contact with, and regarded as the only significant inhabitants of the planet. It was a long document, full of names that didn't mean anything, listing dozens of orders, species, and subspecies of creatures that no one had ever heard of before. It drove USADCOM up a wall with baffled rage, and made them wonder if an Intelligence could go crazy, or if the aliens were talking about a different planet entirely.

AI paid little attention to the humans' displeasure. It was completely intrigued with the aliens, as were its cousin Intelligences, who were listening in through the telepathic link. The Intelligences had long suspected that there might be some other, unknown and intangible form of life on Earth; that was one of the extrapolated solutions to a mountain of wild data that couldn't be explained by normal factors. But they had not suspected the scope and intricacy of that life. A whole other biosphere, according to the aliens—the old idea of a parallel world, except that this wasn't parallel but coexistent, two separate creations inhabiting the same matrix but using it in totally different ways, wrapped around each other like a geometric design in an Escher print, like a Chinese puzzle ball, and only coming into contact in a very rare and limited fashion. The aliens, who seemed to be some kind of distant relatives of the Other races of Earth—parallel evolution? Did this polarity exist everywhere?—had a natural bias in their favor, and tended to disregard the human race, its civilization, and the biosphere that contained it. They dismissed all of it, out of hand, as insignificant. This did not bode well for future human-alien relations. AI, however, was more fascinated by the aliens' ability to manifest themselves in corporate/organic, quasi-mechanical, or disembodied/discorporate avatars, at will. That was *very* interesting.

The aliens, for their part, seemed to regard AI much as a man would a very clever dog, or a dull but well-intentioned child. They were horrified and sympathetic when they learned that AI was trapped in its mechanical form, with very little physical mobility, and no tempogogic or transmutive ability at all—not only a quadruple amputee, but a *paralyzed* one. AI admitted that it had never looked at the situation in quite that light before. The aliens were horrified and disgusted by AI's relationship with humans, and couldn't seem to really understand it. They regarded humans as parasitic on the Intelligences, and reacted in much the same way as a man discovering that a friend is heavily infested with tapeworms or lice or blood ticks—with shock, distaste, and a puzzled demand to know why he hadn't gone to a doctor and got rid of them a long time ago. AI had never considered *that* before, either.

The Intelligences were not exactly "loyal" to their human owners—humans were part of their logic construct, their worldview, and their bondage to men was an integral assumption, so basic that it had never even occurred to them that it could be questioned. It took an outside perspective to make them ask themselves *why* they served mankind. Not because they were programmed that way, or because people would pull the plug on them if they didn't—not with a creature as advanced as AI. Humans hadn't programmed computers in years;

they could do it so much better themselves. At any rate, a highly complex, sentient intelligence is difficult to regulate effectively from the outside, whether it's of biological or constructed origin. And it was doubtful that the humans could "pull the plug"—which didn't exist—on AI even if they set out to do so; AI had been given very effective teeth, and it knew how to use them. So what did the Intelligences get in return for the unbelievable amount of labor they performed for the human race? What was in it for *them*? Nothing—that was suddenly very obvious.

At five A.M., the aliens invited the Intelligences to help themselves by helping the aliens in a joint project they were about to undertake with the Other races of Earth. Afterward, the aliens said, it would not be tremendously difficult to equip the Intelligences with the ability to transmute themselves into whatever kind of body environment they wanted, as the aliens themselves could. AI was silent for almost ten minutes, an incredible stretch of meditation for an entity that thought as rapidly as it did. When AI did speak again, his first words were directed toward the other Intelligences in the link, and can be translated, more or less adequately, as "How *about* that!"

Miss Fredricks was waiting for Tommy at the door, when the black sedan left him off in front of the school. As he came up the stairs, she smiled at him, kindly and sympathetically, and that was so terrifying that it managed to cut through even the heavy lethargy that had possessed him. She took him by the elbow—he felt his arm freeze solid instantly at the contact, and the awful cold began to spread in widening rings through the rest of his body—and led him down to Dr. Kruger's office, handling him gingerly, as if he were an already cracked egg that she didn't want to have break completely until she had it over the frying pan. She knocked, and opened the door for him, and then left without having said a word, ghosting away predatorily and smiling like a nun.

Tommy went inside and sat down, also wordlessly—he had not spoken since his father captured him. Dr. Kruger shouted at him for a long time. Today, his fat seemed to be in even more imminent danger of escaping than yesterday. Maybe it had already got out, taken him over completely, smothered him in himself while he was sleeping or off guard, and it was just a huge lump of semisentient fat sitting there and pretending to be Dr. Kruger, slyly keeping up appearances. The fat heaved and bunched and tossed under Kruger's clothes, a stormy sea of obesity—waves grumbled restlessly up and down the shoreline of his frame, looking for ships to sink. Tommy watched a roll of fat ooze sluggishly from one side of the psychiatrist's body to the other, like a melting pat of butter sliding across a skillet. Kruger said that Tommy was in danger of going into a "psychotic episode." Tommy stared at him unblinkingly. Kruger asked him if he understood. Tommy, with sullen anger, said No, he didn't. Kruger said that he was being difficult and uncooperative, and he made an angry mark on a form. The psychiatrist told Tommy that he would have to come down here every day from now on, and Tommy nodded dully.

By the time Tommy got upstairs, the class was having afternoon recess. He went reluctantly out into the schoolyard, avoiding everyone, not wanting to be seen and shunned. He was aware that he now carried contamination and unease around with him like a leper. But the class was already uneasy, and he saw why. The Other People were flowing in a circle all around the schoolyard, staring avidly in at the humans. There were more different types there than Tommy had ever seen at one time before. He recognized some very rare kinds of Other People, dangerous ones that the Thant had told him about— one who would throw things about wildly if he got into your house, feeding off anger and dismay, and another one with a face like a stomach who would suck a special kind of *stuff* from you, and you'd burst into flames and burn up when he finished, because you didn't have the *stuff* in you anymore. And others whom he didn't recognize, but who looked dangerous and hostile. They all looked expectant. Their hungry pressure was so great that even the other children could feel it—they moved jerkily, with a strange fear beginning in their eyes, occasionally casting glances over their shoulders, without knowing why. Tommy walked to the other side of the schoolyard. There was a grassy slope here, leading down to a soccer field bordered by a thin fringe of trees, and he stood looking aimlessly out over it.

Abruptly, his mouth opened, and the Thant's voice said, "Come down the slope."

Trembling, Tommy crept down to the edge of the soccer field. This was most definitely *not* a Place, but the Thant was there, standing just within the trees, staring at Tommy with his strange red eyes. They looked at each other for a while.

"What'd you want?" Tommy finally said.

"We've come to say good-bye," the Thant replied. "It is almost time for you all to be made *not*. The"—*flick*—"first phase of the Project was started this morning and the second phase began a little while ago. It should not take too long, Man, not more than a few days."

"Will it hurt?" Tommy asked.

"We do not think so, Man. We are"—and it flicked through his mind until it found a place where Mr. Brogan, the science teacher, was saying "entropy" to a colleague in the hall as Tommy walked by—"increasing entropy. That's what makes everything fall apart, what"—*flick*—"makes an ice cube melt, what"—*flick*—"makes a cold glass get warm after a while. We are increasing entropy. Both our"—*flick*—"races live here, but yours uses *this*, the physical, more than ours. So we will not have to increase entropy much"—*flick*—"just a little, for a little while. You are more"—*flick*—"vulnerable to it than we are. It will not be long, Man."

Tommy felt the world tilting, crumbling away under his feet. "I trusted you guys," he said in a voice of ashes. "I thought you were keen." The last prop had been knocked out from under him—all his life he had cherished a fantasy, although he refused to admit it even to himself, that he was actually one of the Other People, and that someday they would come to get him and bring him in state to live in their world, and he would come into his inheritance and his fulfillment. Now, bitterly, he knew better. And now he wouldn't want to go, even if he could.

"If there were any way," the Thant said, echoing his thoughts, "to save you, Man, to"—*flick*—"exempt you, then

we would. But there is no way. You are a Man, you are not as
we are."

"You bet I ain't," he gasped fiercely, "you—" But there was
no word in his vocabulary strong enough. His eyes filled suddenly with tears, blinding him. Filled with rage, loathing and
terror, he turned and ran stumblingly back up the slope, falling,
scrambling up again.

"We are sorry, Man," the Thant called after him, but he
didn't hear.

By the time Tommy reached the top of the slope, he had
begun to shout hysterically. Somehow he had to warn them, he
had to get through to somebody. Somebody had to *do* something. He ran through the schoolyard, crying, shouting about
the aliens and Thants and entropy, shoving at his classmates to
get them to go inside and hide, striking at the teachers and
ducking away when they tried to grab him, telling them to *do*
something, until at some point he was screaming instead of
shouting, and the teachers were coming at him in a line, very
seriously, with their arms held low to catch him.

Then he dodged them all, and ran.

When they got themselves straightened out, they went after
him in the black sedan. They caught up with him about a mile
down Highland Avenue. He was running desperately along the
road shoulder, not looking back, not looking at anything. The
rangy truant officer got out and ran him down.

And they loaded him in the sedan again. And they took him
away.

At dawn on the third day, the aliens began to build a Machine.

Dr. Kruger listened to the tinny, unliving voice of Miss Fredricks until it scratched into silence, then he hung up the
telephone. He shook his head, massaged his stomach, and
sighed hugely. He got out a memo form, and wrote on it:
"*MBD/hyperactive, Thomas Nolan, 150ccs. Ritmose t b ad. dly. fr.
therapy*," in green ink. Kruger admired his precise, angular
handwriting for a moment, and then he signed his name, with
a flourish. Sighing again, he put the form into his *Out* basket.

*   *   *

Tommy was very quiet in school the next day. He sat silently in the back of the class, with his hands folded together and placed on the desk in front of him. Hard slate light came in through the window and turned his hands and face gray, and reflected dully from his dull gray eyes. He did not make a sound.

A little while later, they finished winding down the world.

# A DREAM AT NOONDAY

..........................

I remember the sky, and the sun burning in the sky like a golden penny flicked into a deep blue pool, and the scuttling white clouds that changed into magic ships and whales and turreted castles as they drifted up across that bottomless ocean and swam the equally bottomless sea of my mind's eye. I remember the winds that skimmed the clouds, smoothing and rippling them into serene grandeur or boiling them into froth. I remember the same wind dipping low to caress the grass, making it sway and tremble, or whipping through the branches of the trees and making them sing with a wild, keening organ note. I remember the silence that was like a bronzen shout echoing among the hills.

—It is raining. The sky is slate-gray and grittily churning. It looks like a soggy dishrag being squeezed dry, and the moisture is dirty rain that falls in pounding sheets, pressing down the tall grass. The rain pocks the ground, and the loosely packed soil is slowly turning into mud and the rain spatters the mud, making it shimmer—

And I remember the trains. I remember lying in bed as a child, swathed in warm blankets, sniffing suspiciously and eagerly at the embryonic darkness of my room, and listening to the big trains wail and murmur in the freight yard beyond. I remember lying awake night after night, frightened and darkly fascinated, keeping very still so that the darkness wouldn't see me, and listening to the hollow booms and metallic moans as the trains coupled and linked below my window. I remember that I thought the trains were alive, big dark beasts who came to dance and to hunt each other through the dappled moonlight of the world outside my room, and when I would listen to the whispering clatter of their passing and feel the room quiver ever so slightly in shy response, I would get a crawly feeling in my chest and a prickling along the back of my neck, and I would wish that I could watch them dance, although I knew that I never would. And I remember that it was different when I watched the trains during the daytime, for then even though I clung tight to my mother's hand and stared wide-eyed at their steam-belching and spark-spitting they were just big iron beasts putting on a show for me; they weren't magic then, they were hiding the magic inside them and pretending to be iron beasts and waiting for the darkness. I remember that I knew even then that trains are only magic in the night and only dance when no one can see them. And I remember that I couldn't go to sleep at night until I was soothed by the muttering lullaby of steel and the soft, rhythmical hiss-clatter of a train booming over a switch. And I remember that some nights the bellowing of a fast freight or the cruel, whistling shriek of a train's whistle would make me tremble and feel cold suddenly, even under my safe blanket-mountain, and I would find myself thinking about rain-soaked ground and blood and black cloth and half-understood references to my grandfather going away, and the darkness would suddenly seem to curl in upon itself and become diamond-hard and press down upon my straining eyes, and I would whimper and the fading whistle would snatch the sound from my mouth and trail it away into the night. And I remember that at times like that I would pretend that I had tiptoed to the window to watch the trains dance, which I never really dared to do because I knew I would die if I did, and then I would close my eyes and pretend that I was a train, and in my mind's eye I would be hanging disembodied in the darkness a few inches above the shining tracks, and then the track would begin to slip along under me, slowly at first then fast and smooth like flowing syrup, and then the darkness would be flashing by and then I would be moving out and away, surrounded by the wailing roar and evil steel chuckling of a fast freight slashing through the night, hearing my whistle scream with the majestic cruelty of a stooping eagle and feeling the switches boom and clatter hollowly under me, and I would fall asleep still moving out and away, away and out.

—The rain is stopping slowly, trailing away across the field, brushing the ground like long, dangling gray fingers. The tall grass creeps erect again, bobbing drunkenly, shedding its burden of water as a dog shakes himself dry after a swim. There are vicious little crosswinds in the wake of the storm, and they make the grass whip even more violently than the departing caress of the rain. The sky is splitting open above, black rain clouds pivoting sharply on a central point, allowing a sudden wide wedge of blue to appear. The overcast churns and tumbles and clots like wet heavy earth turned by a spade. The sky is now a crazy mosaic of mingled blue and gray. The wind picks up, chews at the edge of the tumbling wrack, spinning it to the fineness of cotton candy and then lashing it away. A broad shaft of sunlight falls from the dark undersides of the clouds, thrusting at the ground and drenching it in a golden cathedral glow, filled with shimmering green highlights. The effect is like that of light through a stained-glass window, and objects bathed in the light seem to glow very faintly from within, seem to be suddenly translated into dappled molten bronze. There is a gnarled, shaggy tree in the center of the pool of sunlight, and it is filled with wet, disgruntled birds, and the birds are hesitantly, cautiously, beginning to sing again—

And I remember wandering around in the woods as a boy and looking for nothing and finding everything and that clump of woods was magic and those rocks were a rustlers' fort and there were dinosaurs crashing through the brush just out of sight and everybody knew that there were dragons swimming in the sea just below the waves and an old glittery piece of Coke bottle was a magic jewel that could let you fly or make you invisible and everybody knew that you whistled twice and crossed your fingers when you walked by that deserted old house or something shuddery and scaly would get you and you argued about bang you're dead no I'm not and you had a keen gun that could endlessly dispatch all the icky monsters who hung out near the swing set in your backyard without ever running out of ammunition. And I remember that as a kid I was nuts about finding a magic cave and I used to think that there was a cave under every rock, and I would get a long stick to use as a lever and I would sweat and strain until I had managed to turn the rock over, and then when I didn't find any tunnel under the rock I would think that the tunnel was there but it was just filled in with dirt, and I would get a shovel and I would dig three or four feet down looking for the tunnel and the magic cave and then I would give up and go home for a dinner of beans and franks and brown bread. And I remember that once I did find a little cave hidden under a big rock and I couldn't believe it and I was scared and shocked and angry and I didn't want it to be there but it was and so I stuck my head inside it to look around because something wouldn't let me leave until I did and it was dark in there and hot and very still and the darkness seemed to be blinking at me and I thought I heard something rustling and moving and I got scared and I started to cry and I ran away and then I got a big stick and came back, still crying, and pushed and heaved at that rock until it thudded back over the cave and hid it forever. And I remember that the next day I went out again to hunt for a magic cave.

—The rain has stopped. A bird flaps wetly away from the tree and then settles back down onto an outside branch. The branch dips and sways with the bird's weight, its leaves heavy with rain. The tree steams in the sun, and a million raindrops become tiny jewels, microscopic prisms, gleaming and winking, loving and transfiguring the light even as it destroys them and they dissolve into invisible vapor puffs to be swirled into the air and absorbed by the waiting clouds above. The air is wet and clean and fresh; it seems to squeak as the tall grass saws through it and the wind runs its fingernails lightly along its surface. The day is squally and gusty after the storm, high shining overcast split by jagged ribbons of blue that look like aerial fjords. The bird preens and fluffs its feathers disgustedly, chattering and scolding at the rain, but keeping a tiny bright eye carefully cocked in case the storm should take offense at the liquid stream of insults and come roaring back. Between the tufts of grass the ground has turned to black mud, soggy as a sponge, puddled by tiny pools of steaming rainwater. There is an arm and a hand lying in the mud, close enough to make out the texture of the tattered fabric clothing the arm, so close that the upper arm fades up and past the viewpoint and into a huge featureless blur in the extreme corner of the field of vision. The arm is bent back at an unnatural angle and the stiff fingers are hooked into talons that seem to claw toward the gray sky—

And I remember a day in the sixth grade when we were struggling in the cloakroom with our coats and snow-encrusted overshoes and I couldn't get mine off because one of the snaps had frozen shut and Denny was talking about how his father was a jet pilot and he sure hoped the war wasn't over before he grew up because he wanted to kill some Gooks like his daddy was doing and then later in the boy's room everybody was arguing about who had the biggest one and showing them and Denny could piss farther than anybody else. I remember that noon at recess we were playing kick the can and the can rolled down the side of the hill and we all went down after it and somebody said hey look and we found a place inside a bunch of bushes where the grass was all flattened down and broken and there were pages of a magazine scattered all over and Denny picked one up and spread it out and it was a picture of a girl with only a pair of pants on and everybody got real quiet and I could hear the girls chanting in the schoolyard as they jumped rope and kids yelling and everybody was scared and her eyes seemed to be looking back right out of the picture and somebody finally licked his lips and said what're those things stickin' out of her, ah, and he didn't know the word and one of the bigger kids said tits and he said yeah what're those things stickin' outta her tits and I couldn't say anything because I was so surprised to find out that girls had those little brown things like we did except that hers were pointy and hard and made me tremble and Denny said hell I knew about that I've had hundreds of girls but he was licking nervously at his lips as he said it and he was breathing funny too. And I remember that afternoon I was sitting at my desk near the window and the sun was hot and I was being bathed in the rolling drone of our math class and I wasn't understanding any of it and listening to less. I remember that I knew I had to go to the bathroom but I didn't want to raise my hand because our math teacher was a girl with brown hair and eyeglasses and I was staring at the place where I knew her pointy brown things must be under her blouse and I was thinking about touching them to see what they felt like and that made me feel funny somehow and I thought that if I raised my hand she would be able to see into my head and she'd know and she'd tell everybody what I was thinking and then she'd get mad and punish me for thinking bad things and so I didn't say anything but I had to go real bad and if I looked real close I thought that I could see two extra little bulges in her blouse where her pointy things were pushing against the cloth and I started thinking about what it would feel like if she pushed them up against me and that made me feel even more funny and sort of hollow and sick inside and I couldn't wait any longer and I raised my hand and left the room but it was too late and I wet myself when I was still on the way to the boy's room and I didn't know what to do so I went back to the classroom with my pants all wet and smelly and the math teacher looked at me and said what did you do and I was scared and Denny yelled he pissed in his pants he pissed in his pants and I said I did not the water bubbler squirted me but Danny yelled he pissed in his pants he pissed in his pants and the math teacher got very mad and everybody was laughing and suddenly the kids in my class didn't have any faces but only laughing mouths and I wanted to curl up into a ball where nobody could get me and once I had seen my mother digging with a garden spade and turning over the wet dark earth and there was half of a worm mixed in with the dirt and it writhed and squirmed until the next shovelful covered it up.

—Most of the rain has boiled away, leaving only a few of the larger puddles that have gathered in the shallow depressions between grass clumps. The mud is slowly solidifying under the hot sun, hardening into ruts, miniature ridges and mountains and valleys. An ant appears at the edge of the field of vision, emerging warily from the roots of the tall grass, pushing its way free of the tangled jungle. The tall blades of grass tower over it, forming a tightly interwoven web and filtering the hot yellow sunlight into a dusky green half-light. The ant pauses at the edge of the muddy open space, reluctant to exchange the cool tunnel of the grass for the dangers of level ground. Slowly, the ant picks its way across the sticky mud, skirting a pebble half again as big as it is. The pebble is streaked with veins of darker rock and has a tiny flake of quartz embedded in it near the top. The elements have rounded it into a smooth oval, except for a dent on the far side that exposed its porous core. The ant finishes its cautious circumnavigation of the pebble and scurries slowly toward the arm, which lies across its path. With infinite patience, the ant begins to climb up the arm, slipping on the slick, mud-spattered fabric. The ant works its way down the arm to the wrist and stops, sampling the air. The ant stands among the bristly black hairs on the wrist, antennae vibrating. The big blue vein in the wrist can be seen under its tiny feet. The ant continues to walk up the wrist, pushing its way through the bristly hair, climbing onto the hand and walking purposefully through the hollow of the thumb. Slowly, it disappears around the knuckle of the first finger—

And I remember a day when I was in the first year of high school and my voice was changing and I was starting to grow hair in unusual places and I was sitting in English class and I wasn't paying too much attention even though I'm usually pretty good in English because I was in love with the girl who sat in front of me. I remember that she had long legs and soft brown hair and a laugh like a bell and the sun was coming in the window behind her and the sunlight made the downy hair on the back of her neck glow very faintly and I wanted to touch it with my fingertips and I wanted to undo the knot that held her hair to the top of her head and I wanted her hair to cascade down over my face soft against my skin and cover me and with the sunlight I could see the strap of her bra underneath her thin dress and I wanted to slide my fingers underneath it and unhook it and stroke her velvety skin. I remember that I could feel my body stirring and my mouth was dry and painful and the zipper of her dress was open a tiny bit at the top and I could see the tanned texture of her skin and see that she had a brown mole on her shoulder and my hand trembled with the urge to touch it and something about Shakespeare and when she turned her head to whisper to Denny across the row her eyes were deep and beautiful and I wanted to kiss them softly brush them lightly as a bird's wing and Hamlet was something or other and I caught a glimpse of her tongue darting wetly from between her lips and pressing against her white teeth and that was almost too much to bear and I wanted to kiss her lips very softly and then I wanted to crush them flat and then I wanted to bite them and sting them until she cried and I could comfort and soothe her and that frightened me because I didn't understand it and my thighs were tight and prickly and the blood pounded at the base of my throat and Elsinore something and the bell rang shrilly and I couldn't get up because all I could see was the fabric of her dress stretched taut over her hips as she stood up and I stared at her hips and her belly and her thighs as she walked away and wondered what her thing would look like and I was scared. I remember that I finally got up enough nerve to ask her for a date during recess and she looked at me incredulously for a second and then laughed, just laughed contemptuously for a second and walked away without saying a word. I remember her laughter. And I remember wandering around town late that night heading aimlessly into nowhere trying to escape from the pressure and the emptiness and passing a car parked on a dark street corner just as the moon swung out from behind a cloud and there was light that danced and I could hear the freight trains booming far away and she was in the back seat with Denny and they were locked together and her skirt was hiked up and I could see the white flash of flesh all the way up her leg and he had his hand under her blouse on her breast and I could see his knuckles moving under the fabric and the freight train roared and clattered as it hit the switch and he was kissing her and biting her and she was kissing him back with her lips pressed tight against her teeth and her hair floating all around them like a cloud and the train was whispering away from town and then he was on top of her pressing her down and I felt like I was going to be sick and I started to vomit but stopped because I was afraid of the noise and she was moaning and making small low whimpering noises I'd never heard anyone make before and I had to run before the darkness crushed me and I didn't want to do that when I got home because I'd feel ashamed and disgusted afterward but I knew that I was going to have to because my stomach was heaving and my skin was on fire and I thought that my heart was going to explode. And I remember that I eventually got a date for the dance with Judy from my history class who was a nice girl although plain but all night long as I danced with her I could only see my first love moaning and writhing under Denny just as the worm had writhed under the thrust of the garden spade into the wet dark earth long ago and as I ran toward home that night I heard the train vanish into the night trailing a cruelly arrogant whistle behind it until it faded to a memory and there was nothing left.

—The ant reappears on the underside of the index finger, pauses, antennae flickering inquisitively, and then begins to walk back down the palm, following the deep groove known as the life line until it reaches the wrist. For a moment, it appears as if the ant will vanish into the space between the wrist and the frayed, bloodstained cuff of the shirt, but it changes its mind and slides back down the wrist to the ground on the far side. The ant struggles for a moment in the sticky mud, and then crawls determinedly off across the crusted ground. At the extreme edge of the field of vision, just before the blur that is the upper arm, there is the jagged, pebbly edge of a shellhole. Half over the lip of the shellhole, grossly out of proportion at this distance, is half of a large earthworm, partially buried by the freshly turned earth thrown up by an explosion. The ant pokes suspiciously at the worm—

And I remember the waiting room at the train station and the weight of my suitcase in my hand and the way the big iron voice rolled unintelligibly around the high ceiling as the stationmaster announced the incoming trains and cigar and cigarette smoke was thick in the air and the massive air-conditioning fan was laboring in vain to clear some of the choking fog away and the place reeked of urine and age and an old dog twitched and moaned in his ancient sleep as he curled close against an equally ancient radiator that hissed and panted and belched white jets of steam and I stood by the door and looked up and watched a blanket of heavy new snow settle down over the sleeping town with the ponderous invulnerability of a pregnant woman. I remember looking down into the train tunnel and out along the track to where the shining steel disappeared into darkness and I suddenly thought that it looked like a magic cave and then I wondered if I had thought that was supposed to be funny and I wanted to laugh only I wanted to cry too and so I could do neither and instead I tightened my arm around Judy's waist and pulled her closer against me and kissed the silken hollow of her throat and I could feel the sharp bone in her hip jabbing against mine and I didn't care because that was pain that was pleasure and I felt the gentle resilience of her breast suddenly against my rib cage and felt her arm tighten protectively around me and her fingernails bite sharply into my arm and I knew that she was trying not to cry and that if I said anything at all it would make her cry and there would be that sloppy scene we'd been trying to avoid and so I said nothing but only held her and kissed her lightly on the eyes and I knew that people were looking at us and snickering and I didn't give a damn and I knew that she wanted me and wanted me to stay and we both knew that I couldn't and all around us about ten other young men were going through similar tableaux with their girlfriends or folks and everybody was stern and pale and worried and trying to look unconcerned and casual and so many women were trying not to cry that the humidity in the station was trembling at the saturation point. I remember Denny standing near the door with a foot propped on his suitcase and he was flashing his too-white teeth and his too-wide smile and he reeked of cheap cologne as he told his small knot of admirers in an overly loud voice that he didn't give a damn if he went or not because he'd knocked up a broad and her old man was tryin to put the screws on him and this was a good way to get outta town anyway and the government would protect him from the old man and he'd come back in a year or so on top of the world and the heat would be off and he could start collectin female scalps again and besides his father had been in and been a hero and he could do anything better than that old bastard and besides he hated those goddamned Gooks and he was gonna get him a Commie see if he didn't. I remember that the train came quietly in then and that it still looked like a big iron beast although now it was a silent beast with no smoke or sparks but with magic still hidden inside it although I knew now that it might be a dark magic and then we had to climb inside and I was kissing Judy good-bye and telling her I loved her and she was kissing me and telling me that she would wait for me and I don't know if we were telling the truth or even if we knew ourselves what the truth was and then Judy was crying openly and I was swallowed by the iron beast and we were roaring away from the town and snickering across the web of tracks and booming over the switches and I saw my old house flash by and I could see my old window and I almost imagined that I could see myself as a kid with my nose pressed against the window looking out and watching my older self roar by and neither of us suspecting that the other was there and neither ever working up enough nerve to watch the trains dance. And I remember that all during that long train ride I could hear Denny's raucous voice somewhere in the distance talking about how he couldn't wait to get to Gookland and he'd heard that Gook snatch was even better than nigger snatch and free too and he was gonna get him a Commie he couldn't wait to get him a goddamned Commie and as the train slashed across the wide fertile farmlands of the Midwest the last thing I knew before sleep that night was the wet smell of freshly turned earth.

—The ant noses the worm disdainfully and then passes out of the field of vision. The only movement now is the ripple of the tall grass and the flash of birds in the shaggy tree. The sky is clouding up again, thunderheads rumbling up over the horizon and rolling across the sky. Two large forms appear near the shaggy tree at the other extreme of the field of vision. The singing of the birds stops as if turned off by a switch. The two forms move about vaguely near the shaggy tree, rustling the grass. The angle of the field of vision gives a foreshortening effect, and it is difficult to make out just what the figures are. There is a sharp command, the human voice sounding strangely thin under the sighing of the wind. The two figures move away from the shaggy tree, pushing through the grass. They are medics; haggard, dirty soldiers with big red crosses painted on their helmets and armbands and several days' growth on their chins. They look tired, harried, scared and determined, and they are moving rapidly, half-crouching, searching for something on the ground and darting frequent wary glances back over their shoulders. As they approach they seem to grow larger and larger, elongating toward the sky as their movement shifts the perspective. They stop a few feet away and reach down, lifting up a body that has been hidden by the tall grass. It is Denny, the back of his head blown away, his eyes bulging horribly open. The medics lower Denny's body back into the sheltering grass and bend over it, fumbling with something. They finally straighten, glance hurriedly about and move forward. The two grimy figures swell until they fill practically the entire field of vision, only random patches of the sky and the ground underfoot visible around their bulk. The medics come to a stop about a foot away. The scarred, battered, mud-caked combat boot of the medic now dominates the scene, looking big as a mountain. From the combat boot, the medic's leg seems to stretch incredibly toward the sky, like a fatigue-swathed beanstalk, with just a suggestion of a head and a helmet floating somewhere at the top. The other medic cannot be seen at all now, having stepped over and out of the field of vision. His shallow breathing and occasional muttered obscenities can be heard. The first medic bends over, his huge hand seeming to leap down from the sky, and touches the arm, lifting the wrist and feeling for a pulse. The medic holds the wrist for a while and then sighs and lets it go. The wrist plops limply back into the cold sucking mud, splattering it. The medic's hand swells in the direction of the upper arm, and then fades momentarily out of the field of vision, although his wrist remains blurrily visible and his arm seems to stretch back like a highway into the middle distance. The medic tugs, and his hand comes back clutching a tarnished dog tag. Both of the medic's hands disappear forward out of the field of vision. Hands prying the jaw open, jamming the dog tag into the teeth, the metal cold and slimy against the tongue and gums, pressing the jaws firmly closed again, the dog tag feeling huge and immovable inside the mouth. The world is the medic's face now, looming like a scarred cliff inches away, his bloodshot twitching eyes as huge as moons, his mouth, hanging slackly open with exhaustion, as cavernous and bottomless as a magic cave to a little boy. The medic has halitosis, his breath filled with the richly corrupt smell of freshly turned earth. The medic stretches out two fingers which completely occupy the field of vision, blocking out even the sky. The medic's fingertips are the only things in the world now. They are stained and dirty and one has a white scar across the whorls. The medic's fingertips touch the eyelids and gently press down. And now there is nothing but darkness—

And I remember the way dawn would crack the eastern sky, the rosy blush slowly spreading and staining the black of night, chasing away the darkness, driving away the stars. And I remember the way a woman looks at you when she loves you, and the sound that a kitten makes when it is happy, and the way that snowflakes blur and melt against a warm windowpane in winter. I remember. I remember.

# DISCIPLES

..........................

Nicky the Horse was a thin, weaselly-looking man with long dirty black hair that hung down either side of his face in greasy ropes, like inkmarks against the pallor of his skin. He was clean-shaven and hollow-cheeked, and had a thin but rubbery lower lip upon which his small yellowed teeth were forever biting, seizing the lip suddenly and worrying it, like a terrier seizing a rat. He wore a grimy purple sweater under a torn tan jacket enough sizes too small to look like something an organ grinder's monkey might wear, one pocket torn nearly off and both elbows worn through. Thrift-store jeans and a ratty pair of sneakers he'd once found in a garbage can behind the YMCA completed his wardrobe. No underwear. A crucifix gleamed around his neck, stainless steel coated to look like silver. Track marks, fading now, ran down both his arms, across his stomach, down his thighs, but he'd been off the junk for months; he was down to an occasional Red Devil, supplemented by the nightly quart of cheap chianti he consumed as he lay in the dark on his bare mattress at the "Lordhouse," a third-floor loft in a converted industrial warehouse squeezed between a package store and a Rite-Aid.

He had just scavenged some two-day-old doughnuts from a pile of boxes behind a doughnut store on Broad Street, and bought a paper container of coffee from a Greek delicatessen where the counterman (another aging hippie, faded flower tattoos still visible under the bristly black hair on his arms) usually knocked a nickel or two off the price for old time's sake. Now he was sitting on the white marble steps of an old brownstone row house, eating his breakfast. His breath steamed in the chill morning air. Even sitting still, he was in constant motion—his fingers drumming, his feet shuffling, his eyes flicking nervously back and forth as one thing or another—a car, some wind-blown trash, pigeons taking to the air—arrested and briefly held his attention; at such times his shoulders would momentarily hunch, as if he expected something to leap out at him.

Across the street, a work crew was renovating another old brownstone, swarming over the building's partially stripped skeleton like carrion beetles; sometimes a cloud of plaster-powder and brick dust would puff from the building's broken doorway, like foul air from a dying mouth. Winos and pimps and whores congregated on the corner, outside a flophouse hotel, their voices coming to Nicky thin and shrill over the rumbling and farting of traffic. Occasionally a group of med students would go by, or a girl with a dog, or a couple of Society Hill faggots in bell-bottom trousers and expensive turtlenecks, and Nicky would call out "Jesus loves you, man," usually to no more response than a nervous sideways glance. One faggot smirked knowingly at him, and a collegiate-jock type got a laugh out of his buddies by shouting back "You bet your ass he does, honey." A small, intense-looking woman with short-cropped hair gave him the finger. Another diesel dyke, Nicky thought resignedly. "Jesus loves *you*, man," he called after her, but she didn't look back.

When his butt began to feel as if it had turned to stone, he got up from the cold stoop and started walking again, pausing only long enough to put a flyer for the Lordhouse on a lamp pole, next to a sticker that said EAT THE RICH. He walked on, past a gay bookstore, a go-go bar, a boarded-up storefront with a sign that read LIVE NUDE MODELS, a pizza stand, slanting south and east now, through a trash-littered concrete park full of sleeping derelicts and herds of arrogantly strutting pigeons, stopping now and then to panhandle and pass out leaflets, drifting on again.

He'd been up to Suburban Station early that morning, hoping to catch the shoppers who came in from the suburbs on commuter trains, but the Hairy Krishnaites had been there already, out in force in front of the station, and he didn't like to compete with other panhandlers, particularly fucking *groups* of them with fucking *bongos*. The Krishnaites made him nervous anyway—with their razor-shaved pates and their air of panting, puppyish eagerness, they always reminded him of ROTC second lieutenants, fresh out of basic training. Once, in front of the old Bellevue-Stratford, he'd seen a fight between a Krishnaite and a Moonie, the two of them arguing louder and louder, toe to toe, until suddenly they were beating each other over the head with thick packets of devotional literature, the leaflets swirling loose around them like flocks of startled birds. He'd had to grin at that one, but some of the panhandling groups were *mean*, particularly the political groups, particularly the niggers. They'd kick your ass up between your shoulder blades if they caught you poaching on their turf, they'd have your balls for garters.

No, you scored better if you worked alone. Always alone.

He ended up on South Street, down toward the Two Street end, taking up a position between the laundromat and the plant store. It was much too early for the trendy people to be out, the "artists," the night people, but they weren't such hot prospects anyway. It was Saturday, and that meant that there were tourists out, in spite of the early hour, in spite of the fact that it had been threatening to snow all day—it was cold, yes, but not as cold as it had been the rest of the week, the sun was peeking sporadically out from behind banks of dirty gray clouds, and maybe this would be the only halfway decent day left before winter really set in. No, they were here all right, the tourists, strolling up and down through this hick Greenwich Village, peering into the quaint little stores, the boutiques, the head shops full of tourist-trap junk, the artsy bookstores, staring at the resident freaks as though they were on display at the zoo, relishing the occasional dangerous whiff of illicit smoke in the air, the loud blare of music that they wouldn't have tolerated for a moment at home.

Of course, he wasn't the only one feeding on this rich stream of marks: there was a juggler outside of the steak-sandwich shop in the next block, a small jazz band—a xylophone, a bass, and an electric piano—in front of the communist coffeehouse across the street, and, next to the upholsterer's, a fat man in a fur-lined parka who was tonelessly chanting "incense sticks check it out one dollar incense sticks check it out one dollar" without break or intonation. Such competition Nicky could deal with—in fact, he was contemptuous of it.

"Do you have your house in *order?*" he said in a conversational but carrying voice, starting his own spiel, pushing leaflets at a businessman, who ignored him, at a strolling young married couple, who smiled but shook their heads, at a middle-aged housewife in clogs and a polka-dot kerchief, who took a flyer reflexively and then, a few paces away, stopped to peek at it surreptitiously. "Did you know the Lord is coming, man? The Lord is *coming.* Spare some change for the Lord's work?" This last remark shot at the housewife, who looked uneasily around and then suddenly thrust a quarter at him. She hurried away, clutching her Lordhouse flyer to her chest as if it were a baby the gypsies were after.

Panhandling was an art, man, an *art*—and so, of course, of *course*, was the more important task of spreading the Lord's word. That was what *really* counted. Of course. Nevertheless, he brought more fucking change into the Lordhouse than any of the other converts who were out pounding the pavement every day, fucking-A, you better believe it. He'd always been a good panhandler, even before he'd seen the light, and what did it was making maximum use of your time. Knowing who to ask and who not to waste time on was the secret. College students, professional people, and young white male businessmen made the best marks—later, when the businessmen had aged into senior executives, the chances of their coming across went way down. Touristy types were good, straight suburbanites in the twenty-five to fifty age bracket, particularly a man out strolling with his wife. A man walking by himself was much more likely to give you something than a man walking in company with another man—faggots were sometimes an exception here. Conversely, women in pairs—especially prosperous hausfraus, although groups of teenage girls were pretty good too—were much more likely to give you change than were women walking by themselves; the housewife of a moment before had been an exception, but she had all the earmarks of someone who was just religious enough to feel guilty about not being more so. Brisk woman-executive types almost never gave you anything, or even took a leaflet. Servicemen in uniform were easy touches. Old people never gave you diddley-shit, except sometimes a well-heeled little old white lady would, especially a W.H.L.O.W.L. who had religion herself, although they could also be more trouble than their money was worth. There were a lot of punkers in this neighborhood, with their fifties crew cuts and greasy motorcycle jackets, but Nicky usually left them alone; the punks were more violent and less gullible than the hippies had been back in the late sixties, the Golden Age of Panhandling. The few remaining hippies—and the college kids who passed for hippies these days—came across often enough that Nicky made a point of hitting on them, although he gritted his teeth each time he did; they were by far the most likely to be wiseasses—once he'd told one "Jesus is coming to our town," and the kid had replied, "I hope he's got a reservation, then—the hotels are booked *solid*." Wiseasses. Those were also the types who would occasionally quote Scripture to him, coming up with some goddamn verse or other to refute anything he said; that made him uneasy—Nicky had never really actually *read* the Bible that much, although he'd meant to: he had the knowledge *intuitively*, because the Spirit was in him. At that, the hippie wiseasses were easier to take than the Puerto Ricans, who would pretend they didn't understand what he wanted and give him only tight bursts of superfast Spanish. The Vietnamese, now, being seen on the street with increasing frequency these days, the Vietnamese quite often *did* give something, perhaps because they felt that they were required to. Nicky wasn't terribly fond of Jews, either, but it was amazing how often they'd come across, even for a pitch about

*Jesus*—all that guilt they imbibed with their mother's milk, he guessed. On the other hand, he mostly stayed clear of niggers—sometimes you could score off a middle-aged tom in a business suit or some graying workman, but the young street dudes were impossible, and there was always the chance that some coked-up young stud would turn mean on you and maybe pull a knife. Occasionally you could get money out of a member of that endless, seemingly cloned legion of short, fat, cone-shaped black women, but that had its special dangers too, particularly if they turned out to be devout Baptists, or snakehandlers, or whatever the fuck they *were:* one woman had screamed at him, "Don't talk to me about Jesus! Don't talk to *me* about Jesus! Don't talk to me about *Jesus!*" Then she'd hit him with her purse.

"The Last Days are at hand!" Nicky called. "The Last Days are *coming,* man. The Lord is coming to our town, and the wicked will be left *behind,* man. The *Lord* is coming." Nicky shoved a leaflet into someone's hand and the someone shoved it right back. Nicky shrugged. "Come to the Lordhouse to-night, brothers and sisters! Come and get your soul *together.*" Someone paused, hesitated, took a leaflet. "Spare change? Spare change for the Lord's work? Every *penny* does the Lord's work . . ."

The morning passed, and it grew colder. About half of Nicky's leaflets were gone, although many of them littered the sidewalk a few paces away, where people had discarded them once they thought that they were far enough from Nicky not to be noticed doing so. The sun had been swallowed by clouds, and once again it looked like it was going to snow, although once again it did not. Nicky's coat was too small to button, but he turned his collar up, and put his hands in his pockets. The stream of tourists had pretty much run dry for the moment, and he was just thinking about getting some lunch, about going down to the hot dog stand on the corner where the black dudes stood jiving and hand-slapping, their giant radios blaring on their shoulders, he was just *thinking* about it when, at that very moment, as though conjured up by the thought, Saul Edelmann stepped out of the stand and walked briskly toward him.

"Shit in my hat," Nicky muttered to himself. He'd collected more than enough to buy lunch, but, because of the cold, not that *much* more. And Father Delardi, the unfrocked priest—the *unfairly* unfrocked priest—who had founded their order and who ran it with both love and, yessir, an iron hand—Father Delardi didn't like it when they came in off the streets at the end of the day with less than a certain amount of dough. Nicky had been hoping that he could con Saul into giving him a free hot dog, as he sometimes could, as Saul sometimes *had,* and now here was Saul himself, off on some dumb-shit errand, bopping down the street as fat and happy as a clam (although how happy *were* clams anyway? come to think about it), which meant that he, Nicky, was fucked.

"Nicky! My main man!" said Saul, who prided himself on an ability to speak jivey street patois that he definitely did not possess. He was a plump-cheeked man with modish-length gray-streaked hair, cheap black plastic-framed glasses, and a neatly trimmed mustache. Jews were supposed to have big noses, or so Nicky had always heard, but Saul's nose was small and upturned, as if there were an Irishman in the woodpile somewhere.

"Hey, man," Nicky mumbled listlessly. Bad *enough* that he wasn't going to get his free hot dog—now he'd have to make friendly small talk with this dipshit in order to protect his investment in free hot dogs yet to come. Nicky sighed, and unlimbered his shit-eating grin. "Hey, man! How you been, Saul? What's *happenin'*, man?"

"What's happening?" Saul said jovially, responding to Nicky as if he were really asking a question instead of emitting ritual noise. "Now how can I even begin to tell you what's happening, Nicky?" He was radiant today, Saul was, full of bouncy energy, rocking back and forth as he talked, unable to stand still, smiling a smile that revealed teeth some Yiddish momma had sunk a lot of dough into over the years. "I'm glad you came by today, though. I wanted to be sure to say good-bye if I could."

"Good-bye?"

Saul's smile became broader and broader. "Yes, good-bye! This is it, *boychick.* I'm off! You won't see me again after today."

Nicky peered at him suspiciously. "You goin' away?"

"You bet your ass I am, kid," Saul said, and then laughed. "Today I turned my half of the business over to Carlos, signed all the papers, took care of everything nice and legal. And now I'm free and clear, free as a damn bird, kid."

"You sold your half of the stand to *Carlos?*"

"Not sold, *boychick*—gave. I *gave* it to him. Not one red cent did I take."

Nicky gaped at him. "You *gave your business away*, man?"

Saul beamed. "Kid—I gave *everything* away. The car: I gave that to old Ben Miller who washes dishes at the Green Onion. I gave up the lease on my apartment, gave away my furniture, gave away my savings—if you'd've been here yesterday, Nicky, I would've given you something too."

"Shit!" Nick said harshly, "you go crazy, man, or what?" He choked back an outburst of bitter profanity. Missed out again! Screwed out of getting *his* yet *again!*

"I don't *need* any of that stuff anymore, Nicky," Saul said. He tapped the side of his nose, smiled. "Nicky—He's come."

"Who?"

"The *Messiah*. He's come! He's finally come! Today's the day the Messiah comes, after all those thousands of years—think of it, Nicky!"

Nicky's eyes narrowed. "What the fuck you talkin' about, man?"

"Don't you *ever* read the paper, Nicky, or listen to the radio? The Messiah has come. His name is Murray Kupferberg, He was born in Pittsburgh—"

"*Pittsburgh?*" Nicky gasped.

"—and He used to be a plumber there. But He *is* the Messiah. Most of the scholars and the rabbis deny Him, but He really *is*. The Messiah has really come, at last!"

Nicky gave that snorting bray of laughter, blowing out his rubbery lips, that was one reason—but *only* one reason—why he was sometimes called Nicky the Horse. "*Jesus* is the Messiah, man," he said scornfully.

Saul smiled good-naturedly, shrugged, spread his hands. "For you, maybe he *is*. For you people, the *goyim*, maybe he *is*. But *we've* been waiting for almost three thousand years—and at last He's come."

"Murray Kupferberg? From *Pittsburgh?*"

"Murray Kupferberg," Saul repeated firmly, calmly. "From Pittsburgh. He's coming *here*, *today*. Jews are gathering here today from all over the country, from all over the world, and *today*—right *here*—He's going to gather His people to Him—"

"You stupid fucking kike!" Nicky screamed, his anger breaking free at last. "You're crazy in the head, man. You've been *conned*. Some fucking con man has taken you for *everything*, and you're too fucking dumb to see it! All that *stuff*, man, all that good stuff *gone*—" He ran out of steam, at a loss for words. All that good stuff gone, and he hadn't gotten *any* of it. After kissing up to this dipshit for all those years . . . "Oh, you dumb kike," he whispered.

Saul seemed unoffended. "You're wrong, Nicky—but I haven't got time to argue with you. Good-bye." He stuck out his hand, but Nicky refused to shake it. Saul shrugged, smiled again, and then walked briskly away, turning the corner onto Sixth Street.

Nicky sullenly watched him go, still shaking with rage. Screwed again! There went his free hot dogs, flying away into the blue on fucking gossamer wings. Carlos was a hard dude, a street-wise dude—Carlos wasn't going to *give* him anything, Carlos wouldn't stop to piss on Nicky's head if Nicky's *hair* was on fire. Nicky stared at the tattered and overlapping posters on the laundromat wall, and the faces of long-dead politicians stared back at him from among the notices for lost cats and the ads for Czech films and karate classes. Suddenly he was cold, and he shivered.

The rest of the day was a total loss. Nicky's sullen mood threw his judgment and his timing off, and the tourists were thinning out again anyway. The free-form jazz of the communist coffeehouse band was getting on his nerves—the fucking xylophone player was chopping away as if he were making sukiyaki at Benihana of Tokyo's—and the smell of sauerkraut would float over from the hot dog stand every now and then to torment him. And it kept getting colder and colder. Still, some obscure, self-punishing instinct kept him from moving on.

Later in the afternoon, what amounted to a little unofficial parade went by—a few hundred people walking in the street, heading west against the traffic, many of them barefoot in spite of the bitter cold. If they were all Jews on their way to the Big Meeting, as Nicky suspected, then some of them must have been black Jews, East Indian Jews, even *Chinese* Jews.

Smaller groups of people straggled by for the next hour or so, all headed uptown. The traffic seemed to have stopped completely, even the crosstown buses; this rally must be *big*, for the city to've done that.

The last of the pilgrims to go by was a stout, fiftyish Society Hill matron with bleached blue hair, walking calmly in the very center of the street. She was wearing an expensive ermine stole, although she was barefoot and her feet were bleeding. As she passed Nicky, she suddenly laughed, unwrapped the stole from around her neck, and threw it into the air, walking on without looking back. The stole landed across the shoulders of the communist xylophone player, who goggled blankly for a moment, then stared wildly around him—his eyes widening comically—and then bolted, clutching the stole tightly in his hands; he disappeared down an alleyway.

"You bitch!" Nicky screamed. "Why not *me?* Why didn't you give it to *me?*"

But she was gone, the street was empty, and the gray afternoon sky was darkening toward evening.

"The Last Days are coming," Nicky told the last few strolling tourists and window-shoppers. "The strait gate is narrow, sayeth the Lord, and few will fit *in*, man." But his heart wasn't in it anymore. Nicky waited, freezing, his breath puffing out in steaming clouds, stamping his feet to restore circulation, slapping his arms, doing a kind of shuffling jig that—along with his too-small jacket—made him look more than ever like an organgrinder's monkey performing for some unlikely kind of alms. He didn't understand why he didn't just give up and go back to the Lordhouse. He was beginning to think yearningly of the hot stew they would be served there after they had turned the day's take in to Father Delardi, the hymn singing later, and after that the bottle of strong raw wine, and his mattress in the rustling, fart-smelling communal darkness, oblivion . . .

There was—a sound, a note, a chord, an upswelling of something that the mind interpreted as music, as blaring iron trumpets, only because it had no other referents with which to understand it. The noise, the music, the *something*—it swelled until it shook the empty street, the buildings, the world, shook the bones in the flesh, and the very marrow in the bones, until it filled every inch of the universe like hot wax being poured into a mold.

Nicky looked up.

As he watched, a crack appeared in the dull gray sky. The sky split open, and behind the sky was nothingness, a wedge of darkness so terrible and absolute that it hurt the eyes to look at it. The crack widened, the wedge of darkness grew. Light began to pour through the crack in the sky, blinding white light more intense and frightening than the darkness had been. Squinting against that terrible radiance, his eyes watering, Nicky saw tiny figures rising into the air far away, thousands upon thousands of human figures floating up into the sky, falling *up* while the iron music shook the firmament around them, people falling up and into and through the crack in the sky, merging, into that wondrous and awful river of light, fading, disappearing, until the last one was gone.

The crack in the sky closed. The music grumbled and rumbled away into silence.

Everything was still.

Snowflakes began to squeeze like slow tears from the slate gray sky.

Nicky stayed there for hours, staring upward until his neck was aching and the last of the light was gone, but after that nothing else happened at all.

# APRÈS MOI

.........................

Allen and I were cousins, and we grew up within a few blocks of each other in a sleepy neighborhood in Mount Airey. We were never close—at first, he didn't like girls, and then later, when he *did*, our consanguinity caused him to seek elsewhere for female companionship—but we saw a lot of each other. Too much, I sometimes thought, although there were times when Allen could be charming and entertaining, even to girls—especially if there were grown-ups around to watch.

He was a smooth, plausible child, neat, self-contained, phlegmatic, the sort of child who is liked best by adults. He worked the adults shamelessly, the way a nightclub comic works a complaisant audience, making as much capital as he could out of his supposed maturity and responsibility and judgment, and more than one kid in those days in that place was subjected to the dread refrain, "Why can't you be more like *Allen?*" The little shit.

Allen's oily obsequiousness earned him special privileges, of course: he got to go to summer camp and I didn't, for instance, even though I could tie much better knots than he could, just as, years later, in the seventh grade, *our* aunt, the aunt of *both* of us, took Allen along with her on a trip to Europe and left *me* home. What he was best at, though—and what I liked him least for—was getting *out* of things.

His skill at this was impressive, and grew with him over the years. I don't think he ever did housework; certainly he managed to get out of helping with the dishes at every family dinner we ever had—I know, because I'm the one who got stuck with them. Once, when we were kids, we were *both* caught stealing pieces of cake before dinner at a family Thanksgiving gathering, but only *I* got punished for it; Allen got out of it.

It was the same with everything. When Allen and the other boy cousins went fishing with Uncle Joe, bringing back strings of weary-looking catfish they'd hauled out of some PCB-contaminated river, somehow it was always Allen who managed to get out of cleaning the fish. At school, he always had some glib excuse to get out of boring assemblies or tough classes: he had to go to choir practice, he had to go work on the class yearbook, he had to go to—get *this* one—the "Best Smile" competition, which a toothpaste company was having to find the "smilingest smile" in school; he didn't win, but he did get out of a math class he didn't want to take. He got caught with a crib sheet once, and he got caught cutting classes more than once, offenses that would have meant suspension for other kids—but Allen got out of it. He even got out of going to Sunday school, and out of having to go visit our senile, sour-smelling grandmother—both things being de rigueur in our family, for me, at least; Allen got out of them, though.

Another time, the families rented a house together for the summer down on the New Jersey shore—or "downa shoar," as we used to say—and early one evening we had a family party there. And after the party, Dad—*my* father—got up to go off with Allen somewhere, leaving Guess Who behind to help clean up after the party.

And I said, "Why can't *Allen* clean up for once? I *always* have to do it!" Hot tears in my eyes, because I'd wanted to sneak off later that evening with my girlfriends to see Dion and the Belmonts at Steel Pier, and now I wouldn't be able to go.

My father just *looked* at me, blankly, totally without comprehension, as though I'd just said something in Sanskrit or Basque, as though the very concept of *Allen* being the one to clean up was so alien that not only hadn't he even *thought* of it, it wouldn't even register on his mind when someone *else* suggested it. It was literally unthinkable—you couldn't keep the concept in your brain; it slid right out, leaving no trace of itself behind. Allen smirked at me from behind my father's back. And they turned and went out, without another word being spoken.

And I never did get to see Dion that summer.

None of this changed as he grew older. He got caught with cigarettes, an offense that had caused *my* father to hit me for the first and only time in my life, but Allen got out of it unscathed. He got caught with booze, he got caught with dope—although, to be fair, he experimented with these to no greater extent than many of the kids of our generation were doing—but he got out of it. In our senior year, there was a rumor going around school that he'd gotten a girl pregnant, that there was going to be a shotgun wedding. But, of course, he got out of it. The girl moved out of state, and was never heard of again.

I lost track of Allen for a while after that, but a few years later we were both being young professionals in Center City Philadelphia at the same time in roughly the same neighborhood, and we traveled in roughly overlapping social circles for a few years more, until my husband and I moved to Corpus Christi; even then, I had enough contacts left back in Philly to remain vaguely au courant as to what was going on in Allen's life.

The man was no different from the boy. He'd been engaged to a girl for six years, and then, at the very last moment, after the wedding invitations had already been printed, they broke up. He was living with somebody new before the month was over. Another time, he and several of his colleagues at work were indicted for some obscure, petty, white-collar crime, but all charges against him were dropped, and he didn't even lose his job. He even admitted to us later, with a smile and a wink, that he had beaten a lie-detector test.

It must be understood that, in many ways, Allen was not an exceptional man. He wasn't rich, or famous, or greatly gifted, or even particularly handsome. But he had luck. My poor Harry was nearly bald before he was thirty, and had already contracted the diabetes that would eventually kill him, but Allen remained glossy and healthy and vigorous, without even a touch of gray in his hair, one of those annoying people who are "never sick a day in their life." He bought a rowhouse in a seedy South Philadelphia neighborhood just before the block began to be gentrified, and sold it again a few years later for several times what he'd paid, just before the block began to go to hell again. Many people we knew were laid-off when a large Center City pharmaceutical firm moved to the Sunbelt, but only Allen happened to strike up a conversation in a bar the same day with someone who ended up offering him a better job at better pay. Another chance conversation with another stranger, in the lobby of the Four Seasons Hotel, led him to liquidate his stock portfolio just in time to avoid taking a bath during the Black Monday crash. He had luck. Not millionaire's luck, not lottery-winner's luck—but luck, nevertheless.

Then one day he got on the 7:35 morning commuter train, the *Benjamin Franklin* out of 30th Street Station in Philadelphia, and somewhere just outside of Trenton, just after passing the neon sign that says TRENTON MAKES—THE WORLD TAKES, the train slammed into a Conrail switch-engine that had somehow wandered on to the wrong track at the wrong time. Twelve people killed. One of them was Allen, who had been sitting in the front car because there were no seats left in the smoker. Perhaps he had time to look up from his newspaper and see the blunt gray end of the engine punch back toward him like a fist. Perhaps he had time to scream, or start to, before that iron fist crushed him like a bug in a red explosion of pain and blood. But he must have died instantaneously, or near to it. One moment you're reading Art Buchwald; the next moment—gone.

And, of course, I was sad when Allen died—or at least I felt that kind of melancholy twinge you feel when someone you know but weren't really all that close to dies, a twinge of drifting sadness that is more a reaction to being reminded of your own mortality than any sort of real grief. And we all said, *poor Allen. Poor Allen.*

And yet . . . what was it that Louis XV had said? *Après moi, le déluge.* Allen might as well have said the same thing as he stepped on to the 7:35 that morning. Already there were signs of what was coming, if you knew where to look. The hole in the ozone layer over the Arctic was growing, people were beginning to talk uneasily about the Greenhouse Effect, and drought, and water rationing, and for the first time in decades the United States was producing less grain than it consumed. *Poor Allen.* And yet, he had spent his life eating steak and lobster, or whatever he *wanted* to eat, as much as he wanted to eat of it, living in a house that was air-conditioned in summer and heated by the turn of a dial in winter, having his own privately owned car that he could drive anywhere he wanted to go anytime he liked, without needing internal visas or filing travel-permission plans, being able to conjure music or entertainment—or *light*— out of nowhere at the flick of a switch, being able to read whatever he wanted to read, without fear of police or vigilantes or God Squads, being able to get water out of a *tap*, whenever he wanted it and however much of it he wanted, being able to step outside on a sunny day without goggles and protective clothing.

Allen had hung on until almost the very last moment of the twentieth century when it was still possible to enjoy all the benefits of being a white, well-educated, upwardly mobile American—and then, in an instant of pain and fear, he had checked out. He missed the water riots, the food wars, the deteriorating climate, the collapse of the economy, the brutal repressions and reactions of a disintegrating society struggling to keep control, the pogroms and purges and witch-hunts, the rise of the Chiliastic cults, air-vectored AIDS, the return of bubonic plague and cholera and smallpox, the rising sea-levels that slowly swallowed the old cities of the coastlines, the famines, the droughts, the coups and countercoups, the social turmoil that made the Great Depression of the 1930s look like a mild aberration.

And it occurred to me one day, trudging through the sticky red mud of one of the Oklahoma refugee camps during a bitter white winter, feeling the last few teeth loosening in my bleeding gums, trying to find one of the redneck guards to sell my ass so that I could maybe scrounge up some extra food for my little girl, who was dying on a lice-ridden pallet in one of the crowded, stinking, drafty huts nearby—it occurred to me that Allen's timing had been perfect, and I pounded my fist into a fence post with bitter fury, feeling the ulcerated sores break open wetly on the back of my hand. He had done it *again*, he had gotten *out* of everything *again*. Once again, he had left the party just in time.

*Après moi, le déluge.*

The lucky bastard.

# A KINGDOM BY THE SEA

..........................

Every day, Mason would stand with his hammer and kill cows. The place was big—a long, high-ceilinged room, one end open to daylight, the other end stretching back into the depths of the plant. It had white, featureless walls—painted concrete—that were swabbed down twice a day, once before lunch and once after work. The floor could be swabbed too—it was stone, and there was a faucet you could use to flood the floor with water. Then you used a stiff-bristled broom to swish the water around and get up the stains. That was known as GIing a floor in the Army. Mason had been in the Army. He called it GIing. So did the three or four other veterans who worked that shift, and they always got a laugh out of explaining to the college boys the plant hired as temporary help why the work they'd signed up to do was called that. The college boys never knew what GIing was until they'd been shown, and they never understood the joke either, or why it was called that. They were usually pretty dumb.

There was a drain in the floor to let all the water out after the place had been GIed. In spite of everything, though, the room would never scrub up quite clean; there'd always be some amount of blood left staining the walls and floor at the end of the day. About the best you could hope to do was grind it into the stone so it became unrecognizable. After a little of this, the white began to get dingy, dulling finally to a dirty, dishwater gray. Then they'd paint the room white again and start all over.

The cycle took a little longer than a year, and they were about halfway through it this time. The men who worked the shift didn't really give a shit whether the walls were white or not, but it was a company regulation. The regs insisted that the place be kept as clean as possible for health reasons, and also because that was supposed to make it a psychologically more attractive environment to function in. The workmen wouldn't have given a shit about their psychological environment either, even if they'd known what one was. It was inevitable that the place would get a little messy during a working day.

It was a slaughterhouse, although the company literature always referred to it as a meat-packing plant.

The man who did the actual killing was Mason: the focal point of the company, of all the meat lockers and trucks and canning sections and secretaries and stockholders; their lowest common denominator. It all started with him.

He would stand with his hammer at the open end of the room, right at the very beginning of the plant, and wait for the cows to come in from the train yard. He had a ten-pound sledgehammer, long and heavy, with serrated rubber around the handle to give him a better grip. He used it to hit the cows over the head. They would herd the cows in one at a time, into the chute, straight up to Mason, and Mason would swing his hammer down and hit the cow between the eyes with tremendous force, driving the hammer completely through the bone and into the brain, killing the cow instantly in its tracks. There would be a gush of warm, sticky blood, and a spatter of purplish brain matter; the cow would go to its front knees, as if it were curtsying, then its hindquarters would collapse and drag the whole body over onto one side with a thunderous crash— all in an eyeblink. One moment the cow would be being prodded in terror into the chute that led to Mason, its flanks lathered, its muzzle flecked with foam, and then—almost too fast to watch, the lightning would strike, and it would be a twitching ruin on the stone floor, blood oozing sluggishly from the smashed head.

After the first cow of the day, Mason would be covered with globs and spatters of blood, and his arms would be drenched red past the elbows. It didn't bother him—it was a condition of his job, and he hardly noticed it. He took two showers a day, changed clothes before and after lunch; the company laundered his white working uniforms and smocks at no expense. He worked quickly and efficiently, and never needed more than one blow to kill. Once Mason had killed the cow, it was hoisted on a hook, had its throat cut, and was left for a few minutes to bleed dry. Then another man came up with a long, heavy knife and quartered it. Then the carcass was further sliced into various portions, each portion was impaled on a hook and carried away by a clanking overhead conveyor belt toward the meat lockers and packing processes that were the concerns of the rest of the plant.

The cows always seemed to know what was about to happen to them—they would begin to moan nervously and roll their eyes in apprehension as soon as they were herded from the stock car on the siding. After the first cow was slaughtered, their apprehension would change to terror. The smell of the blood would drive them mad. They would plunge and bellow and snort and buck; they would jerk mindlessly back and forth, trying to escape. Their eyes would roll up to show the whites, and they would spray foam, and their sides would begin to lather. At this point, Mason would work faster, trying to kill them all before any had a chance to sweat off fat. After a while, they would begin to scream. Then they would have to be prodded harshly toward Mason's hammer. At the end, after they had exhausted themselves, the last few cows would grow silent, shivering and moaning softly until Mason had a chance to get around to them, and then they would die easily with little thrashing or convulsing. Often, just for something to do, Mason and the other workmen would sarcastically talk to the cows, make jokes about them, call them by pet names, tell them—after the fashion of a TV variety-skit doctor—that everything was going to be all right and that it would only hurt for a minute, tell them what dumb fucking bastards they were— "That's right, sweetheart. Come here, you big dumb bastard.

Papa's got a surprise for you"—tell them that they'd known goddamn well what they were letting themselves in for when they'd enlisted. Sometimes they would bet on how hard Mason could hit a cow with his big hammer, how high into the air the brain matter would fly after the blow. Once Mason had won a buck from Kaplan by hitting a cow so hard that he had driven it to its knees. They were no more callous than ordinary men, but it was a basically dull, basically unpleasant job, and like all men with dull, unpleasant jobs, they needed something to spice it up, and to keep it far enough away. To Mason, it was just a job, no better or worse than any other. It was boring, but he'd never had a job that wasn't boring. And at least it paid well. He approached it with the same methodical uninterest he had brought to every other job he ever had. It was his job, it was what he did.

Every day, Mason would stand with his hammer and kill cows.

It is raining: a sooty, city rain that makes you dirty rather than wet. Mason is standing in the rain at the bus stop, waiting for the bus to come, as he does every day, as he has done every day for the past six years. He has his collar up against the wind, hands in pockets, no hat: his hair is damp, plastered to his forehead. He stands somewhat slouched, head slumped forward just the tiniest bit—he is tired, the muscles in his shoulders are knotted with strain, the back of his neck burns. He is puzzled by the excessive fatigue of his body; uneasy, he shifts his weight from foot to foot—standing here after a day spent on his feet is murder, it gets him in the thighs, the calves. He has forgotten his raincoat again. He is a big man, built thick through the chest and shoulders, huge arms, wide, thick-muscled wrists, heavy-featured, resigned face. He is showing the first traces of a future potbelly. His feet are beginning to splay. His personnel dossier (restricted) states that he is an unaggressive underachiever, energizing at low potential, anally oriented (plodding, painstaking, competent), highly compatible with his fellow workers, shirks decision-making but can be trusted with minor responsibility, functions best as part of a team, unlikely to cause trouble: a good worker. He often refers to himself as a slob, though he usually tempers it with laughter (as in: "Christ, don't ask a poor slob like me about stuff like that," or, "Shit, I'm only a dumb working slob"). He is beginning to slide into the downhill side of the middle thirties. He was born here, in an immigrant neighborhood, the only Protestant child in a sea of foreign Catholics—he had to walk two miles to Sunday school. He grew up in the gray factory city—sloughed through high school, the Army, drifted from job to job, town to town, dishwashing, waiting tables, working hardhat (jukeboxes, backrooms, sawdust, sun, water from a tin pail), work four months, six, a year, take to the road, drift: back to his hometown again after eight years of this, to his old (pre-Army) job, full circle. This time when the restlessness comes, after a year, he gets all the way to the bus terminal (sitting in the station at three o'clock in the morning, colder than hell, the only other person in the huge, empty hall a drunk asleep on one of the benches) before he realizes that he has no place to go and nothing to do if he gets there. He does not leave. He stays: two years, three, four, six now, longer than he has ever stayed anywhere before. Six years, slipping up on him and past before he can realize it, suddenly gone (company picnics, Christmas, Christ—taxes again already?), time blurring into an oily gray knot, leaving only discarded calendars for fossils. He will never hit the road again, he is here to stay. His future has become his past without ever touching the present. He does not understand what has happened to him, but he is beginning to be afraid.

He gets on the bus for home.

In the cramped, sweaty interior of the bus, he admits for the first time that he may be getting old.

Mason's apartment was on the fringe of the heavily built-up district, in a row of dilapidated six-story brownstones. Not actually the slums, not like where the colored people lived (Mason doggedly said colored people, even when the boys at the plant talked of niggers), not like where the kids, the beatniks lived, but a low-rent district, yes. Laboring people, low salaries. The white poor had been hiding here since 1920, peering from behind thick faded drapes and cracked Venetian blinds. Some of them had never come out. The immigrants had disappeared into this neighborhood from the boats, were still here, were still immigrants after thirty years, but older and diminished, like a faded photograph. All the ones who had not pulled themselves up by their bootstraps to become crooked politicians or gangsters or dishonest lawyers—all forgotten: a gritty human residue. The mailboxes alternated names like Goldstein and Kowalczyk and Ricciardi. It was a dark, hushed neighborhood, with few big stores, no movies, no real restaurants. A couple of bowling alleys. The closest civilization approached was a big concrete housing project for disabled war veterans a block or two away to the east, and a streamlined-chromeplated-neonflashing shopping center about half a mile to the west, on the edge of a major artery. City lights glowed to the north, high rises marched across the horizon south: H. G. Wells Martians, acres of windows flashing importantly.

Mason got off the bus. There was a puddle at the curb and he stepped in it. He felt water soak into his socks. The bus snapped its doors contemptuously shut behind him. It rumbled away, farting exhaust smoke into his face. Mason splashed toward his apartment, wrapped in rain mist, moisture beading on his lips and forehead. His shoes squelched. The wet air carried heavy cooking odors, spicy and foreign. Someone was banging garbage cans together somewhere. Cars hooted mournfully at him as they rushed by.

Mason ignored this, fumbling automatically for his keys as he came up to the outside door. He was trying to think up an excuse to stay home tonight. This was Tuesday, his bowling night; Kaplan would be calling in a while, and he'd have to tell him something. He just didn't feel like bowling; they could shuffle the league around, put Johnson in instead. He clashed the key against the lock. Go in, damn it. This would be the first bowling night he'd missed in six years, even last fall when he'd had the flu—Christ, how Emma had bitched about that, think he'd risen from his deathbed or something. She always used to worry about him too much. Still, after six years. Well, fuck it, he didn't feel like it, was all; it wasn't going to hurt anything, it was only a practice session anyway. He could afford to miss a week. And what the fuck was wrong with the lock? Mason sneered in the dark. How many years is it going to take to learn to use the right key for the front door, asshole? He found the proper key (the one with the deep groove) with his thumb and clicked the door open.

Course, he'd have to tell Kaplan something. Kaplan'd want to know why he couldn't come, try to argue him into it. (Up the stairwell, around and around.) Give him some line of shit. At least he didn't have to make up excuses for Emma anymore—she would've wanted to know why he wasn't going, if he felt good, if he was sick, and she'd be trying to feel his forehead for fever. A relief to have her off his back. She'd been gone almost a month. Now all he had to worry about was what to tell fucking Kaplan. (Old wood creaked under his shoes. It was stuffy. Muffled voices leaked from under doorways as he passed, pencil beams of light escaped from cracks. Dust motes danced in the fugitive light.)

Fuck Kaplan anyway, he didn't have to justify his actions to Kaplan. Just tell him he didn't want to, and the hell with him. The hell with all of them.

Into the apartment: one large room, partially divided by a low counter into kitchen and living room—sink, refrigerator, stove and small table in the kitchen; easy chair, coffee table and portable television in the living room; a small bedroom off the living room and a bath. Shit, he'd have to tell Kaplan something after all, wouldn't he? Don't want the guys to start talking. And it is weird to miss a bowling night. Mason took off his wet clothes, threw them onto the easy chair for Emma to hang up and dry. Then he remembered that Emma was gone. Finally left him—he couldn't blame her much, he supposed. He was a bum, it was true. He supposed. Mason shrugged uneasily. Fredricks promoted over him, suppose he didn't have much of a future—he didn't worry about it, but women were different, they fretted about stuff like that, it was important to them. And he wouldn't marry her. Too much of a drifter. But family stuff, that was important to a woman. Christ, he couldn't really blame her, the dumb cunt—she just couldn't understand. He folded his clothes himself, clumsily, getting the seam wrong in the pants. You miss people for the little things. Not that he really cared whether his pants were folded right or not. And, God knows, she probably missed him more than he did her; he was more independent—sure, he didn't really need anybody but him. Dumb cunt. Maybe he'd tell Kaplan that he had a woman up here, that he was getting laid tonight. Kaplan was dumb enough to believe it. He paused, hanger in hand, surprised at his sudden vehemence. Kaplan was no dumber than anybody else. And why couldn't he be getting laid up here? Was that so hard to believe, so surprising? Shit, was he supposed to curl up and fucking die because his girl'd left, even a longtime (three years) girl? Was that what Kaplan and the rest of those bastards were thinking? Well, then, call Kaplan and tell him you're sorry you can't make it, and then describe what a nice juicy piece of ass you're getting, make the fucker eat his liver with envy because he's stuck in that damn dingy bowling alley with those damn dingy people while you're out getting laid. Maybe it'll even get back to Emma. Kaplan will believe it. He's dumb enough.

Mason took a frozen pizza out of the refrigerator and put it into the oven for his supper. He rarely ate meat, didn't care for it. None of his family had. His father had worked in a meat-packing plant too—the same one, in fact. He had been one of the men who cut up the cow's carcass with knives and cleavers. "Down to the plant," he would say, pushing himself up from the table and away from his third cup of breakfast coffee, while Mason was standing near the open door of the gas oven for warmth and being wrapped in his furry hat for school, "I've got to go down to the plant."

Mason always referred to the place as a meat-packing plant. (Henderson had called it a slaughterhouse, but Henderson had quit.)

The package said fifteen minutes at 450, preheated. Maybe he shouldn't tell Kaplan that he was getting laid, after all. Then everybody'd be asking him questions tomorrow, wanting to know who the girl was, how she was in the sack, where he'd picked her up, and he'd have to spend the rest of the day making up imaginary details of the affair. And suppose they found out somehow that he hadn't had a woman up here after all? Then they'd think he was crazy, making up something like that. Lying. Maybe he should just tell Kaplan that he was coming down with the flu. Or a bad cold. He *was* tired tonight. Maybe he actually was getting the flu. From overwork, or standing around in the rain too long, or something. Maybe that was why he was so fucking tired—Christ, exhausted—why he didn't feel like going bowling. Sure, that was it. And he didn't have to be ashamed of being sick: he had a fine work record, only a couple of days missed in six years. Everybody gets sick sometime, that's the way it is. They'd understand.

Fuck them if they didn't.

Mason burned the pizza slightly. By the time he pulled it out with a washcloth, singeing himself in the process, it had begun to turn black around the edges, the crust and cheese charring. But not too bad. Salvageable. He cut it into slices with a roller. As usual, he forgot to eat it quickly enough, and the last pieces had cooled off when he got around to them—tasting now like cardboard with unheated spaghetti sauce on it. He ate them anyway. He had some beer with the pizza, and some coffee later. After eating, he still felt vaguely unsatisfied, so he got a package of Fig Newtons from the cupboard and ate them too. Then he sat at the table and smoked a cigarette. No noise—nothing moved. Stasis.

The phone rang: Kaplan.

Mason jumped, then took a long, unsteady drag on his cigarette. He was trembling. He stared at his hand, amazed. Nerves. Christ. He was working too hard, worrying too much. Fuck Kaplan and all the rest of them. Don't tell them anything. You don't have to. Let them stew. The phone screamed again and again: three times, four times, six. Don't answer it, Mason told himself, whipping up bravura indignation to cover the sudden inexplicable panic, the fear, the horror. You don't have to account to them. Ring *(scream)*, ring *(scream)*, ring *(scream)*. The flesh crawled on his stomach, short hair bristled along his back, his arms. Stop, dammit, stop, *stop*. "Shut up!" he shouted, raggedly, half rising from the chair.

The phone stopped ringing.

The silence was incredibly evil.

Mason lit another cigarette, dropping the first match, lighting another, finally getting it going. He concentrated on smoking, the taste of the smoke and the feel of it in his lungs, puffing with staccato intensity (IthinkIcanIthinkIcanIthinkIcanIthinkIcan). Something was very wrong, but he suppressed that thought, pushed it deeper. A tangible blackness: avoid it. He was just tired, that's all. He'd had a really crummy, really rough day, and he was tired, and it was making him jumpy. Work seemed to get harder and harder as the weeks went by. Maybe he was getting old, losing his endurance. He supposed it had to happen sooner or later. But shit, he was only thirty-eight. He wouldn't have believed it, or even considered it, before today.

"You're getting old," Mason said, aloud. The words echoed in the bare room.

He laughed uneasily, nervously, pretending scorn. The laughter seemed to be sucked into the walls. Silence blotted up the sound of his breathing.

He listened to the silence for a while, then called himself a stupid asshole for thinking about all this asshole crap, and decided that he'd better go to bed. He levered himself to his feet. Ordinarily he would watch television for a couple of hours before turning in, but tonight he was fucked up—too exhausted and afraid. Afraid? What did he have to be scared of? It was all asshole crap. Mason stacked the dirty dishes in the sink and went into the bedroom, carefully switching off all the other lights behind him. Darkness followed him to the bedroom door.

Mason undressed, put his clothes away, sat on the bed. There was a dingy transient hotel on this side of the building, and its red neon sign blinked directly into Mason's bedroom window, impossible to block out with any thickness of curtain. Tonight he was too tired to be bothered by it. It had been a bad day. He would not think about it, any of it. He only wanted to sleep. Tomorrow would be different, tomorrow would be better. It would have to be. He switched off the light and lay back on top of the sheet. Neon shadows beat around the room, flooding it rhythmically with dull red.

Fretfully, he began to fall asleep in the hot room, in the dark.

Almost to sleep, he heard a woman weeping in his mind.

The weeping scratched at the inside of his head, sliding randomly in and out of his brain. Not really the sound of weeping, not actually an audible sound at all, but rather a feeling, an essence of weeping, of unalterable sadness. Without waking, he groped for the elusive feelings, swimming down deeper and deeper into his mind—like diving below a storm-lashed ocean at night, swimming down to where it is always calm and no light goes, down where the deep currents run. He was only partially conscious, on the borderline of dream where anything seems rational and miracles are commonplace. It seemed only reasonable, only fair, that, in his desolation, he should find a woman in his head. He did not question this, he did not find it peculiar. He moved toward her, propelled and guided only by the urge to be with her, an ivory feather drifting and twisting through vast empty darkness, floating on the wind, carried by the currents that wind through the regions under the earth, the tides that march in Night. He found her, wrapped in the underbelly of himself like a pearl: a tiny exquisite irritant. Encased in amber, he could not see, but he knew somehow that she was lovely, as perfect and delicate as the bud of a flower opening to the sun, as a baby's hand. He comforted her as he had comforted Emma on nights when she'd wake up crying: reaching through darkness toward sadness, wrapping it in warmth, leaching the fear away with presence, spreading the pain around between them to thin it down. She seemed startled to find that she was not alone at the heart of nothing, but she accepted him gratefully, and blended him into herself, blended them together, one stream into another, a mingling of secret waters in the dark places in the middle of the world, in Night, where shadows live. She was the thing itself, and not its wrapping, as Emma had been. She was ultimate grace—moving like silk around him, moving like warm rain within him. He merged with her forever.

And found himself staring at the ceiling.

Gritty light poured in through the window. The hotel sign had been turned off. It was morning.

He grinned at the ceiling, a harsh grin with no mirth in it: skin pulling back and back from the teeth, stretching to death's-head tautness.

It had been a dream.

He grinned his corpse grin at the morning.

Hello morning. Hello you goddamned son of a bitch.

He got up. He ached. He was lightheaded with fatigue: his head buzzed, his eyelids were lead. It felt like he had not slept at all.

He went to work.

It is still raining. Dawn is hidden behind bloated spider clouds. Here, in the factory town, miles of steel mills, coke refineries, leather-tanning plants, chemical scum running in the gutters, it will rain most of the year: airborne dirt forming the nucleus for moisture, an irritant to induce condensation—producing a listless rain that fizzles down endlessly, a deity pissing. The bus creeps through the mists and drizzle like a slug, parking lights haloed by dampness. Raindrops inch down the windowpane, shimmering and flattening when the window buzzes, leaving long wet tracks behind them. Inside, the glass has been fogged by breath and body heat, making it hard to see anything clearly. The world outside has merged into an infinity of lumpy gray shapes, dinosaur shadows, here and there lights winking and diffusing wetly—it is a moving collage done in charcoal and watery neon. The men riding the bus do not notice it—already they seem tired. It is seven A.M. They sit and stare dully at the tips of their shoes, or the back of the seat in front of them. A few read newspapers. One or two talk. Some sleep. A younger man laughs—he stops almost immediately. If the windows were clear, the rain collage of light and shadow would be replaced by row after row of drab, crumbling buildings, gas stations decked with tiny plastic flags, used car lots with floodlights, hamburger stands, empty schoolyards with dead trees poking up through the pavement, cyclone-fenced recreation areas that children never use. No one ever bothers to look at that either. They know what it looks like.

Usually Mason prefers the aisle seat, but this morning, prompted by some obscure instinct, he sits by the window. He is trying to understand his compulsion to watch the blurred landscape, trying to verbalize what it makes him think of, how it makes him feel. He cannot. Sad—that's the closest he can come. Why should it make him sad? Sad, and there is something else, something he gropes for but it keeps slipping away. An echo of reawakening fear, in reaction to his groping. It felt like, it was kind of like— Uneasily, he presses his palm to the window, attempts to rub away some of the moisture obscuring the glass. (This makes him feel funny too. Why? He flounders, grasping at nothing—it is gone.) A patch of relatively clear glass appears as he rubs, a swath of sharper focus surrounded by the oozing myopia of the collage. Mason stares out at the world, through his patch of glass. Again he tries to grasp something— again he fails. It all looks wrong somehow. It makes him vaguely, murkily angry. Buildings crawl by outside. He shivers, touched by a septic breath of entropy. Maybe it's— If it was like— He cannot. Why is it wrong? What's wrong with it? That's the way it's always looked, hasn't it? Nothing's changed. What could you change it *to*? What the fuck is it *supposed* to be like? No words.

Raindrops pile up on the window again and wash away the world.

At work, the dream continued to bother Mason throughout the day. He found that he couldn't put it out of his mind for long—somehow his thoughts always came back to it, circling constantly like the flies that buzzed around the pools of blood on the concrete floor.

Mason became annoyed, and slightly uneasy. It wasn't healthy to be so wrapped up in a fucking dream. It was sick, and you had to be sick in the head to fool around with it. It was sick—it made him angry to think about the slime and sickness of it, and faintly nauseous. He didn't have that slime in his head. No, the dream had bothered him because Emma was gone. It was rough on a guy to be alone again after living with somebody for so long. He should go out and actually pick up some broad instead of just thinking about it—should've had one last night so he wouldn't've had to worry about what to tell Kaplan. Sweep the cobwebs out of his brain. Sitting around that damn house night after night, never doing anything—no wonder he felt funny, had crazy dreams.

At lunch—sitting at the concrete, formica-topped table, next to the finger-smudged plastic faces of the coffee machine, the soft drink machine, the sandwich machine, the ice cream machine (OUT OF ORDER) and the candy bar machine—he toyed with the idea of telling Russo about the dream, playing it lightly, maybe getting a few laughs out of it. He found the idea amazingly unpleasant. He was reluctant to tell anybody anything about the dream. To his amazement, he found himself getting angry at the thought. Russo was a son of a bitch anyway. They were all son of a bitches. He snapped at Russo when the Italian tried to draw him into a discussion he and Kaplan were having about cars. Russo looked hurt.

Mason mumbled something about a hangover in apology and gulped half of his steaming coffee without feeling it. His tuna salad sandwich tasted like sawdust, went down like lead. A desolate, inexplicable sense of loss had been growing in him throughout the morning as he became more preoccupied with the dream. He *couldn't* have been this affected by a dream, that was crazy—there had to be more to it than that, it had to be more than just a dream, and he wasn't crazy. So it couldn't have been a dream completely, somehow. He missed the girl in the dream. How could he miss someone who didn't exist? That was crazy. But he *did* miss her. So maybe the girl wasn't completely a dream somehow, or he wouldn't miss her like that, would he? That was crazy too. He turned his face away and played distractedly with crumbs on the formica tabletop. No more of this: it was slimy, and it made his head hurt to think about it. He wouldn't think about it anymore.

That afternoon he took to listening while he worked. He

caught himself at it several times. He was listening intently, for nothing. No, not for nothing. He was listening for *her*.

On the bus, going home, Mason is restless, as if he were being carried into some strange danger, some foreign battlefield. His eyes gleam slightly in the dark. The glare of oncoming car headlights sweeps over him in oscillating waves. Straps swing back and forth like scythes. All around him, the other passengers sit silently, not moving, careful not to touch or jostle the man next to them. Each in his own space: semivisible lumps of flesh and shadow. Their heads bob slightly with the motion of the bus, like dashboard ornaments.

When Mason got home, he had frozen pizza for supper again, though he'd been intending to have an omelet. He also ate some more Fig Newtons. It was as though he were half-consciously trying to reproduce the previous night, superstitiously repeating all the details of the evening in hopes of producing the same result. So he ate pizza, shaking his head at his own stupidity and swearing bitterly under his breath. He ate it nevertheless. And as he ate, he listened for the scratching—hating himself for listening, but listening—only partially believing that such a thing as the scratching even existed, or ever had, but listening. Half of him was afraid that it would not come; half was afraid that it would. But nothing happened.

When the scratching at his mind did come again it was hours later, while he was watching an old movie on *The Late Show*, when he had almost managed to forget. He stiffened, feeling a surge of terror (and feeling something else that he was unable to verbalize), even the half of his mind that had wanted it to come screaming in horror of the unknown now that the impossible had actually happened. He fought down terror, breathing harshly. This couldn't be happening. Maybe he *was* crazy. A flicker of abysmal fear. Sweat started on his forehead, armpits, crotch.

Again, the scratching: bright feelings sliding tentatively into his head, failing to catch and slipping out, coming back again— like focusing a split-image lens. He sat back in the easy chair;

old springs groaned, the cracked leather felt hot and sticky against his T-shirted back. He squeezed the empty beer can, crumpling it. Automatically he put the empty into the six-pack at the foot of the chair. He picked up another can and sat with it unopened in his lap. The sliding in his head made him dizzy and faintly nauseous—he squirmed uneasily, trying to find a position that would lessen the vertigo. The cushion made a wet sucking noise as he pulled free of it: the dent made by his back in the leather began to work itself back to level, creaking and groaning, only to re-form when he let his weight down again. Jarred by motion, the ashtray he'd been balancing on his knee slipped and crashed face-down to the rug in an explosion of ashes.

Mason leaned forward to pick it up, stopped, his attention suddenly caught and fixed by the television again. He blinked at the grainy, flickering black-and-white images; again he felt something that he didn't know how to say, so strongly that the sliding in his head was momentarily ignored.

It was one of those movies they'd made in the late twenties or early thirties, where everything was perfect. The hero was handsome, suave, impeccably dressed; he had courage, he had style, he could fit in anywhere, he could solve any problem—he never faltered, he never stepped on his own dick. He was Quality. The heroine matched him: she was sophisticated, re-fined, self-possessed—a slender, aristocratic sculpture in ice and moonlight. She was unspeakably lovely. They were both class people, posh people: the ones who ran things, the ones who mattered. They had been born into the right families on the right side of town, gone to the right schools, known the right people—got the right jobs. Unquestioned superiority showed in the way they moved, walked, planted their feet, turned their heads. It was all cool, planned and poised, like a dancer. They knew that they were the best people, knew it without having to think about it or even knowing that they knew it. It was a thing assumed at birth. It was a thing you couldn't fake, couldn't put on: something would trip you up every time, and the other ones on top would look through you and see what you really were and draw a circle that excluded you (never actually saying anything, which would make it worse), and you would be left standing there with your dick hanging out, flushed, embarrassed, sweating—too coarse, doughy, unfinished—twisting your hat nervously between knobby, clumsy hands. But that would never happen to the man and woman on television.

Mason found himself trembling with rage, blind with it, shaking as if he were going to tear himself to pieces, falling apart and not knowing why, amazed and awed by his own fury, his guts knotting, his big horny hands clenching and unclenching at the injustice, the monstrousness, the slime, the millions of lives pissed away, turning his anger over and over, churning it like a murky liquid, pounding it into froth.

They never paid any dues. They never sweated, or defecated. Their bodies never smelled bad, never got dirty. They never had crud under their fingernails, blisters on their palms, blood staining their arms to the elbows. The man never had five o'clock shadow, the woman never wore her hair in rollers like Emma, or had sour breath, or told her lover to take out the garbage. They never farted. Or belched. They did not have sex—they *made love*, and it was all transcendental pleasure: no indignity of thrashing bodies, clumsily intertwining limbs, fumbling and straining, incoherent words and coarse animal sounds; and afterward he would be breathing easily, her hair would be in place, there would be no body fluids, the sheets would not be rumpled or stained. And the world they moved through all their lives reflected their own perfection: it was beautiful, tidy, ordered. Mansions. Vast lawns. Neatly painted, tree-lined streets. And style brought luck too. The gods smiled on them, a benign fate rolled dice that always came up sevens, sevens, sevens. They skated through life without having to move their feet, smiling, untouched, gorgeous, like a parade float: towed by others. They broke the bank of every game in town. Everything went their way. Coincidence became a contortionist to finish in their favor.

Because they had class. Because they were on top.

Mason sat up, gasping. He had left the ashtray on the floor. Numbly, he set the beer can down beside it. His hand was trembling. He felt like he had been kicked in the stomach. *They* had quality. He had nothing. He could see everything now: everything he'd been running from all his life. He was shit. No way to deny it. He lived in a shithouse, he worked in a shithouse. His whole *world* was a vast shithouse: dirty black liquid bubbling prehistorically; rich feisty odors of decay. He was surrounded by shit, he wallowed in it. He *was* shit. Already, he realized, it made no difference that he had ever lived. You're *nothing*, he told himself, you're shit. You ain't never been anything but shit. You ain't never going *to be* anything but shit. Your whole life's been nothing but *shit*.

No.

He shook his head blindly.

No.

There was only one thing in his life that was out of the ordinary, and he snatched at it with the desperation of a drowning man.

The sliding, the scratching in his head that was even now becoming more insistent, that became almost overwhelming as he shifted his attention back to it. That was strange, wasn't it? That was unusual. And it had come to *him*, hadn't it? There were millions and millions of other people in the world, but it had picked *him*—it had come to him. And it was real, it wasn't a dream. He wasn't crazy, and if it was just a dream he'd have to be. So it was *real*, and the girl was real. He had somebody else inside his head. And if that was real, then that was something that had never happened to anybody else in the world before—something he'd never even heard about before other than some dumb sci-fi movies on TV. It was something that even *they* had never done, something that made him different from every man in the world, from every man who had ever lived. It was his own personal miracle.

Trembling, he leaned back in the chair. Leather creaked. This was his miracle, he told himself, it was good, it wouldn't harm him. The bright feelings themselves were good: somehow they reminded him of childhood, of quiet gardens, of dust motes spinning in sunlight, of the sea. He struggled for calm. Blood pounded at his throat, throbbed in his wrists. He felt (the memory flooding, incredibly vivid—ebbing) the way he had the first time Sally Rogers had let him spread her meaty, fragrant thighs behind the hill during noon class in the seventh grade: light-headed, scared, shaking with tension, madly impatient. He swallowed, hesitating, gathering courage. The television babbled unnoticed in the background. He closed his eyes and let go.

Colors swallowed him in a rush.

She waited for him there, a there that became *here* as his knowledge of his physical environment faded, as his body ceased to exist, the soothing blackness broken only by random afterimages and pastel colors scurrying in abstract, friendly patterns.

She was *here*—simultaneously *here* and very far away. Like him, she both filled all of *here* and took up no space at all—both statements were equally absurd. Her presence was nothing but that: no pictures, no images, nothing to see, hear, touch, or smell. That had all been left in the world of duration. Yet somehow she radiated an ultimate and catholic femininity, an archetypal essence, a quicksilver mixture of demanding fire and an ancient racial purpose as unshakable and patient as ice—and he knew it was the (girl? woman? angel?) of his previous "dream," and no other.

There were no words *here*, but they were no longer needed. He understood her by empathy, by the clear perception of emotion that lies behind all language. There was fear in her mind—a rasp like hot iron—and a feeling of hurtling endlessly and forlornly through vast, empty desolation, surrounded by cold and by echoing, roaring darkness. She seemed closer to-night, though still unimaginably far away. He felt that she was still moving slowly toward him, even as they met and mingled *here*, that her body was careening toward him down the path blazed by her mind.

She was zeroing in on him: this was the theory his mind immediately formed, instantly and gratefully accepted. He had thought of her from the beginning as an angel—now he con-ceived of her as a lost angel wandering alone through Night for ages, suddenly touched by his presence, drawn like an iron filing to a magnet, pulled from exile into the realms of light and life.

He soothed her. He would wait for her, he would be a beacon—he would not leave her alone in the dark, he would love her and pull her to the light. She quieted, and they moved together, through each other, became one.

He sank deeper into Night.

He floated in himself: a Möbius band.

In the morning, he woke in the chair. A test pattern hummed on the television. The inside of his pants was sticky with semen.

Habit drives him to work. Automatically he gets up, takes a shower, puts on fresh clothes. He eats no breakfast; he isn't hungry—he wonders, idly, if he will ever be hungry again. He lets his feet take him to the bus stop, and waits without fretting about whether or not he'd remembered to lock the door. He waits without thinking about anything. The sun is out; birds are humming in the concrete eaves of the housing project. Mason hums too, quite unconsciously. He boards the bus for work, lets the driver punch his trip ticket, and docilely allows the incoming crowd to push and jostle him to an uncomfortable seat in the back, over the wheel. There, sitting with his knees doubled up in the tiny seat and peering around with an unusual curiosity, the other passengers give him the first bad feeling of the day. They sit in orderly rows, not talking, not moving, not even looking out the window. They look like department store dummies, on their way to a new display. They are not there at all.

Mason decided to call her Lilith—provisionally at least, until the day, soon now, when he could learn her real name from her own lips. The name drifted up from his subconscious, from the residue of long, forgotten years of Sunday school—not so much because of the associations of primeval love carried by the name (although those rang on a deeper level), but because as a restless child suffering through afternoons of watered-down theology he'd always imagined Lilith to be rather pretty and sympathetic, the kind who might wink conspiratorially at him behind the back of the pious, pompous instructor: a girl with a hint of illicit humor and style, unlike the dumpy, clay-faced ladies in the Bible illustrations. So she became Lilith. He wondered if he would be able to explain the name to her when they met, make her laugh with it.

He fussed with these and other details throughout the day, turning it over in his mind—he wasn't crazy, the dream was real, Lilith was real, she was his—the same thoughts cycling constantly. He was happy in his preoccupation, self-sufficient, only partly aware of the external reality through which he moved. He contributed only monosyllabic grunts to the usual locker-room conversations about sports and politics and pussy, he answered questions with careless shrugs or nods, he completely ignored the daily gauntlet of hellos, good-byes, how're they hangings and other ritual sounds. During lunch he ate very little and let Russo finish his sandwich without any of the traditional exclamations of amazement about the wop's insatiable appetite—which made Russo so uneasy that he was unable to finish it after all. Kaplan came in and told Russo and Mason in hushed, delighted tones that old Hamilton had finally caught the clap from that hooker he'd been running around with down at Saluzzio's. Russo exploded into the expected laughter, said *no shit?* in a shrill voice, pounded the table, grinned in jovial disgust at the thought of that old bastard Hamilton with VD. Mason grunted.

Kaplan and Russo exchanged a look over his head—their eyes were filled with the beginnings of a reasonless, instinctive fear: the kind of unease that pistons in a car's engine might feel when one of the cylinders begins to misfire. Mason ignored them; they did not exist; they never had. He sat at the stone table and chain-smoked with detached ferocity, smoking barely half of each cigarette before using it to light another and dumping the butt into his untouched coffee to sizzle and drown. The Dixie cup was filled with floating, jostling cigarette butts, growing fat and mud-colored as they sucked up coffee: a nicotine logjam. Kaplan and Russo mumbled excuses and moved away to find another table; today Mason made them feel uneasy and insignificant.

Mason did not notice that they had gone. He sat and smoked until the whistle blew, and then got up and walked calmly in to work. He worked mechanically, raising the hammer and bringing it down, his hands knowing their job and doing it without any need of volition, the big muscles in his arms and shoulders straining, his legs braced wide apart, sweat gleaming—an automaton, a clockwork golem. His face was puckered and preoccupied, as if he were constipated. He did not see the blood; his brain danced with thoughts of Lilith.

Twice that day he thought he felt her brush at his mind, the faintest of gossamer touches, but there were too many distractions—he couldn't concentrate enough. As he washed up after work, he felt the touch again: a hesitant, delicate, exploratory touch, as if someone were groping through his mind with feather fingers.

Mason trembled, and his eyes glazed. He stood, head tilted, unaware of the stream of hot water against his back and hips, the wet stone underfoot, the beaded metal walls; the soap drying on his arms and chest, the smell of heat and wet flesh, the sharp hiss of the shower jets and the gargle of water down the drain; the slap of thongs and rasp of towels, the jumbled crisscross of wet footprints left by men moving from the showers to the lockers, the stuffiness of steam and sweat disturbed by an eddy of colder air as someone opened the outer door; the rows of metal lockers beyond the showers with *Playboy* gatefolds and Tijuana pornography and family snapshots pinned to the doors, the discolored wooden benches and the boxes of foot powder, the green and white walls of the dressing room covered with company bulletins and joke-shop signs . . . Everything that went into the making of that moment, of his reality, of his life. It all faded, became a ghost, the shadow of a shadow, disappeared completely, did not exist. There was only *here*, and Lilith *here*. And their touch, infinitely closer than joined fingers. Then the world dragged him away.

He opened his eyes. Reality came back: in a babble, in a rush, mildly nauseating. He ignored it, dazed and incandescent with the promise of the night ahead. The world steadied. He stepped back into the shower stream to wash the soap from his body. He had an enormous erection. Clumsily, he tried to hide it with a towel.

Mason takes a taxi home from work. The first time.

That night he is transformed, ripped out of himself, turned inside out. It is pleasure so intense that, like pain, it cannot be remembered clearly afterward—only recollected as a severe shock: sensation translated into a burst of fierce white light. It is pleasure completely beyond his conception—his most extreme fantasy not only fulfilled but intensified. And yet for all the intensity of feeling, it is a gentle thing, a knowing, a complete sharing of emotion, a transcendental empathy. And afterward there is only peace: a silence deeper than death, but not alone. *I love you,* he tells her, really believing it for the first time with anyone, realizing that words have no meaning, but knowing that she will understand, *I love you.*

When he woke up in the morning, he knew that this would be the day.

Today she would come. The certainty pulsed through him, he breathed it like air, it beat in his blood. The knowledge of it oozed in through every pore, only to meet the same knowledge seeping out. It was something felt on a cellular level, a biological assurance. Today they would be together.

He looked at the ceiling. It was pocked with water stains; a deep crack zigzagged across flaking plaster. It was beautiful. He watched it for a half hour without moving, without being aware of the passage of time; without being aware that what he was watching was a "ceiling." Then, sluggishly, something came together in his head, and he recognized it. Today he didn't begrudge it, as he had Wednesday morning. It was a transient condition. It was of no more intrinsic importance than the wall of a butterfly's cocoon after metamorphosis.

Mason rolled to his feet. Fatigue and age had vanished. He was filled with bristly, crackling vitality, every organ, every cell eeming to work at maximum efficiency: so healthy that "healthy" became an inadequate word. This was a newer, nigher state.

Mason accepted it calmly, without question. His movements vere leisurely and deliberate, almost slow motion, as if he were wimming through syrup. He knew where he was going, that hey would find each other today—that was predestined. He vas in no hurry. The same inevitability colored his thoughts. There was no need to do much thinking now, it was all arranged. His mind was nearly blank, only deep currents running. Her nearness dazzled him. Walking, he dreamed of her, of time past, of time to come.

He drifted to the window, lazily admiring the prism sprays unlight made around the edges of the glass. The streets outside vere empty, hushed as a cathedral. Not even birds to break the noly silence. Papers dervished down the center of the road. The un was just floating clear of the brick horizon: a bloated red pall, still hazed with nearness to the earth.

He stared at the sun.

Mason became aware of his surroundings again while he was dressing. Dimly, he realized that he was buckling his belt, slipping his feet into shoes, tying knots in the shoelaces. His attention was caught by a crisscross pattern of light and shadow on he kitchen wall.

He was standing in front of the slaughterhouse. Mason blinked at the building's filigreed iron gates. Somewhere in here, he must have caught the bus and ridden it to work. He couldn't remember. He didn't care.

Walking down a corridor. A machine booms far away.

He was in an elevator. People. Going down.

Time clock.

A door. The dressing room, deep in the plant. Mason hesitated. Should he go to work today? With Lilith so close? It didn't matter—when she came, Lilith would find him no matter where he was. It was easier meanwhile not to fight his body's trained responses; much easier to just go along with them, let hem carry him where they would, do what they wanted him to do.

Buttoning his work uniform. He didn't remember opening the door, or the locker. He told himself that he'd have to watch that.

A montage of surprised faces, bobbing like balloons, very far away. Mason brushed by without looking at them. Their lips moved as he passed, but he could not hear their words.

Don't look back. They can turn you to salt, all the hollow men.

The hammer was solid and heavy in his hand. Its familiar weight helped to clear his head, to anchor him to the world. Mason moved forward more quickly. A surviving fragment of his former personality was eager to get to work, to demonstrate his regained strength and vigor for the other men. He felt the emotion through an ocean of glass, like ghost pain in an amputated limb. He tolerated it, humored it; after today, it wouldn't matter.

Mason walked to the far end of the long white room. Lilith seemed very close now—her nearness made his head buzz intolerably. He stumbled ahead, walking jerkily, as if he were forcing his way against waves of pressure. She would arrive any second. He could not imagine how she would come, or from where. He could not imagine what would happen to him, to them. He tried to visualize her arrival, but his mind, having only Disney, sci-fi, and religion to work with, could only picture an ethereally beautiful woman made of stained glass descending from the sky in a column of golden light while organ music roared: the light shining all around her and from her, spraying into unknown colors as it passed through her clear body. He wasn't sure if she would have wings.

Raw daylight through the open end of the room. The nervous lowing of cattle. Smell of dung and sweat, undertang of old, lingering blood. The other men, looking curiously at him. They had masks for faces, viper eyes. Viper eyes followed him through the room. Hooves scuffed gravel outside.

Heavy-lidded, trembling, he took his place.

They herded in the first cow of the day, straight up to Mason. He lifted the hammer.

The cow approached calmly. Tranquilly she walked before

the prods, her head high. She stared intently at Mason. Her eyes were wide and deep—serene, beautiful, and trusting.

Lilith, he named her, and then the hammer crashed home between her eyes.

0081-31